SINGER

"WRITES BEAUTIFULLY AND HIS PAGES ARE FILLED WITH LOVE, HATE, JOY AND DESPAIR—ALL THE FACETS OF THE HUMAN CONDITION."

—*Associated Press*

Aaron Greidinger was an aspiring young writer and son of a rabbi growing up in Warsaw between the two world wars. He knew many men—and women—whose lives had already been twisted by the impending Nazi horror.

Suddenly the Nazis threatened to invade Poland and Aaron was faced with the most important decision of his life. Should he go to New York with the only two people who could guarantee his safety and success? Or should he stay in Poland and face the Holocaust with his people and with Shosha—his childhood sweetheart who had never really grown up?

Fawcett Crest Books
by Isaac Bashevis Singer:

A CROWN OF FEATHERS   23465-7 $2.50

ENEMIES, A LOVE STORY   24065-7 $2.50

PASSIONS   24067-3 $2.50

SHORT FRIDAY   24068-1 $2.50

Isaac Bashevis Singer

SHOSHA

FAWCETT CREST • NEW YORK

SHOSHA

THIS BOOK CONTAINS THE COMPLETE TEXT OF
THE ORIGINAL HARDCOVER EDITION.

Published by Fawcett Crest Books, a unit of CBS
Publications, the Consumer Publishing Division of CBS Inc.,
by arrangement with Farrar, Straus & Giroux, Inc.

ISBN: 0–449–23997–7

Alternate Selection of the Book-of-the-Month Club
Selection of the Jewish Book Club

Printed in the United States of America

10   9   8   7   6   5   4   3

Author's Note

This novel does not represent the Jews of Poland in the pre-Hitler years by any means. It is a story of a few unique characters in unique circumstances. It appeared in the *Jewish Daily Forward* in 1974 under the title *Soul Expeditions*. A great part of it was translated into English by my nephew Joseph Singer. A number of chapters I dictated to my wife, Alma, and to my secretary, Dvorah Menashe. The entire work was edited by Rachel MacKenzie and Robert Giroux. My gratitude and love to all of them.

I.B.S.

PART ONE

ONE

1 I was brought up on three dead languages—Hebrew, Aramaic, and Yiddish (some consider the last not a language at all)—and in a culture that developed in Babylon: the Talmud. The cheder where I studied was a room in which the teacher ate and slept, and his wife cooked. There I studied not arithmetic, geography, physics, chemistry, or history, but the laws governing an egg laid on a holiday and sacrifices in a temple destroyed two thousand years ago. Although my ancestors had settled in Poland some six or seven hundred years before I was born, I knew only a few words of the Polish language. We lived in Warsaw on Krochmalna Street, which might well have been called a ghetto. Actually the Jews of Russian-occupied Poland were free to live wherever they chose. I was an anachronism in every way, but I didn't know it, just as I didn't know that my friendship with Shosha, the daughter of our neighbor Bashele and her husband, Zelig, had anything to do with love. Love affairs took place between worldly young men who shaved their beards and smoked cigarettes on the Sabbath and girls who wore blouses with short sleeves and dresses with a décolleté. Such follies did not touch a cheder boy of seven or eight from a Hasidic house.

Still, I was drawn to Shosha and I passed through the dark hall that led from our apartment to Bashele's as often as I could. Shosha was about my age, but while I was considered a prodigy, knew several pages of the Gemara and chapters of the Mishnah by heart, could write in Yiddish as well as in Hebrew, and had already begun to ponder God, providence, time, space, and infinity, Shosha was considered a little fool in our building, No.

10. At nine, she spoke like a child of six. She was left behind two years in a class in the public school to which her parents sent her. Shosha had blond hair that fell to her shoulders when she undid her braids. Her eyes were blue, her nose straight, her neck long. She took after her mother, who had been known as a beauty in her youth. Her sister Yppe, two years younger than Shosha, was dark, like her father. She wore a brace on her left leg and limped. Teibele, the youngest, was still a baby when I began to visit at Bashele's. She had just been weaned and slept in a cradle.

One day Shosha came home from school crying—the teacher had dismissed her, with a letter saying there was no place there for her. She brought home two books—one in Russian, one in Polish—as well as some exercise books and a box with pens and pencils. She had not learned any Russian but could read Polish slowly. The Polish schoolbook had pictures of a hut in a village, a cow, a rooster, a cat, a dog, a hare, and a mother stork feeding her newly hatched offspring in their nest. Shosha knew some of the poems in the book by heart.

Her father, Zelig, worked in a leather store. He left home early in the morning and returned late in the evening. His black beard was always short and round, and the Hasidim in our building said that he had it trimmed —a violation of Hasidic practice. He wore a short gaberdine, a stiff collar, a tie, and kid shoes with rubber tops. Saturday he went to a synagogue frequented by tradesmen and workers.

Though Bashele wore a wig, she did not shave her head as did my mother, the wife of Rabbi Menahem Mendl Greidinger. Mother often told me it was wrong for a rabbi's son, a student of the Gemara, to be the companion of a girl, and one from a common home at that. She warned me never to taste anything there, since Bashele might feed me meat that was not strictly kosher. The

Greidingers came from generations of rabbis, authors of sacred books, while Bashele's father was a furrier and Zelig had served in the Russian Army before they married. The children in our house mimicked Shosha's speech. Shosha made silly mistakes in her Yiddish; she began a sentence and rarely finished it. When she was sent to the grocery store to buy food, she lost the money. Bashele's neighbors told her she ought to take Shosha to a doctor because her brain didn't seem to be developing, but Bashele had neither time nor money for doctors. And how could they help? Bashele herself was as naïve as a child. Michael the shoemaker said about her that you could make her believe she was pregnant with a kitten and that a cow flew over the roof and laid brass eggs.

How different Bashele's apartment was from ours! We had almost no furniture. The walls were lined with books from floor to ceiling. My brother, Moishe, and I did not have toys. We played with my father's volumes, with a broken pen, an empty ink bottle, or pieces of paper. Our living room had no sofa, no upholstered chairs, no chest of drawers—only an ark for scrolls, a long table, and benches. People prayed there on the Sabbath. My father stood at a lectern all day long and looked into large books that lay open in a great pile. He wrote commentaries, trying to answer the contradictions that one commentator found in the works of another. He was short, had a red beard and blue eyes, and he smoked a long pipe. From the time I can first remember, I heard him repeat the phrase "It is forbidden." Everything I wanted to do was a transgression. I was not allowed to draw or paint a person—that violated the Second Commandment. I couldn't say a word against another boy—that was slander. I couldn't laugh at anyone—that was mockery. I couldn't make up a story—that represented a lie.

On Sabbaths we weren't allowed to touch a candlestick, a coin, any of the things we amused ourselves with. Father reminded us constantly that this world was a corridor in which one had to study the Torah and perform virtuous deeds, so that when one made one's way to the palace that was the next world, rewards would be waiting to be collected. He used to say, "How long does one live, anyhow? Before you turn around it's all over. When a person sins, his sins turn into devils, demons, hobgoblins. After death they chase the corpse and drag it through forsaken forests and deserts where people do not go or cattle tread."

Mother occasionally got angry at Father for talking so depressingly to us, but she was a moralizer herself. She was lean, with sunken cheeks, a pointed chin, and large gray eyes that expressed both sharpness and melancholy. My parents had lost three children before I was born.

At Bashele's, before I even opened the door, I could smell her stews, roasts, and desserts. Her kitchen contained rows of copper and brass pots and pans, painted and gold-rimmed plates, a mortar and pestle, a coffee mill, all kinds of pictures and knickknacks. The children had a crate filled with dolls, balls, colored pencils, paints. The beds were covered with pretty bedspreads. Embroidered cushions lay across the sofa.

Yppe and Teibele were too young for me, but Shosha was just right. Neither of us went down to play in the courtyard, which was controlled by rough boys with sticks. They bullied any child younger or weaker than they. Their talk was mean. They singled me out in particular because I was the rabbi's son and wore a long gaberdine and a velvet cap. They taunted me with names like "Fancypants," "Little Rabbi," "Mollycoddle." If they heard me speak to Shosha, they jeered and called me "Sissy." I was teased for having red hair, blue eyes, and unusually white skin. Sometimes they flung a rock at me, a chip of wood, or a blob of mud. Sometimes they tripped me so that I fell into the gutter. Or they might sic the house watchman's dog on me because they knew I was afraid of it.

But inside Bashele's I received neither teasing nor roughness. The moment I arrived Bashele offered me a plate of groats, a glass of borscht, a cookie. Shosha took down her toy box with her dolls, doll-sized dishes and cooking things, her collection of human and animal figurines, shiny buttons, gaudy ribbons. We played jacks, knucklebones, hide-and-seek, husband and wife. I made believe I went to the synagogue and when I returned Shosha prepared a meal for me. Once I played the role of a blind man and Shosha let me touch her forehead, cheeks, mouth. She kissed the palm of my hand and said, "Don't tell Mama."

I repeated to Shosha stories I had read or heard from my mother and father, embellishing them freely. I told her of the wild forests of Siberia, of Mexican bandits, and of cannibals who ate their own children. Sometimes Bashele would sit with us and listen to my chatter. I boasted to them that I was familiar with the cabala and knew expressions so sacred they could draw wine from the wall, create live pigeons, and let me fly to Madagascar. One such name I knew contained seventy-two letters, and when it was uttered the sky would turn red, the moon topple, and the world be destroyed.

Shosha's eyes filled with alarm. "Arele, don't ever say the word!"

"No, Shoshele, don't be afraid. I will make it so that you'll live forever."

2 Not only could I play with Shosha, but I could also tell her things I dared not speak of to anyone else. I could describe all my fantasies and daydreams. I confided that I was writing a book. I often saw this book in my dreams. It was written by me and also by some ancient scribe in

Rashi script on parchment. I imagined that I had done it in a former life. My father had forbidden me to look into the cabala. He admonished me that anyone who indulges in the cabala before the age of thirty is in danger of falling into heresy or insanity. But I believed that I was a heretic and half mad anyhow. There stood on our shelves volumes of the Zohar, *The Tree of Life, The Book of Creation, The Orchard of Pomegranates,* and other cabalistic works. I found a calendar where many facts about kings, statesmen, millionaires, and scholars were set down. My mother often read *The Book of the Covenant,* which was an anthology packed with scientific information. There I could read about Archimedes, Copernicus, Newton, and about the philosophers Aristotle, Descartes, Leibnitz. The author, Reb Elijah from Wilna, engaged in long polemics with those who denied the existence of God, and so I learned their opinions. Though the book was forbidden to me, I used every opportunity to read it. Once my father mentioned the philosopher Spinoza—his name should be blotted out—and his theory that God is the world and the world is God. These words created turmoil in my mind. If the world is God, I, the boy Aaron, my gaberdine, my velvet cap, my red hair, my shoes were part of the Godhead. So were Bashele, Shosha—even my thoughts.

That day, I lectured to Shosha about Spinoza's philosophy as if I had studied all his works. Shosha listened while she laid out her collection of gilded buttons. I was sure that she didn't grasp a single word, but then she asked, "Is Leibele Bontz also God?"

Leibele Bontz was known in our courtyard as a hoodlum and a thief. When he played cards with the boys, he cheated. He had all kinds of tricks and excuses to beat up a weaker boy. He would approach a little boy and say, "Someone told me that my elbow stinks. Do me a favor and smell it." When the little boy obliged, Leibele Bontz punched him in the nose. The idea that he could be part of

God destroyed my enthusiasm for Spinoza's philosophy and I immediately developed a theory that there were two Gods—a good one and a bad one—and Leibele Bontz belonged with the bad one. Shosha accepted my new version of Spinoza willingly.

Every day there used to come to the Radzymin studyhouse, where my father prayed, a man called Joshua the herring merchant. He also had a nickname—Joshua the philosopher. He was short, slight, with a beard that had all colors: yellow, gray, brown. He sold marinated herring and smoked herring, and his wife and daughters pickled cucumbers. He prayed late and with great speed after the other worshippers had left. One minute he put on his prayer shawl and phylacteries; a minute later—or so it seemed to me—he took them off. I had stopped going to cheder because my father could not afford the tuition; besides, I was now able to read a page of the Gemara by myself. I often went to the Radzymin studyhouse to converse with this man. He dabbled in logic and told me about the paradoxes of the Greek philosopher Zeno. He also told me that even though the atom was supposed to be the smallest particle of matter, from a mathematical point of view it could be divided infinitely. He explained the meaning of the words "microcosm" and "macrocosm."

The next day I spoke about all this to Shosha. I told her that each atom is a world in itself, with myriads of tiny human beings, animals, and birds. There are Gentiles there and Jews. The men build houses, towers, towns, bridges, without realizing how infinitely small they are. They speak many languages. "In one drop of water there may be myriads of such worlds."

"Don't they get drowned?" Shosha asked.

In order not to make things too complicated, I said, "They all know how to swim."

A day did not pass without my coming to Shosha with new stories. I had discovered a potion that, if you drank

14

it, made you as strong as Samson. I had drunk it already and I was so strong I could drive the Turks from the Holy Land and become King of the Jews; I had found a cap that, if you put it on your head, made you invisible. I was about to grow as wise as King Solomon, who could speak the language of birds. I told Shosha about the Queen of Sheba, who came to learn wisdom from King Solomon and brought with her many slaves, as well as camels and donkeys bearing gifts for the ruler of Israel. Before she came King Solomon ordered that the palace floor be replaced with glass. When the Queen of Sheba entered, she mistook the glass for water and lifted up her skirt. King Solomon sat on his golden throne, and when he saw the queen's legs, he said, "You are famous for your great beauty, but you have hair on your legs like a man."

"Was this true?" Shosha asked.

"Yes, true."

Shosha lifted up her skirt to look at her own legs, and I said, "Shosha, you are more beautiful than the Queen of Sheba." I promised her that when I was anointed and sat on Solomon's throne, I would take her for a wife. She would be the queen and wear on her head a crown of diamonds, emeralds, rubies, and sapphires. The other wives and concubines would bow before her with their faces to the earth.

"How many wives will you have?" Shosha asked.

"Together with you, a thousand."

"Why so many?"

"King Solomon had a thousand wives. It is written so in the Song of Songs."

"Is this allowed?"

"A king may do anything."

"If you have a thousand wives, you will have no time for me."

"Shoshele, for you I will always have time. You will sit near me on the throne and rest your feet on a footstool of topaz. When the Messiah comes, all Jews will mount a cloud and fly to the Holy Land. The Gentiles will become slaves to the Jews. The daughter of a general will wash your feet."

"Oh, it will tickle." Shosha began to laugh, showing her white teeth.

The day that Zelig and Bashele moved from No. 10 to No. 7 Krochmalna Street was like Tisha Bov for me. It happened suddenly. One day I stole a groschen from my mother's purse and bought a piece of chocolate for Shosha in Esther's candy store; a day later movers opened the door of Bashele's apartment and carried out the wardrobes, the sofa, the beds, the Passover dishes, the all-year-round dishes. I didn't even have a chance to say goodbye to the family. Actually, I had become too old to have a girl for a friend. I was studying not only Gemara now but also Tosaphot. The morning they moved, I was reading with my father *Rabbi Chanina, the Assistant of Priests*. From time to time I glanced out the window. Bashele's possessions were loaded on a platform harnessed to two Belgian horses. Bashele carried Teibele. Shosha and Yppe walked behind the wagon. The distance from No. 10 to No. 7 was only two blocks, but I knew that this meant the end. It was one thing to sneak out of the apartment, pass quickly through a dark hall, and knock on Shosha's door, and quite another thing to pay a visit in a strange building. The members of the community that paid my father his weekly remuneration were watchful, always ready to find some sign of misconduct in his children.

It was summer 1914. A month later, a Serbian assassin shot the Austrian Crown Prince and his wife. Soon the Czar mobilized all the armed forces. I saw men who worshipped in our living room on the Sabbath pass by our house with round shiny buttons on their lapels as a sign that they had been called up and would have to fight against the Germans, the Austrians, and the Italians. Policemen entered Elozar's tavern at No. 17 and poured all his vodka into the gutter—in time of war, citizens should be sober. The storekeepers refused to sell merchandise for paper money; they demanded silver coins or gold pieces. The doors of the stores were kept half closed, and only customers with such coins were allowed in.

At home we soon began to go hungry. In the time between the assassination in Sarajevo and the outbreak of the war, many wealthy housewives had stocked their larders with flour, rice, beans, and groats, but my mother had been busy reading morality books. Besides, we had no money. The Jews on our street stopped paying my father. There were no more weddings, divorces, or lawsuits in his courtroom. Long lines formed at the bakeries for a loaf of bread. The price of meat soared. In Yanash's Bazaar the slaughterers stood with knives in their hands, looking out for a woman with a chicken, a duck, or a goose. The price of fowl went up from day to day. Herring could not be bought at all. Many housewives began to use cocoa butter instead of butter. There was a lack of kerosene. After the Succoth holiday the rains, the snow, the frosts began, but we couldn't afford coal for heating the oven. My brother Moishe stopped going to cheder because his shoes were torn. Father became his teacher. Weeks passed by and we never tasted meat, not even on the Sabbath. We drank watery tea without sugar. We learned from the newspapers that the Germans and Austrians had invaded many towns and villages in Poland, among them those where our relatives lived. The Czar's great-uncle Nikolai Nikolaievitch, the chief commander, decreed that all Jews be driven from the regions behind the front; they were considered German spies. The Jewish streets in Warsaw teemed with thousands of refugees. They slept in the studyhouses, even in synagogues. It wasn't long before we began to hear the shooting of heavy guns. The Germans attacked at the river Bzura, and the Russians launched a counterattack. In our apartment the windowpanes rattled day and night.

3 Our family left Warsaw in the summer of 1917. My parents moved to a village occupied by the Austrians. Food was cheaper there. Mother had relatives in that part of the country. The city seemed on the verge of destruction. The war had already lasted three years. The Russians had evacuated Warsaw and in their retreat they had blown up the Praga Bridge. The Germans who ruled Poland were losing on the western front and they let the population starve. We never had enough to eat. Before we left, Moishe fell ill and was taken to the Hospital for Epidemic Diseases on Pokorna Street. Mother and I were taken to the disinfecting station on Szczesliwa Street near the Jewish cemetery. There they shaved off my earlocks and fed me soup flavored with pork. For me—the son of a rabbi—these were spiritual calamities. A Gentile nurse ordered me to strip naked and gave me a bath. When she lathered me, her fingers tickled and I felt like both laughing and crying. It must be that I had fallen into the hands of the demonic Lilith dispatched by her husband, Asmodeus, to corrupt yeshiva students and drag them down into the abyss of defilement. Later when I saw myself in a mirror and caught a glimpse of my image minus earlocks and ritual garment, and wearing some kind of bathrobe I had never seen on a Jewish lad and slippers with wooden soles, I didn't recognize myself. I was no longer formed in the image of God.

I told myself that what had happened to me this day was no mere consequence of the war and German decrees but rather a punishment for my sins—for doubting my faith. I had already read on the sly the works of Mendele Mocher Sforim, Sholem Aleichem, and Peretz, as well as Yiddish or Hebrew translations of Tolstoy, Dostoevsky,

Strindberg, Knut Hamsun. I had glanced into Dr. Shlomo Rubin's Hebrew translation of Spinoza's *Ethics* and had gone through a popular history of philosophy. I had taught myself to read German—so similar to Yiddish—and had read in the original the Brothers Grimm, Heine, and whatever I could lay my hands on. I had kept secrets from my parents.

Simultaneously with the German soldiers, Enlightenment had invaded Krochmalna Street. I had heard of Darwin and was no longer sure that the miracles described in *The Assembly of Saints* had really occurred. Ever since war had broken out on the Ninth Day of Ab, the Yiddish newspaper was brought daily into our house and I read there about Zionism, socialism, and, following the Russian evacuation of Poland when the Russian censorship ceased, a series of articles about Rasputin.

Now revolution had taken over Russia, and the Czar had been deposed. The news was full of the fights and disputes among the Social Revolutionaries, the Mensheviks, the Bolsheviks, the Anarchists—new names and concepts had emerged. I absorbed all this with an eagerness that couldn't be sated. In the years between 1914 and 1917, I didn't see Shosha and I never once met her in the street, not her or Bashele or the other children. I had grown up and had studied one semester in the Sochaczów yeshiva and another semester in Radzymin. Father became the rabbi of a hamlet in Galicia and I had to start to earn my own livelihood.

But I never forgot Shosha. I dreamed of her at night. In my dreams she was both dead and alive. I played with her in a garden which was also a cemetery. Dead girls joined us there, wearing garments that were ornate shrouds. They danced in circles and sang songs. They swung, skated, occasionally hovered in the air. I strolled with Shosha in a forest of gigantic trees that reached the sky. The birds there were different from any I knew. They were as big as

19

eagles, as colorful as parrots. They spoke Yiddish. From the thickets surrounding the garden, beasts with human faces showed themselves. Shosha was at home in this garden, and instead of my pointing out and explaining to her as I had done in the past, she revealed to me things I hadn't known and whispered secrets in my ear. Her hair had grown long enough to reach her loins, and her flesh glowed like mother-of-pearl. I always awoke from this dream with a sweet taste in my mouth and the impression that Shosha was no longer living.

During the years I wandered through the villages of Poland trying to support myself by teaching Hebrew, I seldom thought of Shosha when I was awake. I had fallen in love with a girl whose parents wouldn't permit me to go near her. I began to write in Hebrew and later switched to Yiddish, and the editors rejected everything I submitted to them. I couldn't seem to find a style that might create a literary domain for myself. Discouraged, I gave up literature and concentrated on philosophy, but what I was seeking I did not find there. I knew I must return to Warsaw, but again and again the forces that direct the fate of man hurled me back to the muddy villages. I often considered suicide. When finally I managed to get to the city to find work as a proofreader and a translator, and to be invited to the Writers' Club, first as a guest, then as a member, I felt like one recovered from a state of coma.

Years had gone by, and I didn't know where. Writers my age had achieved fame and immortality, but here I was, still a beginner. My father had died. His manuscripts, like mine, had been scattered and lost, though he had managed to publish one small book.

In Warsaw, I began an affair with Dora Stolnitz, a girl whose goal was to settle in Soviet Russia, the land of socialism. I learned later that she was a functionary of the Communist Party. She had been arrested several times and had spent months in Pawiak and other prisons. I was anti-Communist—anti all "isms"—but I lived in constant fear of being arrested and imprisoned because of my connection with this girl, whom I later began to dislike for her hollow slogans and bombastic clichés about the "happy future," the "bright tomorrow."

The Jewish streets in which I now wandered were close to Krochmalna, but I never went near it. I told myself that I simply had no occasion to go into that section of the city, but there had to be other reasons. I had heard that half the residents of the street had died in the typhus epidemics, of influenza, of starvation. Boys with whom I attended cheder had served in the Polish Army and been killed in the 1920 Polish-Bolshevik War. Later, Krochmalna Street had become a hotbed of Communism. There were always Communist demonstrations in the neighborhood. Young Communists draped red flags over telephone and streetcar wires—even on the windows of the police station. On the Place, an area between No. 9 and No. 13, and in the den where the thieves, pimps, and whores hung out, they now planned the dictatorship of Comrade Stalin. The police were forever conducting raids. This was no longer my street. No one would remember me or my family. When I thought of it, I had the strange feeling that my experience there constituted something removed from the world. I was in my twenties, but it seemed as if I were already an old man. Krochmalna Street was like a deep stratum of an archaeological dig which I would never uncover. At the same time, I recalled every house, courtyard, cheder, Hasidic studyhouse, store; every girl, street loafer, housewife—their voices, gestures, manners of speaking, their peculiarities.

I believed that the aim of literature was to prevent time from vanishing, but my own time I had thrown away. The twenties had passed and the thirties had come. Hitler was fast becoming the ruler of Germany. In Russia, the purges had commenced. In Poland, Pilsudski had created a military dictatorship. Years earlier, America had established an immigration quota. The consulates of nearly all nations refused to issue visas to Jews. I was stranded in a country squeezed between two mighty foes, stuck with a language and culture no one recognized outside of a small circle of Yiddishists and radicals. Thank God, I found friends among members of the Writers' Club and its periphery. The greatest of them all was Dr. Morris Feitelzohn, who was considered by many to be a genius.

TWO

1 Dr. Morris Feitelzohn wasn't widely known. His philosophical works, some written in German and some in Hebrew and Yiddish, were not translated into English or French. To this day I haven't found his name in any philosophical lexicon. His book *Spiritual Hormones* got bad reviews in Germany and in Switzerland. Dr. Feitelzohn was my friend, even though he was some twenty-five years older than I. He could have become famous if he hadn't squandered his energies. His erudition was monumental. For a time he was a lecturer at the University of Berne. He literally invented the Hebrew terminology for modern philosophy. If Feitelzohn was the dilettante one reviewer labeled him, his dilettantism was of the highest order. As a person, he was a brilliant conversationalist and he enjoyed fantastic success with women.

But this same Dr. Morris Feitelzohn often borrowed five zlotys from me at the Writers' Club, Nor did he have any luck with the Yiddish press in Warsaw, where articles that had been accepted were delayed for weeks while the editors changed and corrupted his style. They kept on finding defects in his work. There was much gossip about him. He was the son of a rabbi, but he had fled the house and became an agnostic. He divorced three wives and constantly changed lovers. Someone told me that Feitelzohn sold a sweetheart to a rich American tourist for five hundred dollars. The bearer of this tale called him a charlatan. But the one who slandered Feitelzohn most was Feitelzohn himself. He boasted of his adventures. I once observed that if one combined Arthur Schopenhauer, Oscar Wilde, and Solomon Maimon, one might end up with Morris Feitelzohn. I should have included the Kotzk rabbi, because in his own fashion Feitelzohn was a mystic and a Hasid.

Morris Feitelzohn was of medium height, broad-shouldered, with a square face, thick eyebrows that met over the bridge of his wide nose, and full lips from between which a cigar always jutted. In the Writers' Club they joked that he slept with the cigar in his mouth. His eyes were almost black, but occasionally I saw green glints in them. His dark hair had already begun to recede. Poor as he was, he wore English suits and expensive ties. In his conversation, he had praise for no one and derided world-famous figures. Yet severe critic that he was, he had detected talent in me, and when he told me this, it evoked in me a sense of friendship that bordered on idolization. It didn't prevent me from seeing his faults. At times, I dared to chide him, but he only said, "It won't do you any good. I'll die an adventurer."

Like all skirt-chasers, he had to report his successes. One time when I came to his furnished room, he pointed to the sofa and said, "If you only knew who lay here just yesterday, you'd faint."

"I soon will know," I said.

"How?"

"You will tell me."

"Ah, you're even more cynical than I am." And he told me.

Strangely, Morris Feitelzohn could speak with ardor about the wisdom found in *The Duty of the Hearts, The Path of the Righteous,* and in some of the Hasidic books. He had written a work about the cabala. In his own fashion, he loved the pious Jew and admired his faith and power to resist temptation. He once said to me, "I love the Jews even though I cannot stand them. No evolution could have created them. For me they are the only proof of God's existence."

One of Feitelzohn's admirers was Celia Chentshiner. Celia's husband, Haiml, was descended from the famous Reb Shmuel Zbitkower, the millionaire who during the Kosciusko uprising gave away a fortune to save the Jews of Praga from the Czar's Cossacks. Haiml's father, Reb Gabriel, owned houses in Warsaw and Lodz. Haiml was his only son. In his youth, Haiml had spent half of each day with a Talmud teacher at the Sochaczów study-house, and the other half trying to learn languages— Russian until 1915, German after the Germans occupied Warsaw, and Polish after 1919, when Poland was liberated. But he knew only one language—Yiddish. He liked to discuss Darwin, Marx, and Einstein with Feitelzohn. Haiml read about them all in Yiddish.

Haiml had never had to concern himself with a livelihood. He was a runt of a man and frail. I sometimes thought there wasn't a trade or business for which he would have been suited. Even drinking tea didn't come easy to him. He lacked the dexterity to cut a slice of lemon and Celia had to do this for him. Haiml was capable only of a childlike love for his father and for his wife. His mother was no longer living. Reb Gabriel had a second wife, whose name I didn't dare mention before Haiml. I asked him only once about his stepmother. He turned pale, put his little hand over my mouth, and exclaimed, "Don't talk! Don't talk! Don't talk! My mother is alive!"

Celia was short too, but taller than Haiml. She was related to him on his mother's side. An orphan, she had been raised in Reb Gabriel's house. Haiml fell in love with her while he was still in cheder. When Haiml didn't want to eat, Celia fed him. When he was studying Russian, German, and Polish, Celia studied with him, and while he learned none of these languages, she did. Their marriage took place when Haiml's mother lay on her deathbed.

By the time I met this couple, they were in their late thirties. Haiml looked like a cheder boy who had been dressed in a man's suit, stiff collar, and tie. He spoke in a piping voice, made childish gestures, laughed with a shriek, and when things didn't go his way he burst out crying. He had dark eyes, a small nose, and a wide mouth full of brackish teeth. The black ruff around his bald head hung down in tufts. He was afraid of barbers and Celia cut his hair. She also trimmed his nails. Celia considered herself an atheist, but traces of her Hasidic upbringing lingered. She chose dresses with long sleeves and high collars. She wore her long dark hair in an unfashionable bun. She was pale, with brown eyes, a straight nose, thin lips, and she moved with the lightness of a girl. Haiml used to call her "my empress." Celia had borne Haiml a daughter, who died at the age of two, and Feitelzohn once told her that the child's death contained a measure of divine logic, since Celia already had a child—Haiml. To Celia and Haiml, Feitelzohn represented the big world and European culture. Feitelzohn did not need to suffer want. They were always proposing that he move in with them in their big apartment on Zlota Street, but Feitelzohn refused.

He told me, "All my foibles and aberrations stem from my urge to be absolutely free. This alleged freedom has transformed me into a slave."

2 Because Feitelzohn praised me, the Chentshiners often invited me to dinner, lunch, or for a glass of tea. When Feitelzohn was present, no one else could speak. We were all content to listen. He had traveled throughout the world. He knew practically every important Jewish personality, as well as many non-Jewish scholars, writers, and humanists. Haiml used to say that he was a living encyclopedia. From time to time, Feitelzohn gave lectures in the Writers' Club in Warsaw and in the provinces, and also on short trips he made abroad. On those occasions, Haiml, Celia, and I had a chance to talk among ourselves. Haiml liked opera and was interested in art. He attended exhibitions and bought paintings. Cubism and expressionism had been in fashion many years, but Haiml liked pastoral landscapes of woods, meadows, streams, and huts half hidden behind trees, where, as he put it, one could hide from Hitler, who was threatening to invade Poland. I myself had fantasies about a house in the woods or on an island where I would be safe from Nazis.

Celia's passion was literature. She bought and read nearly every new book that came out in Polish and Yiddish, as well as translations from other languages, and she possessed a sharp critical taste. I often wondered how this woman who had had no formal education could so accurately appraise not only belles lettres but also scientific works. I paid attention to her opinions regarding my writing; invariably they were correct, tactful, and clever.

One time Celia invited me to the apartment on an evening when Haiml was away at a conference of the Poale Zion. We talked so long she revealed a secret to me: she was having an affair with Morris Feitelzohn. That evening I realized that Celia had the same need to confess as everyone else. She was quite frank about the fact that when it came to love, Haiml was as inexpert as a child.

He needed a mother, not a wife, while she was hot-blooded. She said, "I like gentleness, but not in bed."

This remark coming from a woman who dressed and behaved so conservatively and who watched her every word astounded me more than the fact that she was unfaithful to Haiml. Our conversation became nakedly intimate. The essence of what she said was that literature, theater, music, even accounts in the newspapers roused her erotically, yet at the same time her nature was such that she could give herself only to someone to whom she looked up. For a man to utter some foolishness or demonstrate weakness was enough to repel her.

She said, "I could be happy with Feitelzohn, but he's the worst liar I've ever met. He has hoodwinked me so many times that I've lost all respect for myself for still believing him once in a while. He possesses hypnotic powers. He could be the Mesmer or Svengali of our time. If you're convinced that you know him, you're only deluding yourself. Each time I tell myself that the man can no longer surprise me, I get a new shock. Do you know that Morris is superstitious to the point of absurdity? He is terrified of black cats. When he is on his way to a lecture and meets someone holding an empty vessel, he runs back. He carries around all kinds of amulets. When he sneezes he pulls his ear. There are certain words you can't use in his presence. Did you ever try to discuss death with him? He has more idiosyncrasies than a pomegranate has seeds. He considers all women witches. He goes to fortune-tellers who for a zloty tell him he will take a long trip and meet a dark woman. And his contradictions! He breaks every law of the Shulchan Aruch, yet at the same time he preaches Jewishness. He has a wife whom he's never divorced and a daughter he hasn't seen in years. When his mother died he didn't go to her funeral."

I remember that evening and the things Celia said to me, because this was the beginning of our intimacy. I

27

suspected that she had decided to revenge herself upon Feitelzohn through me for his affairs with other women. There was a minute when I was ready to embrace her and whisper those smooth lies that come to the lips on such occasions. But I was sure that Feitelzohn possessed clairvoyant powers. Often when I was about to say something, he plucked the words right out of my mouth. I switched the conversation with Celia to a different topic and her eyes seemed to ask, "You're scared, eh? Yes, I understand."

A while later the doorbell rang. It was Haiml. The conference had been canceled because a quorum wasn't present. Winter had set in and Haiml wore a fur coat, fur boots, and a fur hat resembling a rabbinical *shtreimel*. He looked so funny I barely kept from laughing.

Celia said, "Haiml, our young friend here is as bashful as if he had left the yeshiva only yesterday. I tried to seduce him but he wouldn't cooperate."

"What is there to be bashful about?" Haiml said. "We're all created from the same protoplasm, we all feel the same urges. Don't you find Celia attractive?"

"Both attractive and intelligent."

"So what's the problem? You may kiss her."

"Come here, yeshiva boy!" Celia said, and she gave me a mighty kiss. She said, "He writes like a grown-up but he's still a child. Truly a mystery." After a while she added, "I have a name for him—Tsutsik. That's what I'll call him from now on."

3 Dr. Morris Feitelzohn had spent the years between 1920 and 1926 in America, where he had been on the staff of a Yiddish newspaper in New York and had given courses at some local college. I never found out exactly why he left the Golden Land. Each time I questioned him about it, he gave me a different answer. He said that he couldn't stand the New York climate because he suffered there from hay fever, rose fever, and other allergies. Or he said that he couldn't bear American materialism and reverence for the dollar. He hinted at romantic entanglements. I had heard that the writers at the newspaper conspired against him and got him fired. Also, he had problems at the college where he lectured. In his conversations with me, he often referred to the Yiddish theater in New York, to the Café Royal where the Yiddish intellectuals of the city gathered, and to such Zionist leaders there as Stephen Wise, Louis Lipsky, and Shemaryahu Levin.

In spite of his frequently expressed antipathy toward America and Americans, Morris Feitelzohn never severed his connections with them. He was a friend of the director of HIAS in Warsaw and was known at the American consulate. From time to time, tourists who had either known Feitelzohn in New York or to whom one of his American friends had recommended him came to Poland and Feitelzohn brought them up to the Writers' Club and played the role of guide. He assured me he never took any money from these Americans, but I knew that he went with them to first-class restaurants, to the theater, to museums, and to concerts, and they often left him ties and other gifts. He confided to me that one of the higher officials at the Warsaw American consulate could be bribed to help obtain visas for alleged rabbis, professors, and bogus relatives beyond the quota. The way of transmitting the bribe was to play poker and allow the official to win a large amount. The intermediary was a foreign correspondent in Warsaw who took a percentage for himself. The fact that despite all these contacts Feitelzohn remained a pauper who had to borrow a few zlotys from a poor slob like me seemed proof that he himself was basically honest.

For me that winter in the 1930's was one of the hardest

I had known since I left my parents' house. The literary magazine where I read proof two days a week was on the verge of folding. The publisher who printed my translations was facing bankruptcy. I had sublet a room from a family who now wanted to be rid of me. More than once when people telephoned me they were told that I was out, even though I was right there in my room. In order to go to the bathroom I had to walk through the living room, and the door to this room was often locked at night. I had been planning to move for weeks but hadn't found a room for the little rent I could pay. I was still involved with Dora Stolnitz—I didn't want to marry her, yet wasn't willing to let go.

When I met Dora she had said that she considered marriage a vestige of religious fanaticism. How could you sign a contract for lifelong love? Only capitalists and clerics were dedicated to perpetuating such a hypocritical institution. Although I had never been a leftist, in this I concurred with her. Everything I saw and read bore witness to the fact that modern man didn't take family responsibility seriously. Dora's father, a widower, had gone bankrupt in Warsaw and, to avoid imprisonment, had fled to France with a married woman. Dora had a sister who lived with a journalist, a married man who used to frequent the Writers' Club. Through him I came to know Dora. But in the very first months of our affair she began to insist that we marry. She said she wanted this for the sake of some aunt, a sister of her deceased mother, who was a pious woman.

On that winter day I looked for a room from ten in the morning until nightfall. The rooms I liked cost too much. Others were too small or stank of insecticide and bedbugs. The truth was that the way my affairs were going I couldn't afford even a cheap room. Around five o'clock, I headed for the Writers' Club. It was warm there and I could have a meal on credit. Going to the club gave me a feeling of shame. What kind of writer was I? I hadn't published a single book. It was a cold, wet day. Around evening, snow began to fall. I walked along Leszno Street, shivering under my thin coat, and imagined I had written a work that would startle the world. But what could startle the world? No crime, no misery, no sexual perversion, no madness. Twenty million people had perished in the Great War, and here the world was preparing for another conflagration. What could I write about that wasn't already known? A new style? Every experiment with words turned quickly into a collection of mannerisms.

I opened the door to the club and saw Morris Feitelzohn with an American couple. The man was short and stout, with a wide, ruddy face, a headful of hair white as foam, and a bulging belly. He wore a light-colored coat—a shade of yellow not seen in Poland. The woman was no taller, but young, slim, and dressed in a short fur coat I guessed to be sable. She wore a black velvet beret over her red hair. I wasn't in a mood to meet the Americans and tried to avoid them, but Feitelzohn had already seen me and called out, "Tsutsik, where are you going?"

He had never called me Tsutsik before—obviously he had talked with Celia. I stopped, my eyes bleary from the cold. I tried to dry my palms on the soaked tails of my overcoat.

Feitelzohn said, "Where are you running? I want you to meet my American friends. This is Mr. Sam Dreiman and this is Betty Slonim, an actress. This young man is a writer."

Sam Dreiman's face seemed to have been pasted together from clay. He had a broad nose, thick lips, high cheekbones, and small boring eyes beneath thick white brows. His tie was yellow, red, and gold, pierced with a diamond stickpin. He held a cigar between two fingers and spoke in a loud, grating voice. "Tsutsik?" he bellowed. "What kind of name is that? A pet name, what?"

Betty Slonim might have had the figure of a schoolgirl, but behind the makeup her face revealed maturity. She had hollow cheeks, a narrow chin, and eyes that by the dim glow of the overhead lamps seemed to be yellowish. She reminded me of trapeze artists in the circus. Her voice was that of a boy.

Sam Dreiman shouted at me as if I were deaf. "You write for the papers, eh?"

"For magazines, from time to time."

"What's the difference? In this world we need everything. On the ship I met a man and we played a little pinochle—that's a kind of card game. We got to talking and I asked him, 'What do you do?' and he told me he was going to Africa to capture lions and other wild animals for the zoos in the States. He had a group of hunters with him, and cages, nets, and the devil knows what. This lady, Betty Slonim, is a great actress who has come to Poland to appear in the Yiddish theater. If you have a play, we can do business immediately—"

"Sam, don't talk nonsense," Betty Slonim interrupted him.

"A young man like this could have just the play you're looking for. But before we get down to business, let's first go somewhere for a bite. Come along, young man. What's your real name?"

"Aaron Greidinger."

"Aaron what? That's a hard name. In America we don't go for long European names. There, time is money. A Russian came into our office and his name was Sergei Ivanovich Metropolitansky. You could get asthma just from trying to pronounce a name like that. We called him Met, and that's how it stuck. He's a plumber, a specialist. He puts an ear to a pipe in the basement and he knows what's going on on the top floor. I didn't have any lunch today, and I'm hungry as a dog."

"You can get a bite here," Feitelzohn said, pointing to the lunch counter.

"I'll tell you something. I never trust a writers' restaurant. I ordered dinner at the Café Royal and they gave me a steak as tough as leather. I noticed two restaurants down the street and they both looked pretty good to me. Come, young man, come along with us. May I call you Tsutsik?"

"Yes, of course. But I'm not hungry. I ate not long ago," I lied.

"What did you eat? You don't look like somebody who's overeaten. We'll have a drink of whiskey, too—maybe even champagne."

"Really, I'm not—"

"Don't be so stubborn," Feitelzohn interjected. "Come with us. I think you told me you'd written a play?" he went on, changing his tone.

"I only have the first act and it's just a first draft."

"What kind of play is it?" Betty Slonim asked.

I had stopped blushing when a woman addressed me, but now I felt the blood rush to my face. "Oh, it's not for the theater."

"Not for the theater?" Sam Dreiman shouted. "For who is it then—King Tut?"

"It wouldn't draw an audience."

"What's the subject?" Feitelzohn asked.

"The Maiden from Ludmir. She was a girl who wanted to live like a man. She studied the Torah, wore ritual fringes, a prayer shawl, and even put on phylacteries. She became a rabbi and held court for Hasidim. She covered her face with a veil and preached the Torah."

"If it's well written, it's exactly what I'm looking for," Betty Slonim said. "Can I see the first act?"

"Something will come of this meeting," Feitelzohn observed as if to himself. "Come along; we'll eat, drink, and talk business, as they say in America."

"Yes, come, young man!" Sam Dreiman shouted.

"Keep your wits about you and you'll be swimming in gravy."

4 We sat in Gertner's Restaurant and Sam Dreiman spoke of his and Betty Slonim's plans. He had lost over a million dollars in the Wall Street crash, he said, but only on paper. Sooner or later the stocks would rise again. The economy in Uncle Sam's land was healthy. A good many of the stocks still paid dividends. Besides, he owned houses and was a partner in a factory. The manager was his brother's grandson, Bill, a lawyer. He himself was far from being a young man, so what need was there to worry? God had blessed him with a great love in his late years—he indicated Betty—and what he wanted was to enjoy himself and to provide her with enjoyment. She was a marvelous actress, but the hams on Second Avenue were jealous of her talent. They wouldn't even accept her in the Hebrew Actors Union, but the few times she managed to perform in spite of them, her reviews were sensational —not only from the Yiddish but from the English press as well. She could have appeared on Broadway, but she preferred to act in Yiddish. That was the language that really brought out her talent. Money was no problem. He would rent a theater for her here in Warsaw. The main thing was to find a play that suited her. Betty required dramatic roles. Her first choice was tragedy. She was no comedienne and despised the "dance, song, and strut" of the Yiddish theater in America.

He turned to me. "If you come up with the right goods, young man, I'll give you a five-hundred-dollar advance. If the play goes well, you'll get royalties. If it becomes a hit in Warsaw, I'll take it over to America. The first act is ready, you say? Have you started the second? Betty, you talk to him. You know better what to ask."

Betty was about to speak but Feitelzohn beat her to it:

"Aaron, you'll be a millionaire. You'll become my patron and my publisher. Don't forget that I was the broker who brought it all about."

"If it comes to anything, you'll get your broker's fee from *me!*" Sam Dreiman bellowed. Each time he spoke he spread his hands, and I noticed a big diamond ring on his finger. He also wore a gold-banded wristwatch and jeweled studs.

Now that Betty had taken off her fur coat and sat there in a sleeveless black dress, I could see how thin she was. She had an Adam's apple like a boy's; her arms were like sticks. Warsaw was already talking about how healthy and fashionable it was to be thin, but this Betty seemed to me emaciated. It had become the style for Warsaw women to let their nails grow and cover them with red polish, but Betty's fingernails were uncolored and it was obvious that she bit them. Hair cut *à la garçon* was passé, but Betty still wore hers short. She barely tasted the food before her, and between bites she puffed on a cigarette. She wore a huge diamond bracelet on her left wrist and around her throat a necklace with smaller diamonds.

She leaned toward me and asked, "When did this girl live? In what century?"

"In the nineteenth. She died only a short while ago in Jerusalem. She may have been a hundred years old."

"I never heard of her. Was she that pious?"

"Yes, very pious. Many Hasidim felt that she had been possessed by the dybbuk of an ancient rabbi who uttered the Torah through her lips."

"What else did she do? Is there any action in this play?"

"Very little."

"A drama has to have action. The heroine can't just spout Torah through three or four acts. Something has to happen. Did she have a husband?"

"If I'm not mistaken, she married later on, but it seems she divorced her husband."

"Why don't you write in an affair for her? If a woman like that fell in love, it could create a strong conflict."

"Yes, that's an idea worth considering."

"Have her fall in love with a non-Jew, a Christian."

"A Christian? That couldn't be."

"Why not? Love knows no restrictions. Suppose she were to get sick and go to a Christian doctor. A love might very well develop between them."

"Why couldn't she fall in love with one of her own kind?" Feitelzohn asked. "I'm sure that the Hasidim who sat around her table and swallowed her leavings and listened to her Torah were all mad about her."

"Absolutely!" Sam Dreiman roared. "If I was one of those Hasidim and didn't have my Betty—may she outlive me—I would be mad about her myself! I admit to being an ignoramus, but I love educated women! Betty studied at the Gymnasium. She reads books by the hundreds. She performed in Stanislavsky's theater. Tell them, Betty, who you played with. Let them know who you are!"

Betty shook her head. "There's nothing to tell. I did perform in Russia in Yiddish and in Russian too, but it's just my luck that even before I got going, a whole network of intrigue formed around me. I'll never know why. I don't want power, I'm not rich, I've never tried to steal anyone's husband or lover. The men were attentive to me at first, but when I kept them at a distance, they became my enemies overnight. The women were all ready to drown me in a spoonful of warm water, as the saying goes. That's how it was in Russia and that's how it was in America, and it will be the same here, too—unless there's no competition to conspire against me."

"If anyone dares say a word against my Betty, I'll poke his eyes out!" Sam Dreiman shouted. "Here, they'll kiss your feet!"

"I don't want anyone to kiss my feet. All I want is to be left alone so that I can play with peace of mind."

"You'll play, Betty darling, and the whole world will learn how great you are. They kept all the great ones down. You think Sarah Bernhardt's path was strewn with roses? Well, and what about the others? That one from Italy—whatever her name was. And Isadora Duncan, you think she didn't have trouble? Even Pavlova had it. When people sense the presence of a talent they turn into wolves. I once read in the paper—I forget the writer's name—about Rachel and how the anti-Semites in Paris tried to push her out of—"

"Sam, I want to talk about the play with the young man."

"Talk, darling. I like this play even before I've read it. I feel it was made for you. I bet a dybbuk sits inside you too, Betty darling." He turned to me. "At times when she begins to yell at me, she acts possessed herself—"

"Will you stop or not? Stop it."

"I'll stop. I'll only say one thing more to this young man. I'll give you a few hundred dollars so you can work without worrying where your next meal is coming from. Just make the play so that things happen. Let her fall in love with a doctor or a Hasid or a dogcatcher, you name it. The main thing is, the audience should be curious to know what's going to happen next. I'm no writer, but I would have her get pregnant and—"

"Sam, if you don't stop talking like a clown, I'm leaving."

"So be it. You won't hear another peep from me till we go home."

"I wanted to say something, but he's mixed me up to the point that I hardly know where I am," Betty complained. "Oh, yes—there has to be action. But you're the writer, not I."

"Really, I'm no playwright. I started to write the thing for myself. I wanted to show the tragedy of the intellectual woman, particularly among Jews who—"

"I don't consider myself an intellectual but that is *my* tragedy. Why do you think they conspired against me? Because I had no patience with their gossip, intrigues, and stupidity. Ever since childhood I've been like a foreign element around women. My own sisters didn't understand me. My mother looked at me like a hen that had sat on a duck's egg and hatched a creature drawn to the water. My father was a scholar—a Hasid, a follower of the Husiatiner rabbi—and the Bolsheviks shot him. Why? He was rich once, but the war had ruined him. People fabricated stories and made false accusations against him. My whole family stayed on in Russia, but I couldn't remain among the murderers of my father. The truth is that the whole world is full of evildoers."

"Bettyle, stop talking like that. If I had a million for every good person, Rockefeller would be heating my stove."

"You're the first pessimistic woman I've ever met," Feitelzohn observed. "Pessimism is usually a male trait. I can envision a woman with masculine characteristics and gifts—a female Mozart, say, or even an Edison. But a female Schopenhauer is beyond the stretch of imagination. Blind optimism is essential to the concept of woman. All of a sudden, to hear such words from a female!"

"Maybe I'm not a woman?"

"That's for me to decide!" Sam shouted. "You are one hundred percent a woman—no, not one hundred percent, but a thousand! I've had many women in my life, but what she is—"

"Sam!"

"Well, I'll shut up. Start on the play first thing tomorrow, young man, and don't worry about the money. Betty sweetheart, stop smoking so much. You're on your third pack today."

"Sam, mind your own business."

5 By the time Feitelzohn and I said goodbye to Sam Dreiman and Betty, it was midnight. While shaking hands, Betty squeezed my palm once and then again. She tilted her face toward mine and I caught a whiff of liquor and tobacco. Betty had eaten little, but she had finished several glasses of cognac. She and Sam were staying at the Hotel Bristol and they took a taxi there. Feitelzohn had a room on Dluga Street, but he walked me to Nowo-lipki Street, where Dora Stolnitz lived. He knew about my affairs. He seldom went to bed before two.

He took my arm and said, "My boy, you caught Betty's eye for sure—hoo hah! If that play of yours has anything to it, you're a made man. Sam Dreiman is loaded and he's crazy about Betty. Get out your manuscript and pack it with all the love and sex it can take."

"I don't want to turn it into a piece of trash."

"Don't be an ass. Theater is trash by definition. There's no such thing as a sustaining literary play. Literature must consist of words, just as music must consist of sounds. Once you perform the words on stage or even recite them, they're already secondhand goods."

"The audiences won't come."

"They'll come, they'll come. A guy like Sam Dreiman would think nothing of bribing critics. He may even bribe audiences. The main thing is, don't spare the schmaltz. Today's Jews like three things—sex, Torah, and revolution, all mixed together. Give them those and they'll raise you to the skies. Maybe you have a zloty?"

"Two."

"Well, you're already acting like a millionaire. What do you think about Betty?"

"She seems to be suffering from a persecution complex."

"Probably a lousy actress, too. But I'm having strange fantasies lately. We spoke of dybbuks today—I've been possessed by a dybbuk. He tells me to found an institute of pure hedonism."

"Isn't life itself such an institute?"

"Yes and no. All people are hedonists, yes. From cradle to grave, man thinks only of pleasure. What do the pious want? Pleasure in the other world. And what do ascetics want? Spiritual pleasure or whatever. I go even further. For me, pleasure takes in not only life but the whole universe. Spinoza says that God has two attributes known to us—thought and extension. I say that God is pleasure. If pleasure is an attribute, then it must consist of infinite modes. This would mean that there are myriads of unknown pleasures still to be discovered. Of course, if God happens to have an attribute of evil, woe to us. Maybe He isn't so almighty after all and needs our cooperation. My dybbuk tells me that since we are all parts of Him and since men are the greatest egotists among all creatures—Spinoza says that man's love of himself is God's love for man—the pursuit of pleasure is man's only goal. If he fails here, he must fail in everything else."

"Doesn't your dybbuk know that man has already failed? Isn't the Great War proof enough?"

"It may be proof to me, but not to my dybbuk. He tells me that God suffers from a kind of divine amnesia that made Him lose the purpose of His creation. My dybbuk suspects that God tried to do too much in too short an eternity. He has lost both criterion and control and is badly in need of help."

"Really, you are joking."

"Of course I'm joking, but in some foolish way I am also serious. I see Him as a very sick God, so bewildered by His galaxies and the multitude of laws He established that He doesn't know what He aimed for to start with. Sometimes I look into my own scribblings and discover that I began one kind of work and it turned out to be the opposite of what I intended. Since we are supposed to have been formed in His image, why couldn't such a thing have happened to Him?"

"So you are going to refresh His memory. Is this the topic of your next article?"

"It could be, but these idiotic editors will not take anything from me. Lately they send everything back. They don't even bother to read it. By the way, your memory must also be refreshed. You promised me two zlotys."

"You're right. Here they are. I'm sorry."

"Thank you. Please don't laugh at me. First of all, this crazy Sam gave me too much to drink. Second, after midnight I let go of what is left of my mind. I am not responsible for anything I babble or even think. Since I cannot sleep I must dream with open eyes. Perhaps like me He suffers from insomnia. As a matter of fact, the Good Books tells us He doesn't doze or sleep but watches over the children of Israel. What a watchman! Good night."

"Good night. It was a great pleasure. Thank you."

"Try to write this lousy play. I have lost respect for everything, but I absolutely worship money. If we ever return to idolatry, my temple will be a bank. Here you are."

At Nowolipki Street, Feitelzohn held out a warm hand to me and headed home. I rang and the janitor let me in. All the windows in the courtyard were dark but for one on the third floor. For me, spending the night at Dora's was both a danger (they might raid the apartment and find illegal literature) and a humiliation (we had broken up). She was about to smuggle herself into Russia to take a course in propaganda. Although she denied it heatedly, almost every Communist who crossed the border from Poland was arrested by the Soviets—they were accused of espionage, sabotage, and Trotskyism. More than once I warned her that such a trip was sure suicide, but she said, "Those who have been arrested deserved it richly. Fascists, social Fascists, and all the other capitalist lackeys should be liquidated, the quicker the better."

"Was Hertzke Goldshlag a Fascist? Was Berel Guttman a Fascist? Was your friend Irka a Fascist?" I demanded.

"Innocent people aren't jailed in the Soviet Union! That's done in Warsaw, in Rome, and in New York."

No facts or arguments would convince her. She had hypnotized others and was herself under the spell. In my mind I could see her cross the border at Nieświez, fall to the ground to kiss the soil of the land of socialism, and promptly be dragged off to jail by the Red guards. There she would sit among dozens like her—hungry and thirsty beside a bucket of slops—and keep on asking herself, "Is this possible? What was my crime? I who gave my best years to the socialist ideal."

I walked slowly. I had vowed solemnly not to come here again, but I needed her body. I knew that we would be parting forever. Perhaps she was perplexed by doubts herself. Even the most pious experience occasional heretical thoughts. I stopped for a moment on the dark stairs and indulged in a brief introspection. What if I should be arrested with her this night? What kind of justification could I offer myself? Why, as the saying goes, did I crawl with a healthy head to a sickbed? Well, and should I try to refashion my play to suit Betty Slonim's whims? And what was it Feitelzohn actually wanted? How strange, but during the last few months I heard time and again at the Writers' Club that someone was arranging an orgy. There was a table at the club that young writers had dubbed the "Table of the Impotent." Each night after the theater and movies, the older writers—the classicists, newspaper editors, old journalists, and their ladies —gathered there to discuss politics, Jewish topics, and the eroticism that had come into fashion with Freud and the sexual upheavals in Russia, Germany, and the whole Western world. A famous actor, Fritz Bander, had come to Poland from Germany. The Nazi and conservative newspapers had for a time waged a campaign against Bander for corrupting the German language ("Moischeling," they called it), for making insulting remarks about Ludendorff, and for seducing a German aristocratic young lady and driving her to suicide. Bander, a Galician Jew, fell into such a rage from these attacks, as well as from the poor reviews he had been receiving, that he abandoned Berlin for Warsaw. He wanted to do penance and return to the Yiddish theater. He had brought along his Christian sweetheart, Gretel, the wife of a German film director. Her husband had challenged Bander to a duel and threatened him with a gun. Bander now sat every night with his sweetheart at the Table of the Impotent and told jokes in Galician-accented Yiddish. He had been notorious in Berlin for his sexual prowess. In the Romanisches Café on Grenadierstrasse queer tales were told of his adventures. It was the joke at the Warsaw Writers' Club that Bander's boastings had sparked the ambitions of the old, sick writer, Roshbaum, to become another Casanova.

Before knocking on Dora's door, I stopped to listen. Maybe a meeting of the District Committee was going on inside? Maybe the police were conducting a raid? In this compromised apartment, anything was possible. But no, all was quiet. I knocked three times—a signal between Dora and me—and waited. Soon I heard her footsteps. I never learned why there was no telephone in the apartment, but guessed it was so that the police couldn't tap the wire.

Dora was small, broad in the hips and with a huge bosom. She had a crooked nose. Her big, fluttering eyes were her only attractive feature. They reflected a blend of cunning and the solemnity of one who has assumed the mission of saving mankind. She stood at the door now in her nightgown, with a cigarette stuck between her lips. "I thought you'd left Warsaw," she said.

"Where to? Without saying goodbye?"

"I wouldn't put anything past you."

6 Although a Communist is forbidden to reveal Party secrets to a member of the enemy class, Dora told me that everything was ready for her departure. It was a matter of a few days. She had already sold pieces of her furniture to neighbors. A Party functionary was scheduled to take over the apartment. I had stored a bundle of manuscripts with her and she reminded me that I must take them away when I left in the morning. Although I had eaten a heavy dinner, Dora insisted I join her for rolls with marinated herring and tea.

"You brought this situation about yourself," she said accusingly. "If we had lived together like a normal couple, I wouldn't be going away. The Party doesn't compel a husband and wife to part, especially when there is a child. We could have had a couple of children by now."

"And who would suppport them? Comrade Stalin? I've been left without work. I owe two months' rent."

"Our children wouldn't have starved. Well, it's foolish and too late for such talk. You'll have your children with someone else."

"I don't want children with anyone," I said.

"The typical degenerate psychology of capitalist stooges. It's the collapse of the West, the end of civilization. There's nothing left but to lament the catastrophe. However, Mussolini and Hitler will bring order. Mother Rachel will rise from her grave and lead her children back to Zion. Mahatma Gandhi and his goat will triumph over English imperialism."

"Dora—enough!"

"Come to bed. This may well be the last time for us."

The wire springs of the bed had a depression in the middle and we couldn't lie apart even if we wanted to. We rolled toward each other and listened in on our own desire. Her flesh was plump, smooth, warm. Her enormous breasts amazed me each time we were together—how could she carry around such a load? She pressed her plump knees against mine and complained that I was hurting her. Our souls (or whatever they may be called) were battered and at odds, but our bodies had remained friendly. I had learned to curb my lust. We indulged in some foreplay, some during-play, and sometimes even some afterplay.

Dora put a hand on my loin. "Do you have my replacement standing by yet?"

"Well, and what about you?"

"There'll be so much to do there, I won't have time to think of such things. It's a hard course. It's not so easy to adjust to new circumstances. To me love is no game. I have to respect the person first, believe in him, have faith in his thoughts and character."

"A Russky with all these qualities is awaiting you there."

"Look who's talking! You were always ready to trade me for the first available yenta."

We kissed and bickered. I listed all her former lovers while she counted off all those with whom I might have betrayed her. "You don't even know the meaning of the word faithful!" she said. She kissed and bit me. We went to sleep sated and I woke up with lust renewed.

Dora spoke in a crooning chant, "I'll never forget you, never! My last thoughts on my deathbed will be of you, you reprobate!"

"Dora, I'm worried about you."

"What are you worried about, you lousy egotist?"

"Your Comrade Stalin is a madman."

"You're not even worthy to mention his name. Put your

arms around me! It's better to die in a free land than to live among Fascist dogs."

"Will you write me?"

"You don't deserve it, but my first letter will be to you."

I dozed off again, and I was in Warsaw and in Moscow at the same time. I came to a square filled with graves. I knocked on a door and a huge Russian answered. He was mother-naked and uncircumcised. I asked for Dora and he replied, "Rotting in Siberia." A wild party was going on inside. Men played accordions, guitars, balalaikas; nude women danced. A yellow dog came out from the crowd and I recognized her—Jolka, who belonged to the Soltys of Miedzeszyn. But Jolka had died. What was she doing in Moscow? Oh, these trivial dreams, they have no meaning whatsoever, I said in my dream.

I opened my eyes and beyond the window a murky dawn seemed to be pondering its eternal return. Dora was banging pots in the kitchen. She drew water from the tap and mumbled a song about Charlie Chaplin. I lay still, dazed by the world and its absurdities. She appeared in the doorway. "I'm making your breakfast."

"How is it outside?"

"Snowing."

I washed at the kitchen sink. The water was icy.

Dora said, "A pair of your drawers was knocking around here. I washed them."

"Well, thank you."

"Put them on. And don't forget to take your Fascist manuscripts."

She brought me the drawers and from under the bed pulled a bundle of manuscripts tied with a string.

While I ate, Dora preached: "It's never too late to accept the truth. Spit on all this slime and come with me. Stop writing about those rabbis and spirits and see what the real world looks like. Everything here is corrupt. Over there life is beginning."

"It's corrupt all over."

"Is that your world concept? This could be our last breakfast together. Would you happen to have three zlotys?"

I counted out three zlotys and gave them to her. It left me with three zlotys and change. The magazine and the publisher owed me some money, but it was impossible to get so much as a groschen out of them. My only hope was an advance from Sam Dreiman. I said goodbye to Dora and promised to come back that evening. I took the bundle of manuscripts and went out into the cold courtyard. A dry snow was falling. On the top of the garbage bin a cat stood poised. She fixed her gooseberry-green eyes on me and meowed. Was she hungry? Forgive me, pussy, I have nothing for you. Dun the malefactor who created you. I went out the gate. There was an infirmary in the building, where the sick came to buy chits to see doctors. Some elderly women wrapped in shawls entered the gate. I imagined that they smelled of toothache and iodine. They spoke at the same time, each about her own sickness. The clouds hovered low. An icy wind blew. I headed for the street and my furnished room. It was just big enough to hold the bed and a single chair and almost as cold as outside. I opened the bundle of manuscripts and to my amazement saw the beginning of a second act of my play. Had Providence ordained this? Somewhere causality and purpose were firmly bonded. I began to read. The Ludmir Maiden bewailed the fact that God had granted all the favors to men and only the leavings to women— the laws connected with childbirth, ablutions in the mikvah, the lighting of the Sabbath candles. She accused Moses of being antifeminist and blamed the evils of the world upon the fact that God was a male. Should I add love and sex to this play? Whom should she love—a doctor, a Cossack? She could be a lesbian, but the Warsaw Jews weren't ready for this theme. Suddenly I had an idea:

47

she would fall in love with the dybbuk who possessed her. The dybbuk was a man—I'd make him a musician, a cynic, a lecher, an atheist. She would talk in his voice as well as her own. There was a chance that Betty Slonim could play this. She would portray a split personality. She would supposedly wed the dybbuk inside her; he would mistreat her, disappoint her, and she would demand a divorce.

I felt an urge to tell Betty Slonim my idea that very moment. I knew she was staying at the Hotel Bristol, but I couldn't bring myself to drop in on a lady at a hotel unexpectedly. I lacked even the courage to telephone her. I decided to go to the Writers' Club. Feitelzohn might be there and I could describe my plot to him. Although I was tired, a spark of interest in Betty Slonim kindled in me. I had already indulged in a fantasy in which we enjoyed fame together—she as an actress, and I as a playwright. But Feitelzohn wasn't at the club. In the first room two unemployed journalists played chess and I stopped for a while to look on. The one who was winning—Pinie Machtei, a little man who had only one leg —swayed over the chess board, pulled at his goatee, and sang a Russian song:

> *"Happy or not happy*
> *As long as there is vodka and wine*
> *Let us not whine."*

He said to me, "You may look, but don't kibitz."

He had put his knight in such a situation that his opponent, Zorach Leibkes, had to give up his queen for a castle. If not, he would have been checkmated in two moves. Zorach Leibkes was a temporary replacement in the Yiddish press when the proofreaders were on vacation. He was small and round like a barrel. He too swayed, and he was saying, "Machtei, stop singing. Your castle is nothing but an idiot. I'm afraid of him as much as I'm afraid of last year's frost. You have been a botcher and a botcher you'll remain until the tenth generation."

"Where does the queen go?" Machtei asked.

"She will go. She will go. Don't worry your silly head over it. Once she goes she will shatter your pieces to smithereens."

I went into the main room. There were only three writers there. At a small table sat Shloimele, a folk-poet who signed his poems only with his first name. He was writing a poem in a ledger like those used in grocery stores. He was known to write in almost microscopic letters that only he could decipher. While he wrote, he chirped a monotonous tune. At another table sat Daniel Liptzin, nicknamed the "Messiah." In 1905 he had taken part in the revolution against the Czar and was sent to Siberia. But there he became religious and began to write mystic stories. Nahum Zelikowitz—tall, thin, black like a gypsy, a pipe in his mouth—was pacing back and forth. He belonged to a minority in the Writers' Club that believed Hitler was bluffing and there would be no war. He had published twenty novels and all on the same subject: his love for the actress Fania Ephros, who betrayed him and married a union leader. Fania Ephros had been dead for ten years, but he continued to brood about her many treacheries. Zelikowitz had a continuing war with the Warsaw critics, who all put him down. He had slapped one of them across the face. I greeted him, but he didn't answer me. He was angry with young writers and considered them intruders.

I went back to the first room. Perhaps the Maiden should be possessed by *two* dybbuks, I thought, one a slut, the other a whoremonger? I had written a story of a girl possessed by both a whore and a blind musician. I was seized with boldness. From a phone booth I called information for the number of the Hotel Bristol, and when the hotel answered, I asked to be connected with Miss Betty Slonim. The telephone rang once and I heard her voice: "Hello?"

I was momentarily speechless. Then I said, "I'm the young man who had the honor of being with you at Gertner's Restaurant last night."

"Tsutsik?"

"Yes."

"I've been sitting here thinking about you. What's new with the play?"

"I have an idea I would like to talk over with you and Mr. Dreiman."

"Sam has gone to the American consulate, but come over, and you and I can discuss it."

"I won't be disturbing you?"

"Come right over!" She gave me her room number. I thanked her and hung up. I was tingling with delight over my own courage. Forces stronger than I propelled me. I wanted to take a cab but three zlotys might be too little to pay for it. Suddenly I remembered that I hadn't shaved, and fingered my stubble. I would have to visit a barber. I couldn't call on an American lady unshaven.

7 A doorman in livery guarded the entrance of the Hotel Bristol, and going inside felt almost like entering a police station or a courtroom. But everything went off without a hitch. Although there was an elevator, I climbed the stairs to the fourth floor. The steps were made of marble and along the middle ran a carpet. Betty answered my knock at once. Her room had a huge window and was brighter than any room I had ever seen. The snow had stopped and the sun shone in. I seemed to have been transported to a different climate.

Betty wore a long houserobe and slippers with pompons. Having red hair and having been tormented by nicknames through my childhood—red dog, red cheater, red carrot—I had an aversion to redheads, but Betty's hair didn't repel me. In the sun it seemed a blend of fire and gold. Only now did I observe how white her skin was—as white as my own. Her eyebrows were brown.

A moment after I came in, the telephone rang and she conversed for a few minutes in English. How grand and worldly this language sounded! Betty was shorter than I but she carried herself with pride. She hung up and invited me to take off my coat and make myself comfortable. Even her Yiddish smacked of sophistication. She took my coat and hung it on a wooden hanger. This struck me as novel—so much respect for an old rag that was missing a button. When I was with Dora I felt like a mature man, but here I reverted to a youth. Betty waved me to a sofa and sat down in an easy chair facing me. Her robe parted, and for a fraction of a second I saw her dazzling legs. She offered me a cigarette. I didn't smoke but I wouldn't think of refusing her. She brought me a lighter. I took one puff and became intoxicated by the aroma.

She said, "Now tell me more about the play."

I began to talk and she listened. The expression in her eyes kept changing from anticipation to amazement. "This means I'll have to conduct a love affair with myself?"

"Yes, but in a sense we all do."

"True. I could easily play a man and a woman. Why didn't you bring the script along?"

"Everything is too rough to show."

"Couldn't you recall a few lines for me? I'd like to try it out right now. I'll give you paper and pen and you can write a few lines—some words for the musician and some for the harlot. Wait!" She stood up and from her purse that lay on the dresser took out a lady's fountain pen and a notebook.

51

I began to write as if automatically:

MUSICIAN

Come, girl, be mine. You're a corpse and I'm a corpse, and when two corpses dance the bedbugs prance. I'll make you a present of a pouch of earth from the Land of Israel and the shards that covered my eyelids. With the myrtle between my fingers I'll dig you a pit reaching from Tishevitz to the Mount of Olives. On the way, we'll do like Zimri the son of Solu, and Cozby the daughter of Zur.

HARLOT

Hold your tongue, foul whelp of a musician! I left the world a pure virgin while you wallowed with every whore from Lublin to Leipzig. A band of angels awaits me, while myriads of demons lie in ambush for you.

I handed Betty the pen and notebook and she began to read slowly. Her thin eyebrows lifted and remained raised. Her lips formed an inquisitive smile. She read through to the end, then asked, "Is this taken from your play?"

"Not really."

"You composed it right here and now?"

"More or less."

"Well, you're a strange young man. You have an exceptional imagination."

"That's about all I do have."

"What else do you need? Wait, I'll try to play this."

She began to mumble into the notebook, halting here and there over some word. Suddenly she began acting out the parts in two voices. I clenched my teeth to stop them from chattering. The powers that ruled the world had brought me together with a superb actress. It was hard to conceive that talent like this spent night after night in bed with Sam Dreiman. My cigarette had gone out. Betty walked up and down the room, repeating the dialogue over and over. It struck me that she was better as the musician than as the girl. The girl's voice sounded half masculine. Each time Betty concluded, she glanced at me and I nodded.

Finally she came up and said, "This is good to recite, but a play must have a plot. One of the Hasidim, a rich one, must be in love with me."

"I'll write it in."

"He should have a wife and children."

"Definitely."

"Let him offer to divorce his wife and marry the girl."

"Surely."

"But she won't be able to decide between the dead musician and the live Hasid."

"Right."

"What then?" she asked.

"She'll marry the Hasid."

"Aha."

"But on her wedding night the musician won't let her be with her husband."

"Yes."

"And she'll go off with the musician."

"Where to?"

"To be with him in the grave."

"How long will it take you to write the play? Mr. Dreiman is ready to rent a theater. You could become a famous playwright overnight."

"As it is fated, so shall it be," I said.

"You believe in fate?"

"Absolutely."

"So do I. I'm not religious—you see how I live—but I do believe in God. Before I go to sleep I say a prayer. On board ship I prayed to God each night to send me the right play. All of a sudden, along comes a young fellow, a Tsutsik, with a play that can express my soul. Isn't that miraculous?"

53

"Let's hope so."

"Don't you have faith in yourself?"

"How can one have faith in anything?"

"You must believe in yourself. That's my tragedy—I never have had that belief. As soon as something good begins to happen, I foresee nothing but difficulties and mishaps and I spoil whatever there is. That's how it's been in love and that's how it's been in my career. Do you have a director to suggest?"

"There's no point looking for a director until the play is finished."

"You're still doubtful, eh? This time I won't allow doubt. The play has to turn out well. Stick to the outline we put together just now. Sam Dreiman will give you a five-hundred-dollar advance and that's a lot of money here in Poland. Are you married?"

"No."

"You live alone?"

"I had a girl, but we've broken up."

"May I ask why?"

"She's a Communist and is going away to Stalin's land."

"Why didn't you marry?"

"I don't believe two people can make a contract to love each other forever."

"Do you have a comfortable apartment?"

"I have to move. I'm being dispossessed."

"Rent a nice room. Put aside any other work you're doing and concentrate on our play. What do you intend to call it?"

"The Ludmir Maiden and Her Two Dybbuks."

"Too long. Leave it to me to decide on the title. How much time will the rewriting take?"

"If it goes well, three weeks—a week for each act."

"How do you see the three acts?"

"In the first act, the Ludmir Maiden will become what she is and the rich Hasid will fall in love with her. In the second act, the dead musician must emerge and establish the conflict."

"In my opinion, the dead musician should appear in the very first act," Betty said after some hesitation.

"You're absolutely correct."

"Don't agree with me so quickly. Think it over first. A playwright shouldn't be so compliant."

"I'm no playwright."

"If you write a play, then you're a playwright. If you don't take yourself seriously, no one else will either. Forgive me for speaking to you this way, but I'm a few years older. Actually, everything I tell you I should tell myself as well. Sam Dreiman believes in me. He believes too much. He is perhaps the only person who believes in me and in my talent. That's why—"

"I believe in you, too."

"You do? Eh? Well, thank you. What did I do to deserve that? Apparently someone up there doesn't want my end just yet. Some sort of providence directed you to me."

THREE

1 Sam Dreiman offered me the five-hundred-dollar advance he had spoken of, but I refused to accept such a big sum. We agreed I would take two hundred dollars for now, and I traded them at a currency exchange for over eighteen hundred zlotys. This was a real windfall. I found a new place on Leszno Street that cost eighty zlotys a month. I put down three months' rent and got a wall-papered room with central heating, solid furniture, and an Oriental carpet. My landlord, Isidore Katzenberg, a former manufacturer, told me he had been ruined by exorbitant taxes. The apartment house lay close to Iron Street and was relatively new and modern. One floor was a Gymnasium, and there was an elevator at the front entrance, for which I was given a key.

Everything happened quickly. One evening Sam Dreiman handed me the money and the next day I moved into my new place. I had only to pack my possessions in two valises and carry them over. The maid, Tekla, a young country girl with brown hair and ruddy cheeks, had polished the floor until it gleamed. There was a bed in my room, a sofa, upholstered chairs, and in the long, wide corridor a telephone I was permitted to use at eight groschen a call. God in heaven, I had been thrown into the lap of luxury! I went to a tailor to be fitted for a suit. I lent Feitelzohn fifty zlotys. He demurred, but I forced them on him. I invited him to dinner at a café on Bielanska Street. I had told him the theme of the play and he offered suggestions. Feitelzohn was going to earn money from this venture as well—Sam had asked him to do the "publicity." I had never heard this word, and it had to be explained to me.

Feitelzohn sipped his tea, puffed his cigar, and said, "What kind of publicity man will I make, anyway? If I don't like the play, I won't praise it. But Sam Dreiman is apparently a multimillionaire. He is seventy or more, he has a nasty wife and estranged children who are rich in their own right—what else does he have to do with the money? He wants to spend it as long as he can. This Betty must have brought back his potency. I didn't know either of them in America, but I heard about him. It seems I even met him once at the Café Royal. He is a carpenter by trade. He went to America in the 1880's and became a builder in Detroit. When Ford built his automobile factories there and began to pay his workers five dollars a day, men came flocking from all over America—from the whole world, in fact. Sam Dreiman built houses and he built factories. In America when the money starts flowing toward someone, there is no limit to it. In 1929 he lost a fortune but enough remained. You should have taken the whole five hundred. To him that's a trifle. He'll think you're a shlemiel."

"I can't accept money for goods that don't exist yet."

"Well then, write a good play. The American believes in paying. You can give him mud, but if he pays a lot for it, in his mind it becomes gold."

I was anxious to go home and get to work, but Feitelzohn had begun to expound on a "soul expedition" he was preparing to launch. Psychoanalysis wasn't the answer, he said. The patient comes to the analyst to be cured— that is, to become like everyone else. He wants to be rid of his complexes, and the analyst is supposed to help him in this effort. But where is it written that the cure is better than the disease? Those who would take part in his soul expedition wouldn't be bound by any restrictions. We would assemble in a room on an evening, with the lights off, and give our souls free rein. Man has to be granted the courage to reveal to himself and others what it is he truly desires. The real tyrants weren't those who repressed the body (which is confined anyhow) but those who enslaved the spirit. Alleged liberators, they have all been subjugators of the soul! Feitelzohn said, "Moses and Jesus, the author of the Bhagavad-Gita, and Spinoza, Karl Marx, and Freud. The spirit is a game uncontrolled by rules and laws. If Schopenhauer is right—if blind will is really the thing-in-itself, the essence of all—why not let the wanter want?"

"What's the purpose of only wanting?" I asked.

"Where is it written that there must be a purpose? Maybe chaos *is* the purpose. You've glanced into the cabala, and you know that before Ain Sof created the world He first dimmed His light and formed a void. It was only in this void that the Emanation commenced. This divine absence may be the very essence of creation."

Evening had fallen but still Feitelzohn talked. By the

time we went outside, it was night. The street lights were on in Bielanska Street, and a thin snow was falling. As usual after speaking at length, Feitelzohn grew silent and cranky, ashamed of his own verbosity. He shook my hand and went off in the direction of Dluga Street. I walked toward Leszno. It felt strange to have a pocketful of money suddenly, an elegant room, even a maid who would make my bed and bring me breakfast. Feitelzohn's words had stirred me. Yes, what was it, actually, that I wanted? I felt drawn to Betty Slonim. Celia's kiss and confession presaged a new affair. I did not want Dora to leave. But was I in love with these women? Well, what else did I want? I had dreamed of writing a perfect book and now I wanted a perfect play, too. The snow grew denser. It made my eyelids blink and caused spearlike beams to radiate from lamp posts and show windows. Feitelzohn's constant insinuations that Celia desired me were puzzling. Was he trying to palm her off on me, or to share her with me? I had heard him say that man was on the verge of trading the instinct of jealousy for the instinct of participation.

I had resolved to work late into the night, but as I climbed the steps to my room, weariness settled over me. Tekla let me in. She wore a short white apron and a cap with lace over her hair, like a maid at a doctor's. She smiled familiarly and showed me the curtains she had hung in my room. She had already made my bed. She asked if I would like some tea. I thanked her and said not now.

I tried to overcome my weariness and sat down to rewrite the first act of *The Ludmir Maiden*, but instead I started to write a play that was completely new. I seemed to have lost control over my pen. It raced faster than my fingers. Although the mistress of the house had installed a desk covered in green felt and a desk lamp with a green shade, things glared before my eyes. Aha, that inner antagonist and saboteur was launching a campaign against me. I knew his tricks by now. I wanted to succeed, but he sought my downfall. I found I was leaving out letters and whole words. I began to consult the books that were supposed to serve as guides for my behavior: Payot's *The Education of the Will* and Charles Baudouin's work on autosuggestion, the notebook in which I had set down rules for living and means of maintaining spiritual hygiene, but fatigue overcame me and I fell on my bed in my clothes.

At once the dreams and nightmares took over. When I opened my eyes, the clock showed a quarter of two. I hardly managed to undress before drifting off again into a deep sleep. In my dreams I was able to analyze what I was going through. Yes, dreams were precisely what Dr. Feitelzohn sought to restore to man—aimlessness, spiritual anarchy, the whims of idolators, the perversions of madmen. In my sleep, Betty and Celia became one, although not altogether. I mated with this plural female, and Haiml stood by and encouraged us. Even this coupling had some connection with the play. *Is Celia the Ludmir Maiden? Is Betty the dybbuk of the adulteress? And am I myself the blind musician?* But I had never had any special feeling for music.

I had known Betty Slonim less than two days, but here she was participating not only in my daytime fantasies but in my nocturnal visions as well. She was somehow with me and part of me, my deeds and philosophizing. Feitelzohn wanted to return the soul to that primeval chaos from which all things evolved, but how could chaos create anything? Could it be that purpose, not causality was the essence of being? Were the teleologists right after all?

2   I had planned to get up at seven, but when I wakened I heard the clock in the living room toll nine times. Someone knocked on my door with the stippled panes and Tekla came in carrying a tray covered with a napkin. She had brought me eggs, rolls, cheese, and coffee. I had slept more than seven hours. I had gone through a dreamy epoch I had forgotten except for one fragment—sliding down a mountain as a band of wild people awaited below with clubs, spears, poles, and axes. They half shouted, half chanted a melody, a remnant of which still lingered in my ears—a dirge of passion and madness.

The girl started to apologize. "I thought you were up."

"Oh, I overslept."

"Shall I take the tray back to the kitchen?"

"No, I'll wash later."

"You have a pitcher of water and a basin right here. A towel, too."

"Thank you, Tekla. Thank you very much."

I was overcome by the feeling that I was being given more than I deserved. Why should this country girl be waiting on me? She had undoubtedly been on her feet since six that morning. Yesterday, I had seen her washing clothes. I would have liked to give her something, but I couldn't reach the chair where my jacket hung. She smiled, showing a mouthful of teeth without a blemish. She had muscular legs and firm breasts. She placed the tray carefully on the table. She studied me as if trying to fathom my thoughts. "A good appetite!"

"Thank you, Tekla. You're a fine girl."

A dimple showed in her left cheek. "Good health to you." She left the room slowly.

These are the real people, the ones who keep the world going, I thought. They serve as proof that the cabalists are right—not Feitelzohn. An indifferent God, a mad God couldn't have created Tekla. I felt temporarily enamored of this girl. Her cheeks were the color of ripe apples. She gave forth a vigor rooted in the earth, in the sun, in the whole universe. She didn't want to better the world as did Dora; she didn't require roles and reviews as did Betty; she didn't seek thrills as did Celia. She wanted to give, not to take. If the Polish people had produced even one Tekla, they had surely accomplished their mission. I poured a little water from the clay pitcher into the basin on my washstand. I moistened my hands and dried them on the towel. I took a drink of coffee and a bite of the fresh roll. I felt an urge to utter a benediction and thank the powers that made wheat and coffee beans grow, to offer thanks to the chickens that laid these eggs. I had gone to sleep in misery and risen almost happy.

Someone knocked on the door and opened it. It was my landlord's son, Wladek, who, his father had told me, had quit his law studies at Warsaw University and spent all day at home reading trash and listening to the music and chatter on the radio. Wladek was tall, lean, pale, with a high forehead, thin nose. To me, he appeared ill both physically and mentally. The father spoke Polish with a Yiddish accent but Wladek spoke it grammatically and with style. He said, "Excuse me, sir, for disturbing you in the midst of your meal, but you're wanted on the telephone."

I jumped up, nearly spilling my coffee. This was my first call here. I went out into the corridor and snatched up the receiver.

It was Celia. "I know that if Mohammed won't come to the mountain, the mountain must come to Mohammed," she said. "The trouble is, I have never considered myself a mountain. I've heard about your successes and I want to congratulate you. I thought we were friends, but if you prefer to remain aloof, of course that's your privilege. Still, I would like you to know I'm delighted for you."

"Not only am I your friend—I love you!" I exclaimed with the light-minded assurance of those who can afford to say whatever comes to their lips.

"Oh, really? Well, that's good to hear. But if that's the case, why haven't I heard from you? When you come to us you're like a friend, a brother. Then you go away—and silence. Is this your nature or is it a system you use?"

"No system. Nothing of any kind. I know how busy you are."

"Busy? With what am I busy? Our Marianna does everything. I sit and read, but how much reading can you do? Morris has been visited lately by hordes of Americans, so I see nothing of him. The second American ambassador to Poland I call him. Besides you two, there's no one in our circle to exchange a few words with. Haiml, God bless him, has gotten himself too involved with the Poale Zion. I believe in Palestine and all that, but England does what she pleases with her mandate. Days go by that I don't speak a word to anyone."

"Madam Chentshiner, whenever you want to meet me, all you need do is call. I miss you too," my mouth said of its own volition.

Again Celia paused. "If you miss me, what's to keep you away? And call me Celia, not Madam Chentshiner. Come over and we'll talk. If you'd rather, we can meet at a confectionery. You're probably busy with the play. Morris told me all about it. But no writer writes ten hours a day. What kind of woman is this Betty Slonim? I expect you're in love with her already."

"No, not in love."

"I sometimes envy women like her. They go straight to the target. She picked out a rich old man for a lover and he'll do everything to make her famous. To me, this is prostitution, but when have women not sold themselves for money? If she gets two zlotys for it, she's a street-walker, but when it's many thousands, along with diamonds and furs, she's a lady. I didn't know you wrote plays. Morris told me the theme. An interesting subject. When will you be over?"

"When shall I come?"

"Come for lunch today. Haiml went to his father's in Lodz. I'm all alone."

"At what time?"

"Three."

"Fine, I'll see you at three."

"Don't be late!"

I put down the receiver. She was lonely. I had suffered for years from loneliness; now suddenly my luck had changed. But for how long? An inner voice, that unconscious which Hartmann claims is never in error, told me that it wouldn't be for long. Everything would end in catastrophe. Then why not enjoy the moment? Sleep had calmed me somewhat, but now tension returned. I wouldn't make the first move with Celia, I decided. I'd leave all the initiative to her.

I went back to my interrupted breakfast. Yes, I had to find pleasure before I died and returned to nothing. I reminded myself that I hadn't checked the money I had left overnight in my jacket pocket. Someone might have robbed me while I was asleep. Even Tekla could have stuck in her hand and taken everything. I jumped up and tapped the pocket. No, no one had robbed me. Tekla was an honest girl. Still, I began to count the bills even as I felt ashamed of my mistrust.

There was another knock on the door. Tekla had come to see if I wanted more coffee.

"No, Tekla dear, I've had enough." I gave her a zloty and her cheeks turned red.

3 Exactly at three o'clock I arrived at Haiml's house on Zlota Street. To get there I walked down Iron Street to the juncture of Twarda and Zlota, then turned left. Zlota Street was almost always deserted—a residential street, without stores. Most of the residents were well off, with few or married children. The five-story building where Haiml lived was dark gray, with balconies supported on the shoulders of mythological figures. One had to ring a bell to get in the front entrance. The stairs were of marble but worn, and a spittoon stood on every landing. From the landings one looked out onto a square courtyard, a small enclosed garbage bin with snow on its deck, and a tiny garden where the branches of trees were glazed by the frost and reflected the colors of the rainbow. Celia answered when I rang. Marianna, the maid, had gone to visit her sister, Celia explained. She invited me in. The apartment glistened from cleanliness. In the dining room the table was set. A huge china closet sparkled with crystal and silver. Portraits of men with white beards and of women in wigs and jewelry hung on the walls.

Celia said, "I prepared your favorite dish—potatoes with borscht and meatballs."

She showed me to Haiml's place at the head of the table. From the way she had sounded on the telephone, I expected kisses the moment I came in, an immediate physical intimacy. But her expression told me that she was in no mood for this. She had turned formal. We sat facing each other, far apart. Celia served me. I suspected she had sent the maid away so that we could be alone. The cold walk had given me an appetite and I ate a lot. Celia questioned me about the play, and as I outlined the theme to her, I found myself making unexpected changes. This was a magical theme—like the Torah, it seemed to possess seventy different faces.

Celia said, "Where will you find the actors for such a play? And what about the director? If it doesn't come out absolutely right, it can turn into something terribly vulgar. Our Yiddish actors and actresses in Warsaw are of a low breed. You know this yourself. In all these years I haven't seen anything worthwhile on our stage."

"I'm afraid that I've fallen into a trap."

"Not if you don't hand the play over to them until you're satisfied it's just as you want it. That's my advice."

"Sam Dreiman is about to rent a theater and hire a cast."

"Don't let him do it. From what Morris tells me, he's a common man—a former carpenter. If the thing turns out badly it's *your* reputation that will suffer."

This was not the Celia I had seen on my earlier visit, but I was growing accustomed to abrupt changes both in myself and in others. Modern man may be ashamed of emotion, but he is all affect and temperament. He burns wth love and turns cold as ice; he is intimate one moment and aloof the next. I was no longer astonished by these mysterious variations. In fact, I often suspected that I unwillingly hypnotized those with whom I came in contact and inflicted my moods upon them.

After lunch we went into the parlor and Celia offered me cherry liqueur and cookies. The walls were covered with paintings by Jewish artists—Liebermann, Minkowski, Glicenstein, Chagall, Rybak, Rubinlicht, Barlevi. Jewish antiques were displayed in a glass cabinet—spice boxes, a gold-plated wine benediction goblet, Hanukkah candelabra, a Passover bowl, the sheath of a Book of Esther, a Sabbath bread knife with a mother-of-pearl handle, an illuminated marriage contract, a pointer and crown from a Torah scroll. It was difficult for me to accept the fact that this intense Jewishness was merely decoration, its essence long since lost to many of us.

For a while we discussed painting—cubism, futurism, expressionism. Celia had recently attended an exhibition of modern art and been thoroughly disappointed. In what way was a square head and a nose like a trapeze indicative of man and his dilemmas? What could harsh colors that had neither harmony nor basis in reality say to us? As to literature, Celia had read Gottfried Benn, Trackl, Däubler, as well as translations from modern American and French poets. They left her cold. "All they want is surprise and shock," she said. "But we become shockproof so quickly."

She began to look at me quizzically. It seemed that she was wondering, as I was, why we were behaving so conventionally. She said, "I'm sure that you're infatuated with that Betty Slonim. Tell me about her."

"What is there to tell? She wants the same thing we all do—to grab some pleasure before we vanish forever."

"What do you call pleasure? Sleeping, if you'll forgive me, with a seventy-year-old carpenter?"

"It's payment for other pleasures she's getting."

"What, for instance? I know women who would give up everything to perform on the stage. This seems to me a strange passion. Now, to write a good book, that's something I'd like to do, but I realized early that I hadn't the talent for it. It's the reason I admire writers so."

"What are writers? The same kind of entertainers as magicians. As a matter of fact, I admire someone who can balance a barrel on his feet more than I do a poet."

"Oh, I don't believe you. You play the cynic, but you're really a serious young man. Sometimes it seems to me that I can see right through you."

"What do you see?"

"That you're constantly bored. All people bore you except maybe Morris Feitelzohn. He is exactly like you. He can't find a place for himself anywhere. He wants to be a philosopher, but he's basically an artist. He's a child who breaks all its toys, then cries to have them put together again. Though I'm no artist, I suffer from the same sickness. We might have shared a great love, but he doesn't want this. He tells me how he carries on with servant girls. He continually douses me with cold water, enough to put out the hottest fire. You must give me your solemn word that you won't repeat my words to him. He is deliberately driving me into your arms, and he does this out of insanity. His game consists of igniting the fire in a woman, then leaving her to herself. But he has a heart too, and when he sees those close to him being hurt, it touches his conscience. He is also morbidly curious. He wants to try everything. He's afraid that somewhere there may remain an emotion he hasn't tasted."

"He wants to establish a school of hedonism."

"Foolish fantasies. For years I've been hearing about orgies but I'm sure they provide no satisfaction. They're a lark for fifteen-year-old boys and streetwalkers, not for mature people. You have to be drunk or mad to take part in them. In Paris, for five francs tourists can watch acts of perversion. The few writers who babble about this at the Writers' Club are old and sick people. They can barely stand on their feet."

We were still for a while; then Celia asked, "What about your Communist sweetheart? Has she gone to Stalin's land yet?"

"You know about her, too?"

"Morris speaks of you constantly."

"She's due to go any day now. Everything between us is ended."

"How do you end things? I never could end anything. I hear you finally have a nice room."

"Yes, with Sam Dreiman's money."

"Does it have a balcony?"

"No balcony."

"You once told me that you liked a balcony."

"One can't have everything."

"I sometimes feel that the reason some people get nothing is that they never have the courage to reach out their hands. I am one of those."

"What would happen if I reached out my hands to you now?" I asked.

Celia rocked in her chair. "You can try."

I went over and held out my hands to her.

She looked at me ironically. She stood up. "You may kiss me."

I put my arms around her and we kissed silently for a long time. She moved her lips as if to say something. But no words came out.

Afterward she said, "Don't tell Feitelzohn. He's a jealous little boy."

4   Dusk fell. The winter day—the like of which would never occur again, unless Nietzsche was right in his theory of perpetual repetition—flickered out like a candle. For a while, a purple pane reflected on the parlor wall, a sign that some part of the sky in the west had cleared preceding sunset. Celia didn't switch on the lights. Her face was in shadow and her eyes shone out of it as if casting their own glow. Then it darkened again. Through the window a star sparkled within a split in the clouds. From where I was sitting I tried to fix it in my memory before it vanished. I toyed with the notion of how it would be if the sky remained constantly overcast and parted for only one second each hundred years, when someone might catch a glimpse of a star. He would tell of his revelation, but no one would believe him. He would be called a liar or accused of having suffered an hallucination. Behind how many clouds does the truth lie concealed now? And what did I know about the star I was looking at? This was a fixed star, not a planet. It might be bigger than the sun. Who could know how many planets rotated around it, how many worlds drew sustenance from it? Who could conceive what kind of creatures lived there, what plants grew, what thoughts were thought there? Well, and there were billions of such fixed stars in our Milky Way alone. They couldn't be merely physical or chemical accidents. There had to be someone whose commands controlled the infinite universe. His orders traveled faster than light. So omnipotent and omniscient was he that he presided over every atom, every molecule, every mite and microbe. He even knew that Aaron Greidinger had just embarked on an affair with Celia Chentshiner.

The telephone rang and Celia, who had been sitting silently in the easy chair mulling over her own thoughts, lazily stretched out her hand to the small table on which it stood. She drawled in that singsong used in Warsaw exclusively for telephone conversations, "Haiml? Why so late? I thought you'd call earlier . . . What's that? . . . Everything is fine. Haiml, we have a guest—our young friend came for lunch . . . No, *I* called *him*. If he wants to put on airs, I'll be the one to give in. Who am I, a simple housewife, and he a writer, a playwright, and who knows what . . . Yes, we had lunch and I persuaded him to stay to dinner . . . Oh, he has a famous actress now, young and probably pretty, too. What does he need with a woman my age? How is your father? . . . So? Good, let him take his medicine . . . Tomorrow? When tomorrow? On the twelve o'clock train? . . . Good. I'll meet you at the station . . . What else do I have to do with myself. A whole day went by yesterday and no one rang me. So I swallowed my pride and called him . . . Who? To direct? Don't talk nonsense. He knows as much about theater as I do about astronomy . . . You mustn't laugh at me, but a Gentile director would understand the thing better than one of our boors. They at least have studied and seen theater . . . Morris? I haven't heard from him at all. He has forgotten us, too . . . Oy, Haiml, you're one of those types, all right . . . You want to talk to him? I'll give him the phone. Here he is!"

Celia handed me the receiver. The phone had a long cord. Everything in this room was arranged to avoid effort. I heard Haiml's voice, which sounded even more thin and shrill than when we talked directly.

"Tsutsik! How are you? I hear you're working on your play. Good, good. It's high time a young person wrote for our theater. The world goes forward, but we're still stuck with *Chinke Pinke,* and *Dos Pintele Yid.* Each time Celia and I go to the Yiddish theater we vow it's the last. Well, but not to go is no achievement, either. Our conservative Zionists have renounced the diaspora. All good fortune, they say, will come about in Palestine. But let's not forget that Palestine was only our cradle. We should have grown up in those two thousand years. By ignoring the exile they help bring about assimilation. You were kind to spend time with Celia. Who can she entertain herself with? She has nothing to say to the women in our circle. With them, it's always the same—this dress, that dress, this hat or the other. All gossip. Don't be in any hurry to leave. Don't be bashful . . . Did you say jealous? Nonsense! Who was it said that when people rejoice in one another they exalt the creator, too. When I married Celia and even long before, while we were still engaged, I was terribly jealous. If she so much as spoke or smiled at another man I was ready to trample the two of them to dust. But I once read in a Hasidic volume that when one has a harmful trait and overcomes it, it can completely reverse itself. Today I know that if you really love a woman, her friend can be your friend, her pleasure your pleasure, her ecstasy your ecstasy. Tsutsik, I still want to say something to Celia. Be so good as . . ."

I turned the receiver over to Celia and went off to the room the Chentshiners designated as the library. It was dark there except for the reflection of light from a window across the street. I stood and asked myself, "Are you happy now?" I waited for an answer from that deep source called the inner being, the ego, the superego, the spirit— whatever its name—but no answer came.

Celia opened the door. "What are you doing in the dark like a lost soul? We have no secrets from you."

I could not find words to reply to her, and she said, "How can I begin an affair when I'm seriously thinking about suicide? There are people who at a certain age come to a natural end—all words spoken, all deeds done, and nothing remaining but death. I used to get up each morning with hope. Today I no longer expect anything."

"Why, Celia, why?"

"Oh, I don't fit in anywhere. Haiml is a decent person and I love him, but before he even opens his mouth I know what is going to come out of it. Morris is the very opposite, but you never know where you stand with him. He lives close to desperation. You're too young for me, and unstable. I have the feeling that you won't be staying here in Warsaw long. One day you'll simply pick up and disappear. Morris told me that Sam Dreiman wants to take you to America."

"He's a big talker."

"Such things happen fast. If you have a chance to escape from here, don't wait. We're caught between Hitler and Stalin. Whichever invades the country will bring a cataclysm."

"Why don't *you* leave?"

"Where to? I don't see myself in America."

"What about Palestine?"

"Somehow I don't see myself there, either. It's a place we'll be transported to on a cloud when the Messiah comes."

"You believe this?"

"No, my dear."

FOUR

1 Spring arrived early this year. By March, the trees were abloom in the Saxony Gardens. My play wasn't ready,

71

but even if it had been, it was too late to present it. By May all the affluent families went off for the summer to Otwock, Śwíder, Michalin, and Jósefow. The play wasn't the only problem. Sam Dreiman had had trouble obtaining a theater. So the première was put off until Succoth, when the Yiddish theaters regularly commenced their season. Sam Dreiman had advanced me another three hundred dollars, which I reckoned would carry me through until fall. He was considering renting a summer home on the Otwock route and I would be assigned a room there to work on the play under Betty's supervision. Sam confided to me that even as he sat in Warsaw doing nothing, he was earning several thousand dollars each and every week.

He said, "Take as much as you need. I won't spend it all in any case."

By now, I was on a first-name basis with Sam and with Betty, and they both called me Tsutsik. Yet I knew that everything depended on the play. Sam Dreiman often used the word "success." He kept warning me that the play must reach audiences both in Warsaw and in New York, where he still planned to take it, along with me, its author.

He said, "I know the Yiddish theater in America like the back of my hand. What else did we immigrants have except the theater and the Yiddish paper? Each time I came from Detroit to New York, I never failed to enjoy an evening in the theater. I knew them all—the Adlers, Madam Liptzin, Kessler, and Thomashefsky, not to speak of his wife, Bessie. They spoke plain Yiddish—none of that gobbledygook you hear in the art theaters, where they bore the crowds to death with propaganda. People come to the theater to enjoy themselves, not to revolt against Rockefeller's millions."

Betty and I had already kissed, both in front of Sam and behind his back. When we sat over the manuscript, she would take my hand and put it on her knee. Feitelzohn's contention that the instinct of jealousy was becoming vestigial like the appendix, coccyx, and male breasts seemed to hold as true for this couple as for Haiml and Celia. Sam Dreiman smiled and kidded me good-naturedly when Betty kissed me. He often left us alone and went off to play cards with his acquaintance at the consulate.

Feitelzohn went there as well. Recently he had lectured on the subject "Spiritual Vitamins" at the Writers' Club, and he was preparing to launch a series of soul expeditions. A friend of his, the hypnotist Mark Elbinger, had come to Warsaw from Paris. Feitelzohn told me remarkable facts about this man. He could hypnotize his patients over the phone or merely by telepathy. He was also clairvoyant. He had held séances in Berlin, in London, Paris, New York, and South America. He was supposed to take part in the soul expeditions.

Since Sam preferred to play cards rather than to spend his time looking around for a summer place in the still empty resort villages in the Otwock region, he sent Betty and me to find a suitable villa. Sam planned to arrange that the rehearsals of the play take place there. Feitelzohn had promised to hold soul expeditions on "the loin of nature." At the Table of the Impotent there was even talk of an orgy to be organized by that famous master of revelry, Fritz Bander.

One day I met Betty at the Danzig Railroad station. She bought tickets for us, and we waited in line together. It smelled here of beer, sausages, coal smoke, and sweat. Soldiers carrying full field packs waited for a train and passed the time downing huge mugs of beer that a girl drew from a keg. Her cheeks were red and she wore a tight blouse over her bosom. The soldiers joked with her, talked smut, and her pale-blue eyes smiled half in arrogance, half in embarrassment, as if to say, "I'm only one —you can't all have me."

The newspapers talked of how modern the German

Army had become, fully mobilized and equipped with the latest weapons, but these Polish soldiers looked just like the Russian soldiers in 1914. They wore heavy greatcoats and the sweat poured from their faces. Their rifles appeared too long and too bulky. All of them were doomed to be massacred, yet they made fun of the Jews in the long gaberdines. One even tugged at a Jew's beard, and they could be heard hissing, *"Żydy, Żydy, Żydy."*

I hadn't been in a train for years. I never traveled second class, always third or even fourth. But here I sat on an upholstered bench with an American lady, an actress, and looked out at the brick-red buildings of the Citadel, whose roofs were covered with earth and overgrown with grass. This ancient fortress was supposed to defend Warsaw in case of attack. It also contained a prison. The train rode out onto the bridge. The Vistula gleamed, and a strong breeze blew in from it. The sun reflected large and red in the water, and although the hour was long before sunset, a pale moon appeared in the sky. We rode through Wawer, Miedzeszyn, Falenica, Michalin. There were memories connected with each of these stops. In Miedzeszyn I had slept with a girl for the first time—only slept and done nothing else, since she wanted to preserve her virginity for her husband. In Falenica I had delivered a lecture that turned out to be a fiasco.

We got off in Swider, one stop after Jósefow, where Haiml and Celia had their summer house. A real-estate broker was waiting for us at the station. We waded through the sand until we came to a villa that appeared to me the height of luxury, with verandas, balconies, flower beds, even hothouses, all surrounded by woods. Betty seemed so eager to get rid of the broker that almost immediately she handed him a deposit of two hundred zlotys. Only then did we learn that the house had no lights, there was no linen for the beds, and the nearest restaurant or coffee shop in the neighborhood was kilometers away.

The summer hotels were not open. We had to return to Warsaw and wait for the contract to be drawn up and sent to Sam Dreiman. The broker, a little man with a yellow beard and yellow eyes, seemed suspicious of our intentions. He said to us, "It's too early. The nights are cold and dark. The summer is not here yet. Everything has its time."

From a hut a janitor came out with two barking dogs. He asked the broker to give back the keys to him. We were advised to go back to the station, because at this time of year the trains did not run frequently. But Betty insisted that she see the river Świderek and its waterfall, which the real-estate broker in Warsaw had spoken to her and Sam about. As we walked, a blast of icy wind brought winter back to us. In a matter of minutes the sky became overcast, the moon disappeared, and a mixture of driving rain and hail hit our faces. Betty spoke to me, but I could not hear her in the clamor of the wind. We had reached the Świderek River. The beach stretched before us wet and empty. The low waterfall tumbled with a thundering roar. The narrow stream shone strange and mysterious and two large winter birds flew along the surface, all the while screeching warnings, one to the other, not to get lost in the stormy twilight. Betty's straw hat lifted itself into the air and landed on the bank across. Then it started to roll and turn somersaults; it vanished in the shrubs. Betty clutched with both hands at her disheveled hair as if it were a wig, and she shrieked, "Let's go! The demons are after me. It's always like this when a spark of happiness lights up my life!"

She threw her purse on the sand, put her arms around me, and, pressing me to her, hollered, "Keep away from me! I'm cursed, cursed, cursed!"

2 Winter returned for a while, and Betty put on her sable coat once more. Then spring moved in for good. Warm breezes blew from the Praga woods through my open window, carrying with them the fragrance of grass, blossoms, and newly turned earth. In Germany, Hitler had solidified his power, but the Warsaw Jews had celebrated the festival of the exodus out of Egypt four thousand years ago. That day I didn't go to Betty at the Hotel Bristol. She came to me instead. Sam Dreiman had gone to Mlawa to attend the funeral of a cousin. Betty refused to go with him. She said to me, "I want to enjoy life, not mourn the death of some strange woman." She was again dressed in a summery outfit—a pale-blue suit and a straw hat. She brought me a bouquet, and Tekla took it and put it in a vase. I had never heard of a woman bringing a man flowers.

The spring wouldn't let us work. Birds flew past the open window with cries and twitters. We left the manuscript on the table and went to the window. The narrow sidewalks swarmed with pedestrians.

Betty said, "Spring in Warsaw makes me crazy. In New York there is no such thing as spring."

After a while we went down into the street. Betty took my arm with her gloved hand and we strolled aimlessly. She said, "You always speak of Krochmalna Street. Why haven't you ever taken me there?"

I didn't answer immediately. "That street is completely bound up with my youth. For you, it won't be anything more than a dirty slum."

"Just the same, I want to see it. We can go by cab."

"No, it's not so far. I can't believe myself that I haven't been back to visit Krochmalna Street since I left there in 1917."

We could have gone by way of Iron Street, but I preferred to walk to Prezejazd and there to turn south. On Bank Place we stopped momentarily before the gate of the old bank with its heavy columns. Just as in my boyhood, carts of money were being trundled in and out, guarded by armed police. Zabia Street was still the millinery center, with rows of windows showing hats that were modern and hats worn only by older women—hats with veils, nets, ostrich plumes, wooden cherries, grapes, and hats with crepe for those in mourning. Behind the iron fence of the Saxony Gardens the chestnut trees were scattering their blossoms.

There were benches on Iron Gate Square and weary passersby were sitting in the sunshine. God in heaven, this walk was wakening in me the enthusiasm of a boy. We stopped before the building called Vienna Hall, where wealthy men had weddings for their daughters catered. Below, among the columns, women still peddled handkerchiefs, needles, pins, buttons, and yard goods of calico, linen—even remnants of velvet and silk. We came out onto Gnoyna Street and my nostrils were assailed by the familiar odor of soap, oil, and horse manure. In this neighborhood were the cheders, studyhouses, and Hasidic prayer houses where I had learned Torah.

We reached Krochmalna Street and the stench I recalled from my childhood struck me first—a blend of burned oil, rotten fruit, and chimney smoke. Everything was the same—the cobblestone pavement, the steep gutter, the balconies hung with wash. We passed a factory with wire-latticed windows and a blind wall with a wooden gate I never saw open in all my youth. Every house here was bound up with memories. No. 5 contained a yeshiva in which I had studied for a term. There was a ritual bath in the courtyard, where matrons came in the evening to immerse themselves. I used to see them emerge clean and flushed. Someone told me that this building had been the home of Rabbi Itche Meir Alter, the founder of the Gur dynasty generations ago. In my time the yeshiva had been part of the Grodzisk house of prayer. Its beadle was a drunk. When he had a drop too much, he told tales of saints, dybbuks, half-mad squires, and sorcerers. He ate one meal a day and always (except on the Sabbath) stale bread crumbled into borscht.

No. 4 was a huge bazaar, Yanash's Court, which had two gates—one leading into Krochmalna and the other into Mirowska Street. They sold everything here—fruit, vegetables, dairy, geese, fish. There were stores selling secondhand shoes and old clothes of all kinds.

We came to the Place. It always swarmed with prostitutes, pimps, and petty thieves in torn jackets and caps with visors pulled down over their eyes. In my time, the Boss here had been Blind Itche, chief of the pickpockets, proprietor of brothels, a swaggerer and a knife carrier. Somewhere in No. 11 or 13 lived fat Reitzele, a woman who weighed three hundred pounds. Reitzele was supposed to conduct business with white slavers from Buenos Aires. She was also a procurer of servant girls. Many games were played in the Place. You drew numbers from a bag and you could win a police whistle, a chocolate cake, a pen with a view of Cracow, a doll that sat up and cried "Mama."

I stopped with Betty to gape. The same louts, the same flat pronunciation, the same games. I was afraid that all this would disgust her, but she had become infected by my nostalgia. "You should have brought me here the very first day we met!" she said.

"Betty, I'll write a play called *Krochmalna* and you shall play the leading role."

"You're a great promiser."

I didn't know what to show her next—the den in No. 6 where the thieves played cards and dominoes and where the fences came to buy stolen goods; the prayer house in No. 10 where we used to live, or the Radzymin study-house in No. 12, to which we later moved; the courtyards where I attended cheder or the stores where my mother used to send me to buy food and kerosene. The only change I could observe was that the houses had lost most of their plaster and grown black from smoke. Here and there, a wall was supported on logs. The gutters seemed even deeper, their stink even stronger. I stopped before each gate and peered in. All the garbage bins were heaped high with refuse. Dyers dyed clothing, tinsmiths patched broken pots, men with sacks on their shoulders cried, "Ole clo's, ole clo's, I buy rags, ole pants, ole shoes, ole hats; ole clo's, ole clo's." Here and there, a beggar sang a song—of the *Titanic,* which had gone down in 1911, of the striker Baruch Shulman, who had thrown a bomb in 1905 and been hanged. Magicians were performing the same stunts they had in my childhood—they swallowed fire, rolled barrels with their feet, lay down bareback on a bed of nails. I knew it couldn't be, but I imagined that I recognized the girl who went around shaking a tambourine hung with bells to collect coins from the watchers. She wore the same velvet breeches with silver sequins. Her hair was cut like a boy's. She was tall and slim, flat-chested, her eyes were shiny black. A parrot with a broken beak perched on her shoulder.

"If all this could only be transported to America!" Betty said.

I asked her to wait outside and opened the door to the Neustat prayer house—empty, but the holy ark with the two gilded lions on the cornice, the pulpit, the reading table and benches gave witness that Jews still came here to pray. On shelves the holy books lay and stood in black rows, old and ragged. Since no one was inside, I called Betty to join me. I shouted and an echo responded. I pulled apart the curtain before the ark, opened the door, and glanced at the scrolls in their velvet mantelets and the gold embroidery tarnished with the years. Betty and I thrust our heads inside. Her face was hot. We shared a sinful urge to desecrate the sacred and we kissed. At the same time I excused myself before the scrolls and reminded them that Betty was not a married woman.

We left the prayer house and I looked around the courtyard. Shmerl the shoemaker once lived and had his workshop here in a cellar. He had been given the nickname "Shmerl not today." If you came with shoes or boots to be soled or heeled, he always said, "Not today!" He died while we were still living in Warsaw. A cart drove into the courtyard and took him away to the Hospital for Epidemic Diseases. On Krochmalna Street it was believed that they poisoned patients there. The wags in the courtyard joked that when the Angel of Death with his thousand eyes and sharp sword came for him, Shmerl said, "Not today," but the Angel replied, "Yes, today."

At No. 10 the balcony of what had been our apartment was hung with wash. It had once seemed so high to me, but now I could almost reach it with my fingers. I glanced into the stores. Where were Eli the grocer and his wife, Zeldele? Just as Eli was tall, quick, agile, sharp, and argumentative, Zeldele was small, slow-moving, dull, and good-natured. Zeldele had to be told twice what it was a customer wanted. For her to put out her hand, take a piece of paper, slice off a chunk of cheese, and weigh it could take a quarter of an hour. If you asked her the cost, she began to mull it over and scratch under her wig with a hairpin. If the customer bought on credit and Zeldele marked down the amount, she couldn't make out later what she had written. When the war came and German marks and pfennigs came into use, she grew completely bewildered. Eli abused her in front of the customers and called her "Cow." She became sick during the war and they didn't manage to get her to a hospital. She lay down in bed and went off to sleep like a chick. Eli cried, wailed, and beat his head against the wall. Three months later, he married a plump wench who was just as slow and tranquil as Zeldele.

3 We entered Yanash's Court and went to the slaughter-house. The same blood-spattered walls, the hens and roosters going to their deaths shrieking with the same voices: "What have I done to deserve this? Murderers!" Evening had fallen and the harsh light of the lamps re-flected off the slaughterers' blades. Women pushed for-ward, each with her fowl. Porters loaded baskets with dead birds and carried them off to the pluckers. This hell made mockery of all blather about humanism. I had long considered becoming a vegetarian and at that moment I swore never again to touch a piece of meat or fish.

Outside the slaughterhouse, the lamps used to illuminate the courtyard only intensified the darkness. We passed tubs and basins containing live carp, tench, and pike, which the housewives would clean and chop in honor of the Sabbath. We walked on straw, feathers, and slime. The storekeepers scolded and swore the familiar old curses: "A black plague on you!" "A fever in your guts!" "You should lead your daughter to a black wedding can-opy!"

We left the bazaar and went into the street again. Before gates and lamp posts stood streetwalkers—some fat with huge bosoms and flowing hips; others slim, draped in shawls. Workers coming from factories and shops on Wola and Iron Streets stopped to talk to the whores and haggle over prices.

Betty said, "Let's get out of here! Besides, I'm hungry."

Suddenly I saw the No. 7 building, where Bashele and her three daughters had moved. Even if the family was still alive, they would have left their apartment years ago. Well, but suppose they hadn't moved out? And Shosha still remembered the tales I used to tell her, our playing house, hide-and-seek, tag? I stopped in front of the gate.

Betty asked, "Why are you standing there? Let's go."

"Betty, I have to find out if by any chance Bashele still lives here."

"Who is this Bashele?"

"Shosha's mother."

"And who is Shosha?"

"Wait, I will explain."

A woman walked into the gate and I asked her if Bashele lived in the courtyard.

"Bashele? Does she have a husband? What's her surname?" the woman asked.

I couldn't recall, or perhaps I had never known the family's last name. "Yes, her husband has a round beard," I answered. "He used to be a clerk at some store. She has a daughter, Shosha. I hope they're alive."

The woman clapped her hands. "I know the one you mean! Basha Schuldiener. They live on the first floor opposite the gate to the left. You're an American, eh?"

I pointed to Betty. "She is an American."

"Family?"

"Just friends. I haven't seen them for almost twenty years."

"Twenty years? Go straight ahead, but be careful. The kids dug a hole in the middle of the yard. You can fall and break a leg. It's dark there. The landlords grab the rent money but they don't believe in lighting a lamp at night."

Betty began to grumble, but I exclaimed, "It's a miracle! A miracle! Many thanks!" I called after the woman. I stood in the courtyard of No. 7 and looked across it into a window with a burning gaslight behind which I might possibly soon meet Bashele and Shosha. As if she finally realized what I was going through, Betty grew silent. I took her arm and led her along. Despite the darkness I spotted the hole and we avoided it. We came to the short flight of unlit stairs that led to the first-floor apartment, I felt about for a doorknob, pushed the door open, and a second miracle unfolded before me. I saw Bashele. She stood at the kitchen table peeling an onion. She had aged little in all this time. Her wig was still blond; her wide fair face had wrinkled slightly, but her eyes looked up with the amiable half smile I remembered from my childhood. Her dress might have come from those days, too. When she saw me, her upper lip lifted—she still had her broad teeth. Her mortar and pestle, the cooking utensils, the closet with the carved molding, the chairs, the table—all were familiar.

"Bashele! You don't recognize me, but I recognize you!" I said.

She put down the onion and knife. "I do recognize you. You're Arele."

In the Pentateuch, when Joseph recognized his brothers, they kissed and embraced, but Bashele wasn't a woman who would kiss a strange man, not even one she had known as a child.

Betty arched her brows. "Is it true that you haven't seen each other for almost twenty years?"

"Wait—yes, almost as long," Bashele said in a common woman's voice, kind, motherly, and yet unique. I would have known it out of a million other voices. "Many years," she added.

"But he was only a child," Betty protested.

"Yes. He and Shosha are the same age," Bashele said.

Betty asked, "How can you recognize someone who left here as a child?"

Bashele shrugged. "As soon as he started speaking, I knew him. I heard you became a writer for the papers. Don't stand there in the doorway. Come in and be welcome. This is probably your wife," she said, nodding toward Betty.

Betty smiled. "No, I'm not his wife. I'm an actress from America and he's writing a play for me."

"I know," Bashele said. "We have a neighbor who reads your things. Every time your name appears in the paper he comes and reads to us. Once it said that a piece by you will be played in the theater."

"Where is Shosha?" I asked.

"Went to the store for sugar. She'll be right back."

As Bashele spoke, Shosha came in. God in heaven— what surprises this day had brought, each greater than the other! Were my eyes deceiving me? Shosha had neither grown nor aged. I gaped at this mystery. After a while, I did observe a slight change in her face and in her height. She had grown perhaps an inch or two. She wore a faded skirt and sleeveless jacket that I could have sworn she wore twenty years ago. She stood holding a paper cone used by grocers to weigh out a quarter pound and looked at us. In her eyes was the same childish fascination I remembered from the times I told her stories.

"Shosha, do you know who this is?" Bashele asked.

Shosha didn't answer.

"It's Arele, the rabbi's son."

"Arele," Shosha repeated, and it was her voice, although not exactly the same.

"Put down the sugar and take off your jacket," Bashele said.

Slowly Shosha put the cone of sugar on the table and took off her jacket. Her figure had remained childlike, although I detected signs of breasts. Her skirt was shorter than those in style and it was hard to tell by the gaslight whether it was blue or black. This was how garments looked that had passed through the disinfection station during the war—shrunken, steamed, faded. Shosha's neck was long, her arms and legs thin. Everyone in Warsaw wore sheer, glossy, colored stockings, but Shosha's appeared to be made of coarse cotton.

Bashele began, "The war, the miserable war destroyed us. Yppe died shortly after you moved to the country. She caught a fever and took to bed. Someone snitched and the hospital wagon came for her. For eight days the fever consumed her. They let none of us into the hospital. On the last day I went to ask about her and the guard at the gate said, *'Bardzo kiepsko,'* and I knew that she was gone. Zelig wasn't in Warsaw. He didn't even go to his daughter's funeral. Four years went by before we could put up a tombstone. Teibele grew up a young lady, God spare her, smart, pretty, educated—everything you could want. She went to the Gymnasium. She is a bookkeeper now in a mattress business. They sell everything wholesale. On Thursdays she figures out what's coming to all the employees and gives the slips to the cashier. If she doesn't sign them, nobody gets paid. The boys run after her but she says, 'I've got plenty of time.' She doesn't live here with us, comes only on Sabbaths and holidays. She has an apartment with a roommate on Grzybowska Street. If you tell people you live on Krochmalna Street it ruins your chances for a good match. Shosha lives at home, as you can see for yourself. Arele, and you, young lady, take off your coats. Shosha, don't stand there like a clod! The lady is from America."

"From America," Shosha repeated.

"Have a seat. I'll make tea. Have you eaten supper?" Bashele asked.

"Thanks, we're not hungry." Betty winked at me.

"Sit down. Arele, your parents still live in the provinces?"

"Father is no longer living."

"He was a dear man, a saint. I used to consult him on questions of religious law. He wouldn't even look at a female. The moment I came in he turned away. He was always at the lectern. Such big books, like in a studyhouse. What did he die of? There are no such Jews any more. Even the Hasidim dress like dandies today—cutaway gaberdines, polished boots. Mother still living?"

"Yes."

"And your brother, Moishele?"

"Moishele is a rabbi."

"Moishele a rabbi? You hear, Shosha? He was such a tiny thing. Didn't even go to cheder then."

"He did go to cheder," Shosha said. "Here in the courtyard at the crazy teacher's."

"Eh? The years go by. Where is Moishele a rabbi?"

"In Galicia."

"In Galicia? Where is that? There are such faraway towns," Bashele said. "When we lived in No. 10, Warsaw was Russia. All the signs had to be in Russian. Then the Germans came, and with them the hunger. Later, the Polacks raised their heads and shouted, 'Nasza Polska!' Some boys around here went to join Pilsudski's legion and were killed. Pilsudski went with his men to Kiev; then they were pushed back to the Vistula. The people thought the Bolsheviks were coming and the ruffians began to talk about knifing all the rich and taking their money. Then the Bolsheviks were driven back. They were driven here, driven there—the shortages grew. Zelig is never at home any more. Things happened I will tell you about some other time. People have become selfish. They stopped caring even for their nearest. The zloty is falling, the dollar rises. Here they call dollars 'noodles.' And everything is dearer, dearer. Shosha, set the table."

"With the tablecloth or the oilcloth?"

"Let it be the oilcloth."

Betty signaled that she wanted to tell me something in private. I leaned toward her and she whispered, "I can't eat here. If you want to stay with them, I'll go back to the hotel alone."

I said, "Bashele, Shosha, the fact that I lived to see you again is a great joy to me, but the lady has to leave and I can't let her go alone. I'll come back later. If not tonight, then tomorrow."

"Don't go away," Shosha said. "You went away once and I thought you were never coming back again. One time, our neighbor—Leizer, his name is—said you were in Warsaw and showed us your name in the newspaper, but it didn't say your address. I thought you had forgotten all about us."

"Shosha, a day didn't go by that I didn't think of you."

"Then why didn't you come over? Something you wrote —it had your name on it—was printed in a paper. Not a paper but a book with green covers. Leizer reads everything. He's a watchmaker. He came and read it to us. You described Krochmalna Street accurately."

"Yes, Shosha, I didn't forget anything."

"We moved to No. 7 here and after that you never came over. You got big and you put on phylacteries. I saw you pass by a few times. I wanted to go over to you, but you were walking so fast. You became a Hasid and didn't look at girls. I was shy. Then they said you left the city. Yppe died and there was a funeral. I saw her lying there dead and she was all white."

"Shosha, be quiet!" her mother snapped at her.

"White as chalk. I dreamed about her every night. They made her shroud from my shirt. I got sick and stopped growing. They took me to Dr. Kniaster and he gave me a prescription, but it didn't help. Teibele is tall and pretty."

"You are pretty, too, Shosha," I said.

"I'm like a midget."

"No, Shosha. You have a nice figure."

"I'm grown up and I look like a child. I couldn't go to school. The books were too hard for me. When the Germans took over they began to teach us German. A boy is a *Knabe* to them and how could I remember all that? We were supposed to buy German books and Mama didn't have the money for it. Finally, they sent me home for the second time."

"It's all from not getting enough to eat," Bashele added. "They mixed the bread with turnip or sawdust. It tasted like clay. That winter the potatoes froze and got so sweet you couldn't eat them. I cooked potatoes three times a day. Dr. Kniaster said that Shosha had no blood and he prescribed some brown medicine. She took it three times a day, but when you're hungry, nothing helps. How Teibele —the evil eye spare her—managed to grow up so pretty is God's miracle. When will you be back?"

"Tomorrow."

"Come to lunch tomorrow. You used to be fond of noodles with beans. Come at two. You can bring the lady along. Shosha, this lady is an actress," Bashele said, indicating Betty. "Where do you perform? In the theater?"

"I played in Russia, I played in America, and I hope to appear here in Warsaw," Betty said. "It all depends on Mr. Greidinger."

"He always could write," Shosha said. "He bought a notebook and a pencil and filled three pages. He drew figures, too. One time he drew a house on fire. Flames shot out of every window. He drew the house with a black pencil and the fire with a red pencil. Fire and smoke poured from the chimney. Remember, Arele?"

"I remember. Good night. I'll be here tomorrow at two."

"Don't stay away so long again," Shosha said.

4 I wanted to walk but Betty hailed a droshky. She told the driver to take us to the restaurant on Leszno Street where we had had our first meal in company with Sam Dreiman and Feitelzohn.

In the droshky, Betty put her hand on my shoulder. "The girl is an idiot. She belongs in an institution. But you're in love with her. The moment you saw her, your eyes lit up in a strange way. I'm beginning to think you aren't in your right mind yourself."

"That may be, Betty."

"Writers are all slightly touched. I'm crazy, too. All

talents are. I once read a book about this. I forget the author's name."

"Lombroso."

"Yes, maybe. Or maybe the book was about him. But since each of us is crazy in a different fashion, one can observe the other's madness. Don't start up with that girl. She is sick. If you promise her something and don't keep your word, she'll crack up altogether."

"I know."

"What do you see in her?"

"I see myself."

"Well, you'll fall into a net you'll never be able to untangle yourself from. I don't even believe that such a woman is capable of living with a man. She surely can't have a child."

"I don't need children."

"Instead of your raising her up, she'll drag you down to her level. I know of such a case—a highly intelligent man, an engineer, and he married some unbalanced woman who was older. She bore him a crippled child, a piece of flesh that could neither live nor die. Instead of placing it in an institution, they dragged it to all kinds of clinics, spas, and quacks. It died finally, but the man was ruined."

"I won't have such a freak with Shosha."

"It's typical that the moment something interesting presents itself to me, fate thumbs its nose in my face."

"Betty, you have a lover who is goodness himself, rich as Croesus, and ready to turn the world upside down for you."

"I know what I have. I hope this won't spoil our plans for the play."

"It won't spoil anything."

"If I hadn't seen it with my own eyes, I wouldn't have believed such a thing possible."

I leaned my head against the back of the droshky and looked up above the tin rooftops at the Warsaw sky. It seemed to me that the city had changed. There was something festive and Purim-like in the air. We passed Iron Gate Square again. All the windows of the Vienna Hall were illuminated and I could hear music. Someone must be getting married there this evening. I closed my eyes and put my hand on Betty's lap. The smells of spring came to my nostrils along with the stench of garbage wagons transporting the day's refuse to the fields.

The droshky stopped. Betty wanted to pay but I would not allow it. I helped her out and took her arm. Normally I would have been self-conscious about escorting such an elegant lady to a restaurant, but my encounter with Shosha had dazed me. In the restaurant an orchestra was playing American jazz and hits from Warsaw cabarets. All the tables seemed to be taken. Here they ate the chickens, ducks, geese, and turkeys that had been slaughtered earlier that day. It smelled of roasting, of garlic, horseradish, beer, and cigars. The older men had tucked the huge napkins into their stiff collars. Bellies protruded, necks were thick, and bald pates gleamed like mirrors. The women chattered vivaciously, laughed, and dug their red fingernails into the portions of fowl that couldn't be got at by a fork. Their rouged lips drank from foaming mugs of beer. The headwaiter offered us a table in a niche. They knew Betty here. Sam Dreiman left dollar tips. Skillfully waiters maneuvered among the tables, balancing trays from which steam rose. I sat not facing Betty but alongside her.

The menu didn't feature a single dish that wasn't fish or meat, and I had just vowed to become a vegetarian. After some deliberation I decided the vow would have to wait another day. I ordered broth and meatballs with farfel and carrots, but I had no desire for food. Betty ordered a cocktail and a steak, insisting that it be rare. She took little sips of her drink and looked at me sharply.

She said, "I don't intend to hang around this stinking

world too long. Forty years is the maximum. I don't want to live a day longer. What for? If it works out that I can perform a few years the way I want, all the better. If not, I'll put an end to it sooner. Thank God for one gift—the choice to commit suicide."

"You'll live to ninety. You'll be a second Sarah Bernhardt."

"No. Also, I don't choose to be a second anything. It's first or nothing. Sam promises me a huge inheritance, but I'm convinced he'll outlive me, and I hope that he does with all my heart. They don't know how to mix a cocktail here. They try to copy America but imitations are always false. The music's a poor imitation, too. The whole world wants to copy America and America copies the whole world. Why should I be an actress? Actors are all monkeys or parrots. I tried to write once. I still have a bundle of poems lying around—some in Yiddish, some in Russian. Nobody wanted to publish them. I read the magazines and I see that they print the worst rubbish, but from me they demand that I be another Pushkin or Yesenin. Why are you looking at my steak like that? What you said about vegetarianism today is nonsense. If God created the world this way, then that is His will."

"The vegetarians only express a protest."

"How can a bubble protest against the sea? It's arrogant. If a cow lets herself be milked, she must be milked, and if she lets herself be slaughtered, she should be slaughtered. That's what Darwin said."

"Darwin didn't say that."

"No matter, someone said it. Since Sam gives me money, I must take it from him, and since he goes to Mlawa and leaves me alone, I must spend time with someone else."

"Since your father let himself be shot, then—"

"That's vile!"

"Forgive me."

"Basically, you're right. But man must have regard for his fellow man. Even animals don't devour their own species."

"In my uncle's house a tomcat killed his own kittens."

"A tomcat does what nature tells him. Or this could have been a mad tomcat. You're a mad tomcat yourself, and you too will devour somebody. You looked at that stunted girl today with the eyes of a tomcat looking at a canary. You'll give her a few weeks of happiness, then you'll abandon her. I know this as well as I know it's night now."

"All I did was promise her I'd come for lunch tomorrow."

"Go to her tomorrow and tell her you're married. Actually you do have a wife—that Communist you told me about. What's her name? Dora. Since you don't believe in marriage, then the woman you're with *is* your wife."

"In that case, every modern man has dozens of wives."

"Yes, every modern man has dozens of wives and every modern woman has dozens of husbands. If laws no longer have meaning, let the lawlessness apply to everybody."

The music stopped and we grew silent. Betty tasted a piece of her steak and pushed the plate away. The headwaiter noticed and came over to ask if he could bring her something else. She said that she was not hungry. She complained that the cook used too many spices. Our waiter came over and the two men began to discuss the chef. The headwaiter said, "He'll have to go."

"Don't fire him on my account," Betty said.

"It's not a question of only you. He's been told a hundred times not to use so much pepper, but it's like a madness in him. Because he likes pepper he'll end up without a job—isn't that madness?"

"Oh, every chef is half mad," the waiter said.

Both he and the headwaiter lingered around the table

while we ate dessert. They were apparently afraid of losing their usual tip, but Betty took out two dollars and gave one to each of them. Both men began to bow and scrape. In Warsaw a family could have eaten for half a week on that sum. A millionaire's mistress apparently had to act like the millionaire himself.

"Come, let's go," Betty said.

"Where?"

"To my place."

5 I got home at eight in the morning. On the way to catch my trolley I glanced in a mirror—a pale face, a bristly beard; I had had to leave the hotel early, before the maid brought breakfast. The trolley was full of men and young women going to factories and shops, with lunches under their arms. I yawned and tried to stretch, but there was no room to extend my legs. It had rained during the night and the sky hung overcast and dark as dusk; in the trolley the lights had been turned on. All the faces appeared grim and preoccupied. Everyone seemed to be taking account, wondering at the start of another day, what's the sense of all this effort, and where does it lead to? I imagined that by some common sensitivity they all realized the same mistake and were asking, "How could we have missed something so obvious and why is it too late to correct it?"

At home Tekla let me in. In the corridor her eyes expressed a reproof that seemed to say, "You wild man!" She asked if I wanted breakfast and I told her thanks, but later.

She said to me, "A glass of coffee would be good."

"So be it, dear Tekla." And I handed her a half zloty.

"No, no, no," she protested.

"Take it, Tekla, I like you."

Her cheeks flushed. "You are too good."

I opened the door to my room. My bed stood made and untouched, the shades were lowered—a bit of yesterday lingering and demanding its due. I stretched out on the bed and tried to snatch a few moments' rest. Never had a night seemed as long as this. Once my mother told me the story of a bewitched yeshiva boy who bent down over a water tub to wash his hands before supper and in the second it took him to obtain a pitcher of water lived through a reincarnation of seventy years. Something of this kind had happened to me. During one night I had found my lost love and then succumbed to temptation and betrayed her. I had stolen the concubine of my benefactor, lied to her, aroused her passion by telling her all my lusty adventures, and made her confess sins that filled me with disgust. I had been impotent and then turned into a sexual giant. We got drunk, quarreled, kissed, insulted one another. I had acted like a shameless pervert and an ardent repentant. At dawn, some drunkard tried to break open our door and we were both convinced that Sam Dreiman had come back to surprise us, punish us, perhaps even put us to death. I dozed off and Tekla wakened me with a tray of coffee, fresh rolls, and fried eggs. She no longer paid attention to my wishes but, like a sister or wife, acted on her own initiative. She looked at me knowingly. When she put the tray on the table, I took her around from behind and kissed her nape. She made no move for a moment. Then she turned and murmured, "What are you doing?"

"Give me your mouth."

"Oh, it's forbidden!" She brought her lips to mine.

I kissed her long. She kissed back and her breasts pressed against me. She kept glancing at the door. She risked her reputation, her job. She tore from my arms, panting. She seized my wrists, held them with a peasant's strength, and hissed like a goose, "The mistress could come in!" She shuffled toward the door, dragging her legs with their broad calves. I recalled the phrase from the *Ethics of the Fathers:* "One sin drags another." I sipped the coffee, bit into a roll, tasted the eggs, and took off my shoes. The play lay on my desk, but I couldn't write now. I lay down on the bed and I neither slept nor stayed fully awake. In all the novels I had read, the heroes desired only one woman, but here I was, lusting after the whole female gender.

Finally I dropped off, and in my sleep I wrote the play. The writing became increasingly harder. The pen blotted, ran dry; it scratched the paper and I couldn't make out my own handwriting. I opened my eyes and glanced at my watch—ten past one. I had slept for hours. I was supposed to be at Shosha's at two, and I still must wash and shave. I had decided to take Shosha a box of candy. I no longer needed to steal a groschen or six from my mother to get Shosha chocolate—my pockets were stuffed with Sam Dreiman's banknotes.

I did everything in a hurry. It would take too long to walk to Krochmalna Street, and when I left the confectionary I hailed a droshky. As it pulled up before No. 7, my wristwatch showed five minutes past two. I could feel the mother's and daughter's anxiety. I rushed through the courtyard and nearly fell into the hole I had sidestepped in the dark the evening before. When I opened the door, I walked into a holiday household. The table was set with a tablecloth and china. Shosha wore a Sabbath dress and high-heeled shoes. She no longer looked like a midget, merely a short girl. Her hair was set differently—high, to make her appear taller. Even Bashele had fixed herself up in honor of my visit. I handed Shosha the candy and her blue eyes gazed at me in embarrassed bliss.

Bashele said, "Arele, you are a real gentleman."

"Mama, shall I open it?"

"Why not?"

I helped her. I had asked the confectioner for his best

candy. The box was black with little gold stars. The chocolate lay in fluted paper cups, each of a different size and in its own niche.

The color changed on Shosha's face. "Mama, look!"

"You shouldn't have spent so much," Bashele protested.

"Remember, Shosha, how I used to steal money from my mother to buy you chocolate and was lashed for it at home?"

"I remember, Arele."

"Don't eat any chocolate before lunch. It'll spoil your appetite," Bashele said.

"Just one, Mama!" Shosha pleaded. She studied which piece to select, pointing to one and then another, but she couldn't make up her mind. She stopped, bewildered.

I had read in a book on psychiatry that the inability to decide about even small things was a symptom of a spiritual disorder. I picked out three pieces, one for each of us. Shosha held the candy between her thumb and index finger and lifted her pinky with the gesture of the poseurs of Krochmalna Street. She took a bite. "Mama, it melts in your mouth! How delicious!"

"Say thank you, at least."

"Oh, Arele, if you only knew—"

"Give him a kiss," Bashele told her.

"I'd be ashamed."

"What's to be ashamed of? You're a young lady—may the evil eye spare you."

"Not here, then. In the other room." She held out her hand. "Come with me," she said.

I followed her into the other room, which was crowded with bundles, sacks, and old furniture. There was a metal cot, with a straw mattress but no sheet. Shosha stood on tiptoe and I bent down toward her. She took my face in her childlike hands and kissed me on the lips, on both cheeks, on my forehead, and on the nose. Her fingers were hot. I took her in my arms and we stood there clinging to each other.

I asked, "Shosha, you want to be mine?"

"Yes," Shosha replied.

FIVE

1 It was early summer, the month of May, and Sam Dreiman had rented a cottage for himself and Betty in Świder, not far from Otwock. It wasn't the villa we had seen in March. He had hired a maid and a cook. Every morning, after breakfast, Sam went to bathe in the Świderek River. He stood under the low waterfall with his round shoulders, white-haired chest, swollen belly, and let the water pour over him. He screamed with pleasure, sneezed, gasped, and barked out his gratitude to the cool stream. Betty sat on the beach on a folding chair under a parasol and read a book. Like me, Betty avoided all sports. She could not swim. In the sun, her skin became sickly-red and developed blisters. In the attic, a room with a balcony had been set aside for me, and I used it several weekends. But I stopped going there. There were constant visitors from Warsaw or America—guests came even from the American consulate. The majority of the visitors spoke English, and then when Sam knew I was coming he invited actors and actresses who were scheduled to appear in our play and demanded that I read scenes to them. They were all old, but they dressed like young people—the men in narrow pants, the women in gaudy trousers over their broad hips. They kept praising me and I couldn't stand the excitement and even less the undeserved compliments. I had paid another two months' advance on my room on Leszno Street and wasn't about to let it stand empty. Besides, each time I went, Sam complained because I wouldn't bathe in the little river. I was embarrassed about undressing before strangers. I had never freed myself from a notion inherited from generations: the body is a vessel of shame and disgrace, dust in life and worse in death.

But what really kept me in Warsaw was Shosha. I went to see her now daily. I had laid out a program and tried desperately to stick to it. It required me to rise at eight and wash at the stand. The hours from nine to one were to be spent at my desk with the play. But I had also started a novel, which I shouldn't have done. Besides, the few hours of work were full of interruptions. Feitelzohn phoned every day. He had prepared the first soul expedition, which was to take place at Sam Dreiman's summer house. He was planning to read a paper there, to defend his theory that jealousy was about to vanish from human love and sex and be supplemented by a wish to share libidinous enjoyments with others. Celia called me every other day from Jósefow. Each time, she asked the same thing: "Why do you sit in hot Warsaw? Why not enjoy the fresh outdoors?" She and Haiml both described how balmy the air was in Jósefow, how cool the nights, how sweet the song of the birds. They begged me to come to them. Celia argued, "Let's snatch a little peace before another world war breaks out."

I admitted that they were right and promised them, as I promised Sam Dreiman and Betty, that I would come out that very day or the next, but the moment the clock showed one-thirty I headed for Krochmalna Street. I would enter the gate of No. 7 and see Shosha standing at her window watching for me—a blond girl, blue-eyed, with a short nose, thin lips, a slender neck, her hair braided in pigtails. Thank God, she had all her teeth. She spoke the Yiddish of Krochmalna Street. In her own fashion she denied death. Although they had all died, in Shosha's mind Eli and Zeldele still ran the grocery store, David and Mirale still sold butter, raw and boiled milk, as well as sour milk and cottage cheese, Esther still kept the candy store where you could buy chocolate, cheesecake, soda water, and ice cream. Each day Shosha surprised me with something. She got out her old school textbooks with the familiar pictures and poems. She had kept the notebooks in which I began my literary career and attempted to paint as well. I noticed that when it came to drawing I hadn't made the slightest progress.

Whenever I was with her, I asked myself, How can this be? How can it be explained? Had Shosha found a magical way to stop the advance of time? Was this the secret of love or the power of retrogression? Oddly, Bashele, like Shosha, showed no surprise at my reappearance. I had come back and I was here. I gave Bashele money to prepare meals for me, and when I arrived at two or a bit later, the house already smelled of new potatoes, mushrooms, tomatoes, cauliflower—whatever she had bought that day. She set the table and the three of us sat down and ate as if we had never been parted.

Bashele's dishes tasted as good as they had when I was a child. No one could give to the borscht such a sweet-and-sour zest as Bashele. She added spices to her dishes. She cooked cabbage with raisins and cream of tartar. She kept jars of cloves, saffron, crushed almonds, cinnamon, and ginger on her kitchen shelves.

Bashele took everything in stride. I told her I had just become a vegetarian, and she asked no questions but began to provide meals for me consisting of fruit, eggs, and vegetables. Shosha would go into the alcove to take out her old playthings and lay them out for me as she had done twenty years before. During the meal Bashele and Shosha related all kinds of things. The stone over Yppe's grave had tipped and was leaning on another tombstone. Bashele wanted to set it upright, but the cemetery watchman demanded fifty zlotys. Leizer the watchmaker had a clock with a brass bird that popped out every half hour and sang like a canary. He had a pen that wrote without being dipped in ink and a lens that could light a cigarette when held under the sun. Berl the furrier's daughter had fallen in love with the son of the proprietor of the tough guys' den at No. 6. The mother didn't want to go to the wedding, but the rabbi who came after my father, Joshua the preacher, said this would be a sin. In No. 8, a ditch was dug and they found a dead Russian sapper, with a sword and a revolver. The uniform wasn't yet ruined and medals were still pinned to its lapel. Each time I asked for a person on Krochmalna Street, Bashele knew all about him or her. Most had died. Of those who were still living, many had moved to the provinces or gone to America. One beggar who died in the street was found to be carrying a pouch with golden ducats dating back to the Russian occupation. A whore had been visited by a man from Cracow. He paid her one zloty and went with her to her cellar room. The next day he came again and the day after that, too, and so day after day. He had fallen in love with her. He divorced his wife and married the whore.

Shosha listened in silence. Suddenly she blurted, "She lives in No. 9. She became a decent woman."

It would seem that Shosha understood such things. I glanced at her and she blushed. "Tell me, Shosha," I asked, "did anyone ever propose a match to you?"

Shosha put down her spoon. "They offered me one with a tinsmith from No. 5. His wife died and a matchmaker came to see me."

Bashele shook her head. "Why not tell him about the store manager who wanted you?"

"Who was this manager?" I asked.

"Oh, he worked in a store on Mead Street. A short fellow with a lot of black hair. I didn't like him," Shosha said.

"Why not?"

"He had black teeth. When he laughed, it sounded like 'ech, ech, ech, hee, hee, hee.' "

As Shosha mimicked the man's laughter, she started laughing herself. Then she grew serious and said, "I can't marry without love."

2 No, Shosha hadn't remained completely a child. I kissed her when her mother went shopping and she kissed me back. Her face glowed. I put her on my lap and she kissed my lips and played with my earlobes.

She said, "Arele, I never forgot you. Mama laughed at me. 'He doesn't even know you exist any more,' she told me. 'He probably has a fiancée by now, or a wife and children.' Yppe died, and Teibele went to school. The frosts came, but Teibele always got up early, washed her face, and took her books. She got good grades. Mama was kind to me but she didn't buy me a dress or shoes. When she got angry she said, 'Too bad you didn't die instead of Yppe!' Don't repeat this—she would kill me. During the war Mama began to sell crockery—glasses, ashtrays, saucers, and things like that. She took up a place between the First and the Second Market. She sat there every day and earned next to nothing—a few pfennigs or a mark. I was left alone. They think that I'm a child because I'm small, but I understand everything. Daddy has another woman. He lives with her on Nizka Street. He comes home maybe once every three months. He comes in, counts out some money, and starts right in to yell. He goes to Teibele's—to where she lives. He says, 'She is *my* daughter.' Sometimes he sends the money by her."

"What does your father do? How does he earn money?"

Shosha's face grew solemn. "It's not allowed to say."

"You can tell me."

"I can't tell anybody."

"Shosha, I swear by God I won't tell a soul."

Shosha sat down on a stool next to me and clasped my legs. "With the dead."

"In the burial society?"

"Yes, there. First he worked in a wine and spirits store. When the boss died, the sons pushed him out. On Grzybowska Street there is a society, The True Mercy, and they bury the dead. The boss there went to cheder with Papa."

"Your father drives a hearse?"

"No, a car. This is a kind of car that if someone dies in Mokotów or Szmulewizna, Papa goes and brings him to Warsaw. He has gotten a gray beard but he dyes it and it's black again. The sweetheart—that's what they call her —is with the society, too. Swear that you'll tell nobody."

"Shoshele, whom would I tell? Who of my friends knows you?"

"Mama thinks that no one knows, but they know. There was a lot of trouble about drying the wash in the attic. If you hang it out to dry in the courtyard, it's stolen. Also, a policeman comes and gives a ticket. Whenever it's wash time, a brawl breaks out. The women curse and some-times hit each other. There isn't enough room for every-body. One woman who sells cracked eggs cut a line with wash hanging on it and all the shirts fell down. The others beat her and she ran to snitch to the cops. Oh, there was such a fuss I had to laugh. The woman got mad at Mama and she yelled, 'Go to the dead, with your husband's sweetheart, and rot with them together!' When Mama came home she got spasms. They had to call the barber-surgeon. If Mama knew that I told you, she'd scream terribly."

"Shosha, I'll tell no one."

"Why did he leave Mama? I saw her once, that sweet-heart. She has a voice like a man. It was winter and Mama got sick. We were left without a groschen. You're sure you want to hear?"

"Yes, I do."

"We had to call a doctor, but there was no money for medicine. Or for anything else. Yechiel Nathan, the owner of the grocery store, was still in No. 13 then. You remember him, eh? We used to do all our shopping from them."

"I should say so. He used to pray in the Neustat prayer house."

"Oh, you remember everything! It's good to talk with you—the others know nothing. We were always in debt to them, and when Mama sent me for a loaf of bread, the wife looked into a long ledger and said, 'Enough credit.' I went home, and when I told Mama, she began to cry. She fell asleep and I didn't know what to do. I knew that the society was on Grzybowska Street and I thought maybe Papa would be there. So I went. The windowpanes were white as milk, and a black sign read THE TRUE MERCY. I was afraid to go inside—suppose corpses lay there? I'm a terrible coward. You remember when Yocheved died?"

"Yes, Shoshele."

"They lived on our floor and I was afraid to pass their door at night. During the day too, because it was dark in the hall. At night I dreamed of her."

"Shoshele, I dream about Yocheved till this day."

"You do? She was a little child. What was wrong with her?"

"Scarlet fever."

"You know it all! If you hadn't gone away I wouldn't have gotten sick. I had no one to talk to. Everyone laughed at me. Yes, white panes with black letters. I opened the door and no corpses were lying there. It was a nice room—an office they call it. There was a little window in a wall and people were talking and laughing behind it. An old man carried glasses of tea on a tray. Someone at the little window asked, 'What do you want?' and I told him who I was and that Mama was sick. A woman with yellow hair came in. Her face and hands were covered with freckles. The man said to her, 'This girl is asking about you.' She glared at me and said, 'Who are you?' And I told her. She yelled, 'If you ever come here and bother me again I'll tear out your guts, you little no-good!' She said some filthy words, too. She mentioned that which a girl has—you understand?"

"Yes."

"I wanted to run away, but she opened her purse and dug up some money. When Papa found out about it, he came here and hollered so loud the whole courtyard could hear. He grabbed me by my pigtail and dragged me through the house and spat on me. For three years, maybe, he didn't talk to me when he visited. Mama was angry at me, too. Everyone hollered at me and that's how the years went by. Arele, I could sit with you for a hundred years and not yet finish telling you all of it. Here in our courtyard it's worse than in No. 10. There were bad kids there, too, but they wouldn't beat a girl. They called me names, sometimes they tripped me, but that's all. Remember how we played with nuts on Passover?"

"Yes, Shosha."

"Where was the hole?"

"Inside the gate."

"We played and I won them all. I cleaned you out. I wanted to give you back your nuts, but you wouldn't take them. Velvel the tailor made me a new dress and Mama ordered a pair of shoes from Michael the shoemaker. Suddenly, pious Ytzchokl came out and began to yell at you, 'The rabbi's son plays with a girl! You dreadful boy, I'm going to tell your father this minute and he'll pull out your ears.' Do you remember this?"

"As it happens, this is something I don't remember."

"He chased you and you ran. In those days, Papa still came home all the time. A sheet of matzohs hung in our house. Mama had rendered chicken fat after Hanukkah and we ate so many scraps our bellies nearly burst. They had made you a new gaberdine. Oh, look how I've been chattering away! In No. 10 it wasn't so bad—here, the thugs throw such big rocks they once made a hole in a girl's head. One fellow dragged a girl down the cellar. She screamed, but if you scream in No. 7, no one bothers to see what's wrong. A lot of the hoodlums carry knives. Mama always says, 'Don't mix in.' Here, if you stick up for someone, you could get stabbed. He did, you know what, to the girl."

"And he wasn't jailed for it?"

"A policeman came and wrote in a book and that was that. The fellow—Paysach is his name—ran away. They run away and the policeman forgets what he has written. Sometimes they send the policeman to another street, or to the higher numbers here. When the Germans came, they threw all the bullies and thieves in jail. Later, they let them all out again. People thought it would get better under the Poles, but they take bribes, too. You slip a zloty into the policeman's hand and he erases what he wrote down."

Shosha stood up. "Arele, you must never go away again. When you are here, I become healthy."

3 We took a stroll and Shosha clung to my arm. Her fingers stroked my hand, each finger fondling me in a separate fashion. Warmth spread over me and a prickling hair zigzagged across my spine. I barely kept from kissing her in the street. We stopped before every store. Asher the dairyman was still living. His beard had turned gray. This man who rode each day to the train depot to fetch cans of milk was a charitable person, my father's good friend. When we left Warsaw, my father owed him twenty-five rubles. Father went to say goodbye to him and to apologize for his debt, but Asher took fifty German marks from his purse and gave them to Father.

I was supposed to be sitting polishing the play; instead, I was walking with Shosha through the narrow gate of No. 12 to seek out my chum, Berish's son, Mottel. Shosha didn't know him—he belonged to a later period of my life. In the courtyard, I passed by the Radzymin and the Novominsk prayer houses. Afternoon services were already in progress. I wanted to leave Shosha for a minute and look inside to see which of the Hasidim remained alive from among those I had known, but she held on to my arm and wouldn't let go. She was afraid to remain alone in the courtyard. She had not forgotten the old tales of pimps who rode around in carriages snatching girls to sell into white slavery in Buenos Aires. I didn't dare bring a girl into a Hasidic prayer house while the congregation was praying. Only on Simchas Torah were girls allowed inside a house of worship, or when a relative was deathly ill and the family gathered to pray before the holy ark.

A Gentile man carrying a long pipe at the end of which a flame flared went from lamp post to lamp post lighting the street lamps. A pale light fell over the crowds. They shouted, jostled, pushed. Girls laughed noisily. At every other gate stood streetwalkers, beckoning to the men.

I didn't find my friend Mottel. I climbed the dark stairs to where his father lived with his second wife and knocked on the door, but no one answered. Shosha began to shiver. I stopped with her on the landing and kissed her. I pressed her close and thrust my hand inside her blouse and felt her tiny breasts.

She began to tremble. "No, no, no!"

"Shoshele, when you love, such things are permitted."

"Yes, but—"

"I want you to be mine!"

"For real?"

"I love you."

"I'm so small. I can't write."

"I don't need your writing."

"Arele, people will laugh at you."

"I've longed for you all these years."

"Oh, Arele! Is this true?"

"Yes. As soon as I saw you, I knew that I really haven't loved anyone till now."

"Have you had many girls?"

"Not many, but I've slept with some."

Shosha seemed to think it over. "Did you do it with this actress from America?"

"Yes."

"When? Before you came to me?"

I should have answered yes. Instead, I heard myself say, "I slept with her the night after we met." I regretted my words immediately, but confessing and boasting had become a habit with me. Perhaps I learned it from Feitelzohn or in the Writers' Club. I've lost her, I thought. Shosha tried to move away from me, but I held her tight. I had the feeling of a gambler who risks all he possesses in a game, yet makes himself remain quiet. I could hear the pounding of Shosha's heart behind her little left breast.

"Why did you do it? You love her?"

"No, Shoshele. I can do it without love."

"This is what *they* do—you know who I mean."

"The whores and the pimps. That's what we're all becoming, but I'm still able to love you."

"Do you have others, too?" Shosha asked after a pause.

"It happens. I don't want to lie to you."

"No, Arele. You don't need to fool me. I love you as you are. But don't tell Mama. She would raise a fuss and spoil my happiness."

I had expected Shosha to demand details about my affair with Betty. I was ready to give them to her, as well as the fact that I made love to Tekla, though she had a fiancé in the army to whom I wrote letters for her. But Shosha seemed to have forgotten what I told her or to have dismissed it as of no importance. Was she born with the instinct for sharing Feitelzohn talked about? We continued our walk and we came out on Mirowska Street. The fruit stores had closed, but the sidewalk was littered with straw, slats from broken crates, and tissue paper used to wrap oranges. In the First Market, workers were hosing down the tiled floor. The merchants and customers had already dispersed, but the echoes of their shouts hung in the air. In my time, non-kosher sea creatures without scales or fins used to swim here in enormous tubs. The storekeepers sold lobsters and frogs, which Gentiles ate. Huge electric lights lit the market through the night. I led Shosha into a niche and clasped her shoulders. "Shoshele, do you want me?"

"Oh, Arele, do you still have to ask?"

"You'll sleep with me?"

"With you—yes."

"Did anyone ever kiss you?"

"Never. Some lout tried to once, but I ran away. He threw a chunk of wood at me."

Suddenly I had the urge to show off in front of Shosha, to spend money on her. "Shosha, you said just now that you would do whatever I told you."

"Yes, I will."

"I want to take you to the Saxony Gardens. I want to ride with you in a droshky."

"The Saxony Gardens? They don't allow Jews there."

I knew what she meant—under the Russians, Jews in long gaberdines and women in wigs or bonnets had been banned from the park by policemen guarding the gates. But the Poles had since rescinded that order. Besides, I was wearing modern dress. I assured Shosha that we were allowed to go wherever we chose.

Shosha said, "Why take a droshky? We can take 'street-car No. 11.' Do you know what that means?"

"Yes, go on foot."

"It's a shame to waste money. Mama says, 'Every groschen counts.' You spend a zloty for the droshky and how long is the ride? Maybe half an hour. If you have bundles that's another story."

"Have you ever ridden in a droshky?"

"Never."

"Today you shall ride in a droshky with me. I have a pocketful of zlotys. I told you, I'm writing a play—a theater piece—and they've given me three hundred dollars. I've already spent a hundred and twenty of it, but I've got a hundred and eighty left. A dollar is worth nine zlotys."

"Don't talk so loud. You could be robbed. Once they tried to rob a man from the country, and when he fought, they stabbed him."

We walked down Mirowska Street on the way to Iron Gate Square. On one side was the First Market, on the other a long row of flat shacks where Gentile cobblers sold shoes, boots, even footwear with raised heels and soles for the lame. They were closing up shop for the night.

Shosha said, "Mama is right. God Himself sent you to me. I've already told you about Leizer the watchmaker. Mama wanted to arrange a match between us, but I said, 'I'll stay single.' He's the best watchmaker in all Warsaw. You give him a broken watch and he'll fix it so it will run for years. He saw your name in the paper and he came to us and said, 'Shosha, regards from your fiancé.' That's what he called you. When he said this, I knew that you would come to me one day. He says he knew your daddy."

"Is he in love with you?"

"In love with me? I don't know. He's fifty years old, maybe more."

A droshky came up and I hailed it.

Shosha trembled. "Arele, what are you doing? Mama—"

"Step up." I helped her and got in beside her. The driver in the oilcloth cap with the metal number in back turned around suspiciously. "Where to?"

"Ujazdow Boulevard," I said.

"That's a double fare."

We rode out before Iron Gate Square. Each time the droshky made a turn, Shosha fell against me. "Oh, I'm dizzy."

"I'll bring you home again."

"See how the street looks from a droshky! I feel as if I were an empress. When Mama hears about this, she'll say you're a spendthrift. Arele, I'm sitting with you in a droshky and it seems like a dream to me."

"To me, too."

"So many streetcars! And how bright it is here! Like daytime. Are we going to the elegant streets?"

"You could call them that."

"Arele, since that time I went to The True Mercy I've never been out of Krochmalna Street. Teibele goes everywhere. She goes to Falenica, to Michalin—where doesn't she go? Arele, where are you taking me?"

"To a wild forest where demons cook little children in kettles full of snakes and naked witches with teats on their navels eat them with mustard."

"You're joking, aren't you?"

"Yes, my darling."

"Oh, one never knows what can happen. Mama always teased me, 'Nobody will take *you* except the Angel of Death.' I thought, They'll put me next to Yppe. And then I came home with a cone of sugar and there you were. Arele, what's that?"

"A restaurant."

"Look how many lamps!"

"It's a fancy restaurant."

"Oh, see the dolls in that store window! Like alive! What street is this?"

"The New World."

"So many trees grow here—like a park. And the ladies with the hats, how tall they are! You smell sweetness? What is it?"

"Lilac."

"Arele, I want to ask you something, but don't get mad."

"What do you want to ask?"

"Do you really love me?"

"Yes, Shosha. Very much."

"Why?"

"No whys about it. Just because."

"So long as you weren't there, you weren't there. But if you went away now and didn't come back, I'd die a thousand deaths."

"I'll never leave you again."

"Is that the truth? Leizer the watchmaker once said that all writers are like bums, they walk near the soles of their shoes. Leizer doesn't believe there is a God. He says everything came from itself. How can that be?"

"There is a God."

"Look, the sky is red, just like from a fire. Who lives in these beautiful buildings?"

"Rich people."

"Jews or Gentiles?"

"Mostly Gentiles."

"Arele, take me home. I'm afraid."

"There's no reason to be afraid. If it comes to it that we must die, we'll die together," I said, startled at my own words.

"Is it permitted to put a boy and a girl in the same grave?"

I didn't answer her, and Shosha leaned her head on my shoulder.

4 I rode back in the droshky to the gate of No. 7, having decided to walk from there to Leszno Street, but Shosha clung to my arm. She was afraid to go through the dark gate, the dark courtyard, and to climb the half flight of stairs alone. The gate was locked and we had to wait some minutes for the janitor to come and open it. In the courtyard, we bumped into a short little man—Leizer the watchmaker. Shosha asked him what he was doing out so late and he told us he was taking a walk.

"This is Arele." Shosha introduced me.

"I know. I understand. Good evening. I read what you write—including the translations you have done."

It was hard to see him clearly, but in the dim light coming from a few windows I could make out a pale face with big black eyes. He wore no jacket or hat. He spoke in a soft voice. He said, "Mr. Greidinger—or should I call you Comrade Greidinger? It's not that I'm a socialist, but it says somewhere that all Jews are comrades. I know your Shosha since they moved into this building. I used to visit Bashele at a time when her husband was still a respectable man. I don't want to keep you, but she began talking about you the day we met and she's never stopped. Arele this and Arele that. I knew your father, too, may he rest in peace. I was in your house once. It was during a *din torah*—I came to give testimony. A few years ago when I saw your name in a magazine, I wrote you a letter addressed to the editorial office, but there was no answer. They don't generally answer in editorial offices, I know. It's the same with publishers. Once, Shosha and I went to look for you. In any case, you showed up eventually, and

112

I hear that Romeo and Juliet have found each other again. There are such loves, yes, there are. In this world, there is everything. Nature has a pattern for every piece of goods. If you look for madness, there's no lack of that, either. What do they say in your circles about the world —I mean Hitler and Stalin and that scum?"

"What can they say? Man doesn't want peace."

"Why do you say 'man'? I want peace and Shosha wants peace and so do millions of others. I still maintain that most people in the world don't want wars, even revolutions. They would choose to live out their lives the best way they could. With more, with less, in palaces, in cellar rooms, so long as they had a piece of bread and a pillow to lay their heads on. Isn't that true, Shosha?"

"Yes, true."

"The trouble is that the quiet, patient people are passive and those in power, the malefactors, are aggressive. If a decent majority would decide once and for all to take power in their hands, maybe there would be peace."

"They'll neither decide nor will they ever get power," I said. "Power and passivity don't mix."

"Is that your view?"

"It's the experience of generations."

"Then things are bitter."

"Yes, Reb Leizer, it isn't good."

"What will become of us Jews? Evil winds are blowing. Well, I won't keep you. I sit all day in the house, and before going to bed I take a little stroll. Right here in the courtyard, from the gate to the garbage bin and back again. What can you do? Maybe there are better worlds somewhere else? Good night. For me it was an honor to meet you. I still have respect for the printed word."

"Good night. I hope we meet again," I said.

Only now did I become aware that Bashele was standing at the window watching us. She was obviously worried. I would have to go in for a moment. She opened the door, and as we walked up the stairs she exclaimed, "Where have you been! Why so late? I thought the worst!"

"Mama, we rode in a droshky."

"In a droshky? Why, of all things? Where to? How do you like that!"

Shosha began to tell her mother of our wanderings—we had ridden down the boulevards, gone into a confectionary, eaten cake and drunk lemonade.

Bashele arched her eyebrows and shook her head reproachfully. "For the life of me I can't see the sense of squandering all those zlotys. If I'd known you were going to *those* streets, I would have ironed your white dress. These days you can't be sure of your life. I stopped at the neighbor's and we heard a speech on the radio by that madman Hitler. He screamed so, you could go deaf. Since you haven't eaten supper, I'll make something."

"Bashele, I'm not hungry. I must go home."

"What? Now? Don't you know it's almost midnight? Where will you go so late? You'll spend the night here. I'll fix the bed in the alcove. But you have to eat, too."

Immediately Bashele began to pour water into a pan of flour. She lit the stove. Shosha led me into the alcove to show me the iron bed where Teibele used to sleep. She lit a small gas lamp. There were clothes and laundry piled here, along with baskets and boxes accumulated from the time Zelig was a traveling salesman.

Shosha said, "Arele, I'd like you to spend every night here. I'd like to be with you always—eat with you, drink with you, walk with you. I won't forget this night, not till the day they put shards over my eyelids—the droshky, the confectionary, all of it. I want to kiss your feet!"

"Shosha, what's the matter with you?"

"Let me!" She fell to her knees and began to kiss my shoes. I struggled with her and tried to pick her up, but she kept crying, "Let me! Let me!"

5 Although I was no longer accustomed to a straw pallet, I fell into a deep sleep in Bashele's alcove that night. I opened my eyes in fright. A white image stood at my bed, bending over me and touching my face with thin fingers. "Who is this?" I asked.

"It's me—Shosha."

It took me a while to remember where I was. Had Shosha come to my bed as Ruth went to Boaz?

"Shosha, what is it?"

"Arele, I'm afraid." Shosha spoke in a wavering voice, like a child about to burst out crying.

I sat up. "What are you afraid of?"

"Arele, don't be angry. I didn't want to wake you, but I have been lying there for three hours and I cannot fall asleep. May I sit on your bed?"

"Yes, yes."

"I was lying in bed and my brain turned like a mill. I wanted to wake up Mother, but she would have yelled at me. She's busy with the house all day long and at night she collapses."

"What were you thinking about?"

"About you. Crazy thoughts came into my head—that it wasn't you, that you were already dead and had disguised yourself as Arele. A demon screamed in my ear, 'He's dead, dead!' He made such a racket I thought everybody in the courtyard would hear and there would be a riot. I wanted to recite the Shema, but he spat in my ear and spoke queer words."

"What did he say?"

"Oh, I'm ashamed to repeat them."

"Tell me."

"He said that God is a chimney sweep, and that when we marry I will wet the bed. He butted me with his horns. He tore off the cover and whipped me you-know-where."

"Shoshele, it's all your nerves. When we are together, I'll take you to a doctor and he will make you healthy."

"Can I still sit a little?"

"Yes, but if your mother wakes up she will think that—"

"She will not wake up. Dead people come to me the moment I close my eyes. Dead women tear at my hair. I'm old enough to be a mother but I still haven't gotten my period. A few times I began to bleed and my mother gave me cotton and rags, but then it all stopped. Mother talked about it to a woman peddler—she sold shirts, kerchiefs, bloomers—and this woman told everyone that I'm not a virgin any more and that I'm pregnant. Mother began to pull my hair and call me ugly names. Bullies in the courtyard threw stones at me. This was years ago, not now. When my daddy heard what happened, he gave Mother ten zlotys to take me to a women's doctor, who said it was all a big lie. A neighbor came to us and said that I should be taken to a rabbi, to get a paper saying that I am a *mukasetz* .This means a girl who lost her innocence without a man, by accident. Your father had left Warsaw years before and we went to a rabbi on Smocza Street. He ordered me taken to a mikvah and examined there. I didn't want to go, but Mother dragged me. The woman in charge undressed me until I was naked, and I had to show her everything. I almost died from shame. She touched me and fumbled around. Then she said that I was kosher. The rabbi had asked thirty zlotys for the certificate and we could not afford it, so we let it go. Now that you're here, I'm worried that someone may come and tell you bad things about me."

"Shoshele, no one will come, and I will listen to no one. I didn't know there were still such fanatics in Warsaw."

"Arele, strange things come into my head—perhaps

116

this, perhaps that. Until I was three, I used to wet the bed. Even now, sometimes I wake up in the middle of the night. The room is cold, but I'm soaked with sweat. The pillow is wet. I never drink before I go to bed, but when I wake up I need to go so badly that until I reach the chamber pot I make on the floor. In the daytime, I go to the outhouse in the yard and it is as dark as night, and there are rats as big as cats. You can't sit down. Once a rat bit me. The doors don't close—where there's a chain, there's no hook; where there's a hook, there's no chain. I try not to go, and I've gotten so used to it that days and weeks go by and I don't go. Porters come there from Yanash's Bazaar, and hoodlums, too. When they see a girl, they begin to say nasty words. In some apartments there are water closets. You pull a string and the water flushes. There is light also and toilet paper. Here, there is nothing."

"Shoshele, we are not going to live here forever. I don't earn enough now, but I'm writing a book. And then there's my play for the theater. If I don't succeed this time, I will succeed another time. I will take you away from here."

"Where will you take me? Other girls can read and write, but I never learned how. Maybe you remember when they sent me home from school. I was sitting in class, and the teacher read something to us, but it didn't go into my head. I always saw funny faces. When they called me to the blackboard, I knew nothing and began to cry."

"What did you see?" I asked.

"Oh, I'm afraid to tell you. A woman combing her daughter's hair with a fine comb and putting kerosene on it to get out the lice. Suddenly, lice came from all over—bedbugs, too—and the girl began to scream like mad. I don't remember now if she was a Jewish girl or a shiksa. In a minute the lice ate up the mother and the girl, and

only their bones were left. When I walked on the street
I thought, What will happen if a balcony falls down on my
head? When I passed by a policeman I thought, Perhaps
he will say that I stole something and take me to prison.
Arele, you will think that I'm out of my mind."

"No, Shoshele, it's nothing but nerves."

"What are nerves? Tell me."

"Fear of all the misfortunes that can happen and do
happen to human beings."

"Leizer reads the paper to us, and awful things happen
every day. A man crossed the street and was run over by
a droshky. A girl from No. 9 tried to get into the trolley
car before it stopped, and she lost her leg. Only last week,
a tinsmith fixing a roof fell down and the gutter was red
from blood. With such things in my head, I could not pay
attention to my lessons. When Mother sent me to buy
something, I held the money tight in my fist—then when
I got to the store it was lost. How can this be?"

"Every person has an enemy inside who spites him."

"Then why doesn't Teibele have one? Arele, I want you
to know the truth so that you won't think that we are fooling you."

"Shoshele, no one has fooled me. I will help you."

"How? If it's so bad now, what will happen when Hitler
comes? Oy, Mother is waking up!" Shosha ran from the
alcove. I heard the sound of her shirt tearing as she
caught it on a nail in the door.

SIX

1 Each day—no, each hour—brought a new crisis, but
I had become accustomed to the dangers attending my
lot. I compared myself to a criminal who knows that he
will be punished but until he is seized he squanders his

loot. Sam Dreiman had given me a new advance and Betty had reconstructed my play to suit her whims. She had introduced new characters, even edited my language. I realized with amazement that the passion to write can strike anyone capable of holding a pen. Betty had introduced more action into the drama and added "lyrics," but the play no longer held together. Though Betty mocked and mimicked the American Yiddish, she anglicized mine. The blind musician now declaimed like the villain in a melodrama. Fritz Bander, who had been cast to play a wealthy Hasid in love with the Ludmir Maiden, demanded that his role be larger, and Betty gave him permission to extend it with lengthy monologues. He still retained some Galician Yiddish mixed with German. Fritz Bander also demanded a part for his German mistress, Gretel, who knew no Yiddish. He pointed out that Jews often employed German maids and this was a part she could handle.

Betty had several copies of her version of the play typed up—one for her, one for Sam Dreiman, one for Fritz Bander, one for David Lipman, one for me, and for others. Each person made changes, and the text was typed again and the revisions commenced all over. Sam Dreiman had rented a theater on Smocza Street and ordered the sets, though basic decisions about the production were still to be settled. The Actors Union demanded that jobs be introduced for additional actors as well as for extras. I was forced to write in parts for a beadle, a madman, and an anti-Hasid who berated the Hasidim. The cast grew so large that dialogue essential to its content had to be deleted.

At first, I resisted. I rewrote Betty's and Bander's revisions, corrected their grammar and spelling, but I soon saw that the contradictions, the different styles, and grotesqueries grew faster than I could repair them. I couldn't believe it, but Sam Dreiman also took a hand in the writing. It reminded me of a story I had heard as a child from my mother about a band of spirits who seized a village and turned everything upside down—the water-carrier became the rabbi, the rabbi a bathhouse attendant, the horse thief a scribe, the scribe a teamster. A hobgoblin posed as head of a yeshiva and in the studyhouse preached a sermon filled with blasphemies. The leech, a demon, prescribed goat droppings and calf feathers for the sick, along with moon juice and turkey semen. A devil with the legs of a rooster and the horns of a buck became a cantor and turned the rejoicing of Simchas Torah into the lamentations of Tisha Bov. Such a mystic comedy could have been created from my play.

The telephone in the corridor outside my room never stopped ringing. Tekla no longer bothered to pick up the receiver—invariably the call was for me. The actors and actresses were bickering with each other, with Betty, and with David Lipman, who was threatening to quit. The secretary of the union raised new demands almost daily. The actors complained that the American millionaire had deceived them regarding their wages. The theater owner decided he had signed an unfair contract and would have to have more money. Sam Dreiman screamed at me until I had to hold the receiver away from my ear. If Jews were capable of such deceit and intrigue, he said, then Hitler was right.

I tried to calm the spirits of the others, but I feared a nervous breakdown myself.

The days passed in turmoil. I stopped talking to Shosha and Bashele. When I went to them for lunch, I sat at the table in silence. I even forgot to eat and had to be reminded that the soup was getting cold. At night after two or three hours' sleep I awoke with my heart pounding, the pillowcase drenched in sweat. In my sleep, my own complications had mingled with the problems of the world. Hitler, Mussolini, and Stalin wrangled about my play, and then went to war. Shosha attempted to defend me. I sat up and listened to the echoes of cries and mayhem that still lingered in my brain. My hair pierced my skull. I itched and scratched. I had wakened with a thirst, a gnawing in my intestines, a stinging in my bladder. My nose was stuffed and a shudder kept running down my spine.

Day would be breaking, and I would still sit and take reckoning. I had accepted more money from Sam Dreiman than I had intended. I gave Bashele more for my meals and helped her with her rent as well. I had given Dora a loan I knew I would never get back.

That night I fell asleep at three. At ten to nine, the ringing of the telephone woke me. Tekla poked the door ajar. "It's for you."

It was Betty. She asked, "Did I wake you?"

"Yes, no."

"I had a terrible night. I wouldn't wish it on my worst enemies."

"What happened?"

"Oh, Sam is torturing me. He makes ugly scenes. He says such wild things I'm beginning to think he's losing his mind. Yesterday, he drank maybe a half bottle of cognac. He shouldn't touch it—he has a bad heart and an enlarged prostate."

"What does he want?"

"To destroy himself and everything. He doesn't want the play any more. Every second he gets a new notion. He made such a fuss you could hear him through the whole hotel. I want to remind you that we are rehearsing today. I have about as much strength to perform after last night as you have to dance on the roof, but I can't leave things hanging in the air any longer. At times I'd like to pick myself up and run off to the ends of the earth."

"You too?"

"Yes, me too. He's become jealous all of a sudden.

He seems to know about us!" Betty said, changing her tone.

"What does he know?"

"He's listening right now. I have to stop."

I stood by the telephone with the premonition that presently it would ring again. And so it did. I lifted the receiver and said, "Yes, Celia?"

No one answered and I assumed I had been wrong, but after a while I heard Celia's voice. "Have you become a prophet, or a gypsy?"

"The Gemara says that when the Temple was destroyed God gave the power of prophecy to madmen."

"Is that what the Gemara says? You are crazy, but you are also committing literary suicide. I lay awake half the night worrying about you. Haiml sleeps like a log. The minute his head hits the pillow he begins to whistle through his nose and goes on until morning. But I keep waking up. At times it seems that you wake me. I hear you calling 'Celia!' It's all my nerves. One time it even seemed that I saw you in the doorway. Was it your astral body? There's something not of the ordinary about you. My dear, Morris has read your play. Sam Dreiman gave him a copy. I don't want to repeat what he said. I hear it's no longer your play, everything's distorted. Really, what's the sense of it all?"

"The sense is that I'm losing my senses."

2　When I entered the theater for the rehearsal, coming in from the bright light I bumped against the seats and nearly tripped, but gradually I grew accustomed to the dark. I took a seat in the front row. Sam Dreiman sat two rows behind me. He coughed and grunted and mumbled to himself in English. Celia and Haiml were present, too. Critics aren't usually invited to rehearsals, but I spotted one of them in the audience. In their articles, the critics often decried the state of the Yiddish theater and denounced young writers for allowing kitsch to dominate the stage and for not writing serious plays; yet I knew that they hoped my play would fail. They had launched a campaign against Betty Slonim. In the leftist publications they dubbed Sam Dreiman an American "all-rightnik" and a "Golden Calf." Some theatrical writers pointed out that a mystic play about a girl who presided over Hasidic banquets with a veil over her face, preached the Torah to Hasidim, and was possessed by the dybbuks of a whore and a musician didn't befit the tragic circumstances of Polish Jewry. What was called for were plays that reflected the dangers of Fascism and Hitlerism and the need of resistance by the Jewish masses, not dramas that brought back the superstitions of the Middle Ages.

Two seats away from me sat David Lipman and his wife, Estusia. She peeled oranges and handed sections to him. Because of a heart condition he required constant nourishment. He wore a velour jacket and a flowing tie. The whole play wasn't being performed, merely individual scenes. Fritz Bander, portraying Reb Ezekiel Prager, the Hasid, declared his love for the Ludmir Maiden—Betty. Although I had told Bander time and again not to shout, he thundered away. In those places where he should have lowered his voice, he roared; and he whispered or skipped over those places where he should have been forceful. He swallowed words and improvised. He didn't remember his lines and the prompter had to keep feeding him his speeches. Bander jumbled and fractured the quotations from the Gemara, the Midrash, and the books of the cabala. I had assumed that David Lipman, who was allegedly versed in these matters, would correct him, but he kept silent. He was in awe of Fritz Bander because he had performed in Berlin. Once in a while David Lipman made observations and indicated directions, but he ignored essentials and confined himself to petty details. Betty also had trouble with her lines. She made errors in her Hebrew and even in the Yiddish words. Some of the words she pronounced in a Polish accent, others in a Lithuanian. Where she was supposed to portray both the whore and the blind musician, she lost her bearings altogether.

I sat slumped over, from time to time closing my eyes to lose sight of my disgrace. Betty might be critical of the trash of the American Yiddish theater, but she had adapted its mannerisms. I recalled my mother's saying "words that walk on stilts." Curiously, when Betty spoke to me in private, her Yiddish was fluent and precise. As I gazed at the stage, I knew I had failed completely. My own mistakes were only too clear to me, but I had no idea how to correct them.

The moment the lights went on, Sam Dreiman came charging at me. "We can't put on this monstrosity!"

"No is no."

"I sat there and didn't understand what on earth they were babbling about, and if I didn't understand it, you can't expect anyone else to. I thought you were going to write in plain Yiddish."

"Dybbuks don't speak a plain Yiddish."

Betty, Fritz Bander, and Gretel came up.

"Betty darling, we'll have to postpone the play!" Sam Dreiman shouted.

"Postpone? Until when?"

"I don't know when. I brought you here to be a success, not to have rotten potatoes heaved at you."

"Sam, don't say that."

"Betty darling, the sooner you act on a mistake, the better. Forty years ago I put up a building in Detroit and in the midst of the construction it turned out that the plumbing and everything else wouldn't work. I'd sunk a fortune into the project, but I ordered everything torn down and the building begun all over again. If I hadn't done this, I would have gone to jail. I had a friend, also a builder, and he put up a factory six flights high. Suddenly, while the building was filled with workers, it collapsed and killed seventeen men. He died in prison."

"Well, I knew it! I knew it all! The evil powers have started their tricks again. I'm through as an actress. My luck—"

"Your luck, sweetheart, is as bright as the sun in the sky!" Sam Dreiman hollered. "You will perform in Warsaw, in Paris, in London, and in New York. The name of Betty Slonim will light up Broadway in huge letters, but in a drama that the world wants to see, not in some crazy farce for insane cabalists. Mr. Greidinger, I don't want to be cruel, but what you've given us is unfit for the public. Betty, we'll get another play. He isn't the only writer in Warsaw."

"You can put on all the plays you want, but without me," Betty said. "This is my final card. With my luck, if you put on a masterpiece it would fail. It's all my fault! Mine! Mine!"

"It's mine, too," Sam Dreiman said. "When he brought us the first two scenes and I read them, I saw at once that this wasn't for us. I thought it might be fixed, but not everything can be fixed. It's like that building—the foundation was poorly laid at the start. I fired the architect and began with another. I'll do the same thing right now."

"You can do it, but without me."

"With you, Betty darling, only with you!"

SEVEN

1 At this time, the logic of my pride was that nothing remained to me but to hide from all those involved with me and my profession. I still had over one hundred dollars from Sam Dreiman's third advance—money that I must pay back if I were not to consider myself a thief. My calculations turned around this sum, which was worth about nine hundred zlotys. According to the agreement with the man from whom I sublet my room on Leszno Street, I had to give a month's notice before I moved out, and I certainly did not intend to break this agreement. I considered suicide, but that would be possible only if I could take with me those who had hung all their hopes on me. Meanwhile, I had to be careful with every penny. I stopped sleeping on Leszno Street, which saved me the expense of paying for a taxi when I went home late in the evening. On the bed in Bashele's alcove I covered whole sheets of paper with figures. The publisher for whom I had translated some German books owed me money, but I was far from sure that he would ever pay it. I was working for the literary magazine, but weeks passed without my getting a penny from them. I reminded myself that about three million Jews lived in Poland and managed to make a living somehow. I did not fool Bashele. She knew my situation. I had promised to marry her daughter but we had never set a date. They would not send out warrants for my arrest if I should disappear. Judging by the way Hitler occupied one territory after another and the Allies sat back and did nothing, there was no hope for the Jews in Poland. But running away and leaving at bay those who were dear to me was not in my nature.

Yiddish newspapers in Warsaw reported that the play Sam Dreiman, the American millionaire, had been planning to produce had been canceled. The Yiddish theater season began on Succoth and there was not time for him to find a new play. They also mentioned that he was negotiating with a playwright in America. Of *The Ludmir Maiden,* a journalist wrote in the humor section that it could not be produced because it was possessed by a dybbuk. Leizer the watchmaker read all these stories of my failure to Shosha and Bashele.

In the month of August, a strong heat spell hit Warsaw. When I was a boy, almost no one on Krochmalna Street took vacations and went to the country in the summer. Only the wealthy and rich did this. But times had changed. Workers were now given vacations and they went to Miedzeszyn, Falenica, and even to Zakopane in the mountains. The workers' unions had summer colonies in Karwia at the Baltic Sea in the "corridor" that divided East Germany from West Germany and that Hitler vowed to take back. I heard that Feitelzohn stayed a few weeks in Józefow with Celia and Haiml. I had spoken to Tekla on the telephone and she told me that Celia kept calling me. Tekla asked why I hadn't come home for so long. She also asked for my telephone number and the address where I was staying so that she could tell people how to get in touch with me. I said I was busy with work and didn't want to be disturbed. Even Tekla knew that my play had fizzled. She heard it from Wladek, who read about it in the Polish Jewish newspaper *Nasz Przeglad*.

During the day I seldom left the apartment on Krochmalna Street. My old bashfulness had returned to me, with all its complications and neuroses. Some tenants of No. 7 knew me. From Leizer they had heard about me and my love for Shosha. They had also read of my forthcoming play. The girls used to watch from the windows when I passed with Shosha on the way to the gate. I was ashamed before these girls now and imagined that they laughed at me. I even avoided going to the outhouse during the day. The heels of my shoes were worn down, but I could not pay to have them fixed. My hat was faded and stained. I would put on a fresh shirt and a few hours later it would be soaked with sweat, and dirty. The little hair left on my head began to fall out. When I wiped the perspiration from my skull, I found red hair on my handkerchief. I had begun to have all kinds of mishaps around the house. Bashele would give me a glass of tea and it would slip from my hands. Each time I shaved, I cut myself. I kept losing my fountain pen, my notebook. Money dropped from my pockets. In my mouth a molar began to loosen, but I could not afford to go to a dentist. Anyway, what did I need a dentist for, since my weeks or days were numbered?

I had brought with me a few of the books in which I always sought solace whenever there was a crisis in my life—which was often. This time I couldn't find a trace of comfort in them. Spinoza's "substance" had no will, no compassion, no feeling for justice. He was a prisoner of his own laws. Schopenhauer's "blind will" seemed to be more blind than ever. Of course there was no hope for me in Hegel's *Zeitgeist* or in Nietzsche's Zarathustra. Payot's *Education of the Will* was addressed chiefly to students whose wealthy parents paid for their board and tuition. Coué's and Charles Baudouin's patients had homes, professions, well-to-do families, accounts in the banks. I sat on the edge of the bed all day long and let perspiration run over my hot body. Shosha sat near me on her little stool and talked to me or to herself. Occasionally she spoke to Yppe. For some reason Bashele frequently left the house. Shosha would ask her, "Mommy, where are you going?" And Bashele would say, "Where my eyes carry me."

Now that I had failed for everyone to see, I realized that the failure was my own fault. Instead of working on the play, I had spent hours with Shosha every day. Even though Betty kept warning me that the work on the play was of the highest importance, she made me go with her to museums, to cafés, on long walks, and sabotaged all my plans for work. I should have gone with her in the evenings to see serious plays from which I could learn about the construction of a drama. Instead, she took me to see silly Hollywood movies from which there was nothing to be learned. I wasted precious hours discussing Yiddish

128

literature in the Writers' Club, playing chess, and telling jokes. I even squandered time with Tekla, listening to her complaints about her mistress and her stories about the village where she came from, her unloving stepmother, and of Bolek, to whom she was betrothed and who had left her to go to work in the coal mines of France. Our conversations always ended by our falling down on the bed together. I wasn't really awake in those months. My laziness, my passion, and my empty fantasies had kept me in a hypnotic amnesia. Now I could hear my mother saying, "No enemy can do to a man as much evil as he does to himself."

"Arele, what are you thinking about?" Shosha asked me.

"Nothing, Shoshele. As long as I have you, there is still some sense to my life."

"You will not leave me alone?"

"No, Shoshele, I will stay with you as long as I live."

2　At night I lay awake for hours. From the heat I continuously ran to the sink to drink water and then I had to urinate. Bashele had put a chamber pot under my bed and it soon became full. I stood without any clothes before the window of my alcove—a little window with four panes—and let the breeze that came into the courtyard once in a while blow over me. I looked at the few stars that could be seen moving slowly from one roof to the other. Though I had nothing to expect on earth when the Nazis arrived except starvation and concentration camps, perhaps there was some spark of hope in the heavenly bodies? However, from the popular books about astronomy which I had read, I knew that the stars consisted of the same elements as the sun and the earth. If other planets were inhabited by living creatures, their conditions could be like those on earth: struggle for a bite of food, for a secure place to lay one's head. I was overcome by a rage against creation, God, nature—whatever this wretchedness was called. I felt that the only way of protesting cosmic violence was to reject life, even if I had to take Shosha with me. The animals and the insects did not possess such a choice.

But how would I accomplish this, actually? If I were to throw myself out the window of my room on Leszno Street, I would risk remaining alive with possibly a broken spine. If I were to fling myself under a trolley or a train, I might end up without feet or arms. Should I get rat poison and slowly burn out my insides? Should I hang myself and burden those who loved me with arranging my burial? After much brooding I decided that the best way to end it all would be to throw myself into deep water, where I would molest no one and would even help the fish with a meal. The Vistula was too shallow in the summer. Every day the newspapers wrote about ships that got stuck in the sand. The only way of doing it right would be to go to Danzig or Gdynia and board a ship that sailed the Baltic. A travel agency was advertising a cruise to Denmark for which no foreign passport or visa was necessary. The price was reasonable. It was enough for the passenger to show a Polish inland passport. The trouble was, I didn't possess even this kind of document. In the process of moving from one furnished room to another with my books and confusion of manuscripts, I had lost my draft card, my birth certificate, and all other proof of my citizenship. I would have to travel to the village where I was born and bring to the City Hall witnesses who could attest to the day of my birth or my circumcision feast. The archives of births and deaths had burned down in the German bombardments in 1915. With all my anxiety I had to laugh. I needed to go through a lot of red tape to be able to commit suicide.

That night I fell asleep at dawn. I opened my eyes.

Shosha was shaking my shoulder. I looked at her bewildered. It took me a while to remember where I was and who was waking me. "Arele," she said, "a young lady is waiting for you. The actress from America."

After a while Bashele stuck her head in the room. I asked her and Shosha to please leave and close the door. In a rush I put on my underwear, my pants, my shirt, and my jacket. For a minute I thought I had lost the hundred dollars that I carried in the left pocket of my pants. I needed money to buy a train ticket and ship card to go ahead with my plan. Had someone stolen my money? I touched all my pockets with the turmoil of one who wants to live, not to die. Thank God, the banknotes were in a pocket of my vest. My shirt was crumpled, my collar had a spot, I had lost the cuff link of my right sleeve. I screamed through the closed door, "Betty, wait! I will soon be out." The sun was already scorching me through the open window. From the courtyard I heard the voices: "Bagels, hot bagels! Plums, fresh plums!" A beggar was already scratching out a plaintive melody on a fiddle and his female companion was beating on a little drum with bells, calling for alms. I touched my cheeks. Although I kept on losing the hair on my head, my beard grew with wild impetus. The stubble felt stiff and prickly. Disordered and frowzy, I opened the door and saw Betty freshly made up in a straw hat with a green ribbon, a suit that I had not seen, and white shoes with open toes—a novelty to me. I began to apologize for my appearance.

Betty said, "Everything is all right. You don't have to compete in a beauty contest."

"When I fell asleep day was breaking, and—"

"Stop it. I didn't come to look you over."

"Why don't you sit down?" Bashele said to Betty. "I keep asking the young lady to sit down, but she has been standing all this time. We don't live in luxury but our chairs are clean. I dust them every morning. I wanted to make tea, but the young lady refuses everything."

"I'm sorry. I just had breakfast. Thank you very much. Tsutsik, forgive me for coming so early in the morning. Actually, my watch shows ten minutes to ten. I came, as they say in America, on business. If you like, we can go out somewhere and talk it over."

"Arele, don't go for long," Shosha said. "We have prepared breakfast and later we will have dinner. Mommy bought sorrel and potatoes and sour cream. The lady can eat with us."

"We have enough for both of you," Bashele agreed.

"How can I eat if I've had breakfast already?"

"Shoshele, we will only go out for half an hour," I said. "It's not convenient for us to talk here. Let me find my cuff link and change my collar. One minute, Betty."

I rushed into the alcove and Shosha followed me. She closed the door. "Arele, don't go with her," she said. "She wants to take you away from me. She looks like a witch."

"A witch? Don't talk nonsense."

"She has such sharp eyes. You told me yourself that you lay with her in bed."

"I told you? Well, never mind. Between her and me everything is finished."

"If you want to begin with her again, better kill me first."

"The way things are going, I will kill you anyhow. I will take you on a ship and we will both jump into the sea."

"Is there a sea in Warsaw?"

"Not in Warsaw. We will go to Gdynia or Danzig."

"Yes, Arele, you can do with me whatever you want. Throw me in first or take me to Yppe's grave and bury me there. As long as you do it, it is good. But don't leave me alone. Here is your cuff link."

Shosha bent down and gave it to me. I put my arms around her and kissed her. I said, "Shoshele, I have sworn by God and by the soul of my father that I will never abandon you. It's about time that you trust me."

"Yes, I trust you. But when I saw her, my heart began to pound. She is dressed as if she were going to a wedding. All new to please you. She thinks I don't understand, but I understand everything. When will you be back?"

"As quickly as possible."

"Remember that no one loves you as I do."

"Sweet child, I love you, too."

"Wait, I have a fresh handkerchief for you."

3 Betty and I passed the courtyard; it looked like a marketplace. Peddlers were hawking smoked herring, blueberries, watermelons. A peasant had ridden in with his horse and buggy, and he was selling chickens, eggs, mushrooms, onions, carrots, parsley. In other streets, this kind of business was not allowed, but Krochmalna had its own laws. An old woman carrying a sack on her back stood near the garbage bin and with a stick poked through for rags to make paper and for bones used in sugar factories. Betty tried to take my arm, but I gave her a sign not to do it, since I was sure that Bashele and Shosha were watching us from the window. We were watched from other windows, too. Girls wearing loose dresses over their bouncing breasts were shaking thread-bare carpets as well as featherbeds, pillows, and mangy fur coats that would be worn when winter began. One could hear the noise of sewing machines, cobblers' hammers, the planing and sawing of carpenters. From the Hasidic study-house came the voices of young men chanting the Talmud. In the cheder, little boys recited the Pentateuch. On the other side of the gate Betty took my arm and said, "I didn't know the number of the house, but after I called and called you on Leszno Street and the maid always replied that you were not there, I decided you must be here on your beloved Krochmalna Street. What kind of a swamp have you fallen into? It absolutely stinks here! Please forgive me, but this Shosha of yours is a perfect imbecile. She asked me to sit down at least ten times. I told her I preferred to stand, but she asked over and over again. I really think you are mad."

"You are right. You are right."

"Don't tell me how right I am. You are one of those men who like to sink. In Russia they call them *brodyagi*. Gorky wrote about them. In New York there is a street called the Bowery, and you see them lying on the sidewalk drunk and half naked. Some of them are intelligent, with higher education. Come, let's get out of this sewage. An urchin has already tried to grab my purse. You haven't had breakfast, and I am hungry myself from walking so long around here trying to find the house. All I remembered from my first visit was that there was a ditch in the courtyard. But it seems that they filled it up. Where can we get a cup of coffee?"

"There is a coffee shop at No. 6, but the underworld goes there."

"I don't want to stay on this street another minute. Hurry, here's a droshky. Hey! Stop!"

Betty jumped in and I after her. She said, "Would you like to have breakfast in the Writers' Club?"

"Absolutely not."

"Did you have a quarrel with someone? They say you've stopped coming there. How about Gertner's Restaurant, where we met the first time. My God, it seems so long ago."

"Madame, where to?" The coachman turned his head.

Betty gave him the address. "Tsutsik, why are you hiding from people? I met your best friend, Dr. Feitelzohn, and he told me you've severed connections with him and everybody else. I can understand in a way that you wouldn't want to have anything to do with me, because I'm responsible for what happened, although I had only good intentions. But what's the sense of a young writer burying himself in such squalor? Why don't you at least stay in your room on Leszno Street—you pay the rent, after all. Sam is deeply upset about the way you run away from us."

"I hear he's negotiating a play with some trashy writer from New York."

"Nothing will come of it. I'm definitely not going to play in that kind of junk. I've told you already it's entirely my bad luck. Everyone who's involved with me shares my miserable fate. But I told you I came on business and I'm not lying. The story is this. Sam's not well and I'm afraid he's sicker than I realized. He's planning to go back to America. We've done a lot of talking in the past few days, much of it about you. Now that there's no longer a deadline I've had time and the peace of mind to read your play again. It's not nearly as bad as that short little critic with the tin-framed glasses made it out to be. The insolence of a writer tearing down a piece before it's been performed! That can happen only among the Yiddishists. Such a malicious worm. Someone introduced me to him and I gave him a piece of my mind. He began to excuse himself and flatter me and twist his tongue like a snake. Actually, I think it's a good literary play. The trouble is, you don't know the stage. In America we have men who are called play doctors. They can't write a line themselves, but somehow they know how to rearrange a piece and make it right for the stage. I'll make it short—we want to buy your play and try it out in America."

"*Buy* it? Mr. Dreiman already gave me seven or eight hundred dollars. It's his if he wants it. I'm terribly sorry that I'm not able to give him back the money, but he certainly can do what he likes with the play."

"Well, I can see you're not much of a businessman. I'll

tell you something. He's loaded with money. America is beginning to go through a new period of prosperity, and without lifting a finger, he is making a fortune. If he wants to pay you, take the money. He promised to leave me a large inheritance, but according to the law he has to leave a part of his fortune to his Xanthippe, and perhaps also to his children, though they hate him and defy him. With my luck, I'll probably get nothing. If he's willing to give some to you, there's no reason you should refuse. You won't be able to write if you remain where you are now. I looked into that alcove of yours. It's a hole, not a room. You could suffocate in there. What's the point of it? Even if you want to commit suicide, such a death is too ugly. Here is Gertner's."

Betty tried to open her purse, but I had the fare ready in my hand and I gave it to the coachman.

Betty threw me an angry look. "What's the matter with you? Do you want to finance Sam Dreiman?"

"I don't want to take any more from him."

"Well, everyone is crazy in his own way. Bevies of schnorrers run after him and you are trying to support him. Come, madman. I haven't been here in God knows how long. I even thought they might not be open so early. In New York there are restaurants where the day begins at lunchtime. Now you may kiss me. We can never really be complete strangers."

4 The headwaiter rushed toward us and gave us the table in the niche that Sam and Betty always got when they ate here. He said he was sorry he hadn't seen her and Sam lately. Even though it was still early, there were people already at the tables, eating fish and meat and drinking beer. Betty ordered coffee with cake for herself and made me take rolls with eggs and coffee. The waiter gave us a look of reproach for ordering a late breakfast instead of an early lunch. Those at the other tables gazed at us questioningly. Betty looked too elegant to be my companion. She was saying, "How long is it since we've seen one another? It seems to me an eternity. Sam wants me to return to America, but in spite of all my disappointments I fell in love with Warsaw. What would I do in America? In New York they know everything that is happening everywhere. In the Actors Union they have surely heard of my defeat, and my stock there will have dropped lower than ever. They sit in the Café Royal and make mountains out of molehills. What's left to them except to gossip? Some of them saved when times were good. Those who have nothing get relief from the government. In the summer they play a few weeks in the hotels in the Catskill Mountains. America has become a country where one is not compelled to work if he doesn't want to. They drink coffee and chatter. They play cards. Without cards and gossip they would expire from boredom. My trouble is that I don't play cards. Sam tried to teach me, but I couldn't learn even the names of the suits. A stubborn instinct in me refuses to learn. Tsutsik, I'm as good as finished. This was my last game. I've nothing left except to commit suicide."

"You too?"

"Who else? Is this why you are going to marry Shosha —to make her a widow?"

"I'll take her with me."

"Well, you are, as they say, healthy, fresh, and meshugga. In my case I tried to play year after year after year, and I always failed. Besides, I'm older than you. But why should you fall into such despair? You are a writer of stories, not a playwright. So far as the theater goes, you're still a greenhorn—I think with talent. Oh, here is my cake and your eggs. I used to wonder why those condemned to the electric chair bother to pick out a special last meal. They ask for a rare steak and a tasty dessert. Why should a person care what he eats if he's going to be dead an hour later? It seems that life and death have nothing in common. You may decide to die tomorrow but today you still want to eat for pleasure and sleep in a warm bed. What are your real plans?"

"Really, to get through with the whole botched-up mess."

"My God, when I was on the ship to Europe I never thought I would drive someone into such a state because of my foolish ambitions."

"Betty, it's not your fault."

"Whose fault is it?"

"Oh, it's everything together. The Jews in Poland are trapped. When I said this in the Writers' Club, they attacked me. They had let themselves fall into a stupid kind of optimism, but I know for sure that we will all be destroyed. The Poles want to get rid of us. They consider us a nation within a nation, a strange and malignant body. They lack the courage to finish us off themselves, but they wouldn't shed tears if Hitler did it for them. Stalin will certainly not defend us. Since the Trotskyite opposition began, the Communists have become our worst enemies. Trotsky is called Judas in Russia. The fact is that the Trotskyites are almost all Jews. If you give a Jew one revolution, he demands another revolution—a permanent one. If you give him one Messiah, he asks for another Messiah. As to Palestine, the world doesn't want us to have a state. The bitter truth is that many Jews today don't want to be Jews any more. But it's too late for total assimilation. Whoever is going to win this coming war will liquidate us."

"Maybe the democracies will win."

"The democracies are committing suicide."

"Well, don't let your coffee get cold. If you hadn't decided to carry that silly Shosha on your shoulders, you could easily get yourself to America. There the Jew can still muddle through. I can go back, but the very thought of it makes me shudder. Sam can't stay at home even one night. He always has to go somewhere—usually to that Café Royal. There he meets the writers he supports and the actresses he used to have affairs with. This is the only place where he is somebody. It's funny, but there is only one little place in the whole world—a third-rate restaurant—where he feels at home. He eats the blintzes the doctors have forbidden him. He fills up his belly with twenty cups of coffee each day. He smokes the cigars he knows are poison for him. He demands that I go with him, but for me this café is a nest of snakes. They always hated me, but now that I am with Sam they would like to swallow me alive. The Yiddish theater where he takes me at least twice a week has reached its lowest point. To sit there with him and listen to their stale jokes and see sixty-year-old yentas play eighteen-year-old girls is a physical pain. The sad truth is that for me there isn't *one* place in the whole world where I feel at home."

"Well, we're a well-matched pair."

"We could have been, but you didn't want it. What do you say to this Shosha all day long?"

"I don't say much."

"What is this with you, an act of masochism?"

"No, Betty, I really love her."

"There are things you must see to believe. You can never foresee them in your imagination: you and Shosha, me and Sam Dreiman. At least he finds some comfort among his cronies. Tsutsik, look who's here!"

I raised my eyes and saw Feitelzohn. He stood a few steps from our table with a cigar in his mouth, his Panama hat pushed back, and a cane hooked over his shoulder. I had not seen him with a cane before. He looked older and changed. He smiled with familiar shrewdness, but I imagined that his cheeks had fallen in, as if he had lost his teeth. He approached our table with small steps. "Is this how things are?" he said with a muffled voice, and then took out the cigar. "Well, really, Tsutsik, I begin to believe in your hidden powers." He leaned the cigar in the ashtray on our table. "I passed by and it occurred to me, 'Perhaps Tsutsik is there.' Good morning, Miss Slonim. I've become so mixed up that I forgot to greet you. How do you do? It's nice to see you again. What was it I wanted to say? Yes, Tsutsik. I said to myself, 'What would he do here so early? He only comes here with Sam Dreiman and not this early in the day.' I was about to continue my walk but somehow my feet brought me in by their own choice. You should be ashamed of yourself, Tsutsik. Why are you keeping away from your friends? We have all been looking for you—Haiml, Celia, I. I called you perhaps twenty times, but the maid had one answer: 'Not home.' What's wrong? You have better friends in Warsaw?"

"Dr. Feitelzohn, sit down with us," Betty said. "Why are you standing?"

"Since you two are huddling in a corner, no doubt you have your secrets. But one can say hello in any case."

"We have no secrets. We were talking business and we have finished. Sit down."

"I really don't know what to say," I began to stammer.

"If you don't know, don't say. I will say it for you. You have been a little boy and you will remain one for the rest of your life. Look at you," Feitelzohn said.

"Where did you get a cane all of a sudden?" I asked, just to change the conversation.

"Oh, I stole it. One of my Americans left it to me. Lately my feet have been making monkey business. I walk on a flat road and suddenly my feet begin to run by themselves as if I were ice skating or going downhill. What kind of a malady is this? I will have to ask our literary physician Dr. Lipkin, who understands as much about medicine as he understands about literature. Meanwhile,

I have decided that a cane cannot do any damage. Tsutsik, you look pale. What's the matter? Are you sick?"

"He's perfectly well and crazy," Betty said. "A first-class maniac."

5   Feitelzohn assured us that he had eaten breakfast, and when Betty ordered rolls, an omelette, and coffee for him, he smiled and said, "If one lives in America a few years, one becomes an American. What would the world do without America? When I lived there I complained of Uncle Sam steadily—talked only about his shortcomings. But now that I'm here, I miss America. I could go back if I chose, on a tourist visa. It might even be that I could get a visa as a professor. But in New York and Boston no university would give me a permanent job. And to teach in those small colleges somewhere in the Midwest means dying of boredom. I cannot sit all day long and read like a bookworm. The students there are more childlike than our cheder boys. All they talk about is football, and the professors are not much cleverer. America is a country of children. The New Yorkers are a little more grown up, but not much. Once some friend of mine put me on a ferry to Coney Island. This, Tsutsik, I wish you could see. It is a city in which everything is for play—shooting at tin ducklings, visiting a museum where they show a girl with two heads, letting an astrologer plot your horoscope and a medium call up the soul of your grandfather in the beyond. No place lacks vulgarity, but the vulgarity of Coney Island is of a special kind, friendly, with a tolerance that says, 'I play my game and you play your game.' As I walked around there and ate a hot dog—this is what they call a sausage—it occurred to me that I was seeing the future of mankind. You can even call it the time of the Messiah. One day all people will realize there is not a single idea that can really be called true—that everything

141

is a game—nationalism, internationalism, religion, atheism, spiritualism, materialism, even suicide. You know, Tsutsik, that I am a great admirer of David Hume. In my eyes he is the only philosopher who has not become obsolete— he is as fresh and clear today as he was in his own time. Coney Island fits David Hume's philosophy. Since we are sure of nothing and there is even no evidence that the sun will rise tomorrow, play is the very essence of human endeavor, perhaps even the thing-in-itself. God is a player, the cosmos a playground. For years I have searched for a basis of ethics and gave up hope. Suddenly it became clear to me. The basis of ethics is man's right to play the games of his choice. I will not trample on your toys and you will not trample on mine; I won't spit on your idol and you will not spit on mine. There is no reason why hedonism, the cabala, polygamy, asceticism, even our friend Haiml's blend of eroticism and Hasidism could not exist in a play-city or play-world, a sort of a universal Coney Island where everyone would play according to his or her desire. I'm sure, Miss Slonim, that you have visited Coney Island more than once."

"Yes, but I never came to your philosophical conclusions. By the way, who is David Hume? I've never heard of him."

"David Hume was an English philosopher and a friend of Jean Jacques Rousseau before he became a disgusting schnorrer."

"Here is your omelette, Dr. Feitelzohn," Betty said. "I have heard of Jean Jacques Rousseau. I've even read his *Confessions*."

"It is easy to read David Hume, too. A child can understand him. I'm sure, Tsutsik, you know that $7 + 5 = 12$ has been judged an analytic sentence, not a synthetic a priori one. Hume was right, not Kant. But you still haven't explained what happened to you. You vanished like a wishing ring. I began to think you had gone to Jerusalem and were sitting in a cave trying to bring the Redemption."

"Dr. Feitelzohn, his cave is on Krochmalna Street." Betty turned to me. "May I tell him the truth?"

"If you like. I don't care any more."

"Dr. Feitelzohn, your Tsutsik has found himself a bride-to-be on Krochmalna Street."

Feitelzohn put down his fork. "Is that so? According to the way you used to praise that madman Otto Weininger, I thought you would turn into an old bachelor."

I wanted to answer him, but Betty prevented me. "He could have remained a bachelor, but he found such a treasure—her name is Shosha—that he had to break all his principles and convictions."

"She's making fun of me," I managed to say.

"What? You cannot run away from the female species. Sooner or later you fall into their net. Celia was looking for you desperately. Shosha? A modern girl with such an old-fashioned name? What is she, a fighting Yiddishist?"

Again I tried to answer and again Betty interrupted me: "It would be hard to say just what she is, but if such a connoisseur of women as your Tsutsik decides to marry, you know she has to be something extraordinary. If your David Hume had met her, he would have divorced his wife and run away with Shosha to Coney Island."

"I don't think David Hume had a wife," Feitelzohn said after some hesitation. "Well, mazel tov, Tsutsik, mazel tov."

Only now did Betty let me speak. "She makes fun of me," I said. "Shosha is a girl from my childhood. We used to play together before I went to cheder. We were neighbors at No. 10 Krochmalna. Later I went away and for many years . . ."

Feitelzohn picked up his fork. "Whatever the case, you don't run away from your friends. If you get married, you cannot keep it a secret. If you love her, we want to know her and accept her as one of us. May I call up Celia and tell her the good tidings?"

I saw that Betty was about to come out with some new joke and I said to her, "Do me a favor, Betty, and don't speak in my name. And please don't be so sarcastic. Dr. Feitelzohn, it's not such good tidings and I don't want Celia to know about it. Not yet. Shosha is a poor girl without any education. I loved her as a child and I was never able to forget her. I was sure that she was dead but I found her—thanks to Betty, as a matter of fact."

"I wasn't being sarcastic. I meant it all seriously"— Betty tried to defend herself.

"Why isn't Celia allowed to know the truth?" Feitelzohn asked. "Whenever I expect life to remain status quo, something unexpected pops up. World history is made of the same dough as bagels. It must be fresh. This is why democracy and capitalism are going down the drain. They have become stale. This is the reason idolatry was so exciting. You could buy a new god every year. We Jews burdened the nations with an eternal God, and therefore they hate us. Gibbon tried so hard to find the reason for the fall of the Roman Empire. It fell only because it had become old. I hear that there is a passion for newness in the sky also. A star gets tired of being a star and it explodes and becomes a nova. The Milky Way got weary of its sour milk and began to run to the devil knows where. Does she have a job? I mean your fiancée, not the Milky Way."

"She has no job and she cannot have one," I said.

"Is she sick?"

"Yes, sick."

"When the body gets tired of being healthy, it becomes sick. When it gets tired of living, it dies. When it has enough of being dead, it reincarnates into a frog or a windmill. The coffee here is the best in the whole of Warsaw. May I order another glass, Miss Slonim?"

"Ten glasses, but please don't call me Miss Slonim—my name is Betty."

"I drink too much coffee and I smoke too many cigars. How is it possible that one never gets tired of tobacco and coffee? This is really a riddle."

PART TWO

EIGHT

1   Two days before Yom Kippur eve, Bashele bought two hens with which to perform the sacrificial ceremony, one for herself and the other for Shosha. She wanted to buy a rooster for me, but I refused to let a rooster die for my sins. Certain writers in the Yiddish newspapers had come out against this rite, calling it idolatrous. The Zionist supporters proposed sacrificing money instead, which would go to the Jewish National Fund for Palestine. Still, from all the apartments on Krochmalna Street one could hear the clucking of hens and the crowing of roosters. When Bashele went to Yanash's Court to have the hens slaughtered, she didn't return for two hours. The crowd was so large she couldn't get to the slaughterers. Toward evening, the street emptied even of pickpockets. The den at No. 6 was closed down. Candles were lit in the brothels and no visitors were permitted. Even the Communists were hiding somewhere. Bashele had bought a seat in a synagogue. Toward the evening meal, she lit a large candle stuck in a pot of sand—a "soul candle"—and put on a silk holiday dress that went back to the time we had lived at No. 10. She took out of a chest two prayer books she had received as a wedding present, and went off to services. Before leaving, she blessed Shosha and me. She placed her hands on my head and mumbled the benediction as if I were her son: "God make thee as Ephraim and as Manasseh."

I stayed with Shosha for some time. I tried to kiss her and she admonished me that it was forbidden. She had been busy all day long helping her mother prepare for the after-holiday meal, and she kept yawning and falling asleep. She looked pale. She asked me again and again to read some prayers from her grandmother's prayer book, with its faded pages and spots made by tallow candles and tears, but I refused. After a while I wished her a good holiday and left. Dr. Feitelzohn had invited me to spend the evening with him.

A silence had descended over all the Jewish streets. The trolleys made their way empty, and shops were closed. Overhead, the stars flickered like the flames of memorial candles. Even the prison on Dluga Street, the "Arsenal," appeared veiled in reverent melancholy with its dim glow behind the barred windows. I imagined that the night itself took score of its mission. Feitelzohn's apartment was in a house near Freta Street. He had told me no other Jewish tenants lived there besides him. At times I felt that no Gentiles lived there, either. The front windows were never lit in the evenings, nor were there lights at the gate entrance. I climbed the four flights of stone stairs to his place and not a rustle could be heard from behind a single door. I often played with the idea that this was a house of ghosts.

I knocked, and Feitelzohn opened. The apartment consisted of a huge, almost empty room, with gray walls and a high ceiling with a solitary lamp. A door led to a tiny kitchen. How strange, this erudite man owned hardly a book except for an old German encyclopedia. Nor did he have a desk. He slept not in a bed but on a couch, which was covered with a black blanket. Mark Elbinger sat on the couch now—erect, tense.

I had apparently interrupted a dispute between them, for after a long pause Feitelzohn said, "Mark, of all the errors Jews have made, our greatest was to delude ourselves—and later other peoples—that God is merciful, loves His creatures, hates malefactors, and all the rest of it our saints and prophets preached, from Moses down to Chafetz Chaim. The ancient Greeks never nursed this delusion and that was their greatness. While the Jews accused other nations of idolatry, they themselves served an idol of justice. Christianity is an outcome of this wishful thinking. Hitler, savage that he is, is now trying to de-hypnotize the world from these fallacies, but—oh, the telephone again! On Yom Kippur!"

I was not in a mood to take part in any discussions and I went over to the window. On the right side I could see the Vistula. A three-quarter moon cast silver nets upon the dark water. Elbinger materialized at my side. He murmured, "A strange person, our Feitelzohn."

"What is he?"

"I've known him over thirty years and I don't begin to fathom what he is. All his words have one aim—to cover up what he's really thinking."

"What is he really thinking?"

"Gloomy thoughts. He is disappointed in everything, but mostly in himself. His father was an ascetic. He may still be alive somewhere. Morris has a daughter whom he last saw in her diapers. I myself have known two women who committed suicide over him. One a German in Berlin, and the other a missionary's daughter in London . . ."

Feitelzohn grunted and put down the receiver. "It's my opinion that woman's number-one passion isn't sex but talking," he said.

"What does she want?" Elbinger asked.

"You ought to know, you're the mind reader."

The conversation turned to occultism, and Feitelzohn said, "There are unknown forces here, yes, there are, but they're all part of the mystery called nature. What nature is no one knows, and I suspect that she doesn't know herself. I can easily visualize the Almighty sitting on the Throne of Glory in the Seventh Heaven, Metatron on His right, Sandalphon on His left, and God asking them, 'Who am I? How did I come about? Did I create Myself? Who gave Me these powers? After all, it couldn't be that

I've existed forever. I remember only the past hundred trillion years. Everything before that is hazy. Well, how long will it go on?' Wait, Mark, I'll get you your cognac. Something to nibble on? I have cookies as old as Methuselah."

Feitelzohn went into the kitchen. He came back after a long time with a plate holding two glasses of cognac and a few biscuits. I had told him I was fasting, not because I believed that this was God's will, but to remain in some way a part of my family and all the other Jews. Feitelzohn clinked his glass with Elbinger's. *"L'chaim!* We Jews keep on wishing ourselves eternal life, or at least immortality of the soul. In fact, eternal life would be a calamity. Imagine some little storekeeper dying and his soul flying around for millions of years still remembering that once it sold chicory, yeast, and beans, and that a customer owes it eighteen groschen. Or the soul of an author ten million years later resenting a bad review he got."

"Souls don't stay the same. They grow," Elbinger said.

"If they forget the past, they are no longer the same. And if they remember all of the pettiness of life, then they cannot grow. I have no doubt that soul and body are two sides of the same coin. In this respect Spinoza had more courage than Kant. Kant's soul is nothing but a false figure in a false system of bookkeeping. *L'chaim!* Let's sit down."

The conversation turned again and again to the secret powers, and Elbinger said, "Yes, they exist, but what they represent I do not know. My own experience with them started when I was still a child. We were living in a village so small I could never find it on any map—Sencymin. Actually, it was a hamlet into which two to three dozen Jewish families had moved. My father, a *melamed,* was a pauper. We occupied two rooms—one used for the cheder; the other for the kitchen, the bedroom, and everything else. I had an older sister, Tzipa, and an older brother, Yonkel. I was named Moshe Mottel after a great-grandfather, but I was called Mottele, which later evolved into Mark. I recall a number of episodes in my life as far back as the age of two. My bed was set up in the cheder room, where the children studied by day. The two windows there had shutters and they must have faced east, because the sun shone through them in the mornings. What I'm speaking of now has no connection with the so-called occult but with a feeling that everything is full of mysteries. I recall that once I woke quite early—my parents, brother, and sister were still asleep. The rising sun shone through the cracks in the shutters, and columns of dust rose from sunbeams. I remember that morning with remarkable clarity. Obviously, I was too young to think in the context of words, but I wondered, 'What is all this? Where does it all come from?' Other children no doubt go through the same thing, but on that morning my feeling was unusually strong, and I knew instinctively that I shouldn't ask about this and that my parents couldn't supply any answers. Our ceiling had beams, and a web of sun and shadow played across it. I realized that I myself and what I was seeing— the walls, the floor, the pillow on which I rested my head—were all one. In later years I read about cosmic consciousness, monism, pantheism, but I never experienced it with such impact. More, it provided me with a rare pleasure. I had merged with eternity and I relished it. At times I think it was like the state of passing over from life to what we call death. We may experience it in the final moments or perhaps immediately after. I say this because no matter how many dead people I have seen in my life, they have had the same expression on their faces: *Aha, so that's what it is! If I had only known! What a shame I can't tell the others about it!* Even a dead bird or mouse presents this expression, although not as distinctly as man.

"My first psychic experiences—if you can call them that—were of a kind that might have come in a dream or while I was awake, although I'm as convinced that they weren't dreams as I am that my sitting here with you now is no dream. I remember one time leaving our house at night. Our house—actually, all the Jewish houses were built around a sandy area called the Market. The shops were there, the prayer house and a ritual bath, as well as the tavern. I couldn't say how late it was, but the Market was deserted, all the stores were shut, and the shutters closed. I managed to slip out of bed and open the door. The night was bright—if not from the moon, perhaps from the stars.

"Across the way from us stood another house. The peasant shacks had roofs of straw, while the Jewish houses had crooked shingle roofs. Needless to say, the houses were low. The moment I stepped outside I saw something sitting on the roof across the way. I imagined it was a man, yet different. For one thing, he had no arms or legs. For another, he didn't stand on the roof, he didn't sit—he hovered there. He didn't speak to me, but I understood that he wanted me to come up to him, and I knew that to go up would be the same as going to where my dead brother and sister had gone. Just the same, I felt a strong urge to go to him. I stood gaping in indecision, frightened and disbelieving my own eyes.

"Suddenly I was aware that the man or monster had begun berating me—still in silence—and he lowered a spade toward me. The spade was not a spade at all but something that emerged from his body. It was a kind of tongue, so long and wide that it couldn't have come from any mouth. It stretched out so close to me that I knew it would catch me at any moment. I was overcome by a dreadful fear and ran back into the house screaming. The household wakened. They blew on me and, it seems, uttered incantations over me. My mother, father, Tzipa, and Yonkel—all of them barefoot and in their nightclothes—asked why I was crying so desperately, but I neither could nor wanted to answer them, knowing that I wouldn't be able to find the right words for it, that they would not believe me, and above all, that it would be better for me if I said nothing. Actually, I'm telling this for the very first time tonight. From then on, I became a kind of secret visionary. I saw things that some sense told me not to reveal. In the daytime I often saw shadows on the walls of our house, shadows not connected to the phenomena of light and shade. These were beings that crawled over the walls and into the walls. At times, two came together from opposite directions and one swallowed the other. Some were tall; their heads touched the ceiling—if you could call them heads. Others were small. At times I saw them on the floor, too, and outside on other houses, and in the air. They were always busy—coming, going, rushing. Rarely did one stop for a moment. I tell myself today that I saw ghosts, but this is merely an appellation. One thing does come to mind—I separated them into males and females. I wasn't afraid of them. It would be more accurate to say that I was curious.

"One night after I had gone to sleep and my mother had put out the light and the moon shone in through the cracks in the shutters, I heard a rustling. How shall I describe it? It was like a dried palm leaf shaking, like beating osier branches, like spraying water, and like something else to which there is no comparison. The walls began to hum and buzz, particularly in the corners, and the shapes that till then I had seen only by day now raced in thick whirls. Today, I would express it as a kind of panic among them. They hurried here and there, merged in the corners from which the noise came, raced over the beams and across the floor. My bed began to vibrate. Everything beneath me shook and tossed, and the straw in my mattress seemed animated. For once I was terrified, but I didn't dare cry out, fearing a blow or some other punishment. When I grew older, I speculated that this vibration might have been the result of an earthquake, but when I casually asked my parents and other townspeople if they had ever been through an earthquake, they all replied in the negative. I don't know if Poland has ever suffered an earthquake. The noise and dashing about lasted a long time. You can tell me my venture outside the house and the experiences that night were dreams or nightmares, but I know this isn't so.

"In later years I almost ceased having these visions, or whatever they may have been, but others evolved. I got an urge for girls—for Gentile girls, too—and I gradually realized that if I thought about a girl long enough or intensely enough, she grew magnetized and came to me. I'm not one to ascribe unusual powers to myself. Essentially, I'm a rationalist. I know coincidences occur that, in terms of probability, couldn't happen. When I play the game of dreidel with myself and the dreidel falls on the same letter five or six times because I will it to do so, I can assume that it happened by chance. However, when I spin the dreidel ten times and it comes out the same, I know that chance has nothing to do with it. I'm sure you'd rather hear about girls than dreidels. It came to the point where I would mentally order a woman to come to this and that street, and this and that number—we were then living in Warsaw—and she would come. I can't prove this to you. I can't even demonstrate with a dreidel each and every time. These powers are strangely inclined to be spiteful. They are mischievous, and they hate to be put to the test with pencils and watches. I would say that they hate science and scientists. Believe me, even to my own ears this sounds like nonsense. Who are these powers? Are they living beings? And why should they hate science and statistics? It sounds like a pretext for lying, and I've been called a liar more than once. I myself considered mediums liars if they couldn't demonstrate their powers when they were being controlled, so to say, scientifically. Well, but aren't our sex organs full of caprices, and aren't they, in a sense, antiscience? Morris, if you were told to sleep with a woman in the presence of ten professors with cameras and meters and all kinds of measuring instruments, you wouldn't be such a Don Juan. Well, and what would have happened to poets like Goethe or Heine, if they had been placed at a table surrounded by professors and instruments and ordered to write a great poem? You can play a violin in a bright hall before hundreds of people, but it's a moot point whether Beethoven or Mozart could have written their symphonies under such circumstances. I tell you that although I've managed many things under strict controls and before huge crowds, I've experienced my most significant events only when I've been alone. No one watched for results, and I didn't have to worry that I would be jeered or whistled at. Shyness is a tremendous force—occasionally a negative one. There are many men who would go to brothels, but they don't because with a prostitute they would become impotent. Why should the occult powers be any less capricious than the genitals? I can hypnotize in front of an audience today. I had to learn to do this. I've conquered my fear of failure, but not altogether. If I bang my fist on the table, the table bangs the fist back in return. This is true in spiritual matters as well. Every hypnosis has its counterhypnosis. If I'm afraid that I won't be able to sleep, I lie awake all night, and if professors from another planet sat around me on a single visit, they might conclude that I never slept at all. Why is it so hard to be a good actor and to speak and behave naturally onstage? At home, every woman is a Sarah Bernhardt. I've seen great scholars face an audience unable to utter a lucid sentence on a subject in which they were world experts.

"Yes, I did things that amazed me and convinced me I could dominate other souls, often those whom I barely knew—perhaps they had glanced at me just once. My success with women was so great that it frightened me. What is hypnotism, anyway? My theory is that it's a language with which one soul communicates directly with another.

"Our conscious hypnotic powers have limits. I don't believe that I hypnotized the dreidel. Perhaps I hypnotized my hand to spin the dreidel in such a way that it fell where I wanted it to. But who says that hypnotism is merely a biological force? Maybe it's physical, too? Maybe gravity is a kind of hypnotism? Maybe magnetism is hypnotism? Maybe God is a hypnotist with such strong hypnotic powers that He can say, 'Let there be light,' and there is light? I heard of a woman who ordered a chair to walk, and the chair walked from wall to wall and even danced. A poltergeist lifts plates and breaks them, throws stones, and opens locked doors. A woman came to me once and swore on all that was holy to her that one time when she entered her kitchen a pot rose, soared toward her, and slowly came to rest at her feet. This was an elderly woman, a lawyer's widow, a mother of grown sons and daughters, a person of education and dignity. She had no possible reason to make up such a story. She came to me hoping I could explain the mystery. It had plagued her for years. She told me that the pot didn't *fall* at her feet but laid itself down carefully. From that day on, she was afraid of the pot. She waited for it to pull another stunt, but no, it remained a pot like all pots. The woman cried as she spoke to me. Could this have been a greeting from her late husband? She spent two hours with me, hoping I could provide her with an explanation, but the only thing I could tell her was that the pot hadn't acted on its own, but that some force—an unseen hand— had lifted it and laid it down at her feet. I recall her saying, 'Maybe the pot wanted to play a joke?' "

"If this story is true, we must reexamine all our values, our concept of the world," Feitelzohn said. "Still, why doesn't it happen that a pot or some other object rises in the presence of a physicist or a chemist or at least a photographer with a camera? How is it that these wonders always occur in quiet widows' kitchens? Why don't they happen in a kitchen where there are several cooks present? Can it be that pots are bashful, too?"

At ten-thirty, Elbinger announced that he must leave. He had an appointment. I wanted to leave with him, but Feitelzohn insisted I stay.

He lit a cigar and said, "That big hero is a hypochondriac. He has hypnotized himself into believing that he suffers from a dozen ailments. He is convinced that he hasn't slept in years. He has ulcers. He is supposedly impotent, too. Women are crazy for him, but he practices celibacy. The history of mankind is the history of hypnotism. It's my firm conviction that all epidemics are mass hypnosis. When the papers announce an outbreak of influenza, people start to die from influenza. I myself talked all kinds of insanities into myself. I can't even read a book any more. At the end of the first sentence, I start to yawn. I'm sick of women. Their talking puts me off. Take our Celia. She would come here for an hour or two, and for an hour or two she would chatter. That Haiml is a homosexual. At times it seems to me I'm another. Don't be afraid, I wouldn't lay a hand on you."

Again the telephone rang. Feitelzohn let it ring. He stood there and looked at me in a new way—there was something fatherly and older-brotherly in his look.

He said, "It's Celia. I see you're tired. Go home if you want. Tsutsik, don't stay in Poland. A holocaust is coming here that will be worse than in Chmielnitsky's time. If you can get a visa—even a tourist visa—escape! A good holiday."

Then he walked over to the telephone, which had kept on ringing.

2 Warsaw was so quiet I could hear the echo of my own footsteps. Candles still burned in the windows. The gate in the house on Leszno Street was closed, and the janitor was slow in coming to open it. He grumbled, as if he knew that I intended to move out soon. Although I had my key to the elevator with me, I walked up the dark stairs.

I knocked at the apartment door and Tekla opened it. She said, "The phone rang for you today maybe a hundred times. Miss Betty."

"Thank you, Tekla."

"You don't go to the synagogue on such a holy day?" she asked with reproof.

I didn't know how to answer her. I went to my room. Without putting on the lights, I took off my clothes and lay down, but even though I was tired I couldn't sleep. What would I do after the few zlotys I had left were gone? I saw no possibility of earning money. I lay there, frightened by my situation. Feitelzohn had at least a semblance of a living from his lectures. He took money from Celia and from other women, too. He had a rent-controlled apartment, for which he paid no more than thirty zlotys a month. I had accepted the responsibility for a sick girl.

I fell asleep and wakened with a start. The phone in the corridor was ringing. On my watch the luminous hands showed a quarter past two. I heard the sound of bare feet —Tekla was running to answer. I heard her whispering. The door to my room opened. "It's for you!" Her voice expressed the indignation of a Jew forced to desecrate the holiest day of the year.

I got out of bed and bumped into her. She was wearing only her nightgown. In the hall I picked up the receiver and heard Betty's voice. It was hoarse and grating, like that of someone in the midst of a quarrel. She said, "You must come over to the hotel at once! If I call you in the middle of Yom Kippur night, it's not because of some trifle."

"What's happpened?"

"I've been calling you all day. Where do you wander off to on Yom Kippur eve? I didn't sleep a wink last night and I haven't closed my eyes tonight. Sam is very sick. He has to have an operation. I told him all about us."

"What's the matter with him? Why did you need to tell him?"

"Last night he got up to go to the toilet, but he couldn't pass water. He was in such pain I had to call the First Aid. They relieved him with a catheter, but he requires an operation. He refuses to go to the hospital here and insists on returning to America to his own doctor. The doctor who saw him today told me that he has a weak heart and is not likely to recover from surgery. My dear, I have a feeling he won't make it. He called me to his side and said, 'Betty, I'm cashing in my chips, but I want to provide for you.' He talked in such a way that I couldn't withhold anything from him. I told him the whole truth. He wants to talk to you. Catch a cab and come right over. He's acting like a father to me—closer than a father. I know it's Yom Kippur, but this can't wait. Will you come?"

"Yes, of course, but you shouldn't have told him!"

"I shouldn't have been born! Be quick!" She hung up the receiver.

I tried to put on my clothes in a hurry, and they slipped from my fumbling fingers. The button fell out of my collar and rolled under the bed. I stooped to pick it up and knocked my forehead against the rail. The room was warm, but I felt a chill. I closed the door behind me and began to race down the unlit stairs. For the second time that night I rang the bell and waited for the janitor to open the gate. The pavement outside was wet—it must have been raining. The street lay deserted. I stood at the curb hoping for a taxi to come by but soon realized I could stand all night without one coming. I went in the direction of Bielanska Street and the Cracow suburb. The only streetcar that passed was headed in the opposite direction. I didn't walk but ran. I came to the hotel. The clerk dozed before the honeycomb of key boxes. I knocked on Betty's door. No one answered. I knocked again, this time on Sam Dreiman's door, and Betty let me in. She was wearing pajamas and slippers. Inside, the lights glared with a middle-of-the-night tension. Sam lay with his eyes closed, his head resting on two pillows, seemingly asleep. From under the bedding a little hose ran into a container. Betty's face was sallow and drawn, her hair disordered. "What took you so long?" she asked in a choked voice that hid a scream.

"I couldn't get a cab. I ran all the way."

"Oh. He just now fell asleep. He took a pill."

"Why do you have the room so bright here?"

"I don't know. I'll turn the lights down. I don't know what's happening to me any more. One calamity after another—look at my eyes. Come closer!"

She took me by the arm and pulled me to the other end of the room near the window. She gestured to me to be quiet. She began to talk in a whisper, but from time to time she emitted a shriek as if so many words had collected in her they could no longer be contained.

"I started calling you at ten this morning and on into the night. Where were you—still with that Shosha? Tsutsik, I have no one here but you. I tell you, Sam is a saint. I never knew he had such a noble soul. Oh, if I had known, I would have been nicer to him. I would have been faithful. But I'm afraid it's too late now. He had a hemorrhage in his nose. Tomorrow they're holding a consultation here. I called the American consulate and they arranged everything. They wanted to check him into a private clinic, where he can have the best doctors, but he insisted he would only be operated on in America. In the midst of the commotion he called me to him and said, 'Betty, I know that you love Tsutsik and there's no point in your denying it.' This was such a blow to me that I confessed everything. I began to cry and he kissed me and called me 'daughter.' He has children, but their mother filled them with hate against him. They dragged him to court and tried to grab their inheritance while he was still alive. Wait, he's waking up."

I heard a tossing about and a groan.

"Betty, where are you? Why is the room so dark?"

She ran to the bed. "Sam darling! I thought you would sleep longer. Tsutsik is here!"

"Tsutsik, come over. Betty, turn up the lights. So long as I can draw breath I don't want to be in the dark. Tsutsik, you can see for yourself I'm a sick man. I want to talk to you like a father. I have two sons, both lawyers, but all my life they treated me not like a father but worse than a stranger. I have a son-in-law, and he's no better. Living with him has turned my daughter into a bitch. I haven't felt good for a long time. Old age has suddenly caught me—the head, the stomach, the legs. Twenty times a day I run—if you'll excuse me—to the toilet, but my bladder is blocked up. In New York I have a doctor who watches over me. He gives me a checkup every three months, treats me with massages. He didn't want me to have an operation because my heart is making monkey business. In Warsaw I have no doctor. Besides, we were so busy with the theater I put off everything. My doctor ordered me not to drink—whiskey irritates the prostate and isn't good for the bladder, either—but you don't want to admit you're washed up. Take a chair, sit down. That's it. You, too, Betty darling. What was I saying, eh? Well, I'm afraid God wants me up there with Him. He's probably in the real-estate business and wants Sam Dreiman to advise Him. When the time comes, you got to go.

Even if I survive the operation, it won't be for long. I was supposed to lose weight while I was here. Instead, I gained twenty pounds. How can you diet when you're away from home? I love your Warsaw dishes—they have that homey taste. Well . . ."

Sam Dreiman closed his eyes, then shook himself and opened them again. "Tsutsik, today is Yom Kippur. I thought I'd be able to go to the synagogue. I wanted to go to the one on Tlomacka Street as well as to the Hasidim on Nalewki. I bought the tickets. But man proposes and God disposes. I'll be frank with you—if I should pass away, I don't want to leave Betty to the fates. I know about your affair—she confessed everything to me. I knew about it even before. After all, she's a young woman and I'm an old man. I used to be a great lover, I could raise hell with the best of them, but once you pass into your seventies and have high blood pressure you're no longer the big hero you were. She kept on praising you. She accused herself of having brought you bad luck. I hoped the play would be a success, but it wasn't fated. We did a lot of talking. Hear me out, don't interrupt, I beg you, and think over what I'm going to say, because I look at things in a clear-headed way. You're a poor young man. You have talent, but talent is like a diamond—it has to be polished. I've been told you're involved with some sick, undeveloped girl. She is poor, too, and what is the saying? Two corpses go dancing. Things will not end well in Poland. That beast Hitler will soon come with his Nazis. There'll be a great war. Americans will lend a hand and they'll do what they did in the last war, but before that the Nazis will attack the Jews and there'll be nothing but grief for you here. The Yiddish papers are in trouble already, there are no book publishers, and what goes on on the stage is disgusting. How will you make a living? A writer has to eat, too. Even Moses had to eat. That's what the holy books say.

"Tsutsik, Betty loves you and I gather you don't hate her, either. I'm going to leave her a lot of money—exactly how much I'll tell you another time. I want to make a deal with you—a regular business transaction. I don't know yet what's going to happen to me. It's possible I'll leave this world soon, though if God is willing, I may be around for another few years yet. If they remove my prostate I may not be left a whole man in the true sense of the word. Here is my plan: I want you two to marry. I'll establish a trust fund. A lawyer will explain it all to you. You won't be a parasite supported by his wife but just the opposite—you'll support her. I only ask one promise from you—that as long as I live she can remain my friend. I'll be your publisher, your manager, anything you like. If you write a good play, I'll produce it. When you have a book ready, I'll publish it or give it to another publisher. In America, writers have agents to represent them, and I'll be your agent. You'll be my son and I'll be a father to you. I'll hire people who'll see to it that everything is in order."

"Mr. Dreiman—"

"I know, I know what you want to say. You want to know what will happen to the girl—what's her name? Shosha. Don't think I would leave her to God's mercy in Warsaw so she should starve. Sam Dreiman doesn't do such things. We'll bring her over to America. She is sick and should have help—a psychiatrist maybe. The consul is my friend, but he can't issue a permanent visa. There is a quota and not even the President can get around it. But I've figured how we can manage. We'll take her along as our maid. She won't be anyone's maid, but saying she is can get her a visa. If she's cured there, this would be a hundred times better for her than if she becomes your wife and starves to death here. You have only to agree that Betty can remain my friend and not leave me alone when I'm old and sick, and she won't take you to court if

164

you should want to give your Shosha a kiss or whatever. Isn't that so, Betty?"

"Yes, Sam darling, anything you say is all right with me."

"Do you hear? So that's my plan. It's her plan, too. We talked frankly. Just one thing more—I must leave for America soon, so everything has to be done fast. If you say yes, you'll have to marry at once. If not, we'll say goodbye, and may God help you."

Sam Dreiman closed his eyes. After a while, he opened them and said, "Betty, take him to your room. I have to . . ." He mumbled a few words in English that I didn't understand.

3 In the hallway between her room and Sam's, Betty began to kiss me. Her face was wet from crying, and within a moment my face was drenched. She whispered, "My husband, that's the way God intended it!"

She opened the door to her room for me and immediately went back to Sam's side. She hadn't put on the lights and I stood in the dark. After a while, I lay down on the sofa, my mind blank. I assumed that Betty would come right back, but she was away a long time. The shade was drawn over the window, but it seemed to me that day had started to break. Gradually, I began to take account of the situation. After I had given up on everything, a perspective had opened such as I never dared dream of— a visa to America and the chance to write without worrying about money! I could take Shosha along, too. Something inside me both laughed and marveled. From the time I reached manhood, I had told myself I would marry a girl just like my mother—a decent, chaste Jewish daughter. I always felt pity for men with dissolute wives. They lived with harlots and could never be sure that their children were their own. These women sullied their homes.

Now I was considering taking one of this ilk for my own. What Betty had told me about her adventures in Russia and in America stayed in my mind. During the Revolution she had carried on with a Red Army man, with some sailor, with the director of a traveling actors' troupe. She had sold herself to Sam Dreiman for money. Not only did she have an ugly past, but Sam Dreiman had now stipulated that as long as he lived she would remain his friend—which was to say his lover. "Run!" a voice cried within me. "You'll sink into a slime from which you'll never be able to get out. They'll drag you into the abyss!" It was my father's voice. In the light of dawn I saw his high brow and piercing eyes. "Don't shame me, your mother, and your holy ancestors! All your deeds are noted in heaven." Then the voice began to abuse me. "Heathen! Betrayer of Israel! See what happens when you deny the Almighty! 'You shall utterly detest it and you shall utterly abhor it, for it is a cursed thing!' "

I lay there shaken. Since my father had died, I had been unable to conjure up his face. He never appeared in my dreams. His death had brought with it a kind of amnesia. Often, before going to sleep, I implored him to reveal himself to me wherever he might be and to give me a sign, but my pleas had not been answered. Suddenly here he was beside Betty's sofa, and on the Day of Atonement. Glowing and awesome, he shed his own light. I recalled what the Midrash said of Joseph: as he was about to sin with Potiphar's wife, his father, Jacob, appeared before him. These apparitions come only in the height of distress.

I sat up, my eyes wide open. "Father, save me!" As I pleaded, Father's image dissolved.

The door opened. "Are you asleep?" Betty asked.

It took a while before I could answer. "No."

"Shall I turn on the light?"

"No, no!"

"What's the matter with you? Today is more than Yom

Kippur for me. Before you came, I took a nap on the sofa and my father came to me in a dream. He looked just as I knew him in life, only handsomer. His eyes glistened. The murderers shot him in the face and crushed his skull, but he stood before me unmarked. Well, what's your answer?"

I could only say, "Not now."

"If you don't want me, I won't throw myself at you. I've still retained some pride. One has to be a saint to treat us the way Sam Dreiman is offering to do. But if it's a disgrace for you to become my husband, say so and don't leave me dangling. I've done some ugly things in my time, but I didn't have anyone then and I owed nothing to anyone. My blood burned like fire. Those men weren't even real to me. I swear to you that I've forgotten them all. I wouldn't recognize them if I saw them on the street. Why was I fool enough to tell you about them? I've always been my own worst enemy."

"Betty, Shosha would die if I did this to her," I said.

"Eh? The truth is, she'd be cured in America, but here she'll starve to death. Already their house reeks of decay. She looks ready for the grave. How long can she go on like that? I don't have to get married—not to you or to anybody. That was purely Sam's idea. A real father wouldn't be as good to me as he has been. I'd sooner cut off my hand than just leave him. I've already told you he is barely a man now. All he needs is a kiss, a pat, a kind word. If you can't even let him have that, then be on your way. If I am ready to take Shosha into my house—that ninny—then you needn't act so superior toward Sam. He has more insight in his little finger than you have in your whole body, you goddamn idiot!"

She went out and slammed the door behind her. A moment later she was back. "So what shall I tell Sam? Give me a straight answer."

"Well, all right, we'll marry," I said.

Betty paused a moment. "Is this your decision or are you just trying to make a fool out of me? If you're going to go around burning with jealousy and thinking of me as a whore, we'll call the whole thing off right now."

"Betty, if I can look after Shosha, you can be with Sam."

"What do you think—that I'd post a guard by your bed like that sultan in the *Thousand and One Nights?* I realize you feel close to her. I'm prepared to accept it. But I demand the same from you. The times when a man could indulge all his swinish urges while the woman remained a slave are over. So long as Sam lives—and may God grant him the years he deserves—we must all live together. Try to think of him as my father. That's what he has become. I haven't given up on the theater—I still plan to make another try at it. In America we can revise this play. There no one will harass us or rush us. The fact that you'll be diddling around with your Shosha bothers me as much as last year's frost. I doubt if she's even capable of *being* a woman. Have you got her started yet?"

"No, no."

"Well, a lion can't be jealous of a fly. All I can tell you is that in a hundred and twenty years, when Sam is no more, I won't be looking for anyone else. This, I could swear to before black candles."

"You don't need to swear."

"We must get married at once. Whatever happens, I want Sam to be there."

"Yes."

"I know that you have a mother and a brother, but this can't be put off. If things go well, we'll bring your family over to America, too."

"Thank you, Betty, thank you."

"Tsutsik, I'll be better to you than you can imagine. I've already had enough filth in my life. I want to wipe the slate clean and start fresh. What it is I see in you I'm not sure myself. You have a thousand faults. But there is something about you that draws me. What is it? You tell me."

"I wouldn't know, Betty."

"When I'm with you, things are interesting. Without you, I'm miserable and bored. Come here, wish me mazel tov!"

4 I had fallen into a deep sleep on Betty's sofa. When I opened my eyes, I saw her standing beside me. It was day. She looked bedraggled and upset. She said, "Tsutsik, get up!"

I had wakened with a headache. It was a few seconds before I could remember what I was doing here.

Betty bent over me with maternal concern. "They're taking Sam to the hospital. I'm going with him."

"What happened?"

"He has to be operated on immediately! Where shall I look for you? You'd better stay in this room so I can call you."

"I will, Betty."

"You remember our agreement?"

"Yes."

"Pray to God for him! I don't want to lose him. If, God forbid, something should happen, I'd be left in the cold." She leaned down and kissed me on the mouth. She said, "The ambulance is downstairs. If you need to go out, leave the key with the desk clerk. If you want to go to Shosha's, you can, but you have to break off with that Celia once and for all. I won't stand for a fifth wheel on the wagon. I would have liked you to say goodbye to Sam, but I don't want him to know you spent the night here. I told him you went home. Pray to God for us!"

She left and I stayed on the sofa. I glanced at my wristwatch. It had stopped at the hour of four. I closed my eyes again. From what Betty said, I couldn't understand whether Sam had already made a new will or was planning to. Even if he had, his family would destroy it. I was dismayed at the trend my thoughts were taking. Money matters had always been alien to me. In none of my fantasies had it ever occurred to me to marry for money or for any practical reason. *It's the visa, not the money,* I justified myself—*the fear of falling into the hands of the Nazis.*

Suddenly I felt as if something had bitten me. Break off with Celia? Betty had no right to make such a demand on me while she remained Sam's mistress. I'd go straight to Celia's! I rubbed my jowls—a heavy stubble had sprouted. I stood up, but my legs had grown wobbly from sleeping on the sofa. A mirror hung over the wash-stand. I raised the window shade and gazed at my reflection: withered face, bloodshot eyes, a wrinkled collar. I went to the window and looked out. There was no vehicle of any kind at the hotel entrance. The ambulance had already carried them to the hospital. Betty hadn't even given me its name. From the slant of the sun's rays, I estimated that it was not early.

"What shall I tell Shosha?" I asked myself. "All she would understand was that I married someone else. She wouldn't live through it." I stood looking out at the street, the empty streetcars and droshkies. Even the Gentile neighborhoods seemed deserted in honor of Yom Kippur. I took off my jacket and washed my face, even though it was forbidden on this sacred holiday. I went out. I walked downstairs step by step. There was no reason to hurry. For the first time I felt close to Sam. He wanted the same as I—the impossible.

I passed a barbershop and went in. I was the only patron and the barber treated me with particular politeness. He wrapped me in a white sheet, like a corpse in a shroud. He stroked my beard before he began to lather.

He said, "What kind of city is this Warsaw? It's Yom Kippur by the sheenies and the whole city acts dead. And this is supposed to be the capital, the crown of our Polish nation. It's really funny!"

He had mistaken me for a Gentile. I wanted to answer him, but realized that the moment I spoke more than a word or two my accent would give me away. I nodded, grunting a single word that wouldn't compromise me: "*Tak*."

"They've taken over all Poland," he went on. "The cities are lousy with them. Once, they only stank up Nalewki, Grzybowska, and Krochmalna Streets, but lately they swarm like vermin everywhere. They've even crawled as far as Wilanów. There's one consolation—Hitler will smoke them out like bedbugs."

I barely kept from trembling. The man held the edge of the razor at my throat. I looked up, and his greenish eyes briefly held mine. Did he suspect that I was a Jew?

"I'll tell you something, dear sir. The modern Jews, those who shave, who speak a proper Polish, and who try to ape real Poles, are even worse than the old-fashioned Hebes with their long gaberdines, wild beards, and earlocks. They, at least, don't go where they aren't wanted. They sit in their stores in their long capotes and shake over their Talmud like bedouins. They babble away in their jargon, and when a Christian falls into their clutches, they swindle a few groschen out of him. But at least they don't go to the theater, the cafés, the opera. Those that shave and dress modern are the real danger. They sit in our Sejm and make treaties with our worst enemies, the Ruthenians, the White Russians, the Lithuanians. Every one of them is a secret Communist and a Soviet spy. They have one aim—to root out us Christians and hand over the power to the Bolsheviks, the Masons, and the radicals. You might find it hard to believe this, dear sir, but their millionaires have a secret pact with Hitler. The Rothschilds finance him and Roosevelt is the middleman. His real name isn't Roosevelt but Rosenfeld, a converted Jew. They supposedly assume the Christian faith, but with one goal in mind—to bore from within and infect everything and everybody. Funny, don't you think?"

I emitted a half grunt, half sigh.

"They come here for a shave and a haircut all year, but not today. Yom Kippur is a holy day even for those that are rich and modern. More than half the stores are closed here and on Marshalkowska Street. They don't go to the Hasidic prayer houses in fur-edged hats and prayer shawls like the old-fashioned sheenies—oh no, they put on top hats and drive to the synagogue on Tlomacka Street in private cars. But Hitler will clean them out! He promises their millionaires that he'll protect their capital, but once the Nazis are armed he'll fix them all—ha, ha, ha! It's too bad that he'll attack our country, but since we haven't had the guts to sweep away this filth ourselves, we have to let the enemy do it for us. What will happen later, no one can know. The fault for it all lies with those traitors, the Protestants, who sold their souls to the devil. They're the Pope's deadliest enemies. Did you know, dear sir, that Luther was a secret Jew?"

"No."

"It's an established fact."

The barber had gone over my face twice with the razor. He now splashed me with eau-de-cologne and dusted me with powder. He brushed off my suit and with two fingers removed some stray hairs from my shoulders. I paid him and left. By the time I closed the shop door my shirt was soaked. I began to race, not knowing in what direction I was going. *No, I wouldn't stay in Poland! I'd leave at any price!* I crossed the street and a car nearly ran me down. This was the most tragic day of my life. I, too, had sold my soul to the devil. Maybe go to a synagogue? No, I would desecrate the holy place. My stomach churned and I felt an urge to urinate. Sweat ran from me, and pain stabbed my bladder. I knew that if I didn't void immediately I would wet myself. I came to a restaurant and tried to enter, but the glass door wouldn't give. Was it locked? It couldn't be—I could see diners inside and waiters carrying trays.

A man with a dog on a leash came up and said, "Don't pull, push!"

"Oh, many thanks!"

I asked the waiter for the way to the restroom and he pointed to a door. But when I walked in that direction the door vanished as if by magic. People looked up from their breakfasts and stared at me. A woman laughed aloud.

The waiter came up. "Here!" And he opened a door for me.

I ran to the urinal, but just as with Sam Dreiman, the urine had become blocked inside me.

NINE

1 I didn't go to Celia. I spent Yom Kippur with Shosha. Bashele had gone to the synagogue. The big commemorative candle she had lit the day before still burned, casting almost no light. I lay on the bed next to Shosha in my clothes, dulled by the sleepless night. I dropped off, began dreaming, and awoke. Shosha spoke to me, but even though I heard her voice I didn't follow what she was saying. It had to do with the war, the typhus epidemics, the hunger, Yppe's death. Shosha placed her childlike hand on my loins. We both had fasted.

From time to time I opened an eye and noticed how the sunlight moved up across the opposite wall. A Yom Kippur quiet lay over the courtyard, and I could hear the twittering of a bird. I had made a decision and knew

173

that I would keep it, but why I had made it was something I couldn't explain to myself or to anyone else. Did it have to do with the vision—or hallucination—of my father? Had the barber influenced me with his poisonous words? I was rejecting a woman of passion, of talent, with the capability of taking me to wealthy America, and condemning myself to poverty and death from a Nazi bullet. Had it been jealousy of Sam Dreiman? Such great love for Shosha? Did I lack the courage to disappoint Bashele? I posed a question to my subconscious or unconscious, but no answer came back. This is precisely the case with those who commit suicide, I said to myself. They find a hook in the ceiling, fashion a noose, place a chair underneath, and until the final second they don't know why they are doing it. Who says that everything nature or human nature does can be expressed in motives and words? I had been aware for a long time that literature could only describe facts or let the characters invent excuses for their acts. All motivations in fiction are either obvious or false.

I fell asleep. It was dusk when I awoke. A final sliver of sunset blazed in the pane of a garret window. Shosha said, "Arele, you slept nicely."

"And you, Shoshele?"

"Oh, I slept."

The room filled with shadows. On the table the memorial candle began to flicker. The flame flared up once and soon grew so small it barely touched the wick. Shosha said, "Last year I went with Mommy to the synagogue on Yom Kippur night. A man with a white beard blew the ram's horn."

"Yes, I know."

"When three stars appear in the sky, we'll be able to eat."

"Are you hungry?"

"When you are with me, it's better than eating."

174

I said, "Shoshele, we'll soon be husband and wife. After the holidays."

As I spoke, I wanted to caution Shosha to say nothing of this to her mother for now, but just then the door opened, Bashele came in, and Shosha ran to meet her. "Mommy, Arele is going to marry me after Succoth!" She shouted this in a louder voice than I had ever heard from her. She hugged her mother and began to kiss her. Bashele quickly put down her two prayer books and cast a questioning look at me that was full of joyful astonishment.

"Yes, it's true," I said.

Bashele clapped her hands. "God the merciful has heard my prayers. I stood on my feet all day and prayed only for you, daughter, and for you, Arele, my son. Only God in heaven knows how many tears I shed for you two today. Daughter, apple of my eye, mazel tov!"

They kissed, hugged, and swayed, as if unable to break apart. Then Bashele held out her arms to me. There came from her the aroma of the fast, of the naphthalene in which her dress had been lying a whole year, and of something womanly and festive—an aroma familiar from my childhood, when our living room was turned into a women's synagogue during the Days of Awe. Bashele's voice, too, had grown louder and stronger. She began to speak in the style of the Yiddish supplication book: "It's all from heaven, from heaven. God has seen my grief, my broken spirit. Father in heaven, this is the happiest day of my wretched life. Help us, God, for we have suffered enough. Sweet Father, let me live to enjoy the satisfaction of leading my first-born child to the wedding canopy!" She raised her hands high. A motherly bliss shone in her eyes. Shosha burst into tears. Then Bashele exclaimed, "What's wrong with me? He fasted all day, this treasure of mine, my precious heir. You'll soon have food!"

She raced to the credenza and came back with a beaker

of cherry brandy. The liqueur must have been standing there from long ago, awaiting some joyous occasion. Shosha received the same offering. We drank a toast and kissed. Shosha's lips did not feel like those of a child but like those of a ripe woman. The door opened and Teibele came in, pretty, in a dress that looked new to me. I had met her for the last time on Rosh Hashanah, when she came to share the holiday feast with her mother and sister. Teibele was tall, erect, and resembled her father with her dark hair and brown eyes. Although she had been only three when the family moved from No. 10 to No. 7, she remembered me and called me Arele. On Rosh Hashanah she had brought a slice of pineapple with which to make the New Year benedictions. As soon as she heard the news, something like a mixture of happiness and laughter appeared in her eyes. "Arele, is this true?"

Before I could answer, she embraced me, held me close, and began kissing me. "Mazel tov! Mazel tov! It's a fated thing! And on Yom Kippur! Somehow my heart told me—Arele, I never had a brother, and from now on you'll be my brother, even closer than a brother. When Daddy hears this, he will . . ." Teibele trotted to the door on her high heels.

Bashele asked, "Where are you running in such a hurry?"

"To telephone Daddy," Teibele called back from the hallway.

"Why him? What does this happy event have to do with him?" Bashele shouted after her. "He abandoned us, sick and lonely, and went off to live with a slut—may all the fires of hell consume her. That's no father but a murderer. If it had been left to him, you'd have all starved to death. I was the one who fed you and gave my last bit of strength so that you should live. God in heaven, You know the truth. It was because of that rascal and his filthy ways that we lost Yppe—may she rest in paradise with the sainted souls."

Bashele said all this to herself, to Shosha, and to me, since Teibele had slammed the door behind her.

Shosha asked, "Where will she call from? Is the delicatessen open?"

"Let her call. Let her suck around him, that old whoremonger. To me he's as *trayf* as pork. I never want to see his face again. He was no father when we starved and ailed and spat out our lungs, and I don't want him as a father now when luck has come to us, may it only stay with us. Shoshele, why are you standing there like a ninny? Kiss him, hold him! He is already as good as your husband and to me he's as dear as my own child. We never forgot him, never. A day didn't go by that we didn't think of him. We didn't know where he was or if he lived, so many young people perished in all the fires. When Leizer brought us the good news that he was alive and writing for the newspaper, it was like a holiday in the house. How long ago was this? My head is so muddled I don't know what or when. *I* will lead you to the wedding canopy, my darling daughter—not your cruel father. Arele, my child, God should only grant you as much happiness as you have granted us this night." Bashele began to cry, and Shosha cried with her.

After a while, Bashele put on an apron and started fussing with pots, pans, plates. The two chickens that had been offered in sacrifice on Yom Kippur eve lay already cooked, and Bashele quickly sliced them and served them with challah and horseradish. Later, she scolded herself that she had forgotten to serve the gefilte fish first.

She hovered over me. "Eat, child of mine. You're probably weak from fasting. For myself, my soul was so burdened I didn't even realize I was fasting. To me fasting is no novelty. More than one night I went to bed without a bite in my stomach so that my little swallows should have bigger portions. Eat, Shoshele, eat, my bride! God hearkened to your longing. Worthy ancestors interceded in your behalf. For you, today is not the end of Yom Kippur but Simchas Torah. What happened to Teibele? Why is she staying away so long? He blotted her out as a daughter and still she keeps herself close to him just because he has a nice apartment and throws her a trinket from time to time. A shame and a disgrace! A sin before God."

Bashele sat down to eat, but every few seconds she turned to face the door. Finally, Teibele came back. "Mommy, I have good news for you, but first swallow your food, because when you get excited, you start to choke."

"What news? I don't want news from him."

"Mommy, listen to me! When Daddy heard of Shosha and Arele he became another person. He fell in love with that redhead, and love makes people mad. Daddy told me two things, and I want you to hear carefully, because he's waiting for an answer. First, he said that he would provide Shosha with a trousseau for the wedding and he would give her one thousand zlotys for a dowry. This isn't much, but it's better to begin with a little money than with none. Second, he said that if you, Mother, will agree to a divorce, he'll give you a thousand zlotys, too. Hush! I know how little this is for all your years of suffering, but since you two can't ever be together again, what's the point of spiting each other? You're not that old, and if you dressed yourself up you could still find a suitor. Those were *his* words, not mine. My advice is, forget the past wrongs and come to a settlement once and for all."

The whole time Teibele was talking, Bashele's face twisted with revulsion and impatience. "*Now* he's going to divorce me—when my blood is congealed and the marrow is dried in my bones? I no longer need a husband and have no desire to please anyone. All my life I lived only for you children, only for you. Now that Shosha has found her destined one, I have but one wish—that you should do the same, Teibele. He doesn't have to be a writer or a scholar. What does a writer earn, anyway? Nothing with nothing. I would be satisfied with a merchant, a clerk, even a tradesman. Does it make any difference what a husband does? The main thing is, he should be decent and have one God and one wife, not—"

"Mommy, decency is *not* everything. You have to feel something for a husband, to love him, to be able to talk to him. To tie up with some tailor or clerk and begin cooking and washing diapers is not for me. But why waste time talking about that? Better think over what I told you. I promised Daddy an answer."

"An answer already? I waited for him longer. Hoo-hah, the great squire! The only reason he's got so much gall is that he has money and we're paupers. He'll get no answer today. Sit down and eat with us. In this house, today is a double holiday. We're poor but we don't come from dirt. We had a preacher in our family—Reb Zekele Preacher, they called him. Your father, that skirt-chaser, will have to wait."

"Mommy, there's an expression—strike while the iron is hot. You know Daddy—all moods. Tomorrow he may change his mind. What will you do then?"

"I'll do what I've done all these years—suffer and place my hope in the Almighty. Arele loves Shosha, not her clothes. You can put a dress on a mannequin, too. An educated person considers the soul. Isn't that true, Arele?"

"Yes, Bashele."

"Oh, please call me Mother. May your mother live to a hundred and twenty, but you haven't a better friend than me in the whole world. If someone told me to lay down my life for your tiniest fingernail, as God is my witness, I wouldn't hesitate." Bashele began to cough.

"Arele, there are no words for how much we all love you," Shosha said.

"Well, you two love, but don't try to sell me to some clerk," Teibele said. "I want to love, too. If only I could meet the right person, my soul would open to him fast enough."

That night, Bashele set the date for the wedding—the week of Hanukkah. She suggested that I write a letter to my mother at once in Old Stykov, where my brother Moishe was now rabbi in my father's place.

Teibele, ever practical, asked, "Where will the newlyweds live? An apartment is like gold these days."

"They'll live here with me," Bashele replied. "And when I cook for two, there'll be enough for three."

2   I had committed the worst folly of my life, but I had no regrets. Neither was I elated, as those in love usually are. The day after Yom Kippur I gave notice at Leszno Street that I would be moving out at the end of the month. I might have condemned myself to penury but not yet to death. I still had my room for four weeks. I could pay Bashele for my food until some time after the holidays. I was amazed by my light-mindedness, but not shocked. I had heard that Sam Dreiman had been operated on at the Jewish hospital on Czysta Street and would go off with Betty to recuperate. When Tekla heard that I would be moving out after the Jewish holiday, she came to ask the reason. Was I dissatisfied with the service? Did she, Tekla, neglect to convey an important message to me? Did she insult me in some way? For the first time I saw tears in her pale-blue eyes. I put my arms around her, kissed her, and said, "Tekla dear, it's not your fault. You were good to me. I'll remember you to my last breath."

"Where will you live? Are you going with Miss Betty to America?"

"No, I'm staying right here in Warsaw."

"Bad times are coming for Jews here," she said, after some hesitation.

"Yes, I know."

"If a war should break out, it won't be good for Christians, either."

"Also true. But the history of all peoples is one long chain of wars."

"Why is it so? What do the educated people say—those who write the books?"

"The best thing they find to say is that if there were no wars, no epidemics, and no famines, people would multiply like rabbits and there soon wouldn't be enough for everybody to eat."

"Doesn't enough rye grow in the fields for bread?"

"Not enough for thousands of millions of people."

"Why didn't God make it so there'd be enough for all?"

"I can't answer that."

"Do you know where you will be staying? I'll miss you. I'm off Sundays, but somehow I can't seem to get close to anybody," Tekla said. "The other maids go out with soldiers, with fellows they meet in the street or in Karcelak Place. But I can't make friends with a lout who kisses you one day and doesn't want to know you the next. They drink and fight. They get a girl pregnant and later they don't want to know her. Is that just?"

"No, Tekla."

"Sometimes I think I'd like to become a Jewess. The Jewish boys read newspapers and books. They know what's going on in the world. They treat a girl better than our fellows do."

"Don't do it, Tekla. When the Nazis come, the Jews will be the first victims."

"Where will you move to?"

"No. 7 Krochmalna Street."

"Can I come visit on Sunday?"

"Yes. Wait for me by the gate at noon."

"Will you definitely be there?"

"Yes."

"Is that a holy promise?"

"Yes, my dear."

"You'll be living there with someone, eh?"

"Whoever I live with, I'll miss you."

"I will come!" Tekla dashed from my room. A slipper fell off her foot. She picked it up with one hand and clapped the other over her mouth so that her employer wouldn't hear her crying.

That afternoon I sat down to work on a sketch, and later on a novel based on the life of the false Messiah, Jacob Frank. I had already gathered a substantial amount of material about him. In two days I completed three sketches and took them to the newspaper that had published things from me earlier. All hope was gone, but so was all tension. To my surprise, the editor accepted all three. He even asked me to write other short pieces for him. The power that guides man's lot had postponed my death sentence.

My success with the sketches gave me the courage to phone Celia. I told her everything. Celia heard me out, sighed; from time to time she laughed a short laugh. When I finished she said, "Bring her and let me look her over. Whatever may be, your room still stands ready for you here. You can move in with anyone you like."

"Celia, she's infantile—physically and mentally backward."

"Well, and what are you? What are all writers? Lunatics."

Things began to happen quietly and as if mechanically, I had given up free choice, and causality took over. I let Tekla and her mistress know that I would be staying on another month, and both of them congratulated me and expressed the hope that I would stay even longer. On the last day of Succoth, Teibele called to invite me to her apartment. Zelig wanted to meet me. I put on my good suit, bought candy for Teibele, and took a droshky, so that I wouldn't arrive in a sweat. The girl who shared Teibele's apartment had gone to the opera. Zelig sat at a table in the living room, which was set with liquor and food. With his dyed hair and beard, he looked not much older than he had twenty years ago. He was broad-shouldered, stocky, with a short neck, a pointed belly. His nose was red and had the broken veins of a drinker. He spoke to me with the crudeness of burial-society members. He smelled of alcohol and smoked one cigarette after another. If he were my age, he said, he wouldn't marry a sluggard like Shosha. He complained that Bashele had refused to divorce him and for so many years had kept him from marrying the woman he loved. He compared Bashele to a dog sitting on a pile of hay he couldn't eat himself but wouldn't let another creature have. He told me what I already knew: that he was prepared to come to Shosha's wedding and give her a thousand zlotys' dowry. Like a proper father-in-law to be, he questioned me about my prospects of earning a living at writing. He poured himself half a glass of the vodka Teibele had put out and asked brusquely, "Be honest, what do you see in my Shosha? No front and no behind—a board and a hole is what we'd call her."

"Papa, you shame me!" Teibele cried.

"What's there to be ashamed of? In the burial society we know the truth. A woman can fix herself up for the outside world, cover everything with rouge and powder and corsets, but when we strip her for the shrouds . . ."

"If you don't stop, I'll leave!" Teibele warned.

"Well, daughter, don't be angry. That's how we are. That's why we drink. Without booze, none of us would last. You don't drink, eh?" he said, turning to me.

"Seldom."

"Tell my wife she's waited long enough. It's now or

never if she wants to marry again. If she puts it off for a few more years, she can become a virgin again, ha, ha, ha!"

"I'm going, Papa."

"All right, I won't say another word. Wait, Arele, I've got a present for you."

Zelig took a watch and chain from his breast pocket. I blushed and he said, "Whatever I may be and whatever they say about me, I'm still Shosha's father. If she ever has a child—and I can't imagine how, unless they perform a Caesarean—I'll be a grandfather. I knew your father, may he rest in peace. We were neighbors for years. At times when there was a wedding at your house, they called me in to make a quorum. He always sat over his Gemaras. I also remember your mother. Not a bad-looking woman, though too skinny for my taste. You look like her. What will be with this Hitler? People are all terrified, but not me. If things get bad enough, I'll dig myself a grave, take a shot of brandy, and go to sleep. When you see death every day, you stop being afraid of it. What's life, anyway? You give the throat a squeeze and it's all over. Here, take this watch. That's my wedding present to you. It's silver and it has seventeen jewels. Bashele's father gave it to me to sleep with *his* daughter, and now I give it to you to sleep with *my* daughter. If you take care of it, one day you may give it to the fellow who'll do the favor for *your* daughter."

"Oh, Papa, what's to be done with you?"

"Teibele, give up—you can't do anything with me. I have a present ready for you too, when you find the right man. There is no God. I went to synagogue on Rosh Hashanah and Yom Kippur, but I didn't do much praying."

"So where does the world come from?" Teibele asked.

Zelig pinched his beard. "Where does everything come from? It's there and that's all. In Praga, there were two friends and one got sick. Before dying, he made a deal with his friend that if there was another world he'd come back to give him greetings. He told his friend to light the candles in the Hanukkah lamp on the last day of the mourning period and he would come put them out. The friend did as he was told. On the last day of mourning he lit the Hanukkah lamp. But he was tired from working and he dropped off. Suddenly he woke up. A candle had fallen from the lamp and started a fire. His gaberdine was burning. He ran outside and rolled in the gutter. He had to spend two months in the hospital."

"And what's to be made from this?"

"Nothing. There is no such thing as a soul. I've buried more rabbis and holy Jews than you've got hairs on your head. You stick them in the grave and that's where they rot."

No one spoke for a while; then Zelig asked, "Shosha doesn't sleep so much any more? That time when she got the sleeping sickness she slept nearly a whole year. They woke her, fed her, and she went right back to sleep. How long ago was it—fifteen years already, eh?"

"Papa, what's wrong with you?" Teibele exclaimed.

"I'm drunk. I didn't say anything. She's recovered now."

TEN

1 Dora was supposed to have gone to Russia months earlier, but she was still in Warsaw. Her sister Liza called me at the Writers' Club to tell me Dora had attempted suicide by drinking iodine. It seemed that Wolf Felhendler, a fellow Communist who had gone to Russia a year and a half before, had broken out of Soviet exile and smuggled his way back into Poland. The news he brought was dismaying: Dora's best friend, Irka, had been shot there. A whole group of comrades who had gone to the Soviet Union were either in prison or had been sent to the north to dig for gold. As word of his report spread, the Stalinists in Warsaw accused Wolf Felhendler of being a Fascist traitor and a spy for the Polish Secret Service. However, within Poland trust in Stalin's justice suffered a mighty blow. Even before this, whole cells had become disillusioned and gone over to the Trotskyites, and many Communists had switched to the Jewish Bund or the Polish Socialist Party. Others had become Zionists or turned to religion.

After Dora's stomach had been pumped out, Liza arranged for her to spend a few days in Otwock. Back in her apartment, Dora telephoned me, and I went to visit her in the evening. Behind the door I heard a man's voice—Felhendler's. I hadn't the slightest urge to meet with him. He used to warn the anti-Communists at the Writers' Club that when the revolution came he would see them hanged from the nearest lamp post. Still, I knocked. In a few minutes, Dora opened the door. Even though it was half dark in the corridor, I could see that she looked pale and wasted. She clasped my hand and said, "I thought you would never want to see my face again."

"I hear you have company."

"It's Felhendler. He'll be leaving soon."

"Don't keep him here. I don't have the patience for him."

"He's not the same person. He's gone through hell."

Dora spoke softly and didn't let go of my hand. She led me into the living room, where Felhendler sat at the head of the table. If I hadn't known who he was, I wouldn't have recognized him. He was thinner, aged; his hair had fallen out. His attitude toward me had always been arrogant—he addressed me as if the revolution already had come and he had been appointed a commissar. But now he jumped to his feet. He smiled and I saw that his front teeth were missing. He held out a clammy hand to me and said, "I called you at your room, but you weren't home."

Even his voice had grown meek. I couldn't bring myself to take revenge upon a person so beaten, although I knew that, if it had been within his power, he would have subjected me to the very treatment he himself had received. He said, "I've thought of you more than you know. Did your ears ever burn?"

"Ears burn when you talk about someone, not when you think of him," Dora observed.

"You're right, of course. Lately, I've begun to forget things. For a time I even forgot the names of my own family. You've probably heard what happened to me. Well, I've paid my dues, as they say. But I didn't only think about you, I actually spoke of you. I shared a cell with a man by the name of Mendel Leiterman, who had once been a reader of *The Literary Magazine*. Forty of us were jammed in a cell made for eight. We sat on the floor and talked. The greatest privilege was to be next to the wall where you could lean your head."

I assumed Felhendler would say goodbye and leave; instead, he settled down again. His suit hung so loosely that it seemed not to be his size. In the past, he had always worn a stiff collar and tie, but now his collar was open, revealing a scrawny neck. He said, "Yes, I recalled your words. You predicted everything in detail—you might have been some kind of prophet who had put a curse on me. I don't mean this in a bad sense—I haven't yet reached such a stage of superstitious nonsense. But words aren't lost. At night when I lay on the bare floor, sick and grimy, my head reeling from the stink of the slop bucket —that is, if they let me lie and didn't drag me off for an interrogation—and I heard the doors being opened to take someone else to be tortured, I thought, what would Aaron Greidinger say if he could see all this? It didn't occur to me for a second that I would live to meet and talk with you again. We were all condemned to death or to work in the gold mines, which is worse than death. No, they don't let you die so fast and easy. One time they questioned me for twenty-six hours straight. This kind of physical torture—I'm not speaking of the spiritual pain— I wouldn't wish on my worst enemies, not even on Stalin's minions. I don't believe they were as cruel during the Inquisition or that it's being done in Mussolini's prisons. A man can take torture from an enemy, but when your friend turns out to be the enemy, then the anguish is beyond endurance. They wanted one thing from me—to confess that I was a spy sent by the Polish Secret Service. They literally begged me to do them the favor and confess, but I swore to myself, anything but this."

"Wolf, stop talking about it. It's making you sick," Dora said.

"Eh? I couldn't be sicker than I am. I said to them, 'How can I be a Polish spy when I did time in every Polish jail for our ideal? How can I be a Fascist when for years I was an editor of a magazine that attacked the Zionists, the Bund, the P.P.S., and that openly preached the dictatorship of the proletariat? My family was from the poorest of the poor, and all my life I've suffered hunger and want. Socialism was my only comfort. Why would I become a spy for the reactionary and anti-Semitic Polish regime? What military institutions was I being allowed to get near? Where has your sense of reason gone? Even in madness there has to be a trace of logic,' I said. But the fellow who sat facing me toyed with his revolver the whole time, smoked cigarettes, and drank tea while I was standing on swollen feet and everything inside me was shriveling from lack of food, water, and sleep. He glared at me. His eyes were murderous. 'I've heard all your lousy excuses,' he said. 'You are a Fascist dog, a counter-revolutionary traitor, and a Hitler spy. Sign the confession before I tear the tongue out of your pig's snout.' He called me 'thou,' that Russky. He lit a candle, took out a needle, held it to the flame, and said, 'If you don't sign, I'll jam this under your filthy fingernails.' I knew what pain that meant, for the Polish Fascists had done it to me, but still I couldn't label myself a spy. I looked at him— someone who should have been the defender of the working class and of the Revolution—and for all my anguish I started to laugh. This was bad theater, the worst kind of trash. Even Nowaczynski in the wildest stretches of his sick imagination couldn't have dreamed up such an idiotic plot.

"I stuck out my hand and told him, 'Go ahead. If this is what the Revolution needs, do with me as you will.' He was called out and a new executioner took his place—a new executioner who was rested and full. That's how they questioned me for twenty-six hours by the clock. I pleaded with them, 'Shoot me and put an end to it.' "

"Wolf, I can't listen to any more!" Dora cried.

"You can't, can't you? You have to! We are responsible for this. We spread the propaganda to bring it about. In 1926, when the news began to come out against Trotsky, we called him an agent for the Pilsudskis, the Mussolinis, the Rockefellers, the MacDonalds. We stuffed our ears and refused to hear the truth."

"Felhendler, I don't want to rub salt in your wounds," I said, "but if Trotsky was in power, he wouldn't act any differently from Stalin."

A mixture of irony and anger showed in Felhendler's eyes. "How do you know how Trotsky would act? How dare you make assumptions about things that never happened?"

"They've happened in all the revolutions. Whenever blood is spilled in the name of humanity, of religion, or of any other cause, it leads inevitably to this kind of terror."

"So according to you the working class should keep

silent over what is happening in Russia, allow Hitler and Mussolini to seize the world and let itself be trampled like ants. Is this what you preach?"

"I don't preach."

"Yes, you do. If you can say that Trotsky would be no better than Stalin, it means that the whole human race is corrupt and there is no hope—that we must surrender to all the murderers, the Fascists, those who instigate pogroms and turn the clock back to the Dark Ages, to the Inquisitions, to the Crusades."

"Felhendler, England, France, and America haven't resorted to inquisitions and crusades."

"Oh, haven't they? America has locked its gates and is letting no one in. England, France, Canada, Australia— all the capitalist countries—are doing the same. In India, thousands of people die of hunger each day. English travelers admit this themselves. When Gandhi, submissive as he is, uttered a word, they threw him in jail. Is this true or not? Gandhi babbles about passive resistance. What a swindle! How can resistance be passive? It's exactly as if you would say hot snow, cold fire."

"Then you're still for revolution?"

"Yes, Aaron Greidinger, yes! If you went to a dentist and instead of pulling a rotten tooth he purposely pulled three healthy teeth, this would surely be a tragedy and a crime. But the rotten tooth would still have to be pulled. Otherwise it could infect the whole mouth—even lead to gangrene."

"Right! One hundred percent correct!" Dora exclaimed.

"I hate to dash your hopes," I said, "but I will make another prediction for you: Trotsky's permanent revolution, or whatever revolution it may be, will duplicate precisely what the Stalinists are doing now. I do not want you to have to say again that I was right. You've suffered enough."

"No," Felhendler said. "If I were to think in your terms, I'd have to hang myself this very night."

"Enough," Dora said. "I'll put up tea."

2 We drank tea, ate bread with herring, and Felhendler recounted his experiences form the time he crossed the border into Russia and was met by a delegate of the Comintern. He was taken to Moscow and assigned a room with another delegate from Poland, a Comrade Wysocki from Upper Silesia. Every other evening, they attended free performances of the theater or the opera or some new Soviet film. Suddenly in the middle of a night there was a knock on his door and he was placed under arrest. Five weeks he sat behind bars without knowing the charges against him. He comforted himself with the idea that his imprisonment was an error—he had obviously been mistaken for some other Felhendler and everything would be cleared up at the interrogation. He shared a cell with both political and criminal prisoners. The thieves, murderers, and rapists beat the politicals and took away their food rations. They played cards among themselves, using slips of paper, and gambled for each other's rations, clothing, and the right to sleep on the hard bench instead of the floor. When one of the players lost all he possessed, he played for blows—the winner could slug the loser. Many of the criminals practiced homosexuality. A new prisoner who didn't want to participate was raped. The Red authorities made no effort to protect the victims.

Felhendler said, "In the Polish prisons, even in such a tough jail as Wronki, where I spent three years, they gave us books. I went through a whole library there. But in the land of socialism, we—the fighters for justice!— sat for weeks on end going mad. We kneaded chess pieces out of the claylike bread that they gave us, but there wasn't enough room on the floor to set up a board to play on. None of the political prisoners had the slightest notion of what crimes they had been picked up for. Yet nearly every one of them remained dedicated to the cause. They put the blame on the lower officials of the G.P.U. without once accusing Stalin or anyone in the Central Committee or the Politburo. But I slowly became aware of the quicksand in which we were caught. Some of the prisoners confided to me that they had been forced to make false accusations against their closest comrades."

It was midnight when Felhendler left. The moment he closed the door, Dora burst into tears. "What can one do? How is one to live?"

She clasped me by my wrists and drew me to her. She leaned her forehead on my shoulder and sobbed. I stood there gawking at the opposite wall. From the day I had left my father's house I had existed in a state of perpetual despair. Occasionally, I considered the notion of repentance, of returning to real Jewishness. But to live like my father, my grandfathers, and great-grandfathers, without their faith—was this possible? Each time I went into a library, I felt a spark of hope that perhaps in one of the books there might be some indication of how a person of my disposition and world outlook could make peace with himself. I didn't find it—not in Tolstoy or in Kropotkin, not in Spinoza or in William James, not in Schopenhauer, not in the Scriptures. Certainly the Prophets preached a high morality, but their promises of plentiful harvests, of fruitful olive trees and vineyards, protection against one's enemies, made no appeal to me. I knew that the world had always been and would always remain as it was now. What the moralists called evil was actually the order of life.

Dora wiped her tears. "Arele, I must move from here at once. The apartment isn't mine, and even if it was, I couldn't pay for it. Also, I'm afraid that my ex-comrades will turn me in to the Secret Service."

"The Secret Service knows about you, anyway."

"They could provide the necessary proof. You know how it is with the Stalinists—whoever isn't for them must be liquidated."

"You yourself used to preach this."

"To my shame, yes."

"The Trotskyites follow the same principles."

"What shall I do? You tell me!"

"I can't tell you anything."

"I could be arrested any day. The last time you slept here I was still full of expectation. I even dreamed you might sooner or later come to me in Russia. Now I don't look forward to anything."

"A half hour ago, you agreed with Felhendler's Trotskyism."

"I'm no longer sure. I should have thrown myself out the window instead of drinking iodine."

That night I lay next to Dora, but that was all. I couldn't sleep. Each time I heard the bell at the house gate I assumed it was the police coming to take us in. I rose at dawn and before I went I gave Dora some of the money I had with me.

Dora said, "I thank you, but if you should hear that I've done away with myself, don't feel too bad. I've been left with nothing."

"Dora, for the time being, don't get involved with the Trotskyites. A permanent revolution is about as possible as permanent surgery."

"What will *you* do?"

"Oh, live from day to day—or from hour to hour."

We said goodbye. I was afraid that a secret agent might be waiting by the gate to arrest me, but no one was there. I headed back to my room and my manuscript.

On the way, I glanced at the high tower of the church on Nowolipki Street. In buildings around the enormous courtyard encircled by an iron picket fence lived nuns—Jesus's brides. I often saw them pass in their starched cowls, long black robes, and mannish shoes, their bosoms hung with crucifixes. On Karmelicka Street I passed the "Workers' Home," the club of the left-wing Poale Zion. In there, they espoused both Communism and Zionism, believing that only when the proletariat seized power would the Jews be able to have their own homeland in Palestine and become a socialistic nation. In No. 36 Leszno Street was the Groser Library of the Jewish Bund, as well as a cooperative store for workers and their families. The Bund totally rejected Zionism. Their program was cultural autonomy and common socialist struggle against capitalism. The Bundists themselves had split into two factions, one in favor of democracy and one in favor of immediate dictatorship by the proletariat. In another courtyard was the club of the Revisionists, the followers of Jabotinsky, extreme Zionists. They encouraged Jews to learn to use firearms and contended that only acts of terror against the English, who held the mandate, could restore Palestine to the Jews. The Revisionists in Warsaw had a semi-military unit that from time to time paraded through the streets carrying wooden swords and shouting slogans against those Zionists who, like Weizmann, believed in mediation and compromise with England. Nearly all the Jewish parties had their clubs in this area. Each year added some new splinter group and another office.

I had won a moral victory over Dora, Felhendler, and their comrades, but everything had grown so wildly tangled that I could no longer sneer at anyone else's wrongheadedness.

I went to my room, which I now decided to keep until the wedding, but I was too tired to work. I stretched out on the bed, dozed off, and in my mind heard over and over Felhendler's words and Dora's lament: *What can one do? How is one to live?*

ELEVEN

1 A few days before the wedding, my mother and Moishe arrived, and I met them at the Danzig depot. The train pulled in at 8 a.m. I barely recognized them. Mother seemed smaller, stooped, and as old as a crone. Her nose had lengthened; it curved down like a bird's beak. Creases cut deep into her forehead and cheeks. Only the gray eyes still showed a youthful sharpness. She no longer wore a wig; a kerchief covered her head. Her skirt reached the floor, and she had on a blouse that I remembered from the time I lived at home. Moishe had grown tall. He had a ragged blond beard and earlocks hanging to his shoulders. His rabbinical hat was flecked and mangy, and his fur coat was ratty. The unbuttoned shirt collar exposed a soft, childish throat.

He gazed at me with amazement in his blue eyes and said, "A real German."

After I had kissed my mother, she asked, "Arele, are you sick, God forbid? You're as pale and drawn as if you just got out of a sickbed, may it never happen."

"I didn't sleep the whole night."

"We've been on the road two days and nights. The wagon that took us to the train in Rawa Ruska turned over in the mud. It's a miracle we weren't hurt. One woman broke her arm. That's why we missed the train we intended to take and had to wait twenty hours for another. The Gentiles became unruly. They wanted to cut off Moishele's earlocks. The Jew is helpless. If it's this bad now, how will it be when the murderers come? People shake in their skins."

"Mama, the Almighty will help," Moishe said. "There have been many Hamans and they all came to a bad end."

"Before they came to their bad end, they killed off plenty of Jews," Mother replied.

I had rented a room for Mother and Moishe in a kosher boardinghouse on Gnoyna Street. The proprietor was a Hasid. I called a droshky to take them there, but Moishe said, "I don't ride in droshkies."

"Why not?"

"The seat may be linsey-woolsey."

After lengthy discussion it was decided that Mother would spread her shawl over the seat. Moishe had brought along a basket that closed with a wire and a little lock—the kind once used by yeshiva students. Mother carried her things wrapped in a sheet. Passersby stopped to stare at us. The driver went slowly, since the road was blocked by trolleys, taxis, freight wagons, and buses. The nag looked skeletal; it limped. Moishe began to sway and murmur. He was either commencing his morning prayers or reciting Psalms.

Mother said, "Arele, child, for the fact that I've lived to see you again, and about to be a bridegroom at that, I must thank the Almighty, but why didn't your father, too, live to see it? He studied the Torah almost to the last minute. I didn't realize myself what a saint he was. Alas, I plagued him for dragging us off to such a faraway hole, but he accepted it all in good spirits. I eat my heart out now and don't sleep nights on account of this. Whatever punishment is visited upon me I deserve. Arele, I can't stay in Old Stykov any more. I don't want to speak against Moishele's wife, my daughter-in-law—may she stay healthy and strong—but I can't live with her. She's a country girl, her father is a farmer. In Galicia, Jews were always allowed to own land. She does and says things that displease me. I hear well, thank God, but she screams into my ears as if I were deaf. Her mind is always on petty things. It's true that I've sinned, but how much can a person take?"

"Well, ah, well!" Moishe put two fingers to his lips—a sign that Mother's words were slander and that he wasn't permitted to speak now during prayer.

"Well, ah well here, and *well, ah well* there! Certainly my words are sinful, but what flesh and blood can suffer has a limit. She hates me because I read books and she barely knows how to pray. But what do I have now besides my books? When I open *The Duty of the Hearts* I forget where I am and what's become of me in my old age. Arele, I don't want to die in Old Stykov. True, your father is buried there, but the few years or months allotted me to creep around in this world I don't want to spend among boors. It's bitter for Moishele, too. They pay him no wages. On Thursdays the beadle goes around with a sack collecting handfuls of wheat, corn, and groats—the way the Russians pay their priests, beg the comparison. The Gentiles there are Ruthenians and some of them boast that Hitler is on their side. They fight among themselves, too. One of them chopped off a girl's head right outside our window, just because she'd been going around with another fellow. Our lives are in danger every minute. I pray for death. Each day I beg the Almighty to take me from here, but just because you want to die, you live."

"Well, ah well!"

"Stop with those *well, ah's.* You won't go to my Gehenna. Arele, I want to say something to you, but I don't want you to get angry at me. I will not go back to Old Stykov. Even if I have to sleep in the streets, I'll stay here in Warsaw."

"Mama, you won't sleep in the streets," I said.

"Have pity on me. I hear there's no longer a rabbi on Krochmalna Street. Maybe Moishele could get some job here? I myself am ready to go into an old-age home or wherever I can find a place to lay my head. What kind of girl is this Shosha? How did you happen to choose her? Well, it all comes from heaven."

The droshky pulled up before a gate on Gnoyna Street. Some of the courtyards here were over a hundred years old. There were alleys where farmers came at dawn with their produce from the nearby villages. Eggs were stored in lime in the cellars. In No. 3 was Krel's studyhouse, where I went to read a page of the Gemara on my own after I had left cheder. In No. 5 was a synagogue and another studyhouse. The ritual bath where my mother went when she was a young woman was still in operation nearby. Even the oil cakes, the chick-peas with beans, and the potato cakes sold here smelled as I remembered them.

Mother said, "Nothing has changed."

Several wagons were parked in front of the building where we had stopped. The horses were eating a mixture of oats and chopped straw from feedbags. Pigeons and sparrows pecked at the seeds dropped from them. Men in short sheepskin coats and caps carried sacks, crates, baskets. Through the partially frosted-over windows could be seen bottles, pots, diapers hanging to dry. From one window came the sound of children reciting a chant from the Pentateuch—a cheder. Muddy stairs led up to the boardinghouse on the third floor.

After each half flight, Mother paused. "I'm not used to climbing stairs any more."

On the third floor I opened a door leading off the dark hallway. The boardinghouse consisted of a sitting room and a few small rooms. In the sitting room one man prayed in his prayer shawl and phylacteries, another packed paper boxes into a sack, and a third ate his breakfast. Two women, one in a wig and the other in a bonnet, sat on a bench mending a fur coat with a huge needle and string. The proprietor, with a pitch-black beard and wearing a skullcap, showed us to a room with two beds, where Mother and Moishe would spend the night.

Moishe said, "It's getting late and I want to pray. Is there a house of worship here?"

"There are two prayer houses in the courtyard—one of the Kozienica Hasidim, the other of the Blendew Hasidim. There is a synagogue, too, but those who pray there are all Litvaks."

"I'll go to the Kozienica prayer house."

"Would you want some breakfast?" the proprietor asked Mother.

"Is it strictly kosher?"

"What a question! Rabbis eat here."

"Maybe a glass of tea for now."

"Something to nibble with it?"

"I've lost my teeth. Would you have some soft bread?"

"There isn't a thing I don't have." He went to fetch the bread and tea.

A washstand stood in one corner of the room, with a basin of water, a dipper, and a dirty towel hanging on a hook. Mother said, "Compared to Old Stykov, this is a mansion. We live in a shack with a straw roof. It leaks. There is a stove, but the flue is broken and the smoke won't go up through the chimney. When will I get to see the bride?"

"I'll bring her here."

2 It was the first night of Hanukkah. The owner of the boardinghouse lighted and blessed the first of the eight Hanukkah candles for his guests, but my mother and Moishe refused to accept another person performing so holy a ceremony for them. Besides, he had lighted a candle, not a wick in oil. I went down to the street and bought a tin Hanukkah lamp for them, as well as a bottle of oil, wicks, and a special candle called "the beadle," which is used for lighting the wicks. In their room, Moishe poured the oil into the first little bowl, put a wick in place, lit the beadle, touched the wick with it, and recited the benedictions. Then he began to chant the liturgy: "O Fortress, Rock of my Salvation . . ." These were my father's tunes, even his gestures. At first the wick refused to catch fire, and Moishe had to try to light it again and again. When it did burn finally, it smoked and sputtered. Moishe had placed the little lamp on the window according to the law, so that the miracle of Hanukkah should be shown to the world, even though the courtyard below had three blind walls and no one was there. The window was not tight; wind blew in. Every few seconds the little light fluttered, but it did not go out. Moishe said, "Just like the Jewish people. In each generation our enemies rise up to destroy us, and the Holy One, blessed be He, is saving us from their hands."

"It's high time our enemies should be praying for miracles," I said.

Moishe clutched his beard. "Who are we to tell Him what to do and when to do it? Only yesterday you told Mother that the more the astronomers ponder and measure the stars, the larger they become. You said that many of them are larger than the sun. So how can insignificant creatures like us, with our tiny brains, understand what He is doing?"

Moishe spoke with my father's voice. Only a few years ago my father was arguing with me: "You can spill ink but it won't write a letter by itself. The unbelievers are not only vicious but also fools."

Moishe left for the studyhouse after watching the Hanukkah light for half an hour. He found books there that he could never get in Old Stykov. With the little money he had, he bought *The Roar of a Lion, The Responsa of Rabbi Akiva Eiger,* and *The Face of Joshua.* He promised Mother he would not be late. She sat on her bed, propped up by a pillow, and her large gray eyes stared at the flickering light with curiosity, as if she were seeing such a light for the first time. I remembered her being medium in height, even somewhat taller than Father, but now she appeared shriveled. Her head kept nodding in a constant "yes, yes, yes." Then she said to me, "Arele, God forbid, I don't intend to nag you, you are already an adult, I hope you outlive my bones, but what was the sense of it?"

"What do you mean?"

"You know very well what I mean."

"Mother, not everything one does has to make sense."

My mother's eyes showed the beginning of a smile. "What is it? Love?"

"You can call it that."

"There is a saying that love is blind, but even love isn't completely without reason. A shoemaker's apprentice would not fall in love with a princess, and he certainly would not marry her."

"Even this can happen."

"What? In novels, not in real life. When we lived in Warsaw, I used to read the novels serialized in the newspaper. Your father—peace be with him—disliked newspapers and their writers. He said that they defiled the holy Jewish letters. Only when the war broke out and he wanted to know the news did he glance into a paper. Even in those trashy novels there was some logic. Now you come and marry Shosha. True, she's a gentle child, unfortunately sick, perhaps a victim of her father, but couldn't you find something better in the whole of Warsaw? I'm sinning, I know I'm sinning. I shouldn't say these things. I'm losing the world to come. Look, the light is out!"

We sat in silence. The air smelled of burned oil and of something sweet and long forgotten. Then Mother went on, "My child, it's all so destined. My father, your grandfather—he should rest in peace—had the name of a genius. He could have become a rabbi in a big city, but he was content to stay in his little corner in a forsaken village, and there he remained until his end. Your paternal grandfather, the one from Tomaszów, hid from people altogether. All his years he wrote commentaries on the cabala. Before his demise, he called one of his grandchildren and told him to burn his manuscripts. Only one page was left accidentally, and those who read it maintained it was full of the mysteries of the Torah. He was so unworldly he did not know the difference between one coin and another. If your grandmother Temerl hadn't skimped and saved, there wouldn't have been a piece of bread in the house. She was a saint in her own right. When she went to visit the rabbi of Belz, he invited her to sit down on a chair even though she was a woman. What am I in comparison to them? I'm steeped in sin. Of course I love you, and I would like you to get a good wife, but if heaven ordains differently, I should have the power to curb my tongue. I say all this to remind you that you should remember your origin. We didn't come to this world to indulge in our passions. Look at me and see what happens to blood and flesh. I was a beautiful girl. When I passed Lublin Street, people stopped to stare. I had the smallest feet in town and I shined my shoes every day with polish, even when it rained. I used to polish them a hundred times with the brush. I had a pleated skirt, and every second day I ironed the pleats. People denounced me to your grandfather for being vain. How old was I altogether? Fifteen years. At fifteen and a half I became engaged to your father. A year later I was led to the wedding canopy. A girl is not allowed to study Torah, but I stood behind the door and listened as your grandfather lectured to the yeshiva boys. If one of them made a mistake, I knew it. I also began to look into morality books in Hebrew. By that time, I realized that I'm hot-blooded and that I had to control my impulses. How did this come to me? I hope to God that the children will take after you, not after Shosha."

"Mother, we won't have any children."

"Why not? Heaven wants there to be a world and Jews."

"No one knows what heaven wants. If God had wanted the Jews to live, He wouldn't have created Hitlers."

"Woe to me that you speak such things!"

"No one has ascended to heaven and spoken to God."

"One doesn't need to ascend to heaven, one can see the truth right here on earth. Three days before Meitel's Esther won the lottery, I saw in a dream the letter carrier handing me a paper full of numbers. I wanted to take it, but suddenly Meitel materialized—she was already dead then. Her face was yellow and she wore a white cowl. She said to me, 'It's not for you, my daughter Esther is going to win a lot of money on this.' And she handed the letter carrier a bunch of straw stalks. I was only a ten-year-old child at the time, I didn't even know that there was such a thing as a lottery. I told the dream to everybody in our house. They shrugged their shoulders. After three days a telegram came saying Esther had won the grand prize. When I had this dream they had not yet drawn the numbers. Two years later, I witnessed a case of a haunted house. For weeks an evil spirit kept on knocking on the window frame in the house of Abraham the ritual slaughterer. Soldiers were sent to search the rooms, the cellar, the attic, but nothing could be found to account for this racket. My child, the world is full of so many mysteries that if the scholars continued to study for a million years, they could not solve even a millionth part of them."

"Mother, all this cannot give comfort to the tortured Jews in Dachau, and in other such hells."

"The comfort is that there is no death. Your own Shosha told me her dead sister was visiting her. She's not shrewd enough to invent such a lie."

3 Bashele intended to invite my mother and Moishe for either lunch or supper but Mother told me plainly she wouldn't eat in Bashele's house. Neither she nor Moishe had confidence that the food in her kitchen was strictly kosher. However, in order not to shame her, Mother and Moishe agreed to come for tea and fruit. I don't know how they learned that the late rabbi's wife and her two sons would be visiting Bashele's. Around three o'clock in the afternoon when I brought them from the boardinghouse and opened Bashele's door, I saw to my amazement a room full of people: old women in bonnets of beads and ribbons, men with white beards and sidelocks, also a few young men and girls, who, it seemed, read the literary journal. There were tea glasses, Sabbath cookies, and saucers with gooseberry jam on the table, which was covered with a holiday tablecloth. The old women had brought little gifts wrapped in handkerchiefs—gingerbread, cake, and cookies, raisins, prunes, almonds. My God, we were not completely forgotten on Krochmalna Street! The war, the epidemics, and hunger had worked with the Angel of Death, but a few of those who knew our family remained alive. Bonnets shook, shrunken mouths mumbled blessings and greetings, reminisced about former times. Tears rolled down faded cheeks. The men had all been followers of the late rabbi of Radzymin. He had passed away without an heir, and his court had disintegrated. The Hasidim said that if the rabbi had consented to go through an operation, he might still be living, but to the last day he was true to his conviction that a knife is for cutting bread, not human flesh. He gave up his sacred soul after long suffering. Rabbis from the whole of Poland came to his funeral. He was buried near the grave of his grandfather Rabbi Yankele, who waged war with the demons all his life and performed countless miracles. It was known that corpses came to him at night to confess their misdeeds while alive, and that his garret teemed with spirits.

While the Hasidim greeted Moishe and asked him about the Hasidic courts in Galicia—the courts of Belz, Sieniawa, Ropczyca—the young men and girls introduced themselves to me. They praised the sketches and articles I wrote. They spoke to me in a literary Yiddish with illiterate errors. They had heard about my play that had failed and complained about the state of the Yiddish theater. Civilization was on the verge of collapse, but they were still producing the kitsch plays of fifty years ago. Teibele had come to the reception and she had brought with her her lover the bookkeeper, a little man with a pointed belly and gold teeth in the front of his mouth. Some of the girls gathered around Shosha. I heard one of them ask her, "How does it feel to be engaged to a writer?"

Shosha answered, "Nothing, just like a human being."

"How did you two come together?" another girl asked.

"We both lived in No. 10," Shosha said. "Arele lived in the apartment with the balcony. Our windows faced the courtyard just across the horse stable."

The girls looked at one another and smiled. They exchanged side glances that asked, "What does he see in her?"

Bashele had placed Moishe at the head of the table, with the old men on either side of him. Moishe hinted that it was not in the Hasidic tradition for men and women to sit at the same table, and Bashele put chairs for the old women in the middle of the room. The boys and the girls remained standing. The Hasidim continued to discuss Hasidic topics: What is the difference between the court of Belz and the court of Bobow? Why are the Hungarian rabbis against the world organization of Orthodox Jews? What kind of a saint is the rabbi of Rydnik? Is it true that the rabbi of Rozwadow has inherited the sense of humor of his great-grandfather, the rabbi of Ropczyca? They said it was a pity so little was known about the rabbis of Galicia in this part of the country.

"Why is it important to know?" Moishe asked. "Everyone serves God in his own manner."

"What do they say in Galicia about the tribulations of our time?" one of them asked.

Moishe answered the question with a question: "What is there to say? These are the birth pains of the Messiah. The prophet has already foreseen that at the End of Days the Lord will come with fire and with His chariots like a whirlwind to render His anger with fury and His rebuke with flames of fire. The evil ones don't surrender so easily. When Satan realizes that his kingdom is shaky, he creates a furor throughout the universe. There are dark powers even in the higher spheres. What is Nogah? Good and evil mixed together. The roots of evil reach as far as the legs of the Throne of Glory. Since God had to create a vacuum and dim His light in order to create the world, His face has to be hidden. Without diminishing the power of His radiance there would be no free choice. Redemption will not come at once but gradually. God's war with Amalek is going to last long and will bring great distress and many temptations. One of our sages said about the Messiah, 'Let Him come, but I don't wish to live to see Him.' The Mishnah has foreseen that before the Messiah comes human arrogance will reach its height and . . ."

"Woe to us, the water is up to our necks," said an old Hasid, Mendele Wyszkower, with a sigh.

"What? Evil possesses enormous powers," Moishe said. "In quiet times the vicious try to cover up their intentions and disguise themselves as innocent lambs. But in times of decision they reveal their true faces. Ecclesiastes has said, 'I saw under the sun the place of judgment, that wickedness was there.' The men of iniquity aspire to a world of murder, lechery, theft, and robbery. They want the iniquities to be considered virtues. Their aim is to erase the 'Thou shalt not' from the Ten Commandments.

They scheme to put honest men in prison and thieves to be their judges. Whole communities degenerate. What was Sodom, with its judges Chillek and Billek? What was the Generation of the Flood? Who were the rebels who built the Tower of Babel? One sheep can make the whole herd leprous. One spark of fire can burn a mansion. Hitler —his name should be blotted out—is not the only villain. There are Hitlers in every city, in every community. If we forget the Lord for a second, we are immediately on the side of defilement."

"Oy, it's difficult, very difficult," said another old man, and he groaned.

"Where is it written that things have to be easy?" Moishe asked.

"Our strength is waning," a third old man moaned.

" 'They that wait upon the Lord shall renew strength,' " Moishe replied.

The old women kept still and cupped their ears to hear better. Even the young men and girls who had come to debate culture, literature, Yiddishism, and progress with me became silent.

Suddenly Shosha asked, "Mommy, is this really Moishe?"

There was laughter. Even the old women laughed with their toothless mouths.

Bashele became embarrassed. "Daughter, what's the matter with you?"

"Oy, Mommy, Moishele is a real rabbi, just like his daddy." Shosha covered her eyes with a handkerchief and cried.

4 Two days before my wedding it started to snow and went on without letup. When it finally stopped, frost set in. The streets were buried under drifts of snow as dry as salt. Not even sleighs could make their way through them.

Huge icicles hung from the eaves and balconies. The wires running above the rooftops had grown thick and were glittering with sparks of frost. Here and there a bird's beak or a cat's head peeped from the snow. On Krochmalna Street the Place was deserted. Little snow eddies swirled—imps trying to catch their own tails. The thieves, whores, and pimps were hiding in their cellar rooms or garrets. The vendors who usually sat before Yanash's Court vanished.

The wedding was to take place at eight that evening at a rabbi's on Panska Street. With Zelig's contribution, Bashele had been able to prepare a modest trousseau for Shosha—a few dresses, shoes, and underwear—but I had made no preparations of any kind. From the short pieces I sold and a little money I got from my publisher for translating, I had scratched together enough for my mother's and Moishe's expenses at the boardinghouse, but I had very little left.

On my wedding morning, I rose later than usual. I had stayed awake and could hear the chiming of the grandfather clock and the wailing of the wind until daybreak. It was ten by the time I got out of bed and began to wash and shave.

Tekla pushed open the door. "Shall I bring your breakfast?"

"Yes, Tekla—if you feel like it."

She left and soon came back. "A lady has come with flowers for you."

I had planned to keep everything secret. I started to tell Tekla to let no one in, but at that moment the door opened and I saw Dora. She wore a faded coat, boots, and a hat that looked like an upside-down pot. She held a bouquet wrapped in heavy paper. Tekla grimaced and turned her head.

Dora said, "My dear, there are no secrets. Congratulations!"

My cheeks were covered with soap. I put down the razor and asked, "What kind of nonsense is this?"

"Don't you know you can't keep anything from me? It's true you didn't ask me to the ceremony, but there will always be a kinship between us. No one can erase the years we spent together. Here—may it be with happiness and prosperity."

"Who told you about it, eh?"

"Oh, I have connections. Someone who works with the Secret Service would know everything that goes on in Warsaw."

Dora was referring to the Stalinists who, ever since she had left the Party, had accused her of being an agent for the Polish Secret Police.

I took the flowers from her reluctantly and stuck them into the jug that held my wash water.

Dora said, "Yes, I know everything. I've even had the honor of meeting your bride."

"How did you accomplish that?"

"Oh, I knocked on her door and pretended I was collecting for some charitable cause. I spoke Yiddish to her but she didn't understand what I was talking about, and I thought, She speaks only Polish, but I soon saw that she doesn't know Polish too well either. I don't want to needle you. Since you love her, what difference does it make, anyway? People fall in love with the blind, the deaf, the hunchbacked. May I sit down?"

"Yes, Dora, do sit down. You shouldn't have spent money for flowers."

"I wanted to bring something. I have my reasons. I'm getting married too, and if I give you a wedding present, you'll have to give me one. I have an ulterior motive for everything I do." Dora blinked and sat on the edge of the bed. Rivulets of melted snow ran from her boots onto the floor. She took out a cigarette and lit it.

"Felhendler?" I asked.

"Yes, my dearest. We're both renegades, Fascists, traitors, and provocateurs. Could there be a more perfect match? We'll stand together on the barricades and shoot the workers and peasants. That is, if we don't happen to be in prison at the time. Do the reactionaries know that we're their friends? By the way, what happened to that play you were supposed to have written? You drifted away from me, but I remember each hour we spent together. When something of yours is published, I read it not once but three times. I hear that Dr. Feitelzohn is planning to put out a magazine."

"He's been planning this magazine for years."

Tekla opened the door with her toe and brought in my breakfast tray.

I asked, "Would you join me, Dora?"

"I've had breakfast already, thank you, but I would have a glass of coffee." While Tekla went to bring the coffee, Dora looked around. "Will your wife come to live here with you or will you move in with her?" she asked. "I'm nosy as always."

"I don't know anything yet."

"I don't understand you—but what's the point of upsetting you with questions? You don't know the answer, anyway. As for me, I don't love Wolf. We're too much alike. Lately, he's become exceedingly sarcastic. He keeps making those awful jokes. Our being together is futile, anyway. Either he'll be arrested or I'll be arrested. The police play with us like cats with mice. But so long as we remain on this side of the bars, we don't feel like being alone. As soon as he leaves the house, I start looking up at the ceiling for a hook. When I go downstairs I have to cross the street to avoid my former comrades. If they see me, they spit and shake their fists. You once told me things that I didn't grasp at the time, but since all this has happened, they're starting to come back to me."

"What things?"

"Oh, that you can't help mankind and that those who worry too much about the fate of man must sooner or later become cruel. How did you know this? I hardly dare say it, but I lie in bed next to him and I think of you. He's both ironic and grim. He smiles as if he knows the final truth and I can't stand that smirk, because he smiled the exact same smile when he was a Stalinist. Just the same, I can't be alone any more."

"He moved in?" I asked.

"I can't pay the rent by myself. He got some kind of part-time job in a union."

The door opened again and Tekla came in with a glass of coffee. Her eyes sparkled with laughter. "Miss Betty is here with flowers," she announced.

Before I could answer, Betty appeared on the threshold in a blond fur coat, a fur hat to match, and fur-trimmed boots. She carried a huge bouquet. When she saw Dora she took a step backward. An urge to laugh came over me. "You, too?"

"May I come in?"

"Of course, come in, Betty."

"It's some blizzard outside! Seven witches must have hanged themselves."

"Betty, this is Dora. I've told you about her. Dora, this is Betty Slonim."

"Yes, I know—the actress from America. I recognize you from your picture in the newspaper," Dora said.

"What shall I do with the flowers?"

"Tekla, could you bring a vase?"

"All the vases are full. The mistress keeps kasha in them."

"Bring whatever there is. Take the flowers."

Tekla held out her hand. She seemed to be doing everything in a mocking fashion.

Betty began to hop up and down in her boots. "A terrible frost. You can't cross the street. It's the way it used to be in Moscow. It's like this in Canada, too. In New York they clear away the snow—at least on the main streets. Help me off with my coat. Now that you're about to marry, be a gentleman."

I helped Betty off with her coat. She was wearing a red dress that clashed with her red hair. She looked pale and thin. She said, "You're probably wondering why I came. It's because you bring flowers for a bridegroom and you bring flowers for a corpse, and when the bridegroom is also a corpse, he deserves a double bouquet." She spoke the words as if she had prepared them in advance.

Dora smiled. "Not badly said. I'll be running along. I don't want to disturb you."

"You're not disturbing anybody," Betty said. "What I have to say everyone can hear."

"Shall I bring more coffee?" Tekla asked.

"Not for me," Betty said. "I've had maybe ten glasses today already. May I smoke?"

Betty took out a cigarette, lit it, and after a while offered one to Dora. Both women seemed to fence momentarily with the tips of their cigarettes. It was like the remnant of some heathen rite.

5 Dora still sat on the bed. I had given Betty my chair and I sat on a bench by the washstand. Betty spoke of Eugene O'Neill, one of whose plays had been translated into Yiddish. She would be appearing in it in Warsaw. She said, "I know it's going to be a flop. They don't understand O'Neill even in America, so how will the Warsaw Jews understand him? The translation isn't any good, either. But Sam insisted that I appear in Poland before we go back to America. Oh, how I envy a writer! He doesn't have to deal with people all the time. He sits at his desk with paper and pen and says whatever he wants.

But actors are always dependent on others. At times the urge to write comes over me. I've tried to write a play—a novel, too—but I read what I've written and I don't like it, and I tear it up on the spot. Tsutsik—may I still call you Tsutsik?—here in Poland the situation is deteriorating fast. Sometimes I worry about getting stuck here."

"With an American passport, you've got nothing to worry about," Dora said. "Even Hitler wouldn't start up with America."

"What's a passport? A piece of paper. And what's a play? Paper, too. And what are reviews? Again, paper. Well, and traveler's checks and banknotes are also only paper. One time when I couldn't sleep I started thinking —there was once a Stone Age; now we're in the Paper Age. Some tools have remained from the Stone Age, but from the Paper Age nothing will remain. At night the most bizarre thoughts come to mind. Once, I woke up and began musing about my genealogy. I know only a little bit about my grandfathers and nothing at all about my great-grandfathers and great-grandmothers. Well, and what about the great-great-grandfathers? I figured that when you go back enough generations, everyone stems from thousands of forebears, and from each of them he has inherited some trait. By day, this is nothing more than a passing thought, but at night it becomes terribly relevant and even scary. Tsutsik, you write about dybbuks. The past generations are our dybbuks. They sit within us and usually remain silent. But suddenly one of them cries out. The grandmothers aren't so dreadful, but the grandfathers terrify me. A person is literally a cemetery where multitudes of living corpses are buried. Tsutsik, has this ever occurred to you?"

"All kinds of crazy things occur to me."

"Among the generations there have probably been madmen, and their voices must be heard," Betty went on. "I'm not only a cemetery—in my brain there's an insane asylum, too. I hear the lunatics shriek their wild laughter. They pull at the bars and try to escape. Heredity cells aren't lost. If man is descended from an ape, he carries the genes of an ape in him, and if from a fish, there is something of the fish in him, too. Isn't that funny and frightening at the same time?"

Dora crushed the butt of her cigarette. "Excuse me, Miss Slonim, but did you ever consider that such thoughts have a social undertone? If you have the right pieces of paper, as you've described them—the passport, the checks, the ticket to America—you can indulge in the luxury of probing into all kinds of vagaries. But if you must pay the rent the next day and don't have a groschen and you're apt to be forced out into the cold and they're about to put you in jail for some crime you haven't committed and you're hungry besides—that's when you concentrate on reality. Ninety percent of mankind—ninety-nine percent—is uncertain of its tomorrow, and often of its today. What they have to concern themselves with is the most basic needs. When writers like H. G. Wells or Hans Heinz Evers, or maybe even our own Aaron Greidinger, come out with fantasies about wars between planets or about a girl with two dybbuks who want to get married—excuse me for being so blunt—they're talking to each other. I never read the writer O'Neill, but I have a feeling he's one of those who spin dreams. Miss Slonim, you should appear in something that touches everybody. Then you will be understood and you will have an audience. Forgive my frankness."

Betty bristled. "What should I play in? A propaganda piece preaching Communism? First, I'd be arrested and they'd close down the theater. Second, I come from Russia and I've seen what Communism really is. Third . . ."

"I'm not proposing you should do a Communist play," Dora interrupted her. "How could you? No one knows any more where Stalinism ends and Fascism—or whatever

214

you choose to call it—begins. Still, it remains a fact that the masses suffer and their suffering grows steadily worse. If the Nazis attack Poland, it's the poor who will be the victims. The rich will all flee abroad. If you can show a bank book with a hundred thousand dollars and if you travel strictly for pleasure, then the whole world is open to you. They'll even let you into Palestine if you can show one thousand pounds sterling. Is that true or not, Aaron?"

"A novel or a play that said all this wouldn't change anything," I said. "The masses already know that's how things are. Besides, you said before the very opposite of what you're saying now."

"I didn't say the opposite. I have my doubts, but the masses remain dear to me. They should be taught how to resist this exploitation."

"Dora, you speak of the masses as if they were innocent lambs and only a few villains are responsible for the human tragedy. Actually, a large part of the masses themselves want to kill, plunder, rape, and do what Hitler, Stalin, and tyrants like them have always done. Chmielnitsky's Cossacks weren't capitalists, neither were Petlura's murderers. Petlura himself was a pauper right up to the time Schwartzbard did him in. He starved in Paris."

"Who sent a hundred thousand soldiers to die at Verdun? Wilhelm and Foch."

"Wilhelm and Foch couldn't have sent them unless a big enough percentage had been willing to go. The ugly truth is that a great number of men—young men in particular—have a passion to kill. They only need a pretext or a cause. One time, it's for religion; another, it may be for Fascism or to defend democracy. Their urge to kill is so great it surpasses their fear of being killed. This is a truth forbidden to utter, but true nonetheless. Those Nazis ready to kill and die for Hitler would under other circumstances be as ready to do the same for Stalin. There hasn't been a foolish ambition or an insanity for which people weren't ready to die. If the Jews were to become independent, you could start a war between the Litvaks and the Galicianers."

"If that is true, then there is no hope."

"Who says there is?"

"A hypocrite!" Betty said after Dora had gone. "I've seen her ilk in Russia. They put on leather jackets, hung revolvers at their hips, and became Chekaists. Now they're being liquidated. They richly deserve it. Tsutsik, come kiss me. For the last time."

TWELVE

1 In the afternoon more snow began to fall. A dusky murkiness showed through the windowpanes. The sky loomed low, gray, neither cloudy nor clear but looking as if, through some change in creation, the world had acquired another climate. Where was it written that the Ice Age couldn't suddenly come back? What was to prevent the earth's tearing loose from the gravitational force of the sun and straying from the Milky Way in the direction of some other galaxy? After Dora and Betty left, it grew quiet in the apartment. The telephone didn't ring, nor did Tekla come to straighten up and take away the tray. I lay down in my clothes on the unmade bed and closed my eyes.

Around seven-thirty I'd have to take a droshky, a sleigh, or a cab and go to the boardinghouse on Gnoyna Street where my mother and Moishe were waiting for me. Mother was undoubtedly sitting on a chair or on the bed, waiting absorbed in *The Duty of the Hearts,* which she had brought with her. My marriage to Shosha had robbed her of the last hope of returning to Warsaw. Moishe was probably in the studyhouse browsing through books there. He hadn't uttered a word against Shosha, but his eyes laughed momentarily when he first heard her name. The boys in the cheder where he went used to mimic Shosha. I was sure he was thinking that those who strayed from the path of righteousness also strayed when it came to worldly matters. Well, and what about Feitelzohn, Celia, and Haiml? Even Teibele had reacted with a hint of contempt when she heard I would be marrying her sister. I had already determined never to take Shosha to the Writers' Club. They would ridicule her—and me.

Evening fell abruptly. My room grew dark. The sky had acquired a violet tinge. I got up from my bed and stood at the window. The passersby were not walking but struggling against the blizzard; occasionally they danced with the whirlwind. Vast piles of snow transformed the street into valleys and hills. What are the sparrows doing now? I wondered. According to Spinoza, the frost, the birds, and I were all modes of the same substance. But one mode whistled, whined, and drove a cold wave from the North Pole; a second hid in a hole in a wall, shivering and starving; a third was getting ready to marry Shosha.

It wasn't yet seven when I went outside to find a droshky. I had put on my good suit and a fresh shirt. Haiml and Celia had reserved a room in a hotel for us in Otwock, where we would spend a week. This was to be their wedding gift and our honeymoon, and I had packed a satchel with manuscripts, some clothing, and a toothbrush. I did it all with the feeling that it was never my decision but that some unknown power had decided for me. The illusion of free choice had vanished from within me. Perhaps this is the way all people marry? Perhaps this is how men steal, murder, go to war, commit suicide? Something in me laughed. The fatalists are right after all. I'll never blame anyone for anything. I waited in front of the gate for fifteen minutes, but all the sleighs and taxis that passed were taken. Nor were any of the trolleys with their frosted-over windows heading in the direction of Gnoyna. I started off on foot, carrying the satchel, and the snow sprayed my face at an angle. My eyelids became swollen. The snow-covered street lights cast trails of fog. I stumbled along in the wintry chaos with the uncertainty of a blind man. Even though I wore rubbers, my feet were soon wet. I passed Solna and Electoralna Streets, and from Zimna came out on Gnoyna. How would I take Mother and Moishe through such a storm to Panska? She could barely take a step in normal weather. I glanced at my wristwatch, but I couldn't read the numbers on the dial.

I climbed the three flights of wet and slippery stairs that led up to the boardinghouse. Mother sat in the living room in a velvet dress, a silk kerchief over her head, her face pointed and white. I could see in her eyes both a pious acquiescence in God's verdicts and a tinge of worldly irony. Moishe had already put on his rabbinical fur-lined coat with the mangy collar and his broad-brimmed hat. There were other men and women in the place, guests who had spent the night there, possibly stranded in Warsaw by the snowstorm. They apparently knew who was expected and guessed the circumstances, for when I came in a tumult broke out and a clapping of hands.

Someone exclaimed, "Mazel tov, the groom is here!"

A whirl of steam covered my face and for a moment I saw nothing and heard only a mixture of male and female laughter.

A youth—he may have been an employee of the house —volunteered to go downstairs and help us get a sleigh or droshky. Mother wasn't able to climb in, and I had to lift her and place her in her seat. Moishe didn't forget to be suspicious that the seat cover was of forbidden cloth, and he spread his handkerchief over it for a partition. The droshky had already started off when I realized I didn't have my satchel. I began to shout to the driver to stop. At that moment the youth—Mother designated him an angel from heaven—raced up and threw it in beside me. I wanted to reward him, but I had no change. I yelled my thanks and the wind blew my words away. The droshky's canopy was up; it was dark inside. I heard Moishe say, "Well, thank the Almighty you came. It was getting late and we were afraid something had happened. You know how Mother worries."

"I couldn't get a droshky. I had to walk the whole way."

"God forbid you didn't catch a cold," Mother said. "Ask Bashele to give you an aspirin."

"It all comes from heaven, it's all from heaven," Moishe said. "In everything man does there are obstacles so that he can discern the hand of Providence. If everything were to go smoothly, man would say, 'My power and the might of mine hands hath gotten me this wealth.' When evildoers achieve success, they believe it to be due to their own ability, but not always is the path of evil successful. That Hitler—may his name be blotted out—will be dealt his punishment, nor will Stalin, that wicked monster, have his way either."

"Until they receive their deserved punishment, who knows how many innocent people will perish," Mother said.

"Eh? Accounts are kept in heaven. Rabbi Sholom Belzer once said, 'Not a pinch of snuff is ignored in the Celestial Council of Justice!' He who knows the truth relies completely on God."

The droshky dragged along, rocking. From time to time the horse stopped, turned his head, and glanced back, seemingly wondering why people should drive in weather like this. The driver said in Yiddish, "On a night like this, a droshky is no good and a sleigh is worthless, too. On a night like this, it's good to sit by the stove and eat broth with noodles."

"You'll have to give him a few groschen more," Mother whispered.

"Yes, Mama, I will."

When we got to the rabbi's, everyone was waiting: Shosha, Bashele, Zelig, Teibele, Feitelzohn, Haiml, Celia. They greeted me with smiles, winks. Celia's eyes seemed to ask, Are you really so blind? Or do you see something the others can never see? Maybe they had suspected I would change my mind at the last minute. Mother's old-fashioned clothes brought a condescending expression from the rebbitzen, a stout woman in a black curled wig; she had a broad face and a huge bosom. There was not a trace of feminine well-wishing in her stern gaze. Counting the rabbi and his son—a swarthy youth with hardly any earlocks and the stiff collar of a half Hasid, half dandy— there were seven males present, and the rabbi sent his son out to collar three men from the courtyard or the street to complete the quorum.

Shosha had on a new dress. Her hair done in a pompadour and her high-heeled shoes made her look taller. When we came in, she stretched out her arms and made a gesture as if to run up to us, but Bashele indicated to her that she should stand still. Bashele had brought a bottle of wine, a bottle of whiskey, and a bag of cookies. The rabbi, a tall, erect man with a pointed black beard, didn't appear pious like my father or Moishe, but a worldly person, all business. There was a telephone in his apartment. Mother and Moishe looked at each other, surprised. It never occurred to Father to install a gadget like this in his house.

Since Zelig had already deposited a thousand zlotys with a lawyer to be paid to Bashele after the divorce, the former husband and wife avoided each other. Zelig paced to and fro in a black suit, a stiff collar, and a tie with a pearl stickpin. His shoes squeaked. He was smoking a cigar. He was already properly drunk, as befitted a member of the burial society. He called Mother *"mechutay-neste"* (in-law), and reminded her of the time when we had been neighbors. Feitelzohn was having a conversation with Moishe, displaying his knowledge of the Gemara and the Midrash. I heard Moishe say to him, "You are a scholar, but erudition demands practice."

"For that you need what I lack—faith," Feitelzohn replied.

"Sometimes the faith comes later."

Feitelzohn had already met Shosha at Celia's. He had praised her childish beauty to me, said that she reminded him of an English girl friend of his of olden times, even spoke of having Shosha take part in some future soul expedition of his, together with me. He added, "Tsutsik, in my eyes she has a million times more charm than that American actress—what is her name? If you would have married her, I would have considered it a degradation."

The rabbi sat down to fill out the marriage contract. He wiped the point of his pen on his skullcap. When he asked if the bride was a virgin, Zelig replied, "Certified."

The rabbi's son came back with three men dressed in padded jackets, heavy boots, fur caps. One wore a rope tied across his loins. They didn't want to wait for refreshments until after the ceremony and immediately poured themselves glasses of whiskey. Their faces, raw from the cold outside, blackened and wrinkled from age and hard work, expressed disdain for all the hopes of the young. Their moist eyes behind bushy brows were saying, Just wait a few years and you will know what we know. From behind the stove the rabbi's son brought a canopy and four poles. The rabbi quickly read the ketubbah, the marriage contract written in Aramaic. He swallowed words. I promised Shosha two hunderd gulden in the event I divorced her, and the same sum of money from my heirs should she be widowed.

I hadn't bought a wedding ring. Bashele told me that

no jeweler would be able to supply a ring to fit Shosha's index finger, which was as slender as a child's. Bashele now gave me the ring that Zelig had given her over thirty years ago. I would use it just for that occasion. She burst into tears when the rabbi began to chant the holy words. Teibele wiped a tear from her left eye with a corner of her handkerchief. Shosha moved her lips several times, as if about to ask or to say something, but each time Bashele shook her head in warning.

I noticed that my mother was barely able to stand. From time to time she wavered and took hold of Moishe's shoulder. Moishe swayed as if he were mumbling a prayer.

Haiml and Celia had planned a reception for us at a restaurant, but it had to be canceled. Mother and Moishe let it be known that they didn't trust the big-city restaurants to be strictly kosher. Besides, the last train to Otwock, where a room stood ready for Shosha and me, departed too early to leave enough time for a reception. Bashele had packed a supper for us to eat on the train. Mother and Moishe intended to go back to Old Stykov the first thing the next morning. Haiml and Celia would take them to the station. When Shosha and I returned from Otwock, we would move in with the Chentshiners.

I knew that all who were present at the ceremony—perhaps even Bashele and Shosha herself deep down where a vestige of sane judgment always remains—felt that I was committing a terrible folly, but the general mood was a kind of jubilant solemnity. Feitelzohn, who was wont to make jokes even at funerals to show how consistent he was in his cynicism, conducted himself almost paternally. He squeezed my hand and wished me good luck. He bent down and gallantly kissed Shosha on her little hand. Haiml and Celia both cried.

Zelig said, "Getting married and dying are two things you can't avoid." And he handed me a stack of banknotes wrapped in tissue paper.

Mother wasn't crying. I hugged and kissed her, but she didn't kiss me back. She said, "Since you went ahead and did it, it was obviously ordained."

2 The train was scheduled to leave at twenty to twelve, but at midnight it still hadn't moved. The car in which we were seated was empty. The tiny gas lamp blinded more than it illuminated. Bashele and Teibele, who escorted us to the train, had gone home. It was nearly as cold in the car as outside, and I put on the two sweaters I had packed in my satchel. Shosha had brought along a fur collar and a muff that may have come from before the war and had undoubtedly belonged to her mother. The collar had a fox head with two glass eyes. Shosha pressed against me and her body vibrated, like that of some small animal.

Had we made a mistake and boarded an empty train that was scheduled to stand all night in the station? I wanted to take a look in the other cars, but Shosha clung to me and said she wouldn't be left alone. Eventually we heard a whistle and the train began to glide hesitantly over the slippery rails.

Shosha opened the bag Bashele had given us and we ate a cold meal. Everything she did took a long time: untying the bag, deciding which portion was meant for her and which for me. She seemed to waver at every bite. I had promised Haiml and Celia, those generous benefactors of ours, that when we lived with them Shosha would help out with the housekeeping chores, since Celia's Marianna had gone off to be married, but Shosha's indecision each time she had to make the pettiest choice convinced me that she would be of little use. She picked up a slice of sour pickle and it fell from her fingers. She took a crumb of a roll, then put it down again. Her slim fingers had almost no nails and I could not make out whether she had bitten them off or whether they had stopped growing. She began to chew and somehow forgot that she had food in her mouth.

We rode past the Praga cemetery, a city of headstones enveloped in snowy shrouds, and Shosha said, "Here lies Yppe."

"Yes, I know."

"Oh, Arele, I'm afraid!"

"Afraid of what?" I asked.

Shosha didn't answer and I assumed she had forgotten what I had asked. Then she said, "The train may get lost."

"How? A train runs on tracks."

Shosha thought this over.

"Arele, I won't be able to have children. The doctor once said I'm too narrow. You know where."

"I don't want children. You are my child."

"Arele, are you my husband already?"

"Yes, Shoshele."

"And I'm really your wife?"

"According to the law."

"Arele, I'm afraid."

"What are you afraid of now?"

"Oh, I don't know. Of God. Of Hitler."

"So far, Hitler is in Germany, not here. As to God . . ."

"Arele, I forgot to bring along my little pillow."

"We'll be back in a week and you'll have your pillow again."

"Without my pillow I won't be able to fall asleep."

"You'll sleep. We'll lie in one bed."

"Oh, Arele, I'm going to cry." She burst out in a clamor, like a little girl. I put my arms around her. She trembled and I felt the beating of her heart. I counted her ribs through her dress.

The conductor came in to punch the tickets. He asked, "Why is she crying?"

"Oh, she forgot to bring along her pillow."

"Your daughter, eh?"

"No. Yes."

"Don't cry, little girl. You'll get another pillow." He threw her a kiss and left.

In the midst of crying, Shosha began to laugh. "He thought you're my daddy?"

"That's what I am."

"How is that possible? You're fooling!"

She became still and I put my cheek against hers. She shivered from the cold, but her cheek felt hot. I was cold, too, yet at the same time I was overcome by a desire different from any I had felt before—passion without association, without thought, as if the body, the corporeal stuff, were acting on its own. I listened to my desire and it struck me that if metal could feel, my feeling was that of a needle drawn to a magnet.

Shosha must have read my mind, because she said, "Oh, your beard pricks like needles!"

I started to answer her, but the wheels made a scraping sound, then came to a halt. We were somewhere between Wawer and Miedzeszyn. A white wasteland stretched beyond the other side of the pane. It had stopped snowing and the sky reflected the snow. For all the frost, it seemed to glow of an other-worldly summer.

The conductor came by and announced hastily that the rails were iced over.

"Arele, I'm afraid!"

"Afraid of what?"

"Your mother has grown so old. She looks near death."

"She's not that old."

"Arele, I want to go home."

"Don't you want to be with me?"

"Yes, with you and with my mommy."

"In a week, not before."

"I want it now!"

I didn't answer. She laid her head on my shoulder. A

feeling of despair settled over me, together with the comfort brought about by the awareness that I was not responsible for this entanglement. In the half darkness I winked to my other self, my mad dictator, and congratulated him on his droll victory. I closed my eyes and felt the warmth flowing from Shosha's head to my face. What did I have to lose? Nothing more than what everyone loses anyway.

3 We were the only passengers to get off in Otwock. There was no one from whom to ask the way to the hotel, and we wandered into a wooded area. I must have been half asleep. I started to address someone—it turned out to be a tree. Shosha had become strangely silent. All of a sudden a man materialized as if from the ground and conducted us to the hotel. A servant had been sent to meet us at the station but had missed us. He mumbled who he was and remained mute all the way. He walked so quickly that Shosha could barely follow him. Every few minutes he became lost among the trees and then emerged again in a midnight game of hide-and-seek.

The room they gave us was in the attic and was large and cold. It had one big brass bed and a narrow cot, each with huge pillows and heavy blankets. It smelled of pine and lavender. Through a pane that was not frosted over one could see pines laden with snow-covered cones and draped with icicles like the Christmas trees of the Gentiles. Shosha was ashamed to undress before me, and I had to stand facing the window while she got ready for bed. I had assumed that wandering astray through the cold woods would put Shosha in a panic, but the real danger seemed to have left her indifferent. I saw her reflection in the clean part of the windowpane as she took off her camisole and put on her nightgown. After fussing a long time with buttons and hooks, she got into bed. "Arele, it's cold as ice!" she exclaimed.

Shosha demanded that I lie on the cot, but I lay down beside her. Her body was warm, while mine was half frozen. In my cold arms she fluttered like a sacrificial chicken. Except for her little breasts, which were those of a girl just starting to mature, she was skin and bones. We lay together quietly and waited for the bedding to warm up. Cold came in through the window frame, and the panes rattled. From time to time the wind whistled and dropped to a drawn-out moan like that of a woman giving birth. Sometimes a wailing of different voices could be heard, as if packs of wolves were roaming the Otwock forests.

"Arele, it aches."

"What is it?"

"You're sticking me with your knees."

I pulled my knees away.

"My stomach is rumbling."

"It's my stomach, not yours."

"No, it's mine. Do you hear? Like the crying of a baby."

I felt her abdomen. She shook. "Cold fingers!"

"I'll warm myself on you."

"Oh, Arele, you're not allowed to do this to a female."

"Shoshele, you're my wife."

"Arele, I'm ashamed. Oh, you're tickling me!" Shosha began to laugh, but abruptly the laughter turned into a sob.

"Why are you crying, Shoshele?"

"It's all so strange. When Leizer the watchmaker came to read what you wrote in the newspaper, I thought, How can this be? Is he actually there? I took out the papers you had painted with the colors and they had dried out. We went to look for you at the newspaper and an old man, the one who serves the tea, yelled, 'Not here!' We didn't go back. One evening I played with a shadow on the wall and suddenly it jumped down and slapped me. Oh, you have hair on your chest! I lay sick all year and Dr. Kniasler said I would die."

"When was this?"

She didn't answer. Even as she was talking, she fell asleep. Her breath came quick and soft. I pulled her closer, and in her sleep she cuddled up to me with such force it was as if she were trying to bore inside my guts. How can such a weak creature give off so much heat? I wondered. Is there a physiological reason for it? Or does it have to do with the mind?

I closed my eyes. The tremendous urge for Shosha that had seized me in the train had dissipated. Was I suddenly impotent? I fell asleep and dreamed. Someone shrieked wildly. Animals with long teats dragged me, tore chunks from me with fang and claw. I was wandering through a cellar that was also a slaughterhouse and a cemetery strewn with unburied corpses. I awoke excited. I grabbed Shosha, and before she could even wake up, I mounted her. She choked and resisted. A stream of hot blood burned my thigh. I tried to pacify her, but she broke out in a wail. I was sure she had awakened everyone in the hotel. Had I injured her? I got out of bed and searched for the light switch, but I couldn't find it. I tapped around and bumped into the stove. In my distress I prayed to God to protect her.

"Shoshele, don't cry! People will come running! It was all out of love."

"Where are you?"

I found the switch and turned on the light. For a moment I couldn't see. There was a washstand here with a pitcher of water and two towels hanging at the side. Shosha was sitting up in the bed, no longer crying.

"Arele, am I a wife now?"

4   On our third day in Otwock, while I was sitting with

Shosha in the hotel dining room eating lunch, I was summoned to the telephone. The call was from Warsaw. I was sure it would be Celia, but it turned out to be Feitelzohn.

"Tsutsik, I have good news for you."

"Good news for me? That's something I hear for the first time."

"Yes, good news. But first tell me how things are going with the honeymoon."

"Fine, thanks."

"No crises?"

"Yes, but—"

"Your Shosha didn't die of fright?"

"Nearly. But now she is happy again."

"I like her. With her at your side, your talent will grow."

"From your mouth to God's ears."

"Tsutsik, I told Shapiro, the editor of the evening paper —what's it called?—that you're writing a novel about Jacob Frank, and he wants you to write Frank's biography for him. He wants to print it in six installments a week and pay you three hundred zlotys a month. I told him that was too little and he may up it a few zlotys."

"Three hundred zlotys is too little? That's a fortune!"

"Some fortune! Tsutsik, you're made! He told me you'll be able to drag the thing through a year, or as long as your imagination holds out."

"That really is a stroke of fortune!"

"Are you still moving in with the Chentshiners?"

"Now I won't do it. Shosha will pine away without her mother."

"Don't do it, Tsutsik. You know I'm not jealous of you. Just the opposite. But to live there wouldn't be a good idea. Tsutsik, I'll go bankrupt from this call. We'll celebrate when you come back. Regards to Shosha. Adieu."

I wanted to tell Feitelzohn how grateful I was and that I would pay for the call, but he had already hung up. I went back to the table. "Shoshele, you've brought me luck. I have a job on a newspaper. We won't be moving in with Celia!"

"Oh, Arele, God has answered me. I didn't want to be there. I prayed. She tries to take you away from me. What will you do on the paper?"

"Write the life of a false Messiah who preached that God wants people to sin. The false Messiah himself slept with his own daughter and with the wives of his disciples."

"He had such a wide bed?"

"Not all at the same time—or maybe all together, too. He was rich enough to afford a bed as wide as all Otwock."

"You knew him?"

"He died some hundred aand fifty years ago."

"Arele, I pray to God, and everything I ask for He does. When you went to the post office, a blind man came up and I gave him ten groschen, and that's the reason God did all this. Arele, I love you so terribly! I'd like to be with you every minute, every second. When you go to the toilet I start to worry that you may have gotten lost or fallen. I miss Mommy, too. I haven't seen her for so long. I would like to be with you and with her day and night for a myriad of years."

"Shoshele, your mother will be divorced soon and she may remarry. And it will be impossible for me to be with you every minute. In Warsaw I'll have to go to the editorial office, to the library. Sometimes I'll have to meet Feitelzohn. It was he who got me the job."

"He has no wife?"

"He has many women, but not one wife."

"Is he the false Messiah?"

"In a way, Shoshele—that's not a bad comparison."

"Arele, I want to tell you something, but I'm ashamed."

"You have nothing to be ashamed of before me. I've already seen you naked."

"I want more."

"More what?"

"I want to lie in bed. You know what."

"When? Now?"

"Yes."

"Wait, the waitress hasn't brought us our tea yet."

"I'm not thirsty."

The waitress came with two glasses of tea and two slices of sugar cake on a tray. We were the only guests in the hotel. Another couple was expected but not until the next day.

It had stopped snowing and the sun shone. I had been planning to take a walk with Shosha, maybe as far as Świder. I wanted to see if the river was frozen over and how the waterfall looked with its huge icicles gleaming in the sun, but Shosha's words changed everything. The waitress, a short woman with a broad face, high cheekbones, and liquid black eyes, didn't turn back to the kitchen right away. She said, "Mr. Greidinger, you eat everything up, but your wife leaves everything. That's why she's so thin. She barely touched the appetizer, the soup, the meat, the vegetables. It's not good to eat so little. People come here to gain weight, not to lose."

Shosha made a face. "I can't eat so much. I have a small stomach."

"It's not the stomach, Mrs. Greidinger. My grandmother used to say, 'The intestine has no bottom.' It's the appetite. My boss here lost her appetite and she went to a Dr. Schmaltzbaum. He gave her a prescription for iron and she gained back ten pounds."

"Iron?" Shosha asked. "Can you eat iron?"

The waitress laughed, exposing a mouthful of gold teeth. Her eyes contracted to the size of two berries. "Iron is a medicine. No one is told to eat nails." She walked away, scraping her large shoes across the floor. When she reached the kitchen door, she cast an amused glance back toward us.

Shosha said, "I don't like her. I like only you and Mommy. I like Teibele too, but not as much as you two. I would like to be with you a thousand years."

5   The night was long. We went to sleep before nine and at twelve we both awoke. Shosha asked, "Arele, you don't sleep any more?"

"No, Shoshele."

"Neither do I. Every time I wake up I think it was all a fairy tale—you, the wedding, everything. But I touch you and I see you are here."

"Once there was a philosopher and he believed that everything was a dream. God is dreaming and the world is His dream."

"Is this written in the books?" Shosha asked.

"Yes, in the books."

"Yesterday—no, the day before yesterday—I dreamed that I was home and you came in. After you closed the door you came in again. There was not one Arele, but two, three, four, five, ten—a whole row of Areles. What is a dream?"

"No one knows."

"What do the books say?"

"The books don't know, either."

"How can this be? Arele, Leizer the watchmaker said that you are an unbeliever—is this true?"

"No, Shoshele, I believe in God, but I don't believe that He revealed Himself and told the rabbis all the little laws that they added through generations."

"Where is God? In heaven?"

"He must be somewhere."

"Why doesn't He punish Hitler?"

"Oh, He doesn't punish anybody. He created the cat

and the mouse. The cat cannot eat grass, she must eat flesh. It's not her fault that she kills mice. The mice are certainly not guilty. He created the wolves and the sheep, the slaughterers and the chickens, the feet and the worms on which they step."

"God is no good?"

"Not as we see it."

"He has no pity?"

"Not as we understand it."

"Arele, I'm afraid."

"I'm afraid too, but Hitler won't come tonight. Move over to me. So."

"Arele, I want to have a child with you, a little baby with blue eyes and red hair. The doctor said that if they cut up my belly a living child would come out."

"And you would want that?"

"Yes, Arele. Your child. If it should be a boy, he would read the same books as you."

"It isn't worth cutting up a belly to read books."

"It's worth it. I would suckle him and my breasts would grow bigger."

"They are big enough for me."

"What else is written in the books?"

"Oh, all kinds of things. They found out that the stars run away with us. Myriads of miles every day."

"Where do they run?"

"Into empty space far away."

"They will never come back?"

"They will be extinguished and get cold first, and then they will fall back with such might they will grow hot, and the whole swinish business will begin all over again."

"Where do the books say Yppe is?"

"If there is a soul, she is somewhere. And if there isn't any, then—"

"Arele, she was here. She knows about us. She came to wish me mazel tov."

"When? Where?"

"Here. Yesterday. No, the day before yesterday. How does she know that we are in Otwock? She stood at the door, near the mezuzah, and she smiled. She wore a white dress, not a shroud. When she was alive, two of her front teeth were missing. Now she has a full mouth of teeth."

"There must be good dentists in the hereafter."

"Arele, are you making fun of me?"

"No, I'm not."

"She came to me in Warsaw, too. It was before you visited us for the first time—I sat on my stool and she came in. The door was bolted. Mother was out, and she told me to bolt the door because of the hoodlums. Suddenly Yppe was there. How could she do it? She spoke to me, like one sister to another. I had undone my hair, and she braided it. She played cat's cradle with me, but without string. And then that day before Yom Kippur I saw her in the chicken soup. She had a wreath of flowers on her head, like a Gentile bride, and I knew that something was going to happen. You were there, but I didn't want to say anything. When I mention Yppe, Mother screams. She says that I'm crazy."

"You are not crazy."

"What am I?"

"A sweet soul."

"What do you make of it?"

"You might have dreamed it."

"In the middle of the day?"

"Sometimes one dreams in the daytime."

"Arele, I am afraid."

"What are you afraid of this time?"

"The sky, the stars, the books. Tell me the story about the giant. I forget his name."

"Og, the king of Bashan."

"Yes, about him. Is it true that he could not get a wife because he was so big?"

"That is the story. When the flood came and Noah and his sons and all the animals and fowl went into the Ark, Og could not enter because he was so big, and he sat on the roof. Forty days and forty nights it rained on him, but he didn't drown."

"Was he naked?"

"What tailor could sew a pair of pants big enough for him?"

"Oy, Arele, it is good to be with you. What will we do when the Nazis come?"

"We will die."

"Together?"

"Yes, Shoshele."

"The Messiah isn't coming?"

"Not so quickly."

"Arele, I just remembered a song."

"What song?"

Shosha began to sing in a thin voice.

> *"He was called Beans,*
> *Noodles was her name,*
> *They married on Friday*
> *And nobody came."*

She cuddled up to me and said, "Oy, Arele, it's good to lie with you even if we die."

THIRTEEN

1 In the afternoon paper where the biography of Jacob Frank—it was actually a blend of biography and fantasy —had already been dragging on for months, the news worsened. Hitler and Mussolini had met at the Brenner Pass and no doubt reached decisions regarding the destruction of Poland and the Jews, but a large part of the Polish press kept attacking the Jewish minority as if it were the nation's greatest danger. Representatives of the Hitler Government came to Poland and were received by the dictator, General Rydz-Śmigły, and his ministers. In the Soviet Union the purges, mass arrests, and trials of Trotskyites, old Bolsheviks, right- and left-wing dissidents, Zionists, and Hebrewists became a permanent terror. In Polish cities, unemployment grew. In the villages, particularly where Ukrainians and White Russians lived, the peasants starved. Many *Volksdeutschen,* as the Germans in Poland called themselves, proclaimed themselves Nazis. The Comintern had dissolved the Polish Communist Party. The charging of Bukharin, Kamenev, Zinoviev, and Rykov with sabotage and espionage and the designation of them as Fascist lackeys and agents of Hitler evoked protests even from sworn Stalinists. But circulation did not drop in the Yiddish newspapers in Warsaw, including the afternoon daily for which I worked. On the contrary, more newspapers were read now than before. The story of the false Messiah Jacob Frank and his disciples had to end, but I was ready with a list of other false Messiahs— Reuveyni, Shlomo Mulkho, Sabbatai Zevi.

There was a time when I had to make up some pretext whenever I came home late or didn't come home at all, but gradually Bashele and Shosha became accustomed to asking no questions. What did they know about the writing profession? I had told Leizer the watchmaker that I served as night editor a couple of times a week, and Leizer had explained the facts to Bashele and Shosha. Leizer came by each day and read to them the latest installment of my biography of Jacob Frank. Everyone on Krochmalna Street was reading it—the thieves, the street-walkers, the old-line Stalinists, and the new-fledged Trotskyites. Sometimes when I walked down the street I heard the market vendors talking about Jacob Frank—his miracles, orgies, and lunacies. The leftists still complained that this kind of writing was an opiate for the masses, but after they finished reading the political news on the front page and the local news on page 5 the masses needed an opiate.

Before I moved into the alcove at Bashele's she had had the walls painted and installed an iron stove, and thrown out the sacks and rags that had been accumulating for twenty-odd years. Shosha couldn't be by herself even an hour. The moment she was left alone she was overcome by melancholy. On the other hand, I couldn't be with her all the time. I had never given up my room on Leszno Street or told my landlords that I was married. True, I seldom spent nights there, but even Tekla had learned that writers are impulsive and confused creatures. She had stopped asking what I did, whom I spent time with, where I dragged around in the nights. I paid my rent and each week I gave her a zloty. On Christmas and Easter I brought her a gift. Every time I gave her something, she flushed, protested that she didn't need it, that it wasn't necessary. She would seize my hand and kiss it, as peasants had done for generations.

Because I couldn't be with Shosha all the time, coming home to her was always a wonder to me. She and Bashele had food ready for me to eat before I lay down—rice with milk, tea with a Sabbath cookie, a baked apple. Each night before coming to bed Shosha washed herself and often washed her hair as well. She discussed with me the latest installment of the Jacob Frank story. How could a man have so many women? Was it black magic? Had he sold his soul to the devil? How could a father have doings with his own daughter? Sometimes Shosha provided the answer: those were different times. Didn't King Solomon have a thousand wives? She remembered what I had told her when we lived at No. 10.

Basically, Shosha had stayed the same—the same childish face, the same childish figure. Still, changes had become apparent. In former times, Bashele had been the only one to prepare our meals. She hadn't let Shosha go near the kitchen or entrusted her with the marketing. She only sent her occasionally to the nearby store for a half pound of sugar, a few ounces of butter, a piece of cheese, or a loaf of bread—all bought on credit. I doubted whether Shosha knew the value of coins. Suddenly I observed her bustling about in the kitchen. She accompanied her mother to market in Yanash's Court. I heard her discussing with Bashele the vegetarian dishes that wouldn't upset my digestion. This concern for my diet always baffled me. I wasn't accustomed to anyone's paying attention to my needs. But to Shosha I was a husband, and to Bashele a son-in-law. It had never occurred to me that Shosha could sew or darn, but one day I saw her darning my socks over a tea glass. She began to look after my shirts, handkerchiefs, and collars, and to take my shoes to be heeled at the shoemaker's. I couldn't, or didn't want to be a husband in the accepted sense of the word, but Shosha gradually assumed the duties of a wife.

When I came home in the evenings I still found her seated on her stool, but no longer surrounded by playthings. Nor did she read her schoolbook any more. Surprises constantly awaited me. Shosha would be wearing shoes with high heels and flesh-colored stockings not only when she went visiting but also at home. Her mother had bought her dresses and nightgowns with lace. Occasionally she changed the way she wore her hair.

Shosha's interest in my writing increased. The novel about Jacob Frank had come to an end. The new novel, about Sabbatai Zevi, described with much detail the Jewish longing for redemption in an epoch that displayed similarities to our own. What Hitler threatened to do to the Jews Bogdan Chmielnitsky had done some three hun-

238

dred years earlier. From the day they were exiled from their land, Jews had lived in anticipation of death or the coming of the Messiah. In Poland, in the Ukraine, in the lands ruled by the Turks, and most of all in the Holy Land, cabalists sought to bring the End of Days through prayers, fasts, the utterance of holy names. They probed the mysteries of the Book of Daniel. They never forgot the passage in the Gemara which stated that the Messiah would come when the generation was either totally innocent or totally guilty. Every day, Leizer had to read to Shosha the latest installment and explain to her the references to Jewish law and Jewish history. I heard her say to her mother, "Oh, Mommy, it's exactly like today!"

Teibele still hadn't found a husband. She had been choosy so long, Bashele complained, that she had become an old maid. Instead of a husband, she had taken a lover, a married bookkeeper with five children. Any day, he was allegedly going to divorce his wife, who was a common piece, but two years had gone by with no divorce in sight. Instead of satisfaction, Teibele provided her mother only with shame.

Teibele would often visit her mother and sister. She, too, liked to discuss Jacob Frank, Sabbatai Zevi, and their disciples with me. She brought small gifts for Bashele and Shosha, and occasionally for me as well—a book, a magazine, a notebook. Her lover was spending more and more nights at home with his wife. He had turned out to be a hypochondriac, Teibele said. He had convinced himself that he suffered from heart trouble. When Bashele reminded Teibele that it was getting late and she shouldn't be starting for home at such an hour, Teibele said in jest, "I'll lie down with them," pointing at Shosha and me. Or she would say, "What difference does it make? We're all doomed anyhow."

At night in bed, Shosha no longer talked about dolls, toys, children of neighbors she had known twenty years ago, but quite often she spoke of things I cared about. Was there truly a God up in heaven? Did He know every person's thoughts? Was it true that He loved Jews above all other people? Did He create the Gentiles, too, or only the Jews? Sometimes she questioned me about my novel. How could I be sure of what had occurred several hundred years ago? Had I read it in a book or did I make it up in my head? She asked me to tell her what would occur in the installment tomorrow and in the days after. I began to tell her things I hadn't yet written. I conducted a literary experiment with her—let my tongue wag freely and say whatever came to my lips. I had read and heard from Mark Elbinger about automatic writing. I had also read in a literary magazine about the kind of literature called the "stream of consciousness." I could test all this on Shosha. She listened to everything with the same sense of curiosity —children's stories I had heard from my mother when I was five or six; sexual fantasies no Yiddish writer would have allowed himself to publish; my own hypotheses or dreams about God, world creation, immortality of the soul, the future of mankind, as well as reveries of triumph over Hitler and Stalin. I had constructed an airplane of a material whose atoms were so densely compressed, one square centimeter weighed thousands of tons. It flew at a speed of a million miles a minute. It could pierce mountains, bore through the earth, reach to the farthest planets. It contained a clairvoyant telephone that tuned me in to the thoughts and plans of every human being on earth. I became so mighty I rendered all wars obsolete. When the Bolsheviks, Nazis, anti-Semites, swindlers, thieves, and rapists heard of my powers, they promptly surrendered. I instituted a world order based on Dr. Feitelzohn's philosophy of play. In my airplane I kept a harem of eighteen wives, but the queen and sovereign would be no one other than Shosha herself.

"And where would Mommy be?"

"I would give Mommy twenty million zlotys and she would live in a palace."

"And Teibele?"

"Teibele would become a princess."

"I would miss Mommy."

"We'd come to see her every Sabbath."

For a long time Shosha didn't speak. Then she said, "Arele, I miss Yppe."

"I would bring Yppe back to life."

"How is this possible?"

I elaborated to Shosha the theory that world history was a book man could read only forward. He could never turn the pages of this world book backward. But everything that had ever been still existed. Yppe lived somewhere. The hens, geese, and ducks the butchers in Yanash's Court slaughtered each day still lived, clucked, quacked, and crowed on the other pages of the world book—the right-hand pages, since the world book was written in Yiddish, which reads from right to left.

Shosha caught her breath. "Will we live in No. 10?"

"Yes, Shoshele, on the other pages of the book we still live in No. 10."

"But different people have moved in."

"They live there on the open pages, not the closed ones."

"Mommy once said that before we moved in, a tailor used to live there."

"The tailor lives there, too."

"Everyone together?"

"Each in another time."

I had gradually ceased being ashamed of Shosha. She dressed better, she appeared taller, I took her to Celia's, and both Celia and Haiml were enchanted by her simplicity, her honesty, her naïveté. I had taught her how to handle a knife and fork. She spoke in a childish fashion, but not stupidly.

On one visit Celia had detected a similarity between Shosha and her own deceased daughter. She showed me a yellowed photograph of the child and it struck me, too, that there was a certain resemblance. Haiml, who was growing ever more inclined toward mysticism and occultism, played with the idea that the soul of their little girl might have transmigrated into Shosha and that I was actually his and Celia's son-in-law. Souls weren't lost. They came back and sought bodies through which to reveal themselves to their loved ones. There was no such thing as chance. The forces that guided man and his fate always united those who were destined to meet.

Elbinger happened to be visiting the Chentshiners that evening and he repeated what he had said about Shosha on an earlier occasion—that he thought she possessed the qualities of a medium. All true mediums that he had met displayed the same primitivism, directness, sincerity. Once, he made an attempt to hypnotize Shosha, and as soon as he told her to, she fell into a deep sleep. Elbinger had trouble waking her. Before leaving, he kissed Shosha's forehead.

After Elbinger had gone, Shosha said, "He is not a person."

"What is he?" Haiml and Celia asked in unison.

"I don't know."

"An angel? A demon?" Celia asked.

"Perhaps from the sky," Shosha replied.

Haiml clapped his brow. "Tsutsik, this is a memorable evening for me. I won't forget this evening as long as I live!"

2 This Friday night, as always, I came home to Shosha. I did not keep the Jewish laws, Shosha did not go to the ritual bath, but I yielded to Bashele and pronounced the benediction over the wine on Friday night and on

Saturday morning. Bashele prepared vegetarian Sabbath meals for me. She even baked a vegetarian Sabbath stew with kasha and beans and a kugel made of rice and cinnamon. Shosha blessed the candles every Friday before dusk. She put them in silver candlesticks that Haiml and Celia had given us. Two challahs were covered with a cloth that Bashele had embroidered thirty years ago for Zelig. The family also owned a knife with a handle made of mother-of-pearl on which the words "Holy Sabbath" were engraved. That Friday evening Bashele and Shosha ate gefilte fish with chicken, and for me they made noodles with cottage cheese and carrot stew. They put on their Sabbath clothes and dressy shoes. Through the open window I saw the Sabbath candles in other apartments and heard table chants. The simple Jews sang, "Peace and light to the Jews on the day of rest and the day of joy." The Hasidim sang a cabalist poem by the Holy Issac Luria, written in Aramaic, about a heavenly apple orchard, a heavenly bridegroom and bride, heavenly bridesmaids and best men—all in highly erotic verses that would shock readers and critics even today. Bashele and Shosha conversed about the facts that food was getting more expensive and that it was increasingly difficult to find a place to hang the wash in the attic. Bashele mentioned with nostalgia the custom of past years to spread yellow sand on the floors before the Sabbath. Peasants from nearby villages used to bring carts of the sand in wooden kegs. They called out their merchandise in the streets. Now this was out of fashion. Today women liked to shellac their floors. Another thing, pious matrons used to go from house to house on Friday and collect challah, fish, and tripe—even cubes of sugar—for the poor. The new generation did not believe in this kind of charity. The Communists came in and asked for money for the Jews in Birobidjan, a region deep in Russia, somewhere at the edge of the world. They said that there was a Jewish land there. Only God knows if they were telling the truth.

"Mommy, what comes after the edge of the world? Is it dark there?"

Bashele shook her head. "You tell her, Arele."

"There is no edge of the world. The earth is round like an apple."

"Where do the black people live?" Shosha asked.

"In Africa."

"And where is Hitler?"

"In Germany."

"Oh, they used to teach us all this in school but I could never remember," Shosha said. "Is it true that in America there is a big Jewish man who must sign every dollar or the money isn't worth anything? Leizer the watchmaker said so."

"Yes, Shoshele. But he doesn't sign by hand. They print his signature."

"On the Sabbath one shouldn't talk about money," Bashele said. "There was a pious little rabbi, Reb Fivke, and on the Sabbath he spoke only in the Holy Tongue. He lived on Smocza Street, but on Friday he used to go around with a sack in Yanash's Court and collect food for the poor. After twelve o'clock on Friday he stopped talking, because Friday afternoon is almost as sacred as the Sabbath. When they gave him alms he just nodded or he mumbled some words in the Holy Tongue. One Friday he didn't come with his sack and someone said that he was sick in the poorhouse. After a few weeks he came again with his sack, but he had stopped talking altogether. He just went from store to store like a mute man. Someone said that he had had an operation on his throat and they cut out his windpipe. One Friday he entered a butcher shop and the butcher gave him some chicken feet or a gizzard. A man from the burial society—a gravedigger—happened to be in the store, and when he saw Reb Fivke, he let out a terrible scream and fainted. Reb Fivke immediately disappeared. They revived the gravedigger with cold water and by rubbing his temples with vinegar, and when he came to himself he swore a holy oath that Reb Fivke had died, that he had buried him himself. People couldn't believe it and said that the man was mistaken, but Reb Fivke never came again. Some curious men investigated the matter and they found his widow. He had been dead for months when this happened. I know, because Zelig still used to come home once in a while and the gravedigger was his best chum."

"As far as I know, your former husband does not believe in such things," I said.

"Now he believes in nothing. Then he was still a decent person," Bashele said.

"Oh, I will be afraid to go to sleep," Shosha said.

"Nothing to be afraid of," Bashele said. "Good people don't become spiteful after death. Just the opposite. Sometimes a corpse doesn't realize that he is dead and he leaves his grave and walks among the living. I heard of a man who came home when his family was sitting shiva for him. He opened the door and when he saw his wife and daughters sitting on low stools in their stocking feet, the mirror covered with a black sheet, and his sons with rended lapels, he asked, 'What's going on here? Who died?' And his wife, who was a mean shrew, answered, 'You!' At that moment he vanished."

"Oh, I'm going to have bad dreams."

"Just say, 'In Thy hands I commend my soul,' and you will sleep peacefully," Bashele advised.

After the dessert, Bashele served tea with Sabbath cookies she baked herself. Then I went out with Shosha on a walk from No. 7 to No. 25; one could walk that far safely even at night. Farther there was danger of being attacked by some hooligan or drunk. On some streets there were Jewish stores that were kept open on the Sabbath, but not on Krochmalna Street. Only one tea shop had its door half open on the Sabbath, and the customers drank tea on credit. Even the Communists were not allowed to pay in cash. Bashele remembered times when gangsters used to attack young couples or newlywed pairs and make them pay a few groschen a week in order not to be molested. But this took place in past years, she told me. At the time of the revolution in 1905 the socialists waged war with the toughs of the underworld, and many thieves, pimps, and racketeers were beaten up. A number of brothels were destroyed and the whores dispersed. The brothels and the thieves came back, but the racketeers disappeared forever.

Shosha and I walked. We passed the almost empty Place. When we reached No. 13, across the street from No. 10, Shosha stopped. "Here we lived once."

"Yes, you say it every time we pass."

"You stood on the balcony and caught flies."

"Don't remind me of that," I said.

"Why not?"

"Because we do to God's creatures what the Nazis do to us."

"Flies bite."

"They must bite. This is the way God created them."

"Why did God create them this way?" Shosha asked.

"Shoshele, there is no answer to this."

"Arele, I want to look inside the gate of No. 10."

"You've done it a thousand times already."

"Let me."

We crossed the street and looked into the dark courtyard. Everything remained as it had been twenty years before, except that most of the tenants had died. Shosha said, "Is there still a horse in the stable? When we lived here the horse was brown and it had a white patch on its nose. How long can a horse live?"

"About twenty years."

"Why not longer? A horse is so strong."

"Sometimes a horse lives until thirty."

"Why not until a hundred?"

"I don't know."

"When we lived there a demon entered the stable at night and plaited little braids in the horse's tail, and in its mane," Shosha said. "The demon mounted the horse and rode it from wall to wall all night long. In the morning the horse was wet from perspiration. It had foam on its mouth. It almost died. Why do demons do such things?"

"I'm not sure it's true."

"I saw the horse that morning. It was all wet. Arele, I want to look into the stable. I want to see if the horse is still the same."

"It's dark in the stable."

"I see a light there."

"You see nothing. Let's go."

We continued to walk until we reached No. 16. Then Shosha stopped. This was always a sign that she wanted to say something. Shosha could not walk and talk.

"What is it, Shoshele?"

"Arele, I want to have a child with you."

"Why suddenly?"

"I want to be a mother. Let's go home. I want you to do to me you know what."

"Shoshele, I told you, I don't want any children."

"I want to be a mother."

We turned back and Shosha said, "You go away to the newspaper and I am lonesome. I sit there and queer thoughts come to my mind. I see funny faces."

"What faces?"

"I don't know. They grimace and say things I don't understand. They are not people. Sometimes they laugh. Then they all begin to wail like at a funeral. Who are they?"

"I don't know. You tell me."

"They are many. Some of them look like soldiers. They ride horses, too. They sing a sad song, a silent song. I am frightened."

"Shoshele, you're imagining things. Perhaps you're dreaming."

"No, Arele. I want a child to say kaddish for me when I die."

"You'll live."

"No, they call me to go with them."

We passed No. 10 again, and Shosha said, "Let's look inside the gate."

"Again?"

"Let me!"

FOURTEEN

1 Haiml's father died and left Haiml buildings and real estate worth several million zlotys. Friends and relatives advised Haiml to move to Lodz, where he could keep a closer eye on his main properties, but Haiml said to me, "Tsutsik, a person is like a tree. You can't chop it from its roots and plant it in other ground. Here, I have Morris, you, my friends from the Poale Zion. Somewhere in the cemetery here lie the bones of my little daughter. In Lodz I'd have to look at my stepmother's face each day. The main thing is, Celia would feel unhappy there. Who would she have to talk to? Let there only be peace in the world and we'll get through the years somehow where we are."

At one time Feitelzohn planned to go back to America, but he had long since given up this plan. From Palestine a number of his friends wrote that if he were to come there, there was a good possibility of a position at the Hebrew University in Jerusalem, but Feitelzohn refused. "The German Jews run things there," he told me. "Many of them are more Prussian than the Prussians. I would fit in about as well as you would fit in among Eskimos. I'll have to sneak through my years somehow without universities."

We all lived for the present—the whole Jewish community. Feitelzohn compared this epoch to the year 1000, when the Christians in all Europe awaited the Second Coming and the destruction of the world. So long as Hitler didn't attack, so long as no revolution or pogrom erupted, each day was a gift from God. Feitelzohn often recalled his beloved philosopher, Veihinger, and his philosophy of "as if." The day will come when all truth will be recognized as arbitrary definitions, all values as rules of a game. Feitelzohn toyed with the plan of building a play-temple for ideas, for samples of cultural diversions, for systems of behavior, for religions without revelations—a kind of theater where people would come to act out their thoughts and emotions. The audience would be the performers. Those who hadn't yet decided what kind of games they preferred would participate in soul expeditions with him or with someone of his caliber to discover what would amuse or inspire them most.

I heard Feitelzohn say, "Tsutsik, I know very well that it's all sheer nonsense. Hitler wouldn't accept any other game but his own. Neither would Stalin, nor even some of our own fanatics. But I lie in bed at night and imagine a world of all play—play-gods, play-nations, play-marriages, play-sciences. What happened to mathematics after Lobachevsky and Riemann? What is Kantor's ℵ or the "set of all sets" or Einstein's theory of relativity? Nothing but wordplay. And what are all these parts of the atom that grow like mushrooms after a rain? And what is the receding universe? Tsutsik, the world goes in your direction—everything is becoming fiction. Why are you grimacing, Haiml? You're more of a hedonist than I am."

"Hedonist shmedonist," Haiml answered. "If we're

fated to die, let us die together. I have an idea! In the Sochaczów studyhouse the greatest joy came on the second evening of a holiday. Let us establish in our house that *every day* should be the second evening of a holiday. Who can forbid us to create our own calendar, our own holidays? If all life is nothing but make-believe, let us make believe that every night is the second night of a holiday. Celia will prepare a festive meal for us, and we'll make kiddush, sing table chants, and talk about Hasidism. To me, Morris, you are my rebbe. Your every word is filled with wisdom and love of God as well. There is such a thing as heretical fear of God. You can sin and still be God-fearing. Sabbatai Zevi wasn't the liar he was made out to be. The true Hasid isn't so afraid of sin. You can frighten a non-Hasid with Gehenna and the bed of nails, but not us. Since everything is supposed to be a part of the godhead, why is Gehenna inferior to paradise? I'm looking for pleasure, but to be joyous today people need noisy music, vulgar chansonettes, women in chinchilla furs, and who knows what else, and even then gloom prevails. I go to Lurse's, to the Ziemianska. They sit there gazing into magazines with pictures of whores and dictators. There's not even a trace of the bliss we used to have in the Sochaczów studyhouse, with its torn books, a kerosene ceiling lamp, and a bunch of bearded Jews with untidy earlocks and ragged satin gaberdines. Morris, you know it, and Tsutsik, you know it, too. If God needs a Hitler and a Stalin and icy winds and mad dogs, let Him have them. I need you, Morris, and you, Tsutsik, and if there is no merciful truth, I take the lie that gives me warmth and moments of joy."

"One day we will move in with you," Feitelzohn said.

"When? When Hitler stands at the gates of Warsaw?"

Haiml proposed to Feitelzohn that he publish the magazine he had been planning for years and write a book about the revival and modernization of the play called *Hasidis*. Haiml would finance both and have them translated into a number of languages. All great and revolutionary experiments had originated and been conducted in precarious circumstances, Haiml contended. He suggested that the first temple of play be built in Jerusalem, or at least in Tel Aviv. The Jews, Haiml said, unlike the Gentiles, hadn't spilled blood in two thousand years. Jews were perhaps the only group that played with words and ideas instead of with swords and guns. According to Jewish legend, when the Messiah came, Jews would go to the Land of Israel not on a metal bridge but on one made of paper. Well, and could it be mere chance that the Jews dominated Hollywood, the world press, the publishing houses? The Jew would bring the world deliverance of play and Morris Feitelzohn would be the Messiah.

"Before I become the Messiah," Feitelzohn said to me, "maybe you could lend me five zlotys?"

2 I stayed the night with Haiml and Celia. For some time, my relations with Celia had become platonic. There were times when I ridiculed this word and what it meant, but neither Celia nor I had had much interest lately in sexual experiments. Both she and Haiml still tried to persuade Feitelzohn and me, with Shosha, to move into their apartment and live like one family. Lately, Celia had turned gray. Haiml had mentioned that she was under a doctor's care and that in normal circumstances she would have gone to Carlsbad or Franzenbad or some other spa, but he never said what was wrong with her.

That night, as so often before, the conversation ended with the question why were we not leaving Warsaw, and each of us gave more or less the same answer. I couldn't leave Shosha. Haiml wouldn't go without Celia. Besides, what was the sense of running away when three million Jews remained? Some rich industrialists in Lodz had run away to Russia in 1914 and three years later were murdered by the Bolsheviks. I could see that Haiml feared more the bother of travel than the persecution of the Nazis. I heard Celia say, "If I felt that I still had the strength to begin over, I wouldn't remain here another day. My mother and grandmother as well as my father all died at my age—in fact, younger. I keep myself going only with the force of inertia, or call it what you will. I don't want to go to a foreign land and lie sick in some hotel room or hospital. I want to die in my own home. I don't want to rest in a strange cemetery. What more can Hitler do to me? I don't recall who said it, that a corpse is all-powerful, afraid of no one. All the living want and ever hope to achieve the dead already have—complete peace, total independence. There were times when I was terrified of death. You couldn't mention the word in my presence. When I bought a newspaper, I quickly skipped over the obituaries. The notion that I would one day stop eating, breathing, thinking, reading, seemed so horrible that nothing in life agreed with me any more. Then gradually I began to make peace with the concept of death, and more than that—death became the solution to all problems, actually my ideal. Today when I'm brought the newspapers I quickly turn to the obituaries. When I read that someone has died, I envy him. The reasons I don't commit suicide are first, Haiml—I want to go together with him—and second, death is too important to absorb all at once. It is like a precious wine to be savored slowly. Those who commit suicide want to escape death once and for all. But those who aren't such cowards learn to enjoy its taste."

We went to sleep late. Haiml began to snore immediately and I could hear Celia turning in her bed, sighing, murmuring. She put on the night lamp and put it out. She went to the kitchen to make herself tea, perhaps to take a pill. If everything was nothing but a game as Feitelzohn

maintained, our love game was over, or at least postponed indefinitely. It was actually more his game than
ours. I always felt his presence when I was with her. Often
when Celia talked to me she repeated almost literally
things he told me. She had acquired his sex jargon, caprices, mannerisms. She called me Morris and by some of
his pet names. Whenever our love play failed, Feitelzohn
was lying between us. I even imagined that I could smell
the aroma of his cigar. It was dawn when I fell asleep.
The morning came up cloudy and a bit damp—it had
rained in the middle of the night—but there were signs
that it would be clearing later. After breakfast I went to
Shosha's and stayed there for lunch. Then I left for my
room on Leszno Street. Although it would have been
quicker to go down Iron Street, I walked on Gnoyna,
Zimna, and Orla. On Iron Street you were vulnerable to
a blow from a Polish Fascist. I had laid out my own
ghetto. Certain streets were always dangerous. Other
streets you could walk boldly by day but not at night.
Still others had remained more or less safe for the present.
The corner of Leszno and Iron Streets always posed a
measure of danger. Although I had turned away from the
Jewish path, I carried the diaspora upon me.

As I came closer to the gate, I started to run. Safe inside, I caught my breath. I climbed the three flights of
stairs slowly. I had lots of work to do this day and in
the days to come. I was behind with my novel for the
newspaper. I had promised a story for a literary anthology. I had started another novel about the Sabbatai Zevi
movement in Poland. This was intended to be a serious
work, not for serialization in an afternoon daily. I rang
the bell and Tekla opened the door. She was polishing the
corridor floor and had her dress tucked up over her bare
legs.

She smiled and said, "Guess who called three times last
evening?"

"Who?"

"Guess!"

I mentioned several names, but she shook her head. "You give up?"

"I give up."

"Miss Betty."

"Betty from America?"

"She is here in Warsaw."

I was silent a moment. Feitelzohn had learned from one of the American tourists that Sam Dreiman had died and left Betty a large share of his inheritance, and that Sam's widow and children had contested the will. Now Betty had come to Warsaw. And when? At a time when every Jew in Poland was dreaming of escape. Even as I stood there marveling, the telephone rang and Tekla said, "It's her. She said she'd call in the morning."

3   Although it didn't seem to me so long ago since Betty had returned with Sam Dreiman to America, I barely recognized the woman I faced that day at the Hotel Bristol. She looked years older, middle-aged. Her hair had become thin and was no longer naturally red but an ugly mixture of yellow and red. Her face beneath the rouge and powder appeared somehow broader and flatter; there were wrinkles, and traces of hair on her upper lip and chin. Had she been ailing all this time? Had she grieved so over Sam's death? Something had happened to her teeth, and I noticed a spot on her neck she had not had before. She wore a kimono and slippers. She measured me from head to toe and back, then said, "Already completely bald? Who wore you out so? I thought you were taller. Is it possible at your age to start shrinking? Well, don't take it seriously, I live entirely by my impressions. I lack all sense for what they call objective truth. I hardly recognized Warsaw. Even the hotel didn't seem the same.

Before we left Poland I collected a whole stack of photographs of you and the others, but they got lost along with many of my papers. Sit down, we must talk. What can I offer you? Tea? Coffee? . . . Nothing? What's the sense of nothing? I'll order coffee."

Betty ordered coffee by phone. She spoke in a mixture of Polish and English.

She sat down in an easy chair facing me and said, "You're probably wondering why I came, particularly at such a time. I wonder myself or, to put it more accurately, I've stopped wondering not only about what others do but about my own actions as well. You probably know that Sam is dead. He went back to America and I believed he was well. He threw himself into his business as energetically as ever. Suddenly he dropped dead. One second he was alive, the next he was dead. For all my grief, I envied him. To people like me, death is a long process. We begin dying just as we're starting to mature."

Her voice had also changed—it was hoarser, somewhat shrill. The waiter rang and rolled in a silver service on a cart. It had coffee, cream, and hot milk. Betty handed him a dollar.

We drank our coffee and Betty said, "Everyone aboard ship kept asking the same thing: 'Why are you going to Poland?' They were all going to Paris. I told them the truth, that I have an old aunt in Slonim—the very city whose name I bear—and I wanted to see her before she died. They all believe that today or tomorrow Hitler will start the war, but I'm not so sure. What good would a war do him, since whatever he wants they bring him on a silver platter? The Americans and the whole democratic world have lost the most valuable possession—character. There's a form of tolerance that's worse than syphilis, worse than murder, worse than madness. Don't look at me that way. I'm the same person. It's just that in the time we were apart I lived whole ages. I suffered a complete nervous breakdown. I often heard the term used but didn't know what it meant. In my case, it showed itself in total apathy. One night I went to bed ostensibly normal, and when I woke up I was alive physically but I was neither hungry nor thirsty, nor did I have the slightest urge to get up. You should forgive me, but I didn't even want to go to the bathroom. I lay all day and my mind was blank. After Sam's death I had started smoking heavily. I drank too much, too, although alcohol had never been a passion with me. Sam's Xanthippe and his greedy children took me to court over his will and their lawyer was something it would take the devil himself to invent. Just looking at his face made me sick. I gave up everything and fled for my life. When the actors found out that Sam had left me part of his fortune, they became as tender with me as they would be with a boil. They even offered me membership in the Hebrew Actors Union. I was promised leading roles and whatnot. But my ambition for the stage was gone. What is theater, anyway? False mimicry. Literature is the same. Sam—may he rest in peace—never read anything, and we often argued about this, since I was a voracious reader from childhood. Now I'm beginning to understand him. Why didn't you answer my letters?"

"What letters? I got just one letter from you and you didn't even include a return address."

"How is that possible? I wrote several times. I cabled you, too."

"When? I swear on everything that's holy to me that I received nothing but one letter."

"What's holy to you? First I wrote to the address on Leszno, and when you didn't answer I wrote you in care of the Writers' Club."

"I no longer go to the Writers' Club."

"But that was your second home."

"I decided to stop going."

"And you're capable of sticking to a decision? Maybe my letters are still lying there?"

"What was the cable about?"

"Oh, it's no longer important. Life is full of surprises. If a person thinks no more surprises await him, it's only because he has shut his eyes and doesn't want to know. What about you? Did you break up with that freak Shosha?"

"Break up? Where do you get such notions?"

"How is it you've kept your old room? I didn't call there believing I'd find you—I only hoped they might know your new address."

"I work there. It's my study."

"You have an apartment with her?"

"We live with her mother."

A trace of laughter showed in Betty's eyes. "On that foul street among the thieves and brothels?"

"Yes, there."

"What kind of life do you lead with her, if I may ask?"

"A kind of life."

"Do the two of you ever go anywhere?"

"Rarely."

"You never go out of the house?"

"Sometimes. We take a turn around the garbage bin at night. To get a little air."

"Well, you've remained the same. At least you're crazy in your own fashion. In New York I was stopped in the street by an actor who made guest appearances here and he told me that you've become a big success and have published a novel everyone is reading. Is this true?"

"I'm having a novel printed in a newspaper and I barely earn enough to feed us."

"You're probably running around with ten others."

"That's not true, either."

"What is true?"

"How about you?" I asked. "Surely, you've had affairs."

"Are you jealous? I could have had. Men still chase after me. But when you're deathly ill and each day isn't one crisis but a thousand, you don't want affairs. Is that hocus-pocus Elbinger still in Warsaw?"

"Yes. He fell in love with a Gentile woman who was the mistress of the famous medium Kluski."

"I think I heard of him once. What did he do?"

"The dead came to him and left impressions of their hands in a pail of paraffin."

"You're scoffing, eh? I really believe that the dead are all around us somewhere. What has happened to that short, rich fellow—I've already forgotten his name. His wife was your sweetheart."

"Haiml and Celia. They are here."

"Yes, them. How is it they've stayed in Warsaw? I hear many rich Jews have escaped abroad."

"They want to die."

"Well, you're in one of *those* moods today. I've missed you. That's the truth."

4 I couldn't believe my ears, but after all those angry words about theater in general and Yiddish theater in particular, Betty Slonim had come to Warsaw with a play and was seeking a producer. I shouldn't have been surprised. Many of my colleagues, the writers, behaved precisely this way. They announced that they were laying aside (or breaking) their pens, and soon afterward they launched a novel or a long poem—even announced plans for a trilogy. They heaped invective upon a critic, maintained that he had no conception of literature, and the next day they begged him to write a few kind words about them. The play Betty brought was her own. I stayed the night, and we read it. It was the drama of a young woman, an artist (Betty had made her a painter) unable to fit into any environment. She couldn't find the right husband or lover, or even any interesting girlfriend. The play featured a psychoanalyst who tried to convince the heroine that she hated her father and was jealous of her mother, while in fact the woman worshipped her parents. There was a scene in which the heroine searches for an end to her loneliness by trying to become a lesbian and fails. The play contained possibilities for humor, but Betty handled everything in tragic fashion. The long monologues were packed with clichés. It ran some three hundred pages and was full of observations about painting by someone who knew nothing about it.

Dawn had begun to break by the time I got through with the fourth act. I said to Betty, "The play is good in essence, but it's not for Warsaw, just as mine wasn't for any place."

"What is for Warsaw?" she asked.

"I'm afraid nothing is for Warsaw any more."

"It seems to me this play is just right for the Polish Jews. They are like my heroine—they cannot fit in anywhere, neither among the Communists nor among the capitalists. Certainly not among the Fascists. At times I think nothing is left them except suicide."

"Whether that's true or not, the Warsaw Jews don't want to hear it. Certainly not in the theater."

I was so tired from reading that I lay down on the bed and fell asleep in my clothes. I wanted to tell Betty that she herself was proof that no person or collective has the strength fully to resign, but I was too exhausted to bring out the words. In my sleep I reread the play, gave Betty advice, even wrote new scenes. Betty had left the lights on and from time to time I opened an eye. She was busy in the bathroom. She had put on a magnificent nightgown. She came over to the bed and took off my shoes and pulled off my shirt. In my sleep I laughed at her and her urge to seize all the pleasures at once. That's what suicides are, I thought—hedonists who attempt to enjoy more excitement than they are capable of. This possibly was the answer to my own riddle.

I opened my eyes and saw that it was day. Betty sat at the desk in her nightgown and slippers, cigarette in mouth, writing something on a sheet of paper. My wristwatch showed a few minutes before eight. I sat up. "What are you doing? Rewriting the play?"

She turned her head toward me. Her face was ashen, her eyes had become strangely stern and determined. "You slept but I couldn't shut an eye. No, not the play. For me the play is dead. But I could save you."

"What do you mean?"

"The Jews here are all going to perish. You'll sit with that Shosha until Hitler marches in. I've been reading the paper half the night. What sense does it make, eh? Does it pay to die on account of such a moron?"

"What do you suggest I do?"

"Tsutsik, after I see my aunt I have no reason to stay here, but I want to help you nevertheless. Aboard ship I met an official of the American consulate and we spoke of various things. He even began flirting with me, but he wasn't my type. A military man, a drinker. They drown everything with whiskey—it's their answer to all problems. I asked him about bringing someone to America and he told me that outside the quota this is impossible. But it's easy to obtain a tourist visa if you apply with some goal in mind and can prove that you won't become a public charge. In America, when a tourist marries a citizen, he immediately gets a visa outside the quota and is allowed to remain. I want to tell you something. I see in advance that all my plans and hopes will come to nothing. But if I can help someone who is close to me before I die, I want to do it, and even though you told me cold-bloodedly last night that I have nothing to hope for from you, I consider you somebody close. As a matter of fact, you are the closest person I have outside Sam—may he rest in peace—and my sisters and brothers lost somewhere in the Red hell—I don't even know if any of them are still alive. Tsutsik, since you assure me the play is worth a kick in the ground, as the Litvaks say, I have nothing more to do here, and I can't go back to America all by myself. Between a yes and a no I could arrange a tourist visa for you and you could go with me. Do you have official papers with Shosha? Were you married in court?"

"Only by a rabbi."

"Is it written on your passport that you're married?"

"Nothing is written on the passport."

"You can get a tourist visa immediately if I give you an affidavit. I'll say you've written a play and we want to put it on in America. I'll say I will be appearing in it. There is even a chance that this might really happen. I can show them a bank book and whatever they require. I don't consider death a tragedy. It's actually a release from all trouble. But to live day in, day out with death is too much even for a masochist like you."

"But what could I do with Shosha?"

"They wouldn't give Shosha a tourist visa. If they took one look at her, they wouldn't give one to you."

"Betty, I can't leave her here."

"You can't, eh? That means you're ready to give up your life for her."

"If I have to die, I'll die."

"I didn't know you were so madly in love with her."

"It's not only love."

"What is it?"

"I can't kill a child. I cannot break my promise either."

"If you go to America, there might be a chance you

could send for her. You'd at least be able to send her money. As it is, you will both perish."

"Betty, I can't do it."

"If you can't, you can't. According to what you've told me, you never had such consideration for women. When you got tired of one, you found another."

"Those were adults. They had families, friends. Shosha—"

"Well, you don't have to justify yourself. When a person stands ready to offer his life for another, he obviously knows what he's doing. I wouldn't have believed you capable of such a sacrifice, but you never know what a human being is capable of. Not that those who make the sacrifices are always saints. People sacrificed themselves for Stalin, for Petlura, for Machno, for every pogromist. Millions of fools will give their empty heads for Hitler. At times I think men go around with a candle looking for an opportunity to sacrifice themselves."

Neither of us spoke for a while. Then Betty said, "I'm leaving now to visit my aunt and we may never meet again. Tell me, why did you do it? Even if you lie to me, I want to hear what you'll say."

"You mean marrying Shosha?"

"Yes."

"I really don't know, but I'll tell you, anyway. She is the only woman I can trust," I said, shocked at my own words.

Betty's eyes lit up with laughter. For an instant she became young again. "My God, this is the truth. As simple as that!"

"Perhaps."

"You're both a godless lecher and a fanatical Jew—as bigoted as my great-grandfather! How is it possible?"

"We are running away and Mount Sinai runs after us. This chase has made us sick and mad."

"Don't include me. I am sick and mad, but Mount Sinai has nothing to do with it. As a matter of fact, you're lying.

You are no more afraid of Mount Sinai than I am. It's your miserable pride, your silly fear of losing your filthy male honor. You once told me what one of your cronies said about the impossibility of always betraying and never being betrayed. Who was it—Feitelzohn?"

"I don't remember. Either Feitelzohn or Haiml."

"Haiml couldn't have said it. Well, it doesn't matter. You're crazy, but a good many other idiots of your kind went to their deaths to save the reputation of some whore. No, Shosha won't betray you—unless she is raped by a Nazi."

"Goodbye, Betty."

"Goodbye forever."

5 I had left the hotel without breakfast—I couldn't have stayed because the room-service waitress would have seen me. For the second time I had given up the chance to save myself. I walked without a definite direction. My legs led me by themselves from Trebacka Street to Theater Place. I didn't have the slightest doubt that to remain in Warsaw this time meant falling into the hands of the Nazis, but somehow I didn't feel any fear. I was tired from so little sleep, from reading Betty's play, and from her talk. I had given her the opportunity to scold me and so made our parting less solemn. Only now did it occur to me that she had never before mentioned her aunt in Poland and that she never had gone to see her. She certainly would not have come to Poland especially to see her now. Like me, Betty was ready to perish. A passage of the Pentateuch came to my mind: "I am at the point of dying and what profit shall this birthright be to me?"

I had thrown away four thousand years of Jewishness and exchanged it for meaningless literature, Yiddishism, Feitelzohnism. All I was left with was a membership book-let from the Writers' Club and some worthless manuscripts. I stopped at store windows and stared. Any day the destruction might begin, but in the meantime, here they displayed pianos, cars, jewelry, fancy nightgowns, new books in Polish, as well as translations from German, English, Russian, French. One book had the title *The Twilight of Israel*. Well, but the sky was summery blue, the trees on both sides of the street were lusciously green, the ladies wore the latest styles of dresses, hats, shoes, purses. The men looked them over with expert appraisal. Their legs in nylon stockings still promised the never-realized delights. Although I was doomed, I too glanced at hips, calves, breasts, throats. The generations that will come after us, I said to myself, will think that we all went to our death in repentance. They will consider all of us holy martyrs. They will recite kaddish after us and "God Full of Mercy." Actually, every one of us will die with the same passions he lived with.

They still played the familiar operas in the opera house: *Carmen, Aida, Faust, The Barber of Seville*. They were just unloading from a truck the faded sets that in the evening would create the deception of mountains, rivers, gardens, palaces. I went to a café. The smell of coffee and fresh rolls whetted my appetite. With my coffee a waiter brought me two newspapers. Marshal Rydz-Smigly again assured the nation that the Polish armed forces had the means to repulse all attacks from the right and the left. Foreign Minister Beck had received new guarantees from England and France. The old anti-Semite Nawaczynski attacked the Jews, who, together with the Masons, the Communists, the Nazis, and the American bankers conspired to destroy the Catholic faith and to replace it with pagan materialism. He still quoted the Protocols of the Elders of Zion. Somewhere I had had a trace of faith in free will, but this morning I felt sure that man possessed as much choice as the clockwork of my wristwatch or the fly that stopped on the edge of my saucer. The same powers were driving Hitler, Stalin, the Pope, the Rabbi of Gur, a molecule in the center of the earth, and a galaxy billions of lightyears distant from the Milky Way. Blind powers? Seeing powers? It did not matter any more. We were fated to play our little games and to be crushed.

6 Usually when I didn't spend the night at Shosha's I came home the day after for lunch, but this morning I decided to go back to her early. I was too tired to try to work at my desk on Leszno Street. I paid for my breakfast and went by way of Senator Street to Bank Place and from there to Gnoyna and Krochmalna. In the Jewish streets they bustled and rushed as every day. In the brokerage houses on Przechodnia they figured the value of the zloty against the dollar. Those on the black market paid a few pennies more for the dollar. In the yeshivas they studied the Talmud. In the Hasidic studyhouses they conversed on Hasidic topics. That morning I had the feeling I was seeing all this for the last time. I tried to engrave in my memory each alley, each building, each store, each face. I thought that this was how a condemned man would be looking at the world on his way to the gallows. I was taking leave of every peddler, porter, market woman—even of the horses of the droshkies. I saw in each of them expressions I had never noticed before. Even the horses seemed to know that this was their last journey. There was knowledge and consent in their large eyes, dark with pupil.

On Gnoyna Street I stopped for a moment at the large studyhouse in No. 5. The walls were blackened, the books stained and torn, but young men with long sidelocks still swayed over these ancient volumes and chanted the sacred words with the same mournful chant. At the lectern by the Ark the cantor was praising God for his promise to resurrect the dead. A little man with a yellow face and a yellow beard sold boiled chick-peas and beans that he doled out in a wooden cup. Is he the eternal Jew? One of the thirty-six saints that are the pillars of the world? A disguised Elder of Zion in secret pact with Roosevelt, Goebbels, and Léon Blum to bring about the kingdom of Satan?

I entered Krochmalna and the gate of No. 7. The baker's daughter stood there with large baskets of warm bagels. She must have been one of my readers, because she smiled and winked at me. I imagined that she was saying to me: "Like you I must play my game to the last minute." I passed through the yard, opened the door to Bashele's apartment, and what I saw was so bewildering that I stood in the doorway staring. Tekla was sitting at the table drinking tea or coffee with chicory from a large cup. Shosha sat beside her. Something has happened to my mother, I thought. A telegram must have come announcing that she died! Tekla saw me now and jumped to her feet. Shosha rose, too. She clapped her hands. "Arele, God Himself sent you!"

"What's going on here? Am I already in the World of Delusion?"

"What? Come in. Arele, this Gentile girl came and said she was looking for you. She called you by name. She brought a basket with her belongings. There it is. She said something about a fiancé—I don't know what she's talking about. It's a good thing Mommy went shopping or she might have thought who knows what. I told her you wouldn't be home till lunchtime, but she said she'd wait."

Tekla stood there obviously eager to speak, but she waited respectfully until Shosha had finished. Tekla looked pale and disheveled, as if she hadn't slept. She said, "Forgive me, sir, but something bad has happened to me. Last evening someone knocked on the kitchen door. I thought it might be a neighbor returning a glass of salt she had borrowed, or one of the maids from the courtyard. I opened the door and in came a lout—one of our kind, a Christian. He was dressed in city style. He said, 'Tekla, don't you recognize me?' It was Bolek, my ex-fiancé. He's come back from France from the coal mines and he says he wants to marry me. I was scared to death. I said, 'Why didn't you write all these years? You went away and it was as if the earth swallowed you.' And he said, 'I can't write, and neither could any of the other miners.' Well, between this and that, he sat down on my bed and started talking as if nothing had passed since we last saw each other. He brought me a present, too—some trinket. It's God's miracle I didn't die on the spot. I said, 'Bolek, since you didn't write so long, we are no longer engaged and everything between us is finished.' But he started yelling, "What's the matter? Got somebody else? Or are you in love with that Jew who wrote those letters to me for you?' He was drunk and grabbed a knife. My mistress heard the commotion and she came running, and he started cursing the Jews and threatened to kill us all. The mistress said, 'So far, Hitler isn't here yet. So get out of my house.' Wladek called the police, but a policeman didn't show up till three hours later, after Bolek had gone. He swore he would come back again today, and he warned me that if I didn't go with him to a priest straight off and marry him, he'd kill me. After he left, the mistress came in and said, 'Tekla, you've served me faithfully, but I'm old and weak and I don't have the strength for such goings-on. Take your luggage and leave.' I persuaded her to let me spend the night. This morning she paid me what was coming to me, added five zlotys, and sent me on my way. You once gave me your address on Krochmalna Street, so I came here. The young lady said she's your wife and that you'd be back for lunch, but where could I go? I know no one in Warsaw. I was sure you wouldn't throw me out."

"Throw you out? Tekla, I'm your friend for life!"

"Oh, thank you. What shall I do? I can't go home to

our village, because Bolek said if I did he'd come after me. He has a whole gang of thugs who served in the army and came back with revolvers and bayonets. He said he'd saved up a thousand zlotys and some French money besides, but my heart is no longer his. He can get plenty of other girls. He stank of vodka and he talked like a roughneck. I've grown unused to that kind of coarseness."

"Arele, when Mommy comes back and hears this, she'll get nervous," Shosha said. "If the man is threatening with a knife, you mustn't go to that place. But what will she do here? We hardly have space to lay our own heads. Mommy says each time she goes out to let no one in. She used to say the same when we lived at No. 10— remember?"

"Yes, Shoshele, I remember. Tekla is a decent girl and she won't give anyone any trouble. I'll take her away in a minute." In Yiddish I said, "Shoshele, I'm going with her for a while. When your mother comes back, tell her nothing."

"Oh, she'll know it, anyway. Everyone in the courtyard looks out the window, and when someone who doesn't belong here goes in or out they know it and start to gossip: 'What's she doing here? What does she want?' The younger women are busy with their children, but the old ones want to know everything."

"Well, I'll be back around lunchtime. Tekla, come with me."

"Shall I bring my basket?"

"Yes, bring it."

"Arele, don't be late. When you're late, Mommy starts to worry that maybe you no longer want us, and things like that. I start thinking all kinds of things myself. Last night I could barely sleep a wink. If she's hungry, I can give her bread and herring to take along."

"She'll eat. Come, Tekla."

We walked out under the watchful gaze of eyes that

seemed to ask, "Where is he off to so early with this peasant girl? And what is she carrying in the basket?" I answered them in my mind, "You may try to solve the puzzles in the newspaper, but never the mysteries of life. For seven days and seven nights you could rub your brows like the Sages of Chelm and you'd still never figure out the answer."

In front of the gate, I stood for a long time thinking what to do next. Should I try to find a room for her? Should I go with her to some coffee shop and look up advertisements for maids' agencies? I would have let her stay with Shosha for a while, but I had never told either her or Bashele of my room on Leszno Street. They believed that I slept at the newspaper, and Bashele would begin a long interrogation. Suddenly I knew what to do. The solution was so simple I wondered that it hadn't occurred to me immediately. I walked with Tekla to the delicatessen in No. 12, told her to wait for me by the door, and went inside to phone Celia. Only a few days earlier, she had bewailed the fact that ever since Marianna had left her, she hadn't been able to find a decent maid. I heard Celia's dull voice—one that seemed to say without putting it in words, Whoever it may be, I can expect nothing.

I said, "Celia, this is Tsutsik."

"Tsutsik? What's happened? Has the Messiah come?"

"The Messiah hasn't come, but I have a maid for you."

"A maid? You? For me?"

"Yes, Celia, and a part-time boarder in the bargain."

"Bless me if I know what you mean. What boarder?"

"I am the boarder."

"Are you making fun of me?"

I told Celia what had happened. "I can't stay in my room on Leszno Street any longer. A rowdy peasant is threatening Tekla and me." Celia did not interrupt me, apparently stunned by the turn of events. I could hear her breathing on the other side of the line. From time to time I glanced through the glass door to where Tekla waited. She stood with humble patience. She did not put down the heavy basket but held it in both her hands, pressed to her belly. At home on Leszno Street she showed big-city shrewdness, but overnight she seemed to have lost it all and become a peasant again.

"Will you bring Shosha with you?"

"Whenever she is able to stay apart from her mother."

Celia seemed to ponder the implication of my words. Then she said, "Bring her as often as you want to. This is going to be your second home. Where you go she should go."

"Celia, you are saving my life!" I exclaimed.

Again Celia paused. "Tsutsik, take a taxi and come at once. If I live a little longer, something good may happen even to me. If only it isn't too late."

EPILOGUE

1 Thirteen years had gone by. In New York, I had saved two thousand dollars out of my salary from the Yiddish newspaper. I had also received a five-hundred-dollar advance for a novel that would be translated into English, and I took a trip to London, Paris, and Israel. London still had craters and ruins left over from the German bombs. In Paris, I ate in a restaurant that obtained its food from the black market. In Marseilles I boarded a ship bound for Haifa with a stopover in Genoa. The singing of the young passengers rang through the nights—the old familiar songs, as well as new songs that had come out of the war with the Arabs between 1948 and 1951. After six days, we arrived in Haifa. It was an experience to see Hebrew signs over the stores and streets bearing the names of writers, rabbis, and leaders, to hear Hebrew spoken in the Sephardic style, to see Jewish soldiers of both sexes. In Tel Aviv I stopped at a hotel on Yarkon Street. Although Tel Aviv was a new city, the houses looked old and dingy. The telephone didn't work properly, the bathtub seldom had hot water, and the electricity often went off at night. The food was bad.

There was a notice in a newspaper announcing my arrival, and I began to receive visits from writers, journalists, old friends from Warsaw, distant relatives. Some of them had numbers tattooed on their arms from Auschwitz, others had already lost sons in the battles for Jerusalem or Safad. I heard the same horror stories about Nazi brutalities and the savagery of the N.K.V.D. that I had heard in New York, in London, in Paris, and aboard ship.

One morning as I ate breakfast in the hotel dining room, a tiny person with a milk-white beard that extended like a fan came into the room. He wore an unbuttoned shirt with an open collar, a straw hat, shabby trousers, and sandals on his bare feet. I was sure that I had known him once, but I couldn't identify him. How can such a little man have such a large beard? I wondered. He approached my table with hasty steps. He had young black eyes that resembled the olives on my plate. He pointed a finger and said in a familiar Warsaw Yiddish, "There he is! Peace to you, Tsutsik!"

It was Haiml Chentshiner. I got up and we kissed and held each other for a moment. My face filled with beard. I asked him to have breakfast with me but he told me that he had eaten, and I ordered coffee for him. I had heard that he and Celia perished in the Warsaw Ghetto, but encounters with those supposedly dead had ceased to surprise me. Feitelzohn I knew was no longer alive, for I had read of his death in the paper years ago.

We drank the coffee and Haiml said, "Forgive me for

calling you Tsutsik—it remains a term of affection for me."

"Yes, but I'm an old dog now."

"To me you will always remain Tsutsik. If Celia were alive, she'd call you the same thing. How old are you?"

"Forty-three."

"Not so very old. I'm in my late fifties. It seems to me I'm as old as Methuselah. The things we went through during those years! Not one life but a hundred."

"Where were you, Haiml?"

"Where *was* I? Where wasn't I! In Vilna, in Kovno, in Kiev, in Moscow, in Kazakhstan, among the Kalmucks, the Chunchuz, or whatever they're called. A hundred times I virtually looked the Angel of Death in the eye, but when you're fated to stay alive miracles occur. So long as a breath of life remains in the body, it crawls like a worm, and I crawled and avoided the feet that squash worms till I came to the Jewish land. Here again, we suffered war, hunger, steady danger. Bullets flew over my head. Bombs exploded a few steps away. But here no one went like a sheep to the slaughter. Our lads from Warsaw, Lodz, Rawa Ruska, and Minsk suddenly turned into heroes like the fighters in the time of Masada. Piff-poff! The greatest optimist wouldn't have believed it possible. You probably know what happened to Celia."

"Not a thing."

"How could you, after all? How about going out on the terrace? I like to look at the sea."

We went to the terrace and took a table in the shade. A waiter came over and I ordered more coffee and cookies. For a long time we both stared out to sea, which changed color from green to blue. On the horizon a sailboat rocked. The beach swarmed with men and women. Some exercised, others played ball, sunbathed, or lay under umbrellas. Some splashed at the edge of the water, others swam far out. A man urged a dog to go into the water, but the animal was unwilling to bathe.

Haiml said, "Well, a Jewish land, a Jewish sea. Who would have believed this ten years ago? Such a thought was beyond daring. All our dreams centered around a crust of bread, a plate of groats, a clean shirt. Feitelzohn once said something I often repeat: 'A man has no imagination either in his pessimism or his optimism.' Who could have figured that the Gentiles would vote for a Jewish nation? Nu, but the birth throes are far from over. The Arabs haven't made peace with the situation. It's hard here. Thousands of refugees live in tin shacks. I lived in one of them myself. The sun roasts you all day like fire, and at night you freeze. The women are at each other's throats. Refugees have come from Africa who've never seen a handkerchief—literally people from Abraham's time. Who knows what they are—maybe descendants of Keturah. I hear you've become famous in America."

"Far from it."

"Well, you're known. They used to read your books in the camps in Germany. Things were reprinted in the papers there. Each time I saw your name, I cried, 'Tsutsik!' They thought I was crazy. Today when I saw the notice in *Hayom* that you were here, I began to jump in the air. My wife asked, 'What happened—have you gone mad?' I got married again."

"Here?"

"No, in Landsberg. She had lost her husband and the children were taken away from her to the gas chamber. I was wandering around alone. I didn't have anyone to so much as make me a glass of tea. I remember your words: 'The world is a slaughterhouse and a brothel.' At the time it seemed to me an exaggeration, but it's the bitter truth. They consider you a mystic, while the fact is, you're an out-and-out realist. Still, everything is forced upon us, even hope. The dictator on high, the celestial Stalin, says

273

'You must hope!' And if he says you must, you hope. But what can I hope for any more? Only for death. Where is the sugar?"

"Right here."

"This coffee tastes like dishwater. How long is it since I've seen you—thirteen years? Yes, in September it will be exactly thirteen years. Shosha is no longer alive, eh?"

"Shosha died on the second day we left Warsaw."

"Died? On the way?"

"Yes, like Mother Rachel."

"We knew nothing, nothing. News came from others. There were Jews in Bialystok and Vilna who became mail carriers, messengers. They brought letters to wives across the borders. But you vanished like a stone in water. What happened to you? I first found out you were alive in 1946. I came to Munich with a large group of refugees and someone gave me a newspaper published there. I opened it and saw your name. It said that you were in New York. How did you manage to get to New York?"

"Through Shanghai."

"Who sent you the affidavit?"

"Remember Betty?"

"What a question! I remember everybody."

"Betty married a Gentile, a colonel in the American Army, and he sent me the affidavit."

"You knew her address?"

"I learned it by chance."

"Well, I'm not religious, I don't pray, I don't observe the Sabbath, I don't believe in God, but I acknowledge that some hand guides our world—this, no one can deny. A vicious hand, a bloody hand, occasionally merciful. Where does Betty live—in New York?"

"Betty committed suicide a year ago."

"Why?"

"No one knows."

"What happened to Shosha? If it's painful for you to talk about it, you don't have to tell me."

"I'll tell you anyway. She died exactly as I saw it in a dream a few years before. We were walking along a road that led to Bialystok. It was toward evening. The others walked fast and Shosha couldn't keep up. She began to stop every few minutes. Suddenly she sat down, and a minute later she was dead. I had told this dream to Celia. Maybe to you, too."

"Not to me. I would remember it. What a sweet child she was. In her own fashion, a saint. What was it, a heart attack?"

"I don't know. I think she simply didn't want to live any more."

"What happened to her sister—what was her name, Teibele?" Haiml asked. "And how about her mother?"

"Bashele perished for sure. About Teibele, I don't know what happened. She might have run away to Russia. She had a friend—a bookkeeper. Perhaps she's here, although it doesn't seem probable, since I have heard nothing from her in all these years."

"I'm afraid to ask, but what happened to your mother and your brother?"

"After 1941, the Russians saved them by taking them in a cattle train to Kazakhstan. The trip took two weeks. I met a man who was with them in the same train, and he told me the details. They are both dead. How my mother could last several months after the experience of this trip, I still don't grasp. They were taken to a forest in the middle of the Russian winter and told to build themselves log cabins. My brother died almost immediately after he arrived."

"What happened to your Communist girl friend, what was her name?"

"Dora? I don't know. Got crushed somewhere, either by the do-gooders, or by the do-badders."

"Tsutsik, I'll be right back—don't go away."

"What a thing to say!"

Haiml left and I turned toward the sea again. Two women splashed each other and lost their balance from the force of their laughter. A father and son played with a balloon. A Sephardic Jew in a white cloak, barefoot, and with a scraggly white beard and earlocks dangling to his shoulders, went around begging from the people on the beach. No one gave him anything. Who would go begging on a beach? I wondered. He was probably not in his right mind. At that moment I heard my name called on the public-address system. I was wanted on the telephone.

2 I came back from the phone. Haiml sat at the table, facing the door with a childish eagerness. When I came out, he made a move as if to stand, but kept his seat. I sat down and he asked, "Where did you go?"

"I was called to the phone."

"When you come here, they don't leave you alone for a minute. Well, there were notices about you in the newspapers, but how did they know it when *I* came? People called whom I thought were long buried. Every such meeting was like the resurrection of the dead. Who knows? If we could live to see the miracle that the Jews have a country again, maybe we shall see the Messiah come, after all? Maybe the dead *will* be resurrected? Tsutsik, you know I'm a freethinker. But somewhere inside me I have the feeling that Celia is here, that Morris is here, that my father—may he rest in peace—is here. Your Shosha is here, too. How is it possible, after all, that someone should simply vanish? How can someone who lived, loved, hoped, and wrangled with God and with himself just disappear? I don't know how and in what sense but they're here. Since time is an illusion, why shouldn't everything remain? I once heard you say—or quote someone—that time is a book whose pages you can turn forward, not back. Maybe *we* can't, but some forces can. How is it possible that Celia should stop being Celia? For Morris to stop being Morris? I live with them, speak with them. At times I hear Celia talking to me. You won't believe this, but Celia told me to marry my present wife. I lay in that camp near Landsberg, sick, hungry, lonely, dejected. Suddenly I heard Celia's voice: 'Haiml, marry Genia!' That's my wife's name, Genia. Sure, you can explain this psychologically. I know, I know. Nevertheless, I heard her voice. What do you say to that, eh?"

"I don't know."

"You still don't know? How long can you go on not knowing? Tsutsik, I seem to be able to make peace with everything but death. How can it be that all the generations are dead and only we shlemiels are allegedly living? You turn the page and can't turn it back again, but on page so-and-so they're all right there in an archive of spirits."

"What do they do there?" I asked.

"That answer I don't have. Perhaps we are there already, dreaming the same dream. Either everything is dead or everything is alive. I want you to know that it was only after you left that Morris became great—he never had been as great as he was in those months. He lived with us on Zlota Street until the Jews were herded into the Ghetto in October of 1940, which was more than a year after the Germans came in. As you know, before the war he could have gone to England as well as to America. The American consul urged him to leave. The war with America didn't start until 1941. He could have traveled through Rumania, through Hungary, even through Germany. With an American visa they let you pass. But he stayed with us. One time I said to Celia, 'I'm ready to die but I want one

277

favor from you and the Almighty if He exists—that I never see a Nazi.' Celia said to me, 'Haiml, I promise you that you won't see their faces.' How could she have promised such a thing? She herself had grown in stature. She wasn't the same Celia any more. Our situation and Morris's moving in with us uplifted her to a degree that can't be put into words. She became beautiful!"

"Were you jealous of him?"

"Don't talk nonsense. I too grew a bit. The Angel of Death waved his sword but I stuck out my tongue at him. Outside, it was the destruction of the Temple, but inside our house it was Simchas Torah and Yom Kippur rolled into one. Next to them I, too, became cheerful. I'm not telling these things in proper order—how can you speak of such things in order? My only uncle died in the month of October. It wasn't possible to go to Lodz—a Jew couldn't show his face anywhere. Still, I dared the dangers. I walked the whole distance on foot. The trip there and back was a real odyssey.

"As you know, Celia had prepared a room we called the Cave of Machpelah. She started to prepare it while you were still in Warsaw, but the day they announced on the radio that all men were to cross the Praga Bridge and you decided to leave together with Shosha, that day the room became Feitelzohn's and my only place. We ate there, we slept there. Morris did his writing there. I had brought money from Lodz—not paper money, but golden ducats my father left with my uncle for me. They were saved from the time of the Russians. Just the fact that I had returned with such a treasure to Warsaw and wasn't searched or killed on the way is beyond belief. But I did come back. Then Celia had her jewelry. At that time you could get everything for money. A black market developed almost at once.

"After my odyssey, I was so depleted that my last drop

of courage drained away. Like Morris, I wouldn't go into the street, and Celia became our contact with the outside world. Each time she went, we weren't sure we'd see her again. Your Tekla, too, ran errands for us. She risked her life. She had to go back to her village because her father died.

"The days were days of sorrow. Our life started at night. There wasn't much to eat, but we drank hot tea and Morris talked. He talked those nights as I never heard him talk before. The heritage of generations had wakened within him, and he hurled sulphur and brimstone against the Almighty; at the same time the words themselves blazed with a religious fire. He castigated Him for all His sins since the Creation. He still maintained that the whole universe was a game, but he elevated this game until it became divine. That was probably how the Seer of Lublin, Rabbi Bunim, and the Kotzker spoke. The essence of his words was that since God is eternally silent, we owe Him nothing. It seems I once heard similar words from you— or maybe you were quoting Morris. True religion, Morris argued, was not to serve God but to spite Him. If He wanted evil, we had to aspire to the opposite. If He wanted wars, inquisitions, crucifixions, Hitlers, we must want righteousness, Hasidism, our own version of grace. The Ten Commandments weren't His but ours. God wanted Jews to seize the Land of Israel from the Canaanites and to wage wars against the Philistines, but the real Jew, who began to be what he is in exile, wanted the Gemara with its commentaries, the Zohar, *The Tree of Life, The Beginning of Wisdom*. The Gentiles didn't drive us into the ghetto, Morris said, the Jew went on his own, because he grew weary of waging war and bringing up warriors and heroes of the battlefield. Each night Morris erected a new structure.

"We could have escaped up to the time they locked the

Jews in the ghetto; people went back and forth to Russia. In Bialystok there was a Jew from Warsaw, a half writer, half madman, and a whole martyr. His name was Yonkel Pentzak. He kept going from Bialystok to Warsaw and back again—a kind of holy messenger or a divine smuggler. He smuggled letters from wives to husbands and from husbands to wives. You can imagine the risk connected with such journeys! The Nazis finally got him, but until they did, he served as a sacred mail carrier. He brought me a few letters. Some friends of mine had gone there and they begged us to join them, but Celia didn't want to and Morris didn't want to, and after all, I couldn't leave them behind. What was there for me in that alien world? The whole crew of writers and leaders that sent us greetings had overnight turned about and become ardent Communists. Denouncing one's fellow was now the order of the day. Their writing consisted of praising Stalin, and the reward for this was at first a plate of groats and a bed, and later jail and exile and liquidation. I came to the conclusion that what people call life is death and what people call death is life. Don't ask any questions. Where is it written that a bedbug lives and the sun is dead? Maybe it's the other way around? Love? It wasn't simply love. Tsutsik, do you have a match, maybe? I've gotten into the habit of smoking, actually right here in the Jewish land."

I went to get Haiml matches, and at the same time I bought him two packs of American cigarettes.

He shook his head. "Are those for me? So help me, you're a spendthrift."

"I took more from you than two packs of cigarettes."

"Eh? We didn't forget you. Celia kept asking about you —maybe someone had heard something, maybe something of yours had been printed. After you left Warsaw, where did you go—not to Bialystok?"

"To Druskenik."

"You were able to get there?"

"I smuggled myself over."

"What did you do in Druskenik?"

"Worked in a hotel."

"Well, you did the right thing to stay away from the writers. You couldn't become a Communist, and the anti-Communists were soon sent to Siberia. Later they did the same to most zealous Stalinists. What did you do in 1941?"

"Kept on going."

"Where to?"

"I dragged along till I came to Kovno, and from there I went to Shanghai."

"Got a visa, eh? And what did you do in Shanghai?"

"Became a typesetter."

"What did you set?"

"The *Shitah Mekubbetzet*."

"Well, a crazy race, the Jews. I heard there was a Yeshiva there that published books. You didn't write?"

"I did that, too."

"When did you go to America?"

"At the beginning of 1948."

"I left Warsaw in May of 1941. Morris died in March."

"Why didn't you take Celia along?"

"There was no one to take along."

"Was she sick?"

"She died exactly a month after Morris, in what they call a natural death."

3 Haiml and I squeezed our way into a bus going to Hadar Joseph, a suburb of Tel Aviv with housing for new immigrants. The passengers cursed each other in Yiddish, Polish, German, and in broken Hebrew. The women fought over seats and the men took sides. One woman had brought along a live chicken. The bird tore loose from the basket and began to fly over the heads of the passengers. The driver shouted that he would throw out anyone who caused a disturbance. After a while things quieted down and I heard Haiml say, 'Well, a Jewish nation. The newcomers are all out of their minds—victims of Hitler, bundles of nerves. They always suspect they're being persecuted. First they cursed Hitler, now they curse Ben-Gurion. Their children or perhaps their grandchildren will be normal if the Almighty doesn't send a new catastrophe down upon us. What can you know of what we went through! You haven't said anything, but you're probably wondering why I had to marry again after Celia. Before, Genia and I were two worms crawling separately; then we began to crawl together. Until recently we lived in a tin shack. Later, we got the apartment we have now. How much can a body tolerate? She isn't Celia, but she's a good person. Her husband was a teacher in a Yiddish school in Pietrkow. A Bundist. Genia believed in Stalin for a while, until she got a taste of him. Funny, she knew Feitelzohn. She once went to a lecture of his about Spengler and he autographed a book for her. She's an orderly in a hospital where they bring the wounded in ambulances. The Red Mogen David. It just so happens she's off today. She knows all about you. I gave her your books to read."

We came to Hadar Joseph. Lines of wash stretched from one flat roof to the other. Half-naked children played in the sand. Cement steps led directly into Haiml's kitchen. Outside, it stank of garbage, asphalt, and something else sticky and sweetish that was hard to identify. The kitchen smelled of sorrel and garlic. Next to the gas range stood a short woman with short-trimmed hair—black, mixed with gray. She wore a calico dress and over her bare feet cracked slippers. She had apparently undergone surgery, since the left side of her face was compressed, full of scars under the chin, and her mouth was crooked. When we came in she was watering a flower in a pot.

Haiml called out, "Genia, guess who this is!"

"Tsutsik."

Haiml seemed embarrassed. "He has a name."

"It doesn't matter. Just the opposite," I said.

"Excuse me, that's how we refer to you," Genia said. "Four years I've been hearing it day and night—'Tsutsik,' 'Tsutsik.' When my husband thinks well of someone, he speaks of him without stopping. I had the honor of meeting Dr. Feitelzohn, but I only know you from a picture that appeared in the Yiddish paper. Finally I see you in person. Why didn't you tell me you were bringing someone to the house?" she said, turning to Haiml. "I would have put the place in order. We battle here constantly with flies, beetles, even mice. Years ago I didn't consider that insects or mice were God's creatures, too; but since I've been treated as if I were a beetle myself, I've come to accept things one doesn't want to accept. Please, go into the other room. Such an unexpected guest. What an honor!"

"You see her cheek?" Haiml pointed. "That's where a Nazi hit her with a piece of pipe."

"Well, why talk about it?" Genia said. "Go in the other room. Excuse me for the state it's in."

We went into the other room. A big sofa stood there, one of those that serve as a sofa by day and a bed at night. The apartment had no bathtub, only a toilet and a sink. This room seemed to serve both as a bedroom and a dining room. There was a bookcase, where I spotted Feitelzohn's *Spiritual Hormones* and several of my books.

Haiml said, "This is our land, this is our home. Here, maybe we'll have the privilege of dying if we're not driven into the sea."

After a while, Genia came in and began to straighten up. Even as we sat there, she swept the floor and spread a cloth over the table. She excused herself again and again for the mess. Evening was beginning to fall by the time she served dinner—some meat for herself and Haiml, vegetables for me. It struck me that the couple mixed meat dishes with dairy. I had assumed that despite the fact Haiml talked like a heretic he would be observing Jewishness in the Land of Israel.

I asked, "Since you aren't religious, why did you grow a beard?"

Genia put down her spoon. "That's what I want to know."

"Oh, a Jew should have a beard," Haiml replied. "You have to be different from Gentiles in some way."

"The way you have lived, you're a Gentile, too," Genia said.

"As long as I have never beaten or killed anybody, I can call myself a Jew."

"It's written somewhere that whoever breaks one of the Ten Commandments must break them all," Genia said.

"Genia, the Ten Commandments were written by a man, not by God," Haiml said. "As long as you don't harm anyone, you can live any way you want. I loved Feitelzohn. If they told me to give up my life so that he could live again, I wouldn't hesitate. If there is a God, let Him be witness to what I say. I love Tsutsik, too. The time of property will soon pass and there will evolve a man with new instincts—those of sharing: Morris's very words."

"Then why were you such an anti-Communist in Russia?" Genia asked.

"They don't want to share—they want to grab."

It grew silent and I heard a cricket—the same sound that came from the cricket that chirped in our kitchen when I was a boy. The room filled with shadows.

Haiml said, "I am religious—in my own fashion. I am religious! I believe in the immortality of the soul. If a rock can exist for millions of years, why should the human soul, or whatever you choose to call it, be extinguished? I'm with those who died. I live with them. The moment I close my eyes they are all with me. If a ray of light can travel and radiate for billions of years, why can't a spirit? A new science founded on this premise will emerge."

"When does the bus go back to Tel Aviv?" I asked.

"Tsutsik, you can sleep here," Haiml said.

"Thanks, Haiml, but someone is coming to see me early in the morning."

Genia cleared the dishes and went to the kitchen. I heard her close the front door, but Haiml didn't switch on the lights. A pale glow shone in through the windows.

Haiml began speaking to me, to himself, and to no one in particular: "Where did all the years go to? Who will remember them after we're gone? The writers will write, but they'll get everything topsy-turvy. There must be a place somewhere where everything is preserved, inscribed down to the smallest detail. Let us say that a fly has fallen into a spiderweb and the spider has sucked her dry. This is a fact of the universe and such a fact cannot be forgotten. If such a fact should be forgotten, it would create a blemish in the universe. Do you understand me or not?"

"Yes, Haiml."

"Tsutsik, those are your words!"

"I don't remember saying them."

"You don't remember, but I do. I remember everything that Morris said, that you said, and that Celia said. At times you uttered ridiculous foolishness, and I remember that, too. If God is wisdom, how can there be foolishness? And if God is life, how can there be death? I lie at night, a little man, a half-squashed fly, and I talk with the dead, with the living, with God—if He exists—and with Satan, who certainly does exist. I ask them, 'What need was there for all this?' and I wait for an answer. What do you think, Tsutsik, is there an answer somewhere or not?"

"No, no answer."

"Why not?"

"There can't be any answer for suffering—not for the sufferer."

"In that case, what am I waiting for?"

Genia opened the door. "Why are you two sitting in the dark, eh?"

Haiml laughed. "We're waiting for an answer."

Isaac Bashevis Singer

Winner of the 1978 Nobel Prize
for Literature

SHOSHA	23997-7	$2.50
SHORT FRIDAY	24068-1	$2.50
PASSIONS	24067-3	$2.50
A CROWN OF FEATHERS	23465-7	$2.50
ENEMIES: A LOVE STORY	24065-7	$2.50
THE FAMILY MOSKAT	24066-5	$2.95

FREE
Fawcett Books Listing

There is Romance, Mystery, Suspense, and Adventure waiting for you inside the Fawcett Books Order Form. And it's yours to browse through and use to get all the books you've been wanting . . . but possibly couldn't find in your bookstore.

This easy-to-use order form is divided into categories and contains over 1500 titles by your favorite authors.

So don't delay—take advantage of this special opportunity to increase your reading pleasure.

Just send us your name and address and 35¢ (to help defray postage and handling costs).